DI╵╴╴╴╶
RUIN

PRAISE FOR THE

SISTER HOLIDAY MYSTERIES

"Douaihy's poetic prose and incredible voice shine as we rejoin our indomitable sleuth, Sister Holiday, in her hunt for the truth, and find it is every bit as grisly and profane as it is beautiful and sacred"

GILLIAN FLYNN

"[A] showstopper"

NEW YORK TIMES

"Skilfully plotted, propulsive"

DON WINSLOW

"A searing journey through faith, fire, and female rage"

ELIZABETH HAND

"If you're looking for a queer edgy Agatha Christie-type read, then this is one for you"

GAY TIMES

"If you're not sold by a punk rock nun solving mysteries then can your soul even be saved?"

ELECTRIC LITERATURE

© Chattman Photography

MARGOT DOUAIHY is the author of poetry collections *Bandit/Queen: The Runaway Story of Belle Starr*, *Scranton Lace* and *Girls Like You*. She received her PhD in creative writing from the University of Lancaster. Originally from Scranton, Pennsylvania, she is now living in Northampton, Massachusetts. The first two Sister Holiday Mysteries, *Scorched Grace* and *Blessed Water*, are also available from Pushkin Vertigo.

DIVINE RUIN

MARGOT DOUAIHY

Pushkin Press
Somerset House, Strand
London WC2R 1LA

First published by Pushkin Press in 2026

ISBN 13: 978-1-80533-568-9

A CIP catalogue record for this title is available from the British Library

The authorised representative in the EEA is
eucomply OÜ, Pärnu mnt. 139b-14, 11317, Tallinn, Estonia,
hello@eucompliancepartner.com, +33757690241

Offset by Tetragon, London
Printed and bound in the United Kingdom by Clays Ltd, Elcograf S.p.A.

Pushkin Press is committed to a sustainable future for our
business, our readers and our planet. This book is made from
paper from forests that support responsible forestry.

MIX
Paper | Supporting
responsible forestry
FSC® C018072

www.pushkinpress.com

1 3 5 7 9 8 6 4 2

DIVINE
RUIN

For nurses, carers, and nuns

1

NO, I'VE NEVER BEEN afraid of the dark. Not even as a kid, huddled inside my Scooby-Doo sleeping bag. It's the light that wrecked me. When I could see everything, everyone, full blast, full on. The light's the true terror, revealing every seam and shortcut, all the stains and breaks. When you can see the ghost under the mask that's started to slip. Because every façade cracks. It's not a matter of if, but when. The light makes demands. I'd take darkness any day.

Before you throw scripture at me—me, of all people—you know as well as I do that life isn't hell or heaven but both. God isn't only good or bad but both. And the Word isn't one word, it's every end and beginning. The alpha and omega. Winged lions and firestorms and angels of ruin. God gave us choices, then damned us when we chose.

It'd be a banger of a punch line if it wasn't so fucked.

And, yeah, I signed up for it when I joined the convent. Joke's on me.

When the plague struck and my students began to die, even after I touched their cold skin, I knew they weren't gone. Not completely. They're with us in the darkness that's always existed.

A realm that's as real as the Holy Spirit and just as impossible to capture. Whoever we love and lose returns in dreams, visions so pure and real they coat us in smoke. We wake choking, utterly convinced we saw them.

It's simple, really. Energy's neither created nor destroyed, right? Atoms swirl and reassemble in these borrowed containers, in this borrowed time called life. Maybe it's a cheap comfort. Maybe it's bullshit. But I've planted my ripped flag in the fact that we all meet again in the dark, behind eyelids. The dead find other ways to speak.

But here's the problem. My kids left the earthly plane too soon, and they died because we failed them. Because I failed them. Too busy searching for divine signs, I missed the signs of students in crisis. To waste away like that, waiting for help that never came. Not realizing the strength of the spell. To die alone after scoring. Their gaping mouths, the cheap drugs inside them. Chemicals so *unworthy* of their inner worlds. Their wobbly teen bodies stuck between childhood and adulthood. No chance to step into their future selves. No chance to be haunted by lost dreams.

Drugs promise rebirth, but they lie.

That's why I had to do it. To hunt evil and inch so close to the devil I could feel its hiss in my eardrum, at the base of my spine. To stop an influx—any infestation—you have to crawl into the nest and kill it at the source. Creep into the viper's den like dusk and neutralize it. End it. End its offspring too. No mercy.

The mission chose me or I chose the mission, not sure. Avenge or revenge, does it matter? Not that anything could chip away at the everlasting human need of addiction itself, squirming inside like a rabid thing. An un-immaculate conception. And for queer people, addiction's a trapdoor. In a world that hated us, getting high was a precious escape. Relief from the torment and dread. Until refuge became its own prison.

I knew because I got high more times than I could ever count. I'd felt death close in, felt my limbs die one by one. Big toe. Ankle. Pinky finger. Ten years ago, back in Brooklyn, when it was really bad, I did so much heroin I became pure light, until I felt my jaw die. A slack I couldn't pick up. I went too far, almost bit it a hundred times. Some days, I wished I had.

OD'ing is what addiction wants, but maybe I could buy us some time. Though time was one of the few things that could never be bought or sold in this town.

Me and Riveaux, we'd both felt the grip of addiction, and we'd used it to our advantage. Riveaux survived a ladder fall in the line of duty and was introduced to a brand of pain barely dulled by narcotics. Of course, her pathetic ex-husband proved to be the more dangerous poison. But Private Eye Magnolia Riveaux had beaten them both, and her sleuthing obsession was as gnarly as mine. At least it kept us on the righteous path.

Riveaux ran Redemption Detective Agency. She was an ace mentor—with the nose of a Paris perfumier and the investigative chops (and octogenarian fashion) of Miss Marple. At the top of her game, she became the first Black female arson investigator in New Orleans, before demons chased her into a corner. She'd fought her way out, though. We both had unlikely comebacks, but only mine included a nun's uniform, with gloves and a scarf to hide back-alley tattoos. Me and Riveaux, we'd both learned to hone it—that raw ache. We'd track down the sidewinders who brought fentanyl into our city, my school, my home.

Fentanyl. A strangely beautiful word for all its horror. A swan song inside one word. It made my tongue work—*fentanyl*—gave my mouth shape, gave me purpose. A synthetic drug a hundred times more potent than other opioids, a higher high, with a grieving need that fully devours whoever tries it once. Just once and you're hooked. Or dead.

2

ON THE HORRENDOUS DAY we lost Fleur Benoit, my morning began with cleaning the convent bathroom, wondering how a gutter dyke like me ended up as a Sister of the Sublime Blood. Five years ago, if you'd told me I'd be marrying religion for life, preparing for permanent vows as a nun, bleaching a convent john, and teaching kids how to play "Wonderwall" on an acoustic Fender, I would've spit in your face and decked you for insulting me. Teaching music to Catholic schoolkids, channeling young souls through power chords, was equal parts education and exorcism. What a fine line between nurturing talent and wanting to bash my skull against a cinder block wall until I saw stars.

Though, self-harm and fine lines were art forms in which I'd historically excelled. I'd reinvented myself, but old habits die hard.

So, picture me in that fairly ordinary start to a terrible, terrible Monday. My body a tuned instrument of God, as I swept and mopped, scraped and clawed. Sweat soaking through my rough uniform, I cursed at the nature of dirt itself. How it shows up, we disappear it, and it settles right back in. Rinse, repeat. Purgatory lived in many forms. Baptizing the bathroom was a bitch, but it was gloriously absorbing. No thought, just grout scoured to oblivion. Any nun, any mystic, any witch would surely testify that worship is a verb, suffering an offering. Transcendence lives inside humility.

The gift is in the *doing*.

There was a knock at the bathroom door, then Sister Laurel poked in her head. Her smile was a familiar surprise. "Good morning, Sister Holiday!"

"Morning."

"You have a rehearsal tomorrow, dear, and the announcement will go to press next week. You feeling good, feeling ready?" Her veil bobbed as she hunched her bony shoulders over and gave me a quick, birdlike nod, as if answering for me.

I nodded too. Yeah. Sure. Test-driving my permanent vow ceremony. Rehearsal with Father Nathan. The moment that had me in its crosshairs for two years. And I'd even moved it up on the calendar to get it over with. It was the day I'd been yearning for and stressing about since taking a provisional vow with the Sisters of the Sublime Blood. The ultimate commitment to the convent. A lifelong membership with an enticing bonus—a backstage pass to the afterlife.

It wasn't the God part that tripped me up. I was all in with God. It was the forever part. Forever is *forever*. It never stops. Never ends. No wiggle room. No exit.

"Can't wait," I said.

The most effective lies are cousins of the truth.

Sister Laurel, the eldest yet newest nun in the Sisters of the Sublime Blood, had become my ally in the wake of Sister Augustine's death and Sister Honor's perpetual hatred. She joined our Order from Ascension Parish with her kind eyes that looked like she was, at any time of day, low-grade buzzed on brandy. But she was just high on life. On living. The kind of grace you find in vacant lots where wildflowers punch through concrete. She loved to play bingo at the local community center, where she'd become known for her victory dance, a gentle sway she called the holy shuffle. Sister Laurel often covered for me during my smoke breaks and midnight PI prowls with Riveaux. There's no commandment against a thirty-four-year-old nun moonlighting as a private eye.

"Class is starting soon, dear, so do get a move on," Sister Laurel pleaded. "Sister Honor's in a rather peppery manner this morning." She offered a wink, harmless, mischievous even, but inside the wink was a warning: Fall in line quickly before Mother Superior ignites a consecrated wildfire that'd have Moses saying *no thanks.*

I caught my groan before it fully developed in my throat and turned it into an "of course."

Sister Honor, head nun and a scold in humanoid form. A rotting carcass had more humor. We'd reached a truce after the meltdowns of the past year. Pain and loss brought us together. It was a shaky peace, though, and I was always one mistake away from her wrath.

But I was committed. Or I would be, after my permanent vows.

I threw my disgusting apron in the hamper, stowed the mop, bucket, and supplies, and washed my cracked hands. No time to make fresh coffee. No grounds left either. So I drank the dregs in the convent's pot, which tasted like an ashtray left out in the rain since 1982. But some caffeine was better than none at all. The rush, the return of life inside veins. Every cup of coffee a mini resurrection.

As I walked from our convent to school across Prytania Street, I took in the flowers and flowering trees. Magnolias. Oleander. Bougainvillea. And they seemed to regard me too, to notice me and size me up. The sun kept climbing, spilling me into a long shadow. Our shadows change us the way an idea changes us. For a quick moment we see how we could be—our softer, longer, more fluid angels. Silky as air.

And, yeah, I've heard what they've called me. What they've said behind my back. Twisted Sister. Lesbi-nun. Sister Holi*gay*. Folks never knew what to do with me, what box to keep me in. I was the youngest nun in our Order by forty years. Tattoos. A gold tooth. I was a novelty, even in New Orleans, a place where streets have names like Desire, Piety, Religious. Where languages intersect and every word has two meanings. The town where the dead sleep not below ground, but above, in villages of stone. The city that spins you in a Lindy Hop before she slips a shiv between your ribs. My kind of gal.

"We treat our dead better than our living," my brother, Moose, said once as we walked through the Saint Louis Cemetery. He moved to the Big Easy two months ago. An army vet, he'd started as an EMT two weeks after he'd arrived. After I realized I couldn't get rid of my baby brother, I was glad. With him close, I had one less thing to worry about.

We walked and talked a lot on Saturday evenings. Moose'd buy me coffee at the diner and tell me gory details about work. Or I'd watch him in agony as he drank a hazy beer at a café on Magazine Street. My vows: chastity, obedience, poverty, sobriety.

Eight minutes until the start of class. On the sidewalk in front of school, I saw the noodge, Ryan Brown, texting and smoking. Real cigs. No vape pen BS. The floppy-haired student hadn't yet mastered the vital art of concealing contraband. A shortage of cunning I regularly exploited.

I strode up to him. "Mr. Brown," I said, "you know smoking's prohibited on school grounds." I plucked the lit cigarette from his fingers.

He started to stammer some hilarious half-baked excuse, which I enjoyed cutting short. "Run along to class now."

After Ryan scurried off, I savored his Dunhill in the alley. The morning heat circled me like a loan shark—fanged threats and a bad attitude. Nowhere to run, nowhere to hide.

One cigarette. One last vice before I put the day into a head-lock. Cheeks caving as I took a long drag. My neck went rigid until the nicotine hit and, suddenly, everything was perfect. I was a living circuit. Fingertips sparking. The tobacco tasted like dark chocolate, leather, and a stolen kiss. Exquisite smoke too, the way it fluffed around me.

Vice, my great delight and scarlet mark. A fall from grace, like any fall, intentional or not, dialed the adrenaline to eleven. Maybe as a forever Sister I'd choose more wisely. I *should* choose more wisely. But, there and then, I had a duty to confiscate Ryan Brown's contraband, and wasn't waste the more sinful option? What a delicious responsibility.

▪

The rickety AC droned in the classroom I shared with tight-ass science teacher Rosemary Flynn as I handed out chord analysis exercises. It was the last week of school before summer break. What genius thought high school should run up to Memorial Day, into the hellmouth of humidity? No divine intervention in our academic calendar. Panicked seniors scrambled to make up missing assignments, and the worry of final exams already loomed heavy in the air. Sweaty kids with greasy hair, greasier faces, sopping armpits, complaining about the callouses from all the guitar exercises I lobbed at them. Two or three parents harped on me to show leniency. Not a chance, but nice try.

If the students' midterms—each drenched in senioritis and Axe body spray—were any indication, finals would be catastrophic. I recalled slashing through their pathetic drawings of the four clefs with my red pen, disappointed by so much mediocrity.

Except Rebecca Ansett. She strummed on her guitar with ease to demonstrate perfect fifths, and the sound hovered in the sticky air. I side-eyed Ryan Brown as he folded his worksheet into a paper airplane. The disdain in my eyes was enough to make him unfold the plane and get to work.

Prince Dempsey was MIA for the eleventh day in a row. After a month of gold-star attendance with a bizarre lack of back talk, the kid vanished again. I had a stack of notes from his doctor, but something was majorly off with him. Our eighteen-year-old super senior with PTSD and type 1 diabetes who I'd baptized in the Mississippi River just a month ago on Easter. And often wanted to throttle. That kid with a combustible temper and eyes like propane flames. We had a nuanced relationship, me and Prince. He was too familiar, too much like the hell-seeker I used to be. Or still was.

As the students scribbled, Rosemary Flynn's voice grabbed my ear. She had sidled up to my desk, her posture stiff and proper. "Sister Holiday," she said. "I need to chat with you." Her eyes darted to the students, then back to me, indicating this wasn't for their ears.

"Let's step into the hall," I said. As we moved toward the door, I called out to my class, "Keep working. God has decreed thy sheets be done when I return. And, yes, I can feel the waves of enthusiasm from here."

In the hall, I took a deep breath through my nose before facing Rosemary. She was dressed to kill, in an academically appropriate way. Her red lipstick was too loud for her marble complexion, which could've made her look fatally ill, but instead was precisely on trend. The crisp pink blouse strained against her chest, so taut that I could imagine the exact position of each nipple. Her biceps chiseled through the sleeves. Was she lifting weights? At a gym? At home? Her pencil skirt gripped her obscenely. She seemed like the type of woman who'd make someone brush their teeth, gargle, shower, shave, and wax before she let them into her bed. But then she'd fuck them so hard they woke up in the next zip code. For all of my sleuthing skills and two years of knowing Rosemary, she had an X factor I couldn't unlock. Which made me want to investigate every inch of her. With her strawberry-blond hair intimidated into a bun at the crown of her head, I could see the full length of the porcelain column of her throat.

She looked good. Eye-wateringly good.

"What do you need now?" I kept my voice heavy as the old stapler on her desk. She stared me down like I owed her fifty bucks.

Rosemary Flynn had returned to her job after crying wolf on Easter, a dramatic charade of quitting. Back to school the next week, like a moth to a cashmere twinset. Back to teaching science in her corner of our overheated shared classroom. Back to the electric, unnameable chemistry between us.

"We need to talk about this 'arrangement.'" She finger-quoted and moved closer.

"What arrangement?"

"Sharing a classroom again next year."

The arson jamboree at the beginning of the school year had forced the unholy alliance between the science and music departments. I'd drawn the short straw when it came to roommates. That's what it felt like. Punishment.

"It's not an *arrangement*." I dropped my voice lower, safe from student ears. "It's our desperate reality."

Rosemary leaned in, her perfume dismantling me. She smelled like a fresh bar of handmade rose soap and dried apricots. Her freckles were violently adorable against her unsmiling face. Like they were painted there by an elf committed to my undoing. I tried to focus on her words and not imagine the surprisingly strong back muscles that might be rippled with sweat if she were ever to lie on top of me naked. My vow of chastity rang in my mind like an off-key cathedral bell. Loud, annoying, impossible to ignore. A symphonic cockblock orchestrated by the Almighty and signed by yours truly.

She rested the backs of her hands on her hips and said, "I'm finishing up the Diocese grant application today for proper equipment." She closed her eyes and inhaled. "Nine workbenches with compound microscopes"—I swear she swooned—"Bunsen burners, an eyewash station, and—"

"So interesting." I cut her off. "Why should I care?"

"Sharing is caring. And your little guitar circle will have to tighten up," she said. "I need that space."

A message on the PA jolted us from our sexy duel.

"Sister Holiday to the gym *now*." It was Shelly. Our school's secretary, an index more reliable than a calendar, with an agelessness that defied logic. Shelly sounded so clipped on the PA, I hardly recognized her voice.

"Watch my class," I said to Rosemary, and she shot me a look that promised more sparring to come.

Why the gym? That breathless *now* freaked me out. I sprinted into the hallway, down the main steps, and outside where the morning sun bore down and the heat fit like a kidnapper's hood. I had to readjust my gloves and scarf. Even my eyelids dripped.

"Hurry!" Shelly stood outside the main entrance. "Bernard found her, called 911. He said you'd know what to do."

"Who's *her*?" I said into the back of Shelly's cat-themed cardigan, which felt mildly dangerous in the New Orleans heat.

"Just hurry!"

Oh good, a surprise.

"There," said Shelly, who loped ahead like she was dragged by an invisible rope. She led me into the gym where dozens of people had gathered. I saw the back of Bernard Pham, my pal, fellow musician, fellow rebel, school custodian. The students were quiet as we crossed the basketball court, and I studied their faces. Every face tells a story if you look close enough. A parents' marriage on the rocks. Bullying. Depression. New love. All right there. It was my job to notice, read the tells.

"What the hell?" I elbowed my way through the crowd.

Bernard stepped aside, and then I saw it. Rather, I saw her.

A body was cement still, lying on the lowest row of the bleachers.

It was Fleur Benoit, a senior. Popular girl, the rare breed with a good heart and a quick wit. She practically owned Ensemble 1 last semester. One of my favorite students, though we're not supposed to have those. But who was I to disregard her God-given gifts? She looked submerged with that blue skin.

Like she'd been replaced, redacted. Nothing like the firecracker Fleur I knew.

"She's out cold," Bernard said. "I called 911 and said a student fainted or something."

"She didn't *faint*, she's blue." I roared into Fleur's face. "Hey!" I searched her neck for a pulse, then her wrist.

Nothing. I feared I knew what this was.

"Who has Narcan?" I asked the crowd. "Bernard, Narcan? Shelly? Get it now."

"The bishop banned it," Shelly said breathlessly. "Said Narcan promoted drug use."

The fucking Diocese, warlords in the war on drugs. Last month, they fired Nurse Jenny in a budget-cut bonanza. No nurse. No Narcan. What's next? No fire alarms? No first aid kits? No school?

Fleur's eyes were locked open as she stared upward, past me, at heaven.

Mary, Mother of God, bring her back right now. One more miracle and we're square.

I blessed myself out of reflex and hope and started CPR. Push push push. With the heel of my hand on her chest, I pressed and pressed. Time hiccupped and the world narrowed on this one rhythm, this one song, and it felt so right it had to work. It was working, I told myself. Yes. Yes. Yes. Except, no, it wasn't. Fleur wasn't moving. I pushed and pushed as my arms burned.

My vision tunneled and every inch of her was so unimaginably still it felt like I had detached from reality and floated up, up, up, to the ceiling.

Her pupils were like needle jabs as I gave her two rescue breaths. Two puffs trying to jump-start her breathing.

"They're coming!" Bernard said, and I felt the sirens in my spleen before I heard them.

A student behind me whispered, "She's for-real dead?"

"C'mon, Fleur," someone cried. Begged. Insisted.

My presses were getting too heavy, the type of heavy that cracks ribs. I was going to town on Fleur's small frame. Nothing worked, nothing twitched. Her essence itself had slipped into nothing, into everything. The body and the life that lived inside the body had split. Maybe they'd forever try to find their way back to each other.

Thirty compressions. More rescue breaths. No life. The demented stench of cleaners, mold, and old sweat hung sharp as barbed wire in the hot gym air.

"Did anyone see what she took? How much?" I yelled.

Just tears and whispers in reply. The sudden quiet was outrageous. All that energy and all that youth reduced to the wet sound of my breathing and useless meter of CPR.

Fuck no. Our kids, our art, our work should outlive us. What and who we create are supposed to feed the next generation and then they feed the next and the next.

Infinite spirits inside finite bodies.

Three medics burst in with a squeaky gurney and oxygen tank. I looked for Moose but couldn't spot him anywhere. The EMTs pulled out bags, masks, equipment, leaning over Fleur, taking over chest compressions, spraying Narcan up her button nose, shooting her up with steroids, everything short of sawing her open.

At her side lay her purse, and beside it, a lighter with an engraved letter *B*. The attention and panic fixed on the medics who were working on Fleur with savage intensity, I made a split-second decision. With the toe of my sensible nun shoe,

I nudged the lighter toward me and pocketed it with a silent Hail Mary. Could have been hers. *B* for Benoit. But I never saw Fleur smoking in all the time I'd known her. A year of class and months of rehearsals. The spring recitals and holiday pageants. Countless study halls. Not once had I caught even a whiff of smoke on her uniform. So, yeah, I took evidence. Shouldn't have, but nestled against my thigh, it pulsed with the weight of a potential clue.

For ten more minutes the medics worked, trying to restart her heart. I stayed on the perimeter, watching, waiting to see any flame in her eyes. I let my body release, but not too much. Just enough to sip some air.

On the heels of the medics were the cops who powered through the gym with confident movements. A detective seemed to fancy himself the big dog. A face I didn't recognize and empty eyes I didn't trust. "Secure the scene," he instructed his colleagues. "What's the story?" he snapped at me.

"My student, Fleur Benoit."

"You found her?"

"Bernard Pham did." I pointed at Bernard, who was talking to another police officer and gesticulating wildly. "We both work here," I said.

"When'd he find her?"

"About fifteen minutes ago? I'm Sister Holiday."

The detective turned his back to me and leaned down for a closer look. "Fentanyl?" he asked a colleague. My heart caught fire, an ember's red scream, and dropped into my feet. I didn't know much about street fentanyl, only that it was insidious. An unholy power in even the smallest dose.

"We'll know when we run these," replied an officer who took photos and dangled a baggie of orange pills he'd lifted from Fleur's purse.

The medic who took over CPR from me said the terrible words, "Still no pulse. We've done everything we can."

Fleur, don't be scared. It's okay. Wasn't sure I believed it, but I needed her soul to hear it.

Whether we live or die, we belong to the Lord. Romans 14:8.

3

MY STOMACH DRAGGED ANCHOR for the next twenty minutes as I watched men in uniforms poke around Fleur's body and belongings, question students, and run caution tape across the doors. Bernard disappeared before I'd had a chance to talk to him. Detective No Name told me to stick around for a statement. Death had its own bureaucracy and established rhythm. A routine at once spontaneous and rehearsed. One cop picked at his teeth with the blade of a Bic pen cap while his partner took more photographs. They worked around her body like it was a pothole on Canal Street, something to measure and document before patching it over. How could they be so cold, so unmoved by the presence of a dead human being? All the fight, all the electricity drained from her. Surely the cops and first responders would come loose at home later, or at the bar, in the bottom of a glass. Or, like my own father, inside of themselves, locked so deep no crowbar could pry him out. My dad, a man buried so thoroughly in his own flesh you'd think he'd set up camp. His silence was a beast. It chewed through boring days and birthdays and holidays and every family photo showed the same blank-eyed stranger I called *Dad*. Maybe that's how it started, with a moment too heavy to carry. I felt it in my own throat, silence, the weight of no words.

Fleur, I'm so sorry.

Fleur was the kind of kid who said *hi* and *bye* and asked you how you were doing. Someone who strummed "Free Fallin'" on repeat until she nailed it.

But when I ran the mental tape of it backward through my brain, I remembered more. The hollow laugh in the hallways. The way she'd wrap her arms around her torso like she was giving herself a hug. Her absence in the cafeteria as I walked through it last week, gagging at the rank smell of fried fish sticks and cardboard pizza. And then, of course, Ryan Brown. From the frequent fights at her locker, it seemed they might have been dating. Or he was trying to date her—the way a hurricane tries to charm a coastline.

Last month, I caught up with Fleur at that water fountain near the office, the fountain that Bernard was always fixing. She was staring at the wall, filling her bottle covered in PETA stickers. But the bottle was already overflowing and water splashed onto the ground. She didn't seem to notice or care. Trance eyes.

"Looks like the cup runneth over," I'd said. I remember aiming for a cool-nun vibe but missing by a mile. "You all right?"

She'd shrugged with such conviction. A *fuck no* of a shrug.

"What's the point?" Fleur had replied, finally letting go of the tap.

"Of water?"

"Of finals, graduation, school, anything."

"You have potential," I said. "A future. You can do whatever you want."

"More school and a stupid job? No. I'm taking a gap year."

"What's the plan?" I asked.

"Going to Thailand, to an elephant rescue. Will probably fail finals anyway."

"You'll do just fine. And a gap year to help animals is a good idea." I managed a smile. "If that doesn't work, there's always the convent."

I remember how Fleur had forced a smile too. "If you're in a convent, it can't be that bad."

That memory of the waterfall of a fountain would infect me until the day I died. I should've seen the signs sooner, should've tried harder. I'd lived the tells, how could I miss them? How could I fail her so completely?

The devil's finest trick was making sin seem special. I'd seen the face of evil and, let me tell you, it's nothing exciting. It's not unique. It's an empty wall, a blank page that lets us write it into being. I've let its rancid breath taint my own. We're all capable of damage. A whisper of wrongness hides inside all of us, whether we admit it or not. Pain that feels too good to stop. The sweet and bitter thrill of a bloody lip. A delectable need that gets stronger the more you stab it. Doing a bad thing and secretly loving it and telling no one, not even yourself. Lying. Thinking a sick thought, playing out a nasty vision. Giving in to greed. But keeping it in check. Balancing light and darkness, that's God's ask.

Fentanyl slaughtered pain and people too. Cheap, easy to find, mixed with other meds to make them more addictive. A fast track to the edge of death. But there was a limit on how many resurrections we were granted.

The only way to fix it was to cut this snake off at the head, watch its body wither. Dive into the pit and exorcise the fucker.

That's exactly what I tried to do, before it bit me. Hard.

I couldn't hold my own weight anymore, so I sat on the unforgiving gym floor.

Whoever hooked Fleur up with a lethal dose might be long gone. Or still on campus. Maybe in that room. I hated feeling on the back foot, like I was the cartoon coyote stuck in motion, chasing an idea of the thing, because the real thing was never close enough to nab.

A shaken Shelly had shepherded a dozen crying kids behind the police caution tape, and now the gym was empty of students. But I knew this would live with them. Tough girls wouldn't be tough that day. Loud boys would go quiet. Every defense mechanism, every stupid strongman act that kids had built up for the hellhole of high school had failed under the impossibility and weight of an actual death of a peer. No person, no class, no moment had delivered this lesson. Until now.

Rosemary appeared across the sad expanse, showed her school ID to the cops, then walked over. "What's going on?" She placed a hand over her heart like she was about to take the pledge of allegiance.

"Fleur's dead," I said as I stood, almost toppling over with vertigo, or shock, or both. All sensation drained from my legs. Ankle to knee was numb. Heavy metal. "I think she overdosed."

"I . . . I just . . ." She couldn't string words together. "*Our* Fleur? How?"

"Don't know, but I'm going to find out. Where's Sister Honor? Father Nathan?"

"I saw them on their way to the Guild before class. They might not know yet." Rosemary opened her lips and inhaled, like she was about to say something else, but just turned abruptly and left. The sound of her departing heels was quickly drowned out, and I was impaled by the sight of the medics loading Fleur's dead body onto the gurney. Her hand draped over the side, the hand I taught how to play arpeggios. Her muscle memory wiped.

I knew then and there that Riveaux and I would have to step in, deal with it directly. Interrogate students. Scrutinize statements. Look for discrepancies the cops would miss. Search lockers for drugs, for notes passed in halls. If Fleur had a diary, we needed to find it. Riveaux would have to comb the kid's social media. People write different realities depending on the medium.

We had our work cut out for us. Saint Sebastian's School was shrinking after the events of that year, but there were still nearly a hundred students. Security cameras at school might've helped, if the Diocese hadn't been too cheap to install them. Thanks for nothing, Bishop. But we'd shake something free. Follow any lead, every trail. A hunt has to end somewhere.

"Man alive. Never pegged Fleur Benoit for a druggie." Alex Moore suddenly at my elbow. Our school's know-it-all librarian and Rosemary's aspiring gentleman caller. Dare to dream, fucknut. Alex was so white, so thoroughly pale, like he'd been dipped in liquid nitrogen.

Instead of clotheslining him and watching his bow tie spin like a pinwheel, I said, "And I never pegged you as a gawker. But here we are." Detective No Name took this moment to, blessedly, interrupt.

Alex peered over my shoulder as I filled out a witness statement. The twerp fell into a tight step beside me as I left the gym.

The air scalded me as we hit the street. New Orleans—the curse, the cure. The church bells began to bash themselves like solid thunder. How was it only 10 a.m.?

"I can't believe this. I've seen the opioid epidemic covered on the news, but *here*?" Alex asked with a sincerity that surprised me.

"Maybe," I said. My own spit burned me as I swallowed. "Whatever it was, I missed the signs."

Alex shook his head. "These things are so complicated." Every word was cast in bronze. "I mean, I live a very clean life. But I know that street drugs are a collective ill."

"An ill that kills," I said, not intending to be funny, but Alex laughed anyway. Practically choked.

Then he puffed up. "I've studied youth crises extensively. This is why we all need mental health training."

"Where'd you do yours?"

"I didn't," he said. "That's my point." Then he was gripped by a fascination with his thumb knuckle. "It's never been offered to me. See? Systematic failure."

"You put in a request? With the Diocese?"

"I can't possibly be expected to manage everything, can I?"

With my eye on the convent door, I paused. All I needed was a minute alone. A minute to lock myself in the freakishly clean bathroom and throw up.

"You know the Bible's take," he said. "'Be sober-minded and be watchful.'" His nodding turned creepy, like he couldn't turn it off, an overpriced bobblehead doll for sale at a roadside gift shop. He let his eyes slowly travel across my face. It was the first time I noticed how careful Alex could be. "It's true, though. Be mindful, Sister. Someone with your background has to understand the gravity here."

Background? How the hell would Alex douchebag Moore know anything about my background? I wanted to lobotomize any thoughts of me out of his Ivy League brain. "Don't worry about me. I'm two steps ahead," I lied, and with a "God bless you," I sent Alex on his way.

Riveaux would have to hustle to campus so we could get to work. There was not a minute to waste. Then I heard a shout from behind: "Sister Holiday!" It was Ryan Brown with a fresh Dunhill tucked behind his ear. "It's not true, right? Fleur?" His tears sprayed the sidewalk.

"She's gone. Maybe overdosed," I said, as his face dropped then recollected itself into a crimson knot. I reached out and rested my hand on his shoulder. The gesture felt foreign, like borrowing someone else's hands. He was so skinny and bony. Weak. Not the cocky kid trying to be bad, just a boy flailing in a truth too big for him.

"No!"

"I'm sorry, Ryan. I know you were close. It's a pain you'll never get used to." And I did know pain. Different circumstances, same abyss. "If you have any info, you know you can always tell me, right?" I softened up to play "good cop," the only theater I bothered with because it bought me something I needed. Trust.

"Me?" Ryan took a shuddering breath. "I don't know anything!"

You could say that again, I thought. "Surely you noticed something? Always hanging around Fleur's locker."

"Nothing!" Snot rolled onto his lips. He was too undone to wipe his face. "I swear on my mom's grave."

"Your mom's alive, Ryan. She was just in the office renting your graduation gown."

"Figure of speech," he said. His eyes narrowed in anger. Amazing how fury lives in the face before seeping into the rest of the body. What makes the Hulk "incredible" is rage, green as Louisiana rain.

Time to rip off the Band-Aid. "Ever see Fleur take pills?" I asked. "Or give her any?"

"She was the love of my life!" Ryan tweaked in a jittery dance.

"So you and Fleur were an item?"

"I mean, no, not exactly." Ryan came apart completely. Sobbing, gasping, his whole body shaking.

"It's okay," I said, in my best customer-service voice. I let my exhale lengthen and linger, modeling how to breathe. Had to calm him down so I could turn up the heat.

Once Ryan collected himself, I asked, "This your lighter?" I pulled it out and held it up. The *B*, etched like a vow. "*B* for Brown?" If I'd seen that swanky number before, I'd have swiped it too. Maybe Fleur beat me to the punch.

"Not mine."

"Was it Fleur's then? *B* for Benoit?"

"No. She didn't smoke. She hated the smell."

"If you're holding back on me, I'll find out." I took his cigarette. "Understand?" He nodded glumly.

I stuffed the lighter and cig into my pocket where they burned a psychic hole.

Besides being my cigarette source and ever-present noodge, Ryan Brown was seriously into Fleur. How often I'd watch him trailing her, talking into the back of her head in the cafeteria line. Maybe she was into him too. Maybe not. I couldn't see Fleur going for a poser like him, but what did my celibate gay ass know about high school heteronormies. Regardless, the noodge knew more than he was saying—strange for a kid who usually couldn't shut up. This was the boy who wore socks with sandals, whose "switchblade" was actually a comb, who broadcast details about pounding Hard Lemonade after school, thinking nuns couldn't hear teen talk because our saintly ears tuned out the audible grime of life. Ryan Brown's brevity spoke volumes that day.

His crying intensified. I wasn't going to get anything more from him. It was too fresh.

"It'll be okay," I told him.

"Will it?" He looked dehydrated, wrung out.

"Go to the gym." I dismissed him with a jerk of my chin. "Tell the police what you know."

Hard to imagine a turkey like Ryan Brown involved in school-yard drug dealing. But if I'd learned anything from this past year, it was that you can never discount a suspect until you're sure. And even then, absolute certainty was neither absolute nor certain. Had to keep my eye on that kid.

No more tragedy on my watch. But why'd I lie to Ryan Brown, saying it would be okay? Reality is a rough comedown. We want to believe fables and fairy tales and elaborate fictions. A man in a sleigh delivering billions of presents at once. A virgin giving birth to the son of God. A second chance when the world keeps dealing bad hands. Or was lying a first step toward truth? Arriving at knowledge through a side door?

▪

The numbness by then was so paralyzing, I couldn't even throw up. In the convent bathroom, I slapped my face with cold water and cold hands, then I ducked into the kitchen. The industrial fridge clicked. Three generations of Sisters of the Sublime Blood had obediently wiped the counters into submission, but that Monday they felt like autopsy tables. Too brutal and knowing.

I picked up the convent's old corded phone—no modern luxuries for us nuns—and dialed the only number I had memorized.

"Riveaux," I said. Talking, trying to say one word, was a frustrating challenge. Like walking up a down escalator.

"Sister Goldsmobile." Riveaux's voice spun the expected mix of mild amusement and pointed superiority. She loved her nickname for me—a shout out to my gold tooth—and I pretended to be annoyed, but it'd grown on me, just like Riveaux'd grown on me. No BFF bracelets in the pipeline, but I knew she cared about me too. Not that she'd ever fess up to it. "Your school's making news again," she said.

"Heard already?"

"The blotter," Riveaux said. She'd kept some equipment from her days as an arson investigator with the NOFD. "What's the happs?"

"A student died."

"Mary and Joseph." She coughed. "One of yours?"

"Yeah, a good one. Fleur Benoit. Bernard found her."

"I am so sorry, Goldsmobile. What happened?"

I imagined her rubbing her eyes, could practically see it, through the invisible channel.

"Seems like she OD'd," I said. "She had a bag of pills on her."

"Fentanyl. Has to be. That shit is *everywhere*." Riveaux took a series of breaths like she was doing desk yoga. Or maybe she was sniffing some of her perfume concoctions. Then I heard her typing furiously. "I have the police department reports from Q1 here. Lemme see. Car thefts up, homicides up, domestics up." She whistled. "Fentanyl possessions tripled in the last three months."

"Tripled?"

"They're raking it in," Riveaux said. "Who said crime doesn't pay?"

"Tale as old as time."

She huffed. "What's new is that the DA's started charging fentanyl dealers with first-degree murder, for ODs."

"They're peddling death. Why not?"

"Homicide. You know what that means. Decker will be all over this case like hives." In the silence that followed I heard the machinery of Riveaux's brain deciding what words to verbalize next. "She'll probably be at your school soon."

Sergeant Ruby Decker.

Decker lost her wife, Sue, during Easter weekend because of me. Because of my mistake. My good intentions tainted by deadly misjudgment. And a crooked cop. Decker had made bad calls too. Worse than bad. It tracked, blaming me. I'd have done the same. Anything to lessen the weight of guilt and grief. A broken heart makes you want to break everything.

Riveaux prodded, "You all right?" She must have sensed the cliff I was dangling over.

"Been better, but you can help. Let's work this case, Riveaux."

"You never pick the easy path, do you, question mark?"

"It's never picked me," I said. "You did, though."

"All right, Goldsmobile, don't lay it on too thick. I've got your back. But this is one sticky wicket."

"So how soon can you get here?"

"In a jiffy." She cleared her throat. "Actually, need to tie up a few things here. Give me a jiffy and a half."

I grumbled in acknowledgment and gently hung up.

Bernard's number was laminated and taped above the convent phone. I had to call him next.

After Jack died in the fire last year, Bernard became our sole custodian. Our fix-it savior. All the leaky roofs and broken door hinges after gale-force winds. I called his line but it hit dead air. Bernard's voicemail kicked in with that low roll of his voice you could feel your feet, like a subway train approaching. I called three times but he never answered. Where'd he sneak off to?

Wasn't sure what to say in a message, so I didn't leave one. We'd have to debrief later.

What I did notice was a crack in the phone's plastic green shell. One more busted thing in a city full of them.

▪

It was only lunchtime, though every minute had felt like a year. Classes were paused, but the students had to stay on campus. Police were taking statements in the cafeteria before parents and guardians could collect their charges.

I swung by the utility closet on the school's first floor, in the hopes that Bernard was there. No dice. Father Nathan's office in the rectory across the street was empty too, but his phone was ringing off the hook, as usual, morning, noon, and night.

In the narrow gap between the cafeteria's dumpsters and loading dock, where exhaust mixed with the otherworldly stench of rotted collard greens, I fumbled with the mysterious lighter. Should I use potential evidence to light the cigarette I'd just stolen from Ryan Brown? Fuck no. But smoking helped me think. More crucially, I loved smoking. Loved it with the passion of the liturgy. Delivery pallets formed an attractive half-wall between me and anyone who might glance my way. Though

I kept scanning in every direction for a glimpse of Bernard. We had to talk. He was our inside man if there ever was one at Saint Sebastian's. He worked in every corner and on every floor of campus, with intimate knowledge of occupancy patterns, master keys, and access to blueprints. Surely, he had to have seen something of interest.

"Come on, come on," I said to myself, to God, as I flicked the cursed lighter. "Come on," I said to the last working nerve connecting my brain to the rest of my body. The flame finally caught, and I inhaled deeply, smoke filling my lungs, searing me inside out, like a kiss of steam from a busted pipe. I welcomed the burn. Cruel relief. My eyes watered and my throat ached. I should have laid low. To avoid Sergeant Decker. To stay on Sister Honor's good side.

In the filmy cafeteria window, I took inventory of myself. My shabby plain black uniform. And under that, so many tattoos I'd lost count. An inked Hail Mary hummed its cadence under the cuffs of my black blouse. The only pops of color in my new nun life were my blue eyes—same glassy blue as my brother's—my gold tooth, and my bleach-blond hair. Black roots always showing. Always reminding me of my own mess, my various selves. Maintenance was never my thing. Why was follow-through so much harder than starting something new?

4

AFTER THAT PRECIOUS CIGARETTE sesh, on my way to the convent for a check-in with Riveaux, Prince Dempsey's mom walked onto campus. Trish, the mother of the kid whose absence thrummed in my brain like an aneurysm, strutted across our courtyard like she owned the land. And what I'd first taken for a fashion statement—an avant-garde sleeve—was a pink arm sling, loud and angular against her flowing blouse. Broken arm? Sprain? Dislocated shoulder?

"Where's Prince?" I asked. "He okay? You okay?" I nodded to Trish's arm.

"Well, ain't that a fine how do you do." Trish took a drag of what appeared to be a Virginia Slim and blew a fairly impressive smoke ring. Eight out of ten if I had to judge. "Was hoping you'd be here. We need to talk."

"Where's Prince?" I asked again, drawing it out. The effort to keep my face calm was all-consuming. The heat turned the concrete into a griddle.

"Home again with that blood sugar acting up." She swept her blond hair back with her good hand. "He won't be in class for a few more days."

"We're a week from graduation."

"Doctor's orders," she said. "You gotta cut my boy some slack."

"He staying on top of his"—I searched for the word—"wellness?"

"He most certainly is." There was a pause. A completely insulted, leaden pause before a streak of maternal pride lit up her face. "That's something my boy takes real serious. Well, his sugar and that dog." Trish watched an ambulance drive past, followed by two police cruisers. "Why the cops here? One of them mass-shooting exercises?"

"No." I blessed myself. "One of Prince's classmates died today." I tried to deliver the facts gently, though they might have sounded snippy because my throat was painfully tight.

"Goodness gracious. What on earth happened?"

"An overdose," I said, examining her face as she processed the news.

"Oh no." She squinted up at the sun. "What a *tragedy.*"

"Fleur Benoit," I said. "You know her?"

"Can't say that I do. But, that just ain't right." She straightened her sling then dabbed sweat from her cheek and forehead. "No child should be meeting their maker. This world doesn't make a lick of sense, now does it?"

"No." I stared at the bright sun too, until I was momentarily blind. I rubbed my eyes. Everything was extra that day. The pain. The heat. The light. The dark.

"Got any schoolwork for my boy?" Trish asked. "That's what I'm here for." Her green eyes were expertly adorned with gold eye shadow.

"Yeah, but it's theory plus exercises, and better explained in person. I could stop by your place, bring his guitar," I offered.

"Oh, sweetie, that's real kind, but Prince's little body's so desperate for rest. He'll come round when he's fighting fit." She gave a wink that didn't feel forced, but it was compromised by some lower feeling she didn't want to show. Sadness? Fear? Anger?

"It's not a big deal," I said. "I could stop by later. Keep him on track to graduate."

She laughed without smiling. "Don't think strumming on some guitar's going to get him a diploma."

"I'm worried about him."

"Don't you worry your holy head. He's home where I can keep an eye on him. Keep him safe."

"Safe from what?" I had to wrangle my voice back down. "Prince isn't using drugs, right?"

"Please. That boy?" Trish took a long drag. Held it until I felt the smoke burn my own lungs. Spanish moss dripped spookily from the oaks, threatening to fall. Even the trees were sighing. "Prince knows better than to wallow in the mud with the hogs. He's nothing like his daddy."

"Say more."

"Kenneth always ran hard with the wrong pack. Been up the river for dealing for three years, and hand to God, that has been a blessing. He was a real hard-ass on the boy, on us both, even when Prince was a rug rat. My husband burned his fuse to the quick so many times, he doesn't have a stitch of fuse left."

She lit another cigarette almost as fast as she smoked the first, using her good hand to spark the lighter. The flame sent a wave of red across her necklace—*Trish* with a heart over the *i*. Her lipstick was the color of a stop sign in the blazing sun, and it left a perfect circle on the filter. This woman didn't belong on a stodgy campus among the brick and iron with a cheap arm sling. She belonged on a stage singing a heartbreaking ballad in a martini bar. "But like I said, Prince is nothing like his daddy. Just a little dose of that hot temper from time to time, but he's a decent boy."

"That we agree on. But what happened there?" I asked, nodding again to her arm sling, pink as the nose on a bunny rabbit stuffy.

"Oh, *this*?" She was almost tickled. "Took a little tumble. Thou shall not wear four-inch heels on Bourbon Street. Moses should've put that at the tippy top of those commandments."

"Amen to that."

"Well, I don't have much time left on this lunch break." Trish let her shoulders relax.

Lunch break? Cigarettes weren't exactly a balanced meal, though one of my go-to menu options. "Where's your job?" I asked, hoping to tease a few more details out of her.

"Crescent City Repair. Started taking shifts when my Kenneth got himself locked up." She gave me a weak smile and leaned against the obsidian gate. "A rooster may crow his little heart out," she said, "but nine times outta ten, it's the hen that winds up delivering the goods."

What the ever-loving fuck did that mean? I'd have to ask Riveaux, Rosemary, or Bernard, who were constantly translating local codes and idioms, Cajun French, actual French, and Creole words for me. Phrases like *laissez les bons temps rouler*— let the good times roll. And *fais do-do*—originally "go to sleep," but in New Orleans it meant a dance that raged all night long.

In that moment, Prince's mom looked like Saint Teresa of Ávila, practically levitating in that scalding courtyard. I knew women like Trish. I had countless one-night stands with married women like her, happily playing the role of the revenge fuck for payback on some husband who'd stepped out. Mutually assured destruction. From the three times I'd chatted with her, I'd gotten a pretty clear picture. Trish was a spitfire, but a measured one. She seemed like the kind of woman who'd load up the jukebox with a roll of quarters, who knew all the gossip in town, who could talk a jumper down from a ledge with a ridiculous story about a three-legged dog from twenty years ago.

"I built a life for my boy all by myself, and people try to come and pull the damn rug out from under me. Just feels like folks are out to get me whenever I get a break."

Trish Dempsey'd survived devastation. Storms. Ruthless Acts of God, and, by the sound of it, a less-than-easy marriage. Although her arm was in a sling, her face was flawless, smooth, no bruises or cuts or scrapes.

Student voices bounced around the courtyard like birdsong, notes and messages detached from their sources. The massive oak tree shaded us. Moss wrapped around higher branches like thick sweaters. Trish pressed herself against the bark. To steady herself? Feel ancient wisdom? Hide?

"Got an extra?" I asked, miming smoking and glancing over my shoulders to make sure Sister Honor wasn't lurking. Would be my third smoke of the morning, but it was needed. Desperately. Trish seemed to regard my black gloves.

"No," she said, "last one. Take it." She plucked the cigarette from her lips and tucked it between mine. The filter was warm from her mouth. My lips were suddenly on her red lipstick.

The church bell sang over us, inserted itself, spilling its stubborn chorus into the sky.

Trish took three steps away, stopped, then turned back slowly and gave me a hug with her left arm. Her cheek grazed mine, and her skin was so soft it hurt me. "You know, when I was pregnant,

I drank from a wishing well so my boy'd be born lucky. But he's seen more storms than sunshine." Trish straightened up and squared her shoulders, letting some tension roll to the ground.

As she walked away, the oaks complained under their own weight.

▦

Five minutes later, I was back in the convent kitchen. It was empty. I appreciated the quiet after the chaos of the morning, but Riveaux was taking three jiffies too many to arrive.

I grabbed my Steno where I kept addresses and numbers I hadn't memorized. My brain needed free storage space for other matters. Like sleuthing and scripture. I called Moose who answered after two rings. "I heard," he said. "Goose, I'm—"

"Where are you?"

"All the way across town." Moose had an ease I envied. "Fill me in."

I stretched the phone cord into the hallway and told Moose what had happened. How Shelly had paged me, how Bernard found Fleur, the bag of orange pills, the Narcan and CPR, medics swooping into the scene. Kids crumpling into sad piles.

"Narcan. Orange pills," Moose echoed. Moose, the nickname I gave my brother because Gabriel never quite suited him. Though he turned out to be quite the protector. He called me Goose so we'd always rhyme. Always be in sync, even when far apart. He trusted medicine, I trusted God. Between us, we had the bases covered.

He said "orange" again, and I could hear his mind flipping through mental folders, looking for a fit. "Could be fentanyl masquerading as any number of things."

"The police have to test it."

As Moose and I talked, I stood face-to-face with the painting of Saint Margaret Mary Alacoque. In our exceptionally spare convent, art held powerful energy. The saint's halo was so strong, bursting with gold light, I could almost feel it fall onto me. Then I touched other frames in the hall. Tapping corners and edges, like they might disappear if I didn't keep proving they were real. The morning sizzle of terror and rage had run out its charge, leaving an itching restlessness in my blood.

Moose cleared his throat. "Bernard okay?"

"*Bernard?* What about me?"

He inhaled slowly then said, "You're stronger than him, and you know it. Where's he now?"

Moose and Bernard had become friends too. I didn't realize how much Moose had grown to care about my life at Saint Sebastian's, but it was nice to hear him share my concern.

"Bernard gave his statement to the cops," I said, "and now, I don't know where he is. I looked for him, called him a few times but it went to voicemail."

"Uh-huh." I could see him closing his eyes on the other end of the phone, his long eyelashes clasping, casting rivers of shadows down his cheeks. The sound waves crackled. "This sucks."

"Sucks." I laughed, continuing the habit of laughing when it wasn't funny. "It's a fucking nightmare, Moose."

"Promise me you're not going to get mixed up in this."

"Meaning what?"

"You're too smart to play dumb." Moose was already guilting and pleading and chiding. My Moose. Sometimes he felt like my own kid. Other times he sounded so much like Dad it took the breath clean out of my lungs. "Promise you'll stay out of it?" he repeated.

"My student is dead."

"So you won't promise?" A queeny edge nipped his words, a sass I usually loved and wanted to hear more from my brother, except when it was aimed at me.

"I have to go," I said.

"Wait!"

I slammed the phone down though I could hear his voice still trying to grab me.

No, I wasn't going to get "mixed up." Not by myself, at least.

The old me knew that world intimately, like the ridges of the roof of my own mouth. That first high was like the first time I came—feeling exploded out of me. A revelation. A sensation roared where there'd been only emptiness. The void I'd carried my whole life, a howling emptiness like the moaning of a cave. It was filled for one scalding second. Human bodies are built for euphoria. Who'd blame us for wanting to touch the divine, to feel divine ourselves. But chasing a high always cued up a crash.

That's why I'd crack this. I knew a thing or two about getting so blasted you forgot your own name. I perfected the sin of crucifying yourself. Not trusting your own mind. Me, Sister Holiday, nun with no love for authority and a painfully DIY bleach job. A part-time sleuth, music teacher at Saint Sebastian's School, full-time watchdog of God. But I had real faith. A faith that cut me when I held it too tight, but it was still worth carrying all the same.

Fleur was dead, and I had a new mission from God. Always my toughest client.

One clue so far: a lighter with a *B* cut into it. One victim: a good kid who took a bad drug.

Riveaux and I'd get to the bottom of this one too. As if an abyss had a floor.

5

RIVEAUX MARCHED UP TO me at the convent's front door. Her neon-white blouse was efficiently de-wrinkled by the impressive humidity. The air was thick as Drano then, too hot for even the starlings who hid in the shade of the muscular wisteria vines. Riveaux's mom jeans offered pockets so roomy she could easily carry a hammer in one and a tire iron in the other. Just a few months earlier, she'd walked with a cane, but, like Moose, Riveaux had built herself back up and stood taller than ever. Even her shoulders relaxed with some ease. Seeing her strength renewed my faith in her. In Redemption Detective Agency. In us.

"Call 911 again," she said when she saw the state of me. "Looks like someone's been hit by the struggle bus."

"Don't start," I said, annoyance giving my words some well-earned grandeur. Truth was, the sight of Riveaux steadied me more than the prayers I sailed up to the divine on a loop that day.

Her eyes tracked left and right with that oiled focus I'd noticed last year when she was still working arson investigation. When she'd read char patterns like I read the Gospel of

Mark. Now, as a PI, she was reading people. Looking for origin points, mapping how destruction forked through the hours and days and lives of human beings instead of architecture. As we walked across campus, the cops moved around us haphazardly like they were extras in a show too stunningly ridiculous to watch even on a hospital TV. They seemed far more interested in placing lunch orders at Mahoney's than finding relevant evidence of drug dealing. "Decker here yet?" Riveaux asked.

"Hope not." I blessed myself and kissed my gloved knuckles.

"I know you two have beef, Goldsmobile," she said, "but Decker's radar is zeroed in on perps right now. Not grudges."

"Pretty sure I'll always be a suspect in her book."

"Innocent until proven guilty, though I *suspect* you're right." Riveaux paused, so very proud of her zinger. "Where shall we start?" She tightened her already too-tight ponytail.

"I saw a bunch of police herding teachers and students into the cafeteria. The gym's taped off for CSI shit. Maybe we can search lockers. And interview any stragglers."

"Won't the lockers be locked, question mark?" Riveaux used her pinky to slide her glasses up her nose as we entered the west wing.

"Bernard has the universal key."

"A master key? Winning."

Bernard usually was full of win. "Haven't seen him since ten, though. Sometimes he hides in the utility closet." I pointed down the hall. "But he wasn't there when I swung by earlier."

He was in shock, no doubt, and I was worried about him. Despite the upheaval, when I reached for Bernard, I expected to grab him. He was one of my constants. Never had to ask how I took my coffee, and vice versa. I guided Riveaux back toward the utility closet. It was worth another try.

That was the moment I should've told Riveaux about the lighter I found near Fleur. Should have, but the relief of swinging open the closet door and seeing Bernard derailed my train of thought. He looked small amid the towers of toilet paper, paper towels, and red jugs of cleanser so large you could hide a short freshman in them.

"Where you been?" I stood in front of him.

After a silence so hard it could pop out a filling, he said, "Oh, hey." His voice was stripped down, weak, like a wood floor sanded raw. His eyes wouldn't land anywhere for more than a second.

"I called you three times," I said. "We need your help opening up lockers." He backed up when I put my hand on his shoulder. "And I was worried. You okay?"

"Sorry. I, uh. So, yeah. Been trying to—"

"Hey, man." Riveaux moved closer to Bernard. "Hanging in there?"

Bernard stared at her, as if Riveaux's words were on some kind of delay. "You find everything when you're working custodial. Pregnancy tests. Those stupid dye tags from shoplifted clothes. A ferret in a classroom."

"A ferret?" Riveaux's slightly appalled face revealed she wasn't a fan. "*Alive?*"

"Very." Bernard tapped the bun at the crown of his head. "A frisky little guy. I took him to the small mammal shelter in Kenner."

Bernard, the softie. He bounced his key ring, which had its own soundtrack. There was a distinct and silent charge in his eyes, like the wattage was too high and soon a breaker was about to blow. "I find stuff the students think they can hide.

Never thought I'd ever find one of them, though. *A dead body.* Death seems so, so, I don't know, unhuman."

Tragedy makes theologians of us all.

"You're our inside man," I said. "You had to have seen something this morning."

"Yes. I told you what I saw—a dead body," he said. "And I wish—" His voice broke and his face fell. He was shutting down. "I wish—"

"Nothing prepares us." I made the sign of the cross with big theatrical movements, not for drama, but to send the blessing to wash over Bernard.

"Nothing ever could," Riveaux said.

"We may never know why it happened but we need to figure out *how*. If you want some alone time, don't worry about coming with us. But can we use your keys?" I extended my gloved palm.

"No." He snipped, surprising himself. I could tell by how quickly he tried to right the ship, a flash of embarrassment. "Sorry. I mean, I'll come with. I want to help."

Bernard and I'd been raked over hot coals. After we lost our friends Jack and Sister T. After Sister Augustine's flameout, Father Reese's final swim, Father Nathan's missing weekend, and Grogan's revenge clusterfuck. Bernard knew me—my secrets. Most of them, anyway. Trust was a fragile creature.

"Should probably grab an officer to do this right," Riveaux said. "Thank me later."

Bernard looked at me, and then I looked at Riveaux like she was insane. "A cop?" I balked in the whiniest pitch I could access.

"I know, I know. But we need to cover our asses," she said. "If we want anything we find to stand up in court, we need to start thinking like the authorities. Not acting like those fucking clowns, just thinking like them. Yep?" She tapped her canine tooth.

"Yeah," I relented. Of course, she was right.

"Onward," Riveaux said, and waved at the officer near the main entrance. He was leaning against a wall ignoring Shelly, who was crying into her hands. The officer didn't hesitate when Riveaux signaled him over. He walked toward us with a slow, measured pace that matched his excessive height.

"My old pal, Officer Arthur," Riveaux whispered as he approached. "He owes me a favor. Worst fantasy football picks you could possibly imagine. Obsessed with his smartwatch stats."

"Congrats, Maggie." Officer Arthur towered over us with his hands clasped behind his back. "Heard you got licensed."

"So shiny and new." She flashed her PI license. "New letterhead, same crummy hours."

"We miss ya downtown," he said.

"Then let's spend some quality time today," she said. "Can you help us with a locker search?"

"Crew's assigned to that later."

"But we're here now," she said, "and I know your team's busy pulling statements in the cafeteria. The custodian Bernard Pham's got the keys to the kingdom."

Bernard held up a key on his bulky ring. "A master, for the lockers."

Arthur took the keys and gave me an icy look. "Who's she?"

Riveaux smiled with her eyes only. "Sister Holiday works here."

"And?" I wheeled Riveaux.

"And what?" She stared at the ground, thought about it, then twitched as she remembered. "She works with me too. She's my agency apprentice."

"You always did love the strays," Arthur said. I drilled my tongue into the sharp point of my gold tooth.

"The lockers," Riveaux said. "Yes or no?"

"Well—"

"We'll save tons of time, and you'll get your ten thousand steps," Riveaux said, as she pulled on a pair of her own latex gloves. Baller move.

"All right. Then maybe I can actually make it home for dinner for once this year. Lisa's had it with me." Arthur slipped on a pair of gloves, handing two more sets from his pocket to Bernard and me. "Those aren't going to cut it." He pointed to my leather calling cards.

By the time we'd finished snapping on the gloves, Arthur was already headed down the hall like he'd done this a thousand times. "Follow me. And, don't do anything you wouldn't want me to explain to a judge."

"We're on the same side here," said Riveaux.

The search started with the west wing lockers, as we worked our way to number eight, Fleur's. Each door was dented and scratched but never the same way twice. Years of institutional green paint peeling to show primer gray and steel underneath.

By that point in the afternoon, with the news of Fleur's death out there, I'd imagined students would've liberated anything suspicious or problematic from their lockers, but we still had to look.

When Officer Arthur opened Fleur's locker, it smelled like strawberry lip balm. Sweet enough to give you a toothache just standing near its open door. I spotted a partially sucked Jolly Rancher stuck to old homework. On the top shelf sat a makeup bag. Shiny, floral, tacky. It was the kind of thing you'd go home with after a White Elephant exchange if you were unlucky.

I stared. The rose on the gaudy fabric was a nest of swirls, an infinity of pink petals. Inside one petal was another petal and inside that was a smaller petal and on the tiniest petal was a smear of black, mascara, and inside that smear, a single speck of glitter.

Tiny. Perfect. Impossible.

I leaned into the locker to look closer and to pray. To Fleur. Impossibility itself. The glitter.

The speck pulsed. Or maybe I blinked.

"Easy, Goldsmobile." Riveaux pulled me back by my blouse. I felt her knuckles between my shoulder blades. "Gonna go cross-eyed."

I readjusted my layered gloves as Officer Arthur opened the bag. Nothing of note was inside, unfortunately. Just hair ties, Lip Smackers, and mascara.

We continued to follow Officer Arthur down the hall with the master key. Some doors were stuck, needing Arthur's full body weight to pry them open. Others swung loose on hinges with missing screws. Every door opening threw a shadow.

The evidence in Ryan Brown's locker was jack-in-the-box subtle. A pack of Dunhills—a treasure I wasn't able to swipe. A Snapple bottle filled with gin and cranberry juice. A variation of the same nauseating swill I'd chugged before a family dinner or a guitar lesson or a date when I was young myself. A little something to take the edge off. But what if the edge was necessary, a load-bearing wall, the permanent infrastructure?

Prince Dempsey's locker held only a bag of oral hygiene treats for his dog, BonTon, his fur baby. Otherwise, a striking emptiness.

"Prince has been absent for nearly two weeks," I said to Riveaux. "His mom claims he's home sick. And she has her arm in a sling."

She stuck out her bottom lip. "Think Prince is in trouble, question mark?"

"When is he not? I'll stay on it," I said, to her, to my wary brain.

We kept going, carefully as altar servers, through every locker in the wing. They told stories in their silence. Sharpied names half rubbed away. Notes folded into paper boats that looked seaworthy. A condom still in its wrapper—mercifully—tucked inside a math textbook. Two ring lights in one locker. Ring lights, for fuck's sake. So many tools designed to hide "flaws" in our faces, though imperfections were actually miracles, divine clock hands, a way to honor our survival, catalog years lived on this mysterious bundle of sky and sea called a planet. There were so many ways to alter ourselves you'd think God made us all wrong and it was the tech bros and plastic surgeons who got the template right.

We saw flasks and helmets. Corn nuts and protein bars. Trident spearmint gum and powdered Donettes. Community Coffee to-go cups that'd grown fur. Nothing that felt relevant—but that didn't stop Riveaux from meticulously documenting our search on her iPad.

Bernard tapped his chin and looked at his phone like he was late for a job interview, which, perhaps he was. "That's the lot of them," he said.

"No, it's not," I said. "There are dozens of lockers in the east wing."

"East wing?" Riveaux seemed surprised to hear it uttered.

"Yeah," I said, walking in that direction. "It's still out of commission. But you never know."

The east wing had been a no-go zone since the fires at the start of the school year. It was taped off, off-limits, slated for an overhaul and rebuild while the center wing and west wing remained functional. The east wing was another victim of shame and retaliation. Another carcass of collateral damage. And, like most revenge thrillers, it was drowning in ghosts. In that east wing smoke, I'd seen the Holy Ghost. Or so I thought. Now it seemed like an ideal spot to hide drugs.

Officer Arthur studied the crumpled yellow tape that still fluttered from the east wing barricades. "Doesn't look like it's under construction."

"The Diocese is dragging their feet on fixing it," I said.

The smell hit first. The sour, sick sweetness of rot. A stench like vertigo, a violent free fall. Scorch marks crawled the walls, scars that refused to heal.

Some of the lockers hung open, having been rummaged and rifled through by every fireman, officer, and insurance agent this side of the Gulf. Most were empty. Only one was locked. We all looked at each other meaningfully. Arthur opened it with fluid confidence.

Riveaux immediately spotted something. "What do we have here?"

The long-limbed officer reached in and pulled out a paper bag. Nested inside were dozens of clear plastic baggies of pills. A cozy roost of the same orange tablets I'd seen next to Fleur earlier. No labels, no branding. Unmistakable color of a goddamn creamsicle.

"The stash," Riveaux said, her eyes lit with a victorious glow.

"Oh, snap." Bernard blinked.

"Same pills that Fleur had," I said.

"Dead drop?" Riveaux mused aloud. "We should presume these contain fentanyl," she said, inspecting a baggie that Officer Arthur placed in her gloved palm. "Doesn't look like they're masquerading as Oxy or Vicodin. At least not a varietal I was once familiar with," she sighed.

"Not in my former wheelhouse either," I said, remembering the meth I popped like Mentos at pier dances during Pride. Also didn't look like the Ambien Moose took for insomnia.

Riveaux tensed the muscles around her eyes. "Any markings?"

"No stamping on the pills," Officer Arthur said with his flashlight flicking over the contents.

Riveaux tapped the baggie in her hand, one edge crimped like it'd been melted. "Ten pills. Ten pills in each baggie. Goldsmobile, how many did you see this morning?"

"Five? Maybe six?" I replied. "Couldn't count."

"So ten in each bag. At least five accounted for with Fleur, not including the one in her bloodstream. That potentially leaves four out there, from her baggie alone," Riveaux said.

"Bad news," Bernard said.

"These might not *all* be deadly," Arthur said. "The goal is to get users addicted."

"Dealers want return customers," I agreed, "not dead ones."

I looked at the cache in the locker again. "Is someone at Saint Sebastian's dealing?" The thought burned through me.

"Not necessarily," Riveaux asserted. "The whole city heard about the fire. Anyone who knew the east wing was unoccupied could be our dealer. Anyone with a calculating mind."

"You could slip in and out through the east exit without being seen," Bernard said. "It's not like we have a security system."

What if *Fleur* had been dealing? I shook off the question as quickly as it formed. Dealers rarely use themselves. But, what if? No. Arthur and Riveaux had started chatting quietly among themselves. I walked backward a few steps behind the group, turned, and drove my knee into a locker. Hard. The metal shrieked like an animatronic mousebot getting kicked in the stomach. My kneecap yelped in bone-deep anguish, but the feeling was intoxicating, overwhelming. A luxury. A different explosion to scare panic out of my chest.

Before Arthur and Riveaux turned around, Bernard dropped his clipboard and fell. Threw his body to the ground to cover for me. "So clumsy!" he said musically. He stood, making a show of it all. "Sorry."

"Gotta phone this in." Officer Arthur's lemur eyes glistened, then he pivoted. His voice ping-ponged around the hall as he walked a few feet away, talking to a station crew.

"We need to warn everyone," I said, "to trash any questionable pills. Flush every pill now."

Riveaux squinted. "And tip off our dealer? No way. The force should stake out the locker."

"Sister Holiday's right," Bernard said. "We should warn folks now."

Riveaux jogged to catch up with Arthur, and I hung back with Bernard, slowed my step. "You sure you didn't see anything odd this morning?" I asked him. "Find anything weird in the past few weeks?"

"No," he said. "Truly, nothing."

Then we all left the sooty wing. The evidence, now in NOPD custody, would soon be tested. Photographed. Logged. The locker would be dusted for prints. If we were lucky, maybe they'd find something conclusive and nail the fucker fast. But if we were actually lucky, this nightmare wouldn't have happened at all. And I prayed to Mary and Saint Lucy and all the saints that no more kids would die.

■

Back at the main entrance, the air pressurized in a distressing way, like wool drenched by warm rain, never to fit right again. Sister Honor was rounding the corner, striding toward me and Bernard. I'd been doing my best to avoid her. But sometimes our best isn't good enough.

"Why in the name of our perfect Lord are you dawdling in this hallway like a band of vandals?" Sister Honor's voice dropped to that dangerous octave that usually preceded detention. I knew she'd be rattled by Fleur's death. As our Mother Superior. Principal. Fellow human. But her righteous flame was burning extra hot. "There's too much to do. This is a community in *peril* yet again, and here you are playing detective." She looked ruefully at my latex gloves.

"But I've already given the cops my statement, and I'm assisting the officers."

"That is not your role. Your *role* is to be a servant of the Sisters of the Sublime Blood." Her glare alone could ignite the Paschal candle. "You must set an example for the students, their parents, and the police on our campus! You have abandoned your sacred duty of care."

"*Abandoned?*" I wanted to headbutt her, to scream in her face, but I kept my voice cool. "Where were you when I was giving

Fleur CPR? Where were you when they wheeled her dead body away?"

She shut her eyes and crossed herself so theatrically I wondered if she dislocated a shoulder. "How *dare* you question—"

"We have to warn the students immediately," I continued. No matter how much Sister Honor irked me, there wasn't a moment to waste.

"About *what*?" Sister Honor's apocalyptic breath made the air quiver.

"A bad batch of counterfeit pills." I spoke calmly, steadily, like I was approaching a suicide bomber with their thumb on the button, ready to detonate. "Probably laced with fentanyl. Students need to dump whatever they're holding, if they have anything."

She threw her head back. "You know this information how, exactly?" Her cataract-glossed eyes searched the ceiling.

"It's part of my 'duty of care.'" There was so much more to say, to rant about. I wanted to call my Mother Superior out on her bullshit. One of our best kids was dead and she was on a power trip. Pulling myself back felt impossible. Each thought in my head ticked ticked ticked with excruciating loudness. So loud I was convinced everyone else could hear.

"And she knows from all of her time at rock bottom," Bernard offered, his eager tone landing like a brick through a car window. "From her *past*."

Dear sweet Bernard. He really did seem to think he was helping.

Sister Honor drew herself up inch by annoying inch, lassoing me with her cloudy gaze. "Your past is precisely why you should remember your place now, *Sister* Holiday." The way she said *Sister* made it sound radioactive, something that needed handling with a hazmat suit. Every twelve-stepper and former addict knew that tone. The one that said your second chance, your redemption, your grace was always one mistake from evaporating.

Riveaux rejoined us, stepping into the firing line. "Easy now. Emotions are coming in hot today, but we just found evidence of an illicit drug operation at your school."

"Well"—Sister Honor sucked her teeth—"if this is indeed true, which I pray it is not, the police and experts will no doubt endeavor to restore order." She smoothed her tunic, which took her an agonizing amount of seconds. "Our precious school is holding on by the flimsiest thread, and a scandal of this magnitude would undoubtedly lead to our closure."

"We need to warn everyone," I begged. "Shut it all down until the threat passes."

"What good would a *closed school* do for our students?" Sister Honor asked. "We are their spiritual home. Idle hands breed bigger problems."

"And dead students won't?" I asked, and caught a wince flash across Sister Honor's face. She recovered in a heartbeat, but I'd seen it. That raw nerve below the armor. I'd learned over Easter weekend why she could be so fucking cold. Sixty years as God's soldier. All the gaslighting and hard work. But underneath the metal she was bleeding out. Just like the rest of us.

We're all soft targets in the end.

Bernard pressed the whole of his back against a closed locker. He was counting quietly and breathing dramatically, like he was listening to one of those meditation apps Moose used.

"As your Mother Superior, I expressly forbid you from decreeing a school-wide warning."

"You can't." I crossed my arms. "We have to—"

"If any warning does go out, *you* will go out with it." Sister Honor sprayed spit as she talked. "The police will handle this their way. We shall handle it ours—with dignity, discretion, and the bishop's counsel."

"But—"

"Our brief respite will continue tomorrow morning with a special Mass for Fleur Benoit, but we shall otherwise keep our doors open and graduation on schedule." Sister Honor's habit consumed the hallway as she turned.

The air stayed cold after she left. The kind of temperature plunge that comes when something dead walked among the living. Or before betrayal drove the knife home. Sister Honor was serving yet another system protecting itself. No different than the Diocese shuffling predatory priests like a shitty shell game on the boardwalk.

"That went well," Riveaux said.

"She's just playing hard to get." I sighed, could keep sighing, could fill every canyon in the world with my sighs.

"Still no security cameras in this joint?" Riveaux scanned the walls and ceiling.

Bernard shook his head. "No budget."

It was time to address the *B* lighter. I pulled it from my pocket. "I found this in the gym. Don't think it was Fleur's, but it was in her possession."

Riveaux's face glowed at first with excitement and then worry. Her eyes like mesmerizing barber poles. "You took evidence?"

Hell yeah, I did. Sure, I knew that Riveaux was all about PI protocol and shit, but this was a potential *lead.* I was starting to explain when Bernard uncharacteristically interrupted: "Okie dokie, my dudes," he said, clasping his hands, "feels like it's time to leave you both to it. This guy's gotta get back to the mill."

This guy? As he started to give the peace sign, I grabbed his wrist and pressed hard. "Why're you being so wack? What's up with you?"

"Well . . ."

"Well what?" I got in his face so he'd look me in the eye.

"The lighter's mine." Bernard reached for it but Riveaux blocked him.

"Yours? Did you drop it when you saw Fleur?" she asked.

"No. Haven't seen it in weeks."

"But you don't even smoke," I said.

"Auntie gave it to me for my incense."

No wonder the utility closet always smelled like palo santo.

"Think Fleur found it somewhere? Maybe nicked it?"

"Who knows. I totally could have left it somewhere," he said.

Riveaux's nostrils twitched. "Where *exactly* in the gym did you find this?" she asked me.

"Next to Fleur."

"Ah, great. Near the body of the victim." She bagged the lighter and said, "Points for quick thinking, Goldsmobile. But I'll hand this over to Arthur so we keep the case bulletproof, okay? Sorry, Bernard."

I nodded and she sent a nod right back.

Everything about Riveaux that day screamed quirky PI mentor. Clever thinker. She could play both sides of the law. She had a fix for most problems. Riveaux the inventor. Riveaux the survivor. Riveaux the *Miss Congeniality Part 3* sans makeover. Fuck makeover stories anyway. The real triumph wasn't losing the dorky glasses and throwing on a ball gown. Transformation means ripping off the skin "they" force you to wear and bloodletting truth, like Carrie's little party trick. Resurrection isn't about coming back nicer, cleaner, more put together. It's about rising in glory. Fiercer. Ready to slice the air. Like Jesus showed us.

Bernard jumped when his phone buzzed. I couldn't decipher his expression as he stared at the screen. He grumbled about water pressure in the girl's restroom, then in a second he was gone, swallowed by the emptiness of the hall.

"He's acting weirder than usual." Riveaux blinked.

"Who isn't today?" I said, but his discomfort was nagging me. I'd chalked it all up to stress, PTSD from what he'd seen. But why be so cagey about the lighter? I shook my head, refusing to go further down that path. It was Bernard. My Bernard. "And before everyone hightails it out of here, let's interview some students, see what we can learn."

"I believe the children are the future," Riveaux semi-sang. What a great voice. How hadn't I heard it before? "But Sister Honor said Goldsmobiles have to stay in their lane."

"I'm not changing lanes. I'm passing on the fucking shoulder."

"Dangerous as hell." Riveaux shook her head. "And I'm in."

6

JESUS'S ETERNAL PATIENCE AND sublime grace was there,
whenever I needed it. And Holy Mary did I need it that day. The
tiny savior on the crucifix above my desk looked so much like
Moose it startled me. The strong nose. Beard scruffy but soft,
like it was trying to make up its mind, between wild and tame. If
those wooden eyes had opened right then and the statue whispered, *Don't do anything stupid, Goose,* I wouldn't have flinched.

Riveaux stole the swivel chair from Rosemary's desk, which
was so tidy, it was unsettling. Our shared classroom would serve
double duty as our impromptu interrogation site. "You take the
lead here, Goldsmobile. The students trust you, question mark?"

"They do." No wishful thinking, just fact. I was a damned
good teacher, which earned me points with parents. The gold
tooth and the occasional glimpse of ink beneath my sleeves
and gloves sent a different message to their children. A subtle
rebellion despite my nun garb. In an increasingly fake and
algorithm-driven world of starfuckers, maybe my messy con-
tradictions felt real to the kids. A belief in a story bigger than
us and a revolt against Catholicism's grand performance and
arbitrary rules, fashioned and maintained by white men who'd

never had to question their own authority. To actual hell with that nonsense.

One by one we interviewed students. I pulled them as they exited the cafeteria with a soft tap on the shoulder and the implied promise of spiritual counsel. Sister Honor was thankfully occupied with the chaos, and Sergeant Decker hadn't shown her face yet, leaving the coast clear.

Our first interview was with Tyrell. Wearing a Saints jacket over his polo, despite the biblical heat and our dress code, Tyrell told us he saw Fleur in the library "a lot," consorting with kids in "sick kicks." My Steno captured the keywords while Tyrell's knee bounced up and down, conducting its own private earthquake.

Next was Maria, a sophomore, who tearfully confided that Fleur seemed "super sloshed" on class picture day. Fleur was supposed to help lay out the yearbook, but Maria said she "flaked." Maria picked at the fraying hem of her uniform skirt as I wrote.

I asked each student the same set of questions: Have you seen any suspicious interactions around campus lately? Any cash passing hands? Slow-rolling cars? Fleur talking with strangers? Each kid looked at me with roaring bewilderment. Most sales in the modern era were invisible. Digits changing on one screen resulting in changing digits on another.

If we were taking them at their word, no one saw any deals. And no one fessed up to having pills either. It was like trying to catch the dead center of infinity with my gloved hands.

Rachel, a senior with tiny pupils and a distant voice like she was a vole who'd fallen down a well, said that Fleur was "sick of this shit" and wanted to quit school and leave "this dump" early. But David, a skeletal sophomore, reported the exact opposite.

David said he'd swear on the Bible that Fleur was "majorly into graduating" and proving all the "haters" wrong with a triumphant march at commencement and flipping Sister Honor the bird. Dear God, yes. How I would have adored that. The mental image made me want to weep and laugh and scream *praise* all at once.

Two competing narratives. David was right or Rachel was right. Or they were both mistaken. The truth was still so breathlessly far away. Running after it gave me shin splints.

Amber was next. A senior with an uptown accent and a brooding air. From the courtyard she heard Fleur "beefing" with "that sus guy" behind the gym two weeks ago. With no cameras—naturally—we had no corroboration. It was "real intense," Amber said, then her attention drifted to her artful nails, as if reading our fortunes in the lacquer.

"Which *suspicious* guy are we talking about here?" Riveaux asked.

"I mean, I think it was Prince Dempsey." Amber tapped one long nail on the table.

I recoiled when Prince's name hit my ears. Dear God, the terribly sour warmth of it. Communion wine hangover times eleven.

"Prince Dempsey." Riveaux lifted so high in her chair I expected her knees to crack the table.

"Fleur's the only one I heard for real-real, but I'm eighty percent sure it was Prince," she said. "I just can't believe she's gone." Amber created sounds of crying but no tears fell. Her eyes were vacant. Her eyelash extensions weren't as impressive as her hair extensions, which were so high-end they probably had their own trust fund.

"It is a hell of a shock." Riveaux spoke softly, intently. I had to admit, it was an exhilarating pleasure to be in that makeshift interrogation room with her. With her strategic withholding and my who knew what, our interviews had a rhythm, a swing to them. Redemption was earning its name. "Back to Prince Dempsey," she said. "Have you seen him recently?"

"Not since that drama." Amber checked her phone. "My dad sent me an Uber. It's been a shit week. Some asshole stole his car. Can I go now?"

I nodded and said, "Go with God."

Riveaux sighed after Amber walked out. *"Go with God,"* she mocked.

"I'm a nun, remember?"

"That foul mouth and gold piece make it easy to forget." She tapped her canine.

I bared my teeth like a rottweiler. I would have loved to start barking—that was the mood I was in.

"Prince Dempsey got a name drop," Riveaux said, and brought her hands to her lower back. "Did you know Prince and Fleur had a moment?"

"Those two?" I shook my head.

"What if the kid's breaking bad again?"

I calmed myself for a breath, remembered the feeling of elation as I'd baptized the punk in that ill-advised ceremony in storm water. "Prince has really changed. He's not the same kid I met when I moved here. But I would definitely love to lay some questions on him."

"People change and then backslide," Riveaux said. She saw patterns of crime and I saw possibilities for grace. Maybe we were both right, and still screwed all the same.

"It's a small school. Everybody's up in everybody's business. There's more they're not saying, though. I wish we could tap their fucking phones."

"Well, Goldsmobile, we're not the cops." She waved her palm over her private eye credentials on the desk like it was an illuminated manuscript. She had that card out for transparency. Her previous life with the NOFD helped her secure her certification speedily. Unfortunately for me, there was no similar exchange for shredding guitar and blacking out. Would need a few thousand hours to score mine. "And if we want to keep Redemption Agency open long enough to celebrate its first birthday, we'll have to tread lightly."

"For every piece of red tape we have to wrestle, an angel gets her wings."

Some actual intel arrived when an extremely over-it student named Sarah confided that Fleur "popped pills" seemingly "on the reg."

Riveaux gripped her stylus like she was going to snap its neck. "Which pills?"

"Like, the focus ones. Study buddies."

"What are they actually called?" I asked.

"Uh, *study buddies*," she repeated, annoyed, like it was the most obvious fact in the history of facts. "Everyone takes them."

Riveaux coughed. "Everyone?"

I pressed my palms together. *Study buddies*. Finally. A goddamn breakthrough.

"Not me!" Sarah clarified. "I sometimes borrow my brother's weed, but that's all natural."

Then with immediate urgency, she said, "Gotta go," and she left.

"Thanks," Riveaux said into the door as it closed. She turned to me. "I can think of a few things a *study buddy* might be. Speed, Ritalin, Adderall. Something zippier than cold brew."

Adderall. Ritalin. Study drugs. Sanctioned fixes for overwhelmed minds. For overworked and overstimulated teens trying to cram their way to Tulane. Trying to survive a society that demanded always-on, can-do, all-nighter attitudes and offered insomnia in return. And if they couldn't get a prescription, or needed more milligrams to feel the effects, kids were buying knockoffs on the street—knockoffs with lethal ingredients. It made so much sense.

Riveaux read through her notes on her shiny tablet. "Tyrell said Fleur was always in the library. Why don't you mosey on up there, *check out* the scene?"

"Smart thinking, predictable pun." I'd scope it out for as long as I could stand to breathe the same air as Alex Moore.

Riveaux looked at her watch. "It's getting quiet around here. I'm going to head back to the office, call up Arthur, see if any lab work's in yet."

"*Go with God,*" I said in the same voice Riveaux used to mock me. The double imitation, to my surprise, sounded like my mother. I hadn't heard her voice in so long, the recognition made me shrink. Mom'd kick open her urn to tell me to get a decent haircut.

Mom.

For all the ways we fear mothers, loathe mothers, become our mothers, we still need mothering.

Mother Superior.

Mother of God.

The mother lode.

Motherfucker.

"Meet me at the office at seven to trade notes." Riveaux was already moving toward the door before she finished her sentence.

"Can't you pick me up?" I asked. Riveaux had other cases on the agency docket, but she knew I didn't have transportation. Even if a holy benefactor donated a vehicle to the church, the Diocese would eighty-six it. They'd lose their minds if they saw a nun behind the wheel.

Riveaux placed a musical jumble of change in my palm. "The streetcar will be running. Go with God." She whistled her way out.

7

IN THE STAIRWELL TO the library, Father Nathan appeared suddenly, like he'd dropped through a hole in the ceiling. "Sister Holiday." His voice was steady and somber, the way it has to be when you're captaining a ship through the Sea of Bad News. Like God telling Job to buckle the hell up. "It's a truly trying day." He blessed himself. "But it's good to see you."

"Guess we should push back tomorrow's rehearsal," I said. My permanent vows ceremony was two weeks away, next Sunday's holy ripper where everyone'd watch me leave the modern plane, get spiritually anointed, and reintroduced as a bride of Christ. Spectacular timing, considering I was high with rage for Fleur, so amped up that standing still took tremendous effort. The dire need shot up from the ground, into my feet. "In light of everything," I said.

"I've got a much better idea," Father Nathan said, taking a moment before the words leapt fully formed from his mouth. "Let's do it right now."

"I can't." The words were sharp but not as harsh as I felt in my own head. "I'm in the middle of something."

He smiled, but it was a tired, pitted thing, and he just stood at the window studying the late afternoon sky, as if the perfect response lived there and only there. "Mmhmm. I hear you. But if I know you half as well as I think I do, I'd say you're about to walk into the eye of the storm to investigate. Yes? No?"

"Maybe so," I said.

I followed his eyes through the glass. The sky looked stuck, clouds woven in devastating layers and everything stilled.

He stuffed his hands in the pockets of his long cassock. Maybe he was trying to hold himself together too. "It's so hard, but I think we have to trust the process now."

"'Process?' You mean the *police*?"

"We've both had our differences with authority." When he faced me, his eyes were so much softer than I'd expected. "We've almost made a career out of it. But now I think it's best to step aside, let the cops do their cop things."

Memories fired back. A full body shock of remembering. Us on the boat. The gunshots. So much blood on the ground and walls, like it was ladled out by a mad chef.

"Remember when 'their cop things' almost got us both killed?" I asked.

"Grogan's behind bars," he said, "and the good ol' boys on the force know their days are numbered."

"Because of *us*."

"Exactly. Now we're the ones who have to hold the line. And our work here is important too."

"Your grace is annoyingly compelling, but I can't rehearse today. I just can't."

"Five minutes. We'll keep it short and sweet, and we can pray for Fleur right after. Yes?" He glanced back to make sure I was following.

I couldn't say no.

It was also an opportunity to see if Father Nathan'd observed anything peculiar. Like me, he was on campus twenty-four hours a day, but in different zones, for the most part. And he had access to people and places I didn't. Though he did his own laundry on Thursdays in the rectory, praise Jesus. What an odd gift, not making the nuns do every last shred of bitch work in the ministry. As we walked from the school to the church, I asked, "How'd we miss what was happening with Fleur? Was something right under our noses?"

He let out a deep breath and paused. The Coronation of Mary could have started and ended in the duration of that pause. "She was always chatty when I saw her. Always with that impish smile. But toward the end, yes, I think she was struggling."

"With what?" My body tightened.

"Don't know. I never pushed her."

"Tyrell said she hung out in the library a lot. A bunch of students would meet there. Know anything about it?"

"No," said Father Nathan. "But it doesn't surprise me. You wouldn't believe how lonely kids are. Desperate for connection in *real life*, not on a screen."

We'd reached the church then. The stained glass came alive as light spilled through it. Slow-moving beams, like fingers playing a ghostly tune. Mary's eye. Saint Michael the Archangel, a blast of wings and metal, raising his sword to shank the serpent under his feet. That sneaky snake with emerald and gold scales. The devil pushing the next hit, the next shot, egging on the next monumentally stupid decision, confident mere mortals would fall for it.

The wooden kneeler near the altar trembled as I sank into it. During the Hail Mary, it threatened to snap. "You'd think an all-knowing God could pitch in for better furniture," I said.

"That's what collection plates are for." Father Nathan's smile was small and crooked, unlike the tall man himself.

"I promise to live in poverty, chastity, and obedience." I spit out each word. More accurately, I ripped each one out of me like a tapeworm.

"You're rushing. Spiritual oneness isn't a race."

"Hard to think about my ceremony and the Holy See at a time like this."

My mind screamed about Fleur, the pills in the burnt wing. About the Sisters of the Sublime Blood motto—bringing light into a dark world—while Sister Honor played politics with human lives hanging in the balance. I thought Sister Honor had changed after Father Reese's murder. And maybe she had, but, like an empty New Year's resolution, it didn't stick. Keeping up appearances over actual safety. The bishop's approval carried more weight than a dead kid. And there I was, days from permanent vows, about to tether myself to the hypocrisy.

"Believe me, I understand. Even more reason for us—me and you—to speak truth, live truth, *be* truth."

"No pressure," I said.

He pulled out his pocket watch and held it up. "Here."

"You going to hypnotize me?" I watched it swing on the chain.

"If only I were that talented. Would make this job a heck of a lot easier. You're rushing." He smiled warmly again, but there was worry there too. "The watch will help you focus."

Perfect. A ticking clock. Just what that powder keg of a day needed.

But the watch was smooth in my cupped hand, elegant as moonlight. Unutterably fine. A family heirloom? Or maybe a graduation present, placed in younger Nathan's palm with pride. As I flipped it open, it slipped out of my grip. I froze as it smacked the marble floor.

"No!" My face flushed and my body lifted. Light as a grenade the second before it touched ground. "I'm so sorry."

He brought his hands up, into prayer position, to calm me. "It's okay."

Okay. The word people say all the time without intention or meaning. But it sounded genuine from him.

As I picked the watch up, I could see the damage. The glass had cracked into a viscous spider web. "I promise I'll get this fixed."

"Don't worry about it." He blessed himself.

"You sure?"

He nodded.

It was time to loop him in. There was no other choice. I rapid-fired the fresh hell we'd stared down that day. The locker stash, potential deaths in circulation, Sister Honor's disastrous mandate.

"She *really* said that?" Father Nathan shook his head slowly, carefully, as if he was balancing the Bible on his excellent hair.

I nodded. "I thought the whole point of this"—I motioned to the altar, the stained glass, everything in that sacred space— "was helping people."

"It's what Jesus asks of us, to do the right thing." He stared at the altar and I could smell the menthol of the mothballs the rectory used to keep nibbling creatures off priestly vestments. That bright, aggressive scent was weirdly comforting. "I don't agree with her, if it's consolation. Not at all."

"We have to act now."

"You're right, but I swore I'd empower the women of our church, not make decisions for them. I'm not Father Reese. Those days are done." His jaw set.

"What are you saying? Spell it out, please."

"Mother Superior has the last word."

"But what about the kids?" I bent down in the aisle again with the broken clock. A face frozen in its final second of wholeness. "Someone else could die. And I'm worried about Prince— he's been out of class for weeks."

"Trust that he'll return to us in time," Father Nathan said. "Let's pray for Fleur now."

His hands joined mine in prayer. To hold Fleur close, protect her always. I remembered her in class, on campus, during practice, the in-between moments. How she loved to eat Skittles one at a time. How she found four-leaf clovers and yelled at Ryan Brown for throwing recyclables into the trash bin. How she brought in her mom's homemade divinity candy for Teacher Appreciation Day. The little things that make a person a person.

When we finished, as was often the case after praying, I felt better. Still fucked up but less gutted.

"You know what I see when I look at this?" He held up the broken watch. "I don't see damage. I see something ready to be fixed."

"Subtle metaphor."

"Subtlety doesn't galvanize the masses. Look around you." He stood and brushed off his vestments.

Before we left, he dipped his right index finger in holy water and blessed himself. I could see the fire of the cross take shape as he moved, like he was scorching the air with a blowtorch.

I really looked at Father Nathan then. At the dark circles under his eyes mirroring mine. So tired, like his last sleep was in the womb. We were the same generation, almost the same age. Members of the same clerical fam. A white lesbian nun and a Black iconoclastic priest. We were both punk in our own ways, both hot-wired by God, ride or die on the same crazy road.

"Go," he said. "We'll do a final rehearsal soon."

"Thank you."

"One stipulation," he said, "when, or if, you find anything, come to me first. Before you go charging off."

"Promise," I said.

A promise I knew I couldn't keep.

The watch in his hand glowed. The shatter pattern, like pulsing veins. Maybe cracking things open was the only way to really understand them. To go *inside* the tick. It was an invitation. A relief. A sacred breaking to learn the secrets, see how things were unmade.

8

THE LIBRARY CIRCULATION DESK was empty. Alex Moore abdicating his throne? Or just congratulating himself on his awesomeness in the bathroom mirror?

I dropped into the computer station and jabbed the power button. The primitive Dell coughed to life like it was on borrowed time. Ghost in the machine. Every click of the mouse produced a maddening spinning ball. Wait. Click. Curse. Repeat.

As I waited for the computer-poltergeist to open a new browser tab, I replayed the student interviews. Had to keep their words alive in my ears, clear and loud, so I could extract subtext, net any lie. Amber's tearless crying. Prince Dempsey, the "sus guy." How study drugs were the score du jour at Saint Sebastian's.

And, according to the headlines, our school wasn't alone. Across America, record numbers of teens were relying on drugs like Adderall and Ritalin to focus, to do one thing at a time, to make decent grades, even just to read. But they were drag racing with their developing brains. The meds were practical magic for tons, but there were side effects. Migraines, dry mouth, appetite loss, tachycardia, seizures, hallucinations, and an ever-increasing tolerance and need for more.

More, the American affliction.

And even with all of that, the prescriptions were the "safer" option. On the streets, some fucks hawked speed mixed with fentanyl to get their clients more addicted. All the chances people take when we don't know the depth of the risks. Even when I knew the threat—the risk—I still rolled the dice. So ravenous, the human desire to be empty or full, hazy or focused, too busy to think. To be anything but yourself. The computer fan kicked into overdrive and a sconce blinked.

My mind fell backward in time. To a moment so close it lived inside me, like lightning that entered my body but never exited. Back in the hallway with Fleur. The same Fleur who was forever filling her water bottle. The way her expression changed when I'd ask about graduation and future plans. How she'd blinked like she had hot sauce in her eyes. How no breath she took seemed to pull her back to earth. I was realizing that both Rachel's and David's versions of Fleur's last days could be true—she was toggling between extremes.

Just then, a former student of mine, Joey Delachaise, strolled into the library, straight backed, with a basketball under his arm. Perfect timing.

"Hey, Joey," I said.

"Hey."

"You all right?"

"Dunno."

"Worst day today," I said.

"Hasn't really sunk in yet."

"Won't hit for a while," I said. "Need anything?"

"Dunno."

"Take it moment to moment. Just say to yourself, 'What do I need right now?' Then do that thing. Can you do that?"

"Dunno." Was Joey talking, or was it a recording? Hitting play on an audio file? "I guess I could try."

"I know you can," I said.

He shrugged, staring down at his cotton-ball white sneaks. Sick kicks.

"Were you and Fleur friends?"

"I guess," he said.

"Who else do you see hanging here?" God, I sounded square.

"People come and go." Joey was clearly not into talking.

"What's the vibe?"

"We hang." He bounced on his heels.

"What else?"

"Dunno. Study. Alex reads our essays," Joey said. And he used *Alex*, not *Mr. Moore*. I stopped myself from rolling my eyes. Alex dickbag Moore was desperate to be the cool teacher. Like me.

As Joey looked around the library, I could feel the vibrations of words he wasn't sharing. His navy polo smelled, paradoxically, of both strong body odor and deodorant. One dark curl flopped into his right eye.

I lowered my voice. "Joey, if you have any orange pills, don't take them. Just trust me." He looked back at me with an unreadable expression. Couldn't tell if he'd heard me.

Before I had the chance to tell him anything else, he said, "Later," and slinked out the door, abandoning whatever it was he had to do in the library.

A moment later I heard Alex's voice. "Your presence in my stacks is long *overdue*."

"So is equal pay for equal work." I quickly acknowledged his presence then returned to the screen. Alex Moore's sideburns announced his complete fuckery like smug banners. Yeah, I needed to talk to him, but he could wait.

"That is true. Thankfully, the future is female." He angled his pipe cleaner of a neck over my shoulder to get a view of the sad screen. "Why are you still here today?"

"Online gambling," I said, which made him chuckle.

I continued scrolling as quickly as the hailstorm of spinning balls would allow. Reading up on counterfeit study drugs had brought me to stats on the fentanyl epidemic. ODs were up 25 percent in the parish—it was starting to seem like a miracle it had taken this long to strike our campus. I hated how death looked so clear, so unapologetic in numbers and percentages. Sterile.

Finally I looked up at Alex. "Tell me about the kids who study here."

"Most of the students come in at some point, but there are some regulars." He swirled his right wrist in slow, deliberate circles, as though testing its hinges. "No motto or rules. I just assist when I can, for kids who really want to achieve."

"Achieve what?"

"You know, get accepted into Ivies." He radiated a particular breed of male privilege.

"I don't know," I said. "Educate me."

"Extracurriculars, test prep, essays, the full package." He scrunched his nose.

"Those regulars. Tell me about them. Was Fleur here a lot?"

"It's not like I take *attendance* in the library."

"How about Joey Delachaise?"

"Joey? I guess so. He and Fleur"—he stopped for an inhale—"seemed to get a lot out of collaborating."

The library air curved slow and heavy, columns of humidity. Near the rat-fuck Alex's circulation desk, a portrait of Saint

Jerome peered down at us. A signature expression of wonder, some sorrow, and a healthy dose of defiance. Like New Orleans itself. A place where corner stores sold love spells, flowering vines climbed bell towers, and brass bands led funeral processions. The holy refusal of this city to ever quietly call it quits. To ever leave the party without starting a new one.

"How did Fleur seem lately?"

"No red flags to report," Alex said, then pulled a chair over and sat next to me. I was surprised he didn't bring over two more chairs for his heinous sideburns. "Let me." He reached over the keyboard. "Research is one of my areas of expertise. When I was TA'ing at Dartmouth, I found it was most effective to—"

"I'm all set." My words scraped my tongue like the rusty cheese grater Sister Honor won in a barter with the Sisters of Nazareth in 1995.

"No. This is my bread and butter." Alex's toxic cologne was a shocking affront that choked what was left of my restraint. Thank the Lord that Riveaux wasn't there to smell his transgressions, though a front-row seat to her dressing down his essence would be divine. God save me.

"You can help me by really thinking back. I need to get a better handle on Fleur's behavior in the past few months."

"I can't recollect much more there, but, hang on a minute."

"I don't have a minute."

He stood, jogged to his desk like a dipshit, and returned with a single piece of paper. "Heard you guys found something in the closed-off wing."

"Word travels fast around here."

"Little birdie told me." He flapped his arms.

"Huh."

"If you ask me," he said, though no one had, "it's no surprise they'd find something like that there, with all the time they've wasted on the renovation. I hear there's money ready for it too. Ever wonder why it's not being put to use?"

"No."

"Surely you've noticed the Rebuild Fund hasn't been doing much rebuilding."

"Say what you want to say, Alex." I kept my eyes on the spinning ball, clicking and clicking into a delirious oblivion. With the heat that machine was throwing off, the library had to be ninety-nine degrees. My neckerchief was drenched. The sweat was relentless, ridiculous.

"If I were you," he said with nasally excitement, "I would focus on a different set of figures instead of those." He pointed at the screen where percentages represented dead teenagers. Numbers instead of humans.

"To understand what happened to Fleur?" I asked.

"If you want to prevent more catastrophes," Alex said, "the answers might be in here." With his linguine arms he slid the paper, a one-page spreadsheet, across the desk, like he'd been waiting his entire life and every past life to bust out that super-secret spy move.

"You're our school bookkeeper then too?" I asked, then monitored his reaction reflected in the computer glass. But all I could see were his sideburns like skinned pelts. "How do you find the time?"

"I simply realized things weren't adding up. But you didn't hear it from me."

"Ah, a whistleblower then. You'll get a lot of reading time in witness protection." I took the printout and scoffed. But I'd be an idiot not to check out any possible tip, even from Alex Moore.

There were potentially lethal drugs out there. From the same batch that killed Fleur. Tiny tablets. Dots. How could something so small be so powerful, so cruel? A cancer cell. A mold spore. A spider bite. A lie.

Behind me the computer gave up. A frenzy of crashing blue. I grabbed Alex's paper and my Steno with the interview notes. "God bless you," I said, like he was an allergy, and walked out of the library.

▪

At the main office, I watched Shelly through the open door. A pipe had dripped brown water onto her Winnie-the-Pooh calendar. Her face was puffy and red from crying, long past the point where CoverGirl could cover a damn thing.

I went in. "Hi, Shelly." My blouse stuck to the back of my liquifying body. "Holding up?"

"Oh, sure," was all she could say for a moment. Her Diet Coke unopened near her keyboard. "I keep remembering Fleur's funny little ways."

"Me too," I said. Fleur had a biting sense of humor. Her quips. Her sick burns during recitals and the Nativity pageant: *Ryan Brown's one of the Wise Men? Must be a good actor.*

Then I spotted what I was looking for, among the rainbow-labeled drawers of the filing cabinet. FISCAL in mint green. We talked for ten minutes and I swore I heard Fleur's voice echoing down the hallway. "I know how much Fleur adored you," I lied.

"Did she now?" Her eyes welled up and her bottom lip trembled. "*Me?*"

"She talked about you all the time," I said, choosing each word carefully. "At graduation, she was planning to play 'Wind Beneath My Wings,' and—" I looked up and paused. "And—"

"And *what*?" Shelly asked, her mouth open.

"She was going to dedicate it to you."

That dismantled her completely. "Precious angel!" She choked back sobs and mopped tears with her wrists and forearms. "I always *knew* we had a connection." Her face was dripping as if she'd been sprayed with a hose. "Sorry! Would you just look at this mess. My Lord."

"Go," I said, "take a moment for yourself. I'll help anyone who comes by."

"You sure you don't mind?"

"Not at all," I said, with my gloved palm on her heaving shoulder.

"What a comfort, to know we still have guardian angels here." That unleashed a new torrent of tears and hyperventilating, and I heard Shelly saying "angel . . . angel . . ." over and over as she walked to the first-floor ladies' room.

After I heard the door shut, I backed up into the office and grabbed the color-coded key ring from her desk. Mint green. Bingo. With a stealth and silence honed from breaking into my dad's liquor cabinet under a framed Walsh family tree, I quickly unlocked the drawer of the filing cabinet. The picture of her tuxedo cat dressed as the pope stared me down. *Sorry, your excellency.*

There were financial records, invoices from school vendors, utility bills, receipts, all organized and broken up into labeled dividers. *Thanks be to Shelly.* I grabbed as much as I could carry from the Rebuild Fund file, relocked the drawer, and left Shelly a note on the top of a pile of mail, church bulletins, and domestic violence pamphlets. I'd promised I'd stick around, but I couldn't risk a convo about paperwork. *Divine duty calls. Bless you*, it said, with a tiny cross.

Time to see which path—shitty pills or dirty money—would drop me into the next circle of hell.

9

MONDAY, DUSK. SWEET OLIVE and jasmine strangled the air as I walked to catch the streetcar to the Redemption Agency office. Such a lingering wet scent. Close, too close, like a garrote around my neck. The swollen tides of late May flowers sagged, drunk on the heat. Wasps had built empires in their eaves. It seemed like every petal had a pulse, and each sunflower was a head nodding with terrible knowledge. So lush, slow, and crawling it all was. Eden before the Fall.

I passed an abandoned shack and peered inside the warped windows. The sun was still severe then, and the home's interior was a lake of shadows. It looked cave-dark in there, where a lone wolf could hide to lick her wounds. Not that I was a creature who'd ever retreat. But for a moment, the darkness pulled me. I could feel my body relaxing into it.

Into nothing.

Finally at the streetcar stop, I waited the length of a Hail Mary for it to arrive. I stepped on and sat across from a white woman with a face like a dried apple. She clutched her purse tight. To my left, a baby wailed from its mother's arms while the parents laughed at a video on the dad's phone, a video of what sounded like a wrestling match, a coked-up announcer, a riotous crowd. Modern parenting.

The trolley crawled down Saint Charles, under a living canopy of rabid oak branches. The trees were so hyped up, so crazed, I'd expected them to roll out their own traveling revival ministry. The kind with talking serpents and freshly dunked, wild-eyed believers screaming: "Hallelujah! Saved!"

Give me a fucking break.

But was I any better with my Catholicism? Chanting, eating flesh, drinking blood, bringing the Savior's body inside my own. Gilding old bones, pilgrimages to see an undecaying heart. Our incense made from weeping trees. Maybe all believers were nuts—crazy in different ways. The spindly femme man nailed to a cross wasn't a symbol for me. He was as real and mysterious as life itself.

Fleur should have been on that streetcar too, headphones on, canceling the noise, ignoring the world. Or letting the world in, strategically. The Nativity memory blazed again. Last year's Christmas pageant, Fleur Benoit as the Virgin Mary. Her hand reaching for the plastic prop of baby Jesus that Sister Honor forced us to use and refused to replace, though the doll's time-eaten eyes made it look utterly possessed. *Our little Lord Chucky, asleep on the hay,* Fleur had said. I'd laughed so hard I choked.

Now Fleur was gone. Everywhere and nowhere.

Because of a pill? One fucking pill? For all the sincere joy I took in mind-altering substances and their resulting black-outs, I hadn't heard about fentanyl until recently. Synthetic opioids constructed in labs. It came in powder, pill, patch, and liquid forms, with a high that could take down a rhino. With withdrawal that lit your head on fire and made you shit your pants. Fentanyl had the strength to hook you. Could become your entire personality. Could steal your breath forever. Unless Narcan resurrected you.

Medical exorcism of the demon.

Of course, Riveaux had predicted its unholy rise. She was psychic like that. A diviner. Never needed to consult Doppler radar because she knew when rain was coming. Riveaux was an unapologetic nerd, and I was pretty sure her fashion consultant was a Magic 8 Ball, but she owned every choice. She had the courage needed to be herself.

It made me sick. The strip-mining of kids' attention. Every screen begged for their focus and "likes." At Saint Sebastian's, we preached about sitting still in Mass like it was a holy test. Teachers bitched about students spacing out during class, but what did they expect? Kids grew up bombarded. Apps. Games. Notifications every nine seconds. Social media dopamine blasts. Sister Honor's hour-long seminar on the epistle to the Galatians was boring as fuck, but having to suffer through it built stamina. Made you fight to stay awake. Stay sharp.

I found Riveaux holed up in her corner of our Redemption Detective Agency office in Carrollton. She was walled in on all sides by steamy windows, alchemy ingredients, and a blinking monitor. "You're ten minutes late, Goldsmobile," she said as she crushed out a cigarette. "Fleur's preliminary tox screen confirms our suspicions."

"Dear God."

The fan chopped through the silence.

"She had fentanyl in her system," Riveaux said. "We'll get the full toxicology next week."

"That was quick. How'd you access it?"

"Turn around."

When I turned, I saw Fleur's mother walking out of the bathroom. Her eyes were puffy from crying. The bloat of unfathomable pain. Pain that distorts and changes flesh.

"I'm so sorry, Mrs. Benoit." I blessed myself. "I—"

"Look at my precious baby girl." Mrs. Benoit held up her phone and thumbed through photos. Baby Fleur with an even tinier button nose. Kid Fleur with tight braids. Tween Fleur who cut her own bangs too short, a riot grrrl–approved method. "Look," her mother repeated.

I took the phone and swiped to an image of Fleur at her recital last year. She was caught in profile at the piano with her neck curved. A picture of total focus. She had on a string of antique pearls like Rosemary Flynn liked to wear. But it was her hands that haunted me. They were suspended above the keys in that terribly beautiful pre-storm light streaming through the windows. Her hands flexed and fingers spread as if she was trying to pull strings of gold energy from the earth. The scream of each knuckle. I had to look away.

"I can't believe it. I *don't* believe it," Mrs. Benoit said.

"I don't want to believe it either," I said.

"She never even had a cavity." Mrs. Benoit touched the screen. "Not one."

"Fleur was the best kid," I said, as rage slashed through my grief. A hungry dark wave rocked, knocked me so hard I didn't just see stars, I tasted them too. The cross around my neck felt like it weighed ten million pounds. My legs wavered grotesquely. I wanted to grab every saint by their fucking halo and slam their heads together, demand answers, a do-over, an end to suffering.

Just end it.

"This isn't the way it should ever go." Riveaux spoke into the desk. Such sadness in her voice. Anger too. She made a fist with her right hand. Skin over the knuckles strained to the point of tearing.

Mrs. Benoit dropped an envelope onto the desk. "I've never had a problem with the police, but my baby girl wasn't a junkie, and they're acting like she was some kind of criminal."

"How so?" Riveaux asked, then dropped her voice to me and said, "Cops couldn't solve a knock-knock joke without calling for backup."

"Asking if I saw her take drugs, if I'd found 'paraphernalia' in her room. I swear to you, Fleur wouldn't even take Advil. I could barely get her to take echinacea when she had a cold. I can't believe this."

Me neither, I thought. Never suspected it. But the bewilderment meant nothing in the end. Because she did take something. She died of an overdose.

Then Mrs. Benoit reached into her purse for another picture to share. From her wallet, the last school photo of Fleur. The fake clouds behind her. The back covered in hurried cursive: *Fleur, Senior Year. My beautiful girl.* Then the year, like time could ever be stilled, stalled, captured. I held the photo carefully by the edges, this slice of emulsion and paper that pretended to be a person. Photos lie to us so beautifully. They show us what was there but never what happened next. Like crime scene outlines, marking where a body used to be. All that light and shadow tricking us into believing in permanence. Like we're stealing and freezing time. But photos are elegant proof of its passage. Maybe we'd be better off without photographs, without that luminous torture. Mrs. Benoit's hands trembled as she took back the picture and held it to her chest, gently.

"I know this is delicate," Riveaux said, "but I need to ask. Did Fleur ever mention trouble focusing? Academic pressure?"

"She was worried about finals," Mrs. Benoit admitted. "But so was every other senior. And she had already mapped out her gap year. She was flying over to Thailand, to work with elephants."

"She mentioned the plan to me," I said, closing my eyes for a moment. "Last time we spoke. A year to care for rescued animals." I thought about Prince saving BonTon. BonTon's training to save Prince by sniffing out his sugar levels. Rescuers who needed rescuing.

"This is the first day, Lord forgive me, that I've been glad Fleur's father is dead, and didn't have to bear this." She stumbled and grabbed the edge of the desk for support. This woman had lost her husband and her daughter. Her whole family.

"Very sorry to hear that he passed," Riveaux said. "When?"

"Five years ago. Brain cancer." She closed her eyes, and I felt severed. "Just me and my beautiful girl against the world. Until now."

Riveaux started to say something about our process and timeline when I broke in. "We'll find who's responsible for this."

"You have to." Mrs. Benoit's eyes were mutilated but furious. Red as Rahab's scarlet cord. Red as the earth that drank Abel's blood.

"We will," I said. "This is personal for me."

"We'll call as soon as we have anything," Riveaux said, "and thank you." She brought her eyes back to her notes. Ash the color of a Communion wafer fell into a little pile in her ashtray.

As I watched Fleur's mom leave, a flash of grief for my own mother stunned me. The strength and mystery of blood. How we are made from another's body, forged and formed from the deepest places inside. When a loved one is lost, when their soul leaves the physical plane, there are corners of the mind, of the body too, that become rooms you can't unlock. Missing my mom was cellular, an emptiness so constant it wore me down. Some of my genetic code changed when Mom died. A compass robbed of true north.

I closed the door and dropped into the chair in front of Riveaux's beat-up desk. The cash inside Mrs. Benoit's envelope seemed to vibrate.

"We're officially on the clock," Riveaux whispered and counted the money, logging in the amount on a spreadsheet. "Told you this case wouldn't be easy."

"That which does not kill us—"

"Definitely calls for a smoke." Riveaux tossed me her pack.

After I lit one and took a pull, I exhaled a loose ringlet of smoke—which I swear to God morphed into the shape of a question mark before it vanished.

"Hungry?" She pointed at her desk. "Got a Cup O' Noodles in the bottom drawer."

"No. And nothing says I've got my life together like forever chemicals."

"Goldsmobile, I forgot to mention. You dropped this on your way in," she said as she leaned down, but as she stood, all she had was her middle finger up, a snappy lil *fuck you*. "Here you go."

"Ha. Ha."

She turned back to face her computer. "'Forever chemicals' are still better for me than ex-husbands."

I winced. Riveaux's divorce from that gaslighter Rockwell had been a mess. She'd be picking up the maggoty scraps for months. Years, maybe.

"Amen to that," I said.

The box fan whooshed and shook.

"So I checked out Tyrell's tip," I said. "Fleur was studying at the library on the regular. A few kids were. They might have all been taking these pills."

"Study buddy buddies?"

"Maybe. But there's no evidence yet—nothing leading us to the source. Oh, and Alex Moore alleges there's money missing from the school's Rebuild Fund." I pulled the paper from Alex and the files I borrowed from Shelly out of my bag. "I'll follow up on it. But numbers aren't really my thing. Maybe you can take a look too?"

"Tomorrow." She rubbed at the edge of her lip with her thumb. "Not a priority by any stretch. But I did some digging of my own—found an interesting bit."

"Yeah?"

"I toured Fleur's Instagram before her mom arrived," Riveaux said. "Wanna see a fascinating selfie of her smooching 'the goodest girl.'"

"The *what*?"

"BonTon. Fleur posted a picture of herself with Dempsey's dog." She held up her phone showing a photo of Fleur side-eyeing the camera as she planted a kiss on the pit bull's cannon-ball-wide head.

I saw fevered sparks momentarily. Fractals blazing into lightning strikes that forked through my whole being. "BonTon?" Prince hardly let anyone look at his dog let alone get cozy.

For a moment I entertained the idea of Prince as our resident dealer. Motive? Money, of course. Prince needed it. His options didn't leave much room for great decisions. America, where ethics are a privilege.

Then, opportunity. Prince Dempsey was a loner, but he knew the rhythms of the school day. The ins and outs, the exits and entrances. He certainly knew about the east wing abandonment. He could move product right under our noses.

On the other hand, Prince had a good heart beneath the tough-guy act. And he'd been absent for weeks. Trish Dempsey'd said he was sick. Father Nathan'd trusted that he'd resurface. But what if Prince was about to be the next victim? Another client of the bad batch.

Either way, we needed face time with that kid.

"How much do counterfeit pills sell for?" I asked.

"Depends on the dealer and territory," she said, "but as low as two dollars a pop, and up to thirty."

"They have to sell *a lot* of two-dollar pills to make the operation worth their time."

"Yep."

People cooked uppers and cut them with fentanyl. Prettied up the pills with fun, fabulous colors. And sold the counterfeits to kids. Kids who they knew would get hooked. Or end up dead.

The office was terrarium hot, the air spiced with smoke and Riveaux's homemade colognes. Vines from the only not-dead plant cast snaky shadows on the floor.

"You really ready for this?" Riveaux rubbed her left temple like it could summon a séance of suspects in her mind. "This case is going to be a joyless pursuit."

"If we're doing this for joy, we're doing it all wrong."

"Drug rings are like the Hydra. Chop off one head, three more pop up. It's not only dealers we've got to worry about. All the stakeholders. The system. Supply to transport."

"It's the addiction I wish we could address. The need for the fix."

"Let's tackle a problem we can actually solve," Riveaux said in a halting voice.

"If anybody can crack this case, it's us. Two people who found our ways out. Despite the odds."

She pursed her lips and aggressively waved off the praise like it was the reek of hot garbage. "I'm no saint."

"Neither am I. Just a nun with a nose for trouble."

Riveaux guffawed, then a real laugh. Strained but genuine. "More like a tooth for trouble." She tapped her canine. "I'm the nose."

I reached and snagged a tiny vial from her desk, rolling the glass between my gloved fingers. The label read *Frankincense*, a scent fit for the son of God. I unscrewed the tight cap and inhaled deeply. Smell was an ancient portal. A place without words, without borders or edges. I tried to erase the smell of the gym as we failed to save Fleur. The wretched smell of fear.

"Don't drop it." She snatched the vial and I took in the clutter of our agency. A hard-earned comfort in the chaos. A statement.

I stood and walked across the office, making floorboards creak under my feet. A bead of sweat slid down my back as I cracked open a window. The sounds of the city poured in. A rumble of traffic, some babble from overheated tourists, a band on a far corner. "We have to talk to Prince," I said.

She leaned back in her chair and nodded. "Let's track him down."

A cicada flew in through the open window, its impossible wings almost as long as the reach of Riveaux's voice. It landed on the corner of her desk and watched us with its red attention.

"That's a prehistoric situation right there." Riveaux shut one eye. Not into it. No ferrets or cicadas for Riveaux's Christmas present this year.

I scooped up the insect to walk it back to the window. In my gloved palm, our visitor looked like it was floating in black ink. It hesitated—or maybe I'd imagined it—and then raised its wings like a tiny prophet before rejoining the sweltering air. A silent consolation from another lost soul trying to survive that hot mess of a day. Was it a divine sign? An accidental miracle? Eye to eye, creature to creature. All of us so fragile, scared, born into a world that could crush us or cherish us. Every creature, no matter how monstrous or misunderstood or beautiful, was part of the Lord's brutal magnificence. Even crawling things, stinging things, sewer-born things that made people invoke God's name in shock and disgust. The Sisters strived to protect their ecosystems, too. The intelligence of a web, built by one stealthy arachnid. Or a hornet's nest, erected by a telepathic community in a creepy collective line dance of insect architecture.

"Miracle?" I asked.

"What?" Riveaux said as she coughed.

"Sorry, thinking out loud."

"Thinking what?"

"Was our special guest a miracle or a messenger of an impending plague?"

"Plague's here, Goldsmobile. We have to change our perspective." Riveaux grabbed her truck keys and said, "'The only real voyage of discovery consists not in seeking new landscapes but in having new eyes.'"

"Proust again?"

"Marcel never quits."

"Neither does God's wrath."

10

RIVEAUX'S PICKUP RATTLED DOWN the dark Esplanade Avenue like a shopping cart full of loose nails. Her car radio crackled with some unholy jam-band spawn that made my gold tooth ache. We passed houses with porch lights illuminating pink and purple doors. Gingerbread trim hanging on by a prayer. New Orleans defied the structural rules. There were homes perched on stilts. Camelback houses with second stories clad behind the originals. Narrow shotguns standing shoulder to shoulder.

We coasted to the Dempsey trailer with the truck windows rolled down, letting the fermented sweetness of the Domino factory pour in. As Riveaux bit her bottom lip and bopped to the regrettable drums, I couldn't turn my brain off. The hypocrisy of it all. Most politicians and priests treat addiction like a social disorder, something to be criminalized—swept under the rug. But look around the city, the country. We're a nation established on stolen land, built up by stolen labor, with power-hungry men still obsessed with owning women's organs. Why's anyone shocked when people try to numb the surreal reality? Please. The system's not broken. It's working exactly as intended, grinding up the poor and the marginalized to feed the machine while self-declared saviors grift their way to profit and slap their names on ridiculous skyscrapers. It's enough to make anyone want to check out, even for a moment. But that moment can stretch into eternity if you're not careful. And for kids like Prince, who inherited nothing but wreckage, extra care was required.

I leaned on the truck armrest and took a long drag of a Riveaux-gifted cigarette. "Where's the fentanyl coming from?" I asked. "The border?" I hated falling into the vat of so-called religious right bullshit. Whiners whipping up a frenzy about immigrants. But Occam's razor. If I didn't ask all the questions, including about supply routes, one of them would sink me.

"Doesn't matter," Riveaux said. "Tons of product comes over both borders, docks, containers. We need to locate the dealers here first. Our hometown reps."

"No supply without demand," I replied. Through the window I saw the levee. A speed bump to slow unruly and relentless waters. A promise that sometimes breaks.

"You got that right," Riveaux said, "and folks these days consume a hell of a lot."

I took another long drag. Dear Lord, it tasted good, playing in the accordion of the lungs. The lungs, the silk creatures that held air, the Holy Ghost, addiction, grief, smoke. My first cigarette at age thirteen was my first buzz. A quick rip in reality, like slipping sideways into a stranger's life. A better life. Weight lifted, every ragged edge gone for a second.

A block before arriving at our destination, we rolled past the Mardi Mart, a corner store with more bulletproof glass than groceries.

I stuck my arm out of the passenger window, into the sumptuous air. Like the breath of the night. My hand swam the tide of the wind. "Why they putting fentanyl in so many street drugs now?"

"It's cheap," Riveaux said, "and strong. Fentanyl is heroin to the power of a hundred. And if you don't die, you're high all day, living for the next hit."

Shocking but not. Unreal but real. I knew the drill. What separates humans and animals isn't language. Koko the gorilla could communicate. Spoke via sign language. Even named a kitten. What separates humans from animals is our capacity for creative self-annihilation. More than addiction, an endless need. We're our own prey.

We pulled up to the Dempsey trailer and Riveaux killed the engine. We parked down the street, windows open, watching. Before we could exit the truck, Trish Dempsey stormed through the trailer door, yelling, cursing blue blazes. Her right arm nestled in that sling, floated there, a pause between verses.

A peppy frog song grew louder, needling the air, competing with Trish's voice. The thick stench of a nearby swamp was indecent. The trailer was a vestige of the FEMA disaster recovery effort that turned out to be a breeding ground for more disasters.

Trish powered up and down the trailer's metal steps, her pink sling in flight, as she screamed into her phone. "I'm sick of this shit. I'm not going to keep cleaning up your messes." She stumbled on the last step and caught herself on the rusted railing. The too-bright streetlight let us see the scene from our vantage point, but some words were lost to the frogs.

"You looked me square in the eye," Trish said into the phone, "and you *swore*."

Riveaux tapped ash into the congealed air. "Betting it's not a call about her vehicle's extended warranty."

"Press zero for domestic dispute," I said. "But her husband's in jail."

"Sweetie on the side?"

"Don't think he's the sweetest sidepiece," I said. "Note the arm sling."

The intensity ticked up on the phone call. "Run that smooth-talking mouth of yours all you want," Trish said, volume punching up with each word. "But I'm *done* listening, and I'm done with you." She paused and kicked a rock. "You no good son of a bitch."

"Son of a bitch," Riveaux echoed. A person, a curse, a consequence of words.

Trish held the phone in front of her face and primal-screamed into it. Anger. Power. Fear. The few times I'd seen Trish Dempsey in church, she was memorable, for sure, but not hectic. Nothing like that call. Once, I watched her place canned peaches in the offering basket. No money. Just a small can of peaches.

"Should we go talk to her?" I asked Riveaux. The back of my neck burned and my scalp prickled. But before I could open the passenger door, Trish stomped to her car and tore off into the sticky night.

"Stable environment," I said. "No wonder Prince is so reactive."

"Let's get his hot take," Riveaux said.

We walked up to the trailer. The metal siding was studded with shoe-sized dents. The doorbell wouldn't depress, so I knocked on the door and braced for BonTon's howling. *Knock knock knock.* But it was eerily silent. No barking. No cursing. No sound from inside. I pounded on the door again, enjoying the release, the flimsy aluminum losing itself under my fist. But Prince obviously wasn't there. The wind shifted, the air a sweet glaze.

Trish had said that Prince had been home. Was home, sick. Why was the trailer empty? Where was he? Why lie? The brain-blitz fired me up, charged me. I felt fluid and concrete. Ready to break the door. Ready to break wrists.

"Time to talk to locals," I said.

▪

It was almost 10 p.m., so our interrogation options were limited. We started close. A guy taking out the trash across the street from the Dempsey trailer said he'd just moved to the city from Little Rock. Nothing to report about Prince, though he did have a lot to say about vaccines and the deep state. "And here they had us all fooled," Riveaux told him with an annihilating grin. "Deep state can't get anything past you."

A cashier at the nearby Mardi Mart said she hadn't seen Prince in a while, but Trish came in all the time for her Virginia Slims. Trish was "courteous half the time," she said, choosing not to comment on the other half.

"Ever see her with anyone?" I asked.

"Not really. Actually, just one fella sometimes."

"What fella?" Riveaux asked.

"Some blond guy."

"Her son?" I asked. "He's blond. About her height. White pit bull."

"No dog that I recall." She shrugged. Her eyeliner was like a ransom note. Thick and inscrutable but demanding attention.

"Height, weight, unique features?" Riveaux asked.

"Regular?"

"When's the last time you saw Trish with that fella?" I asked.

"Few days ago," she replied, then said, "Sorry, time to start closing up."

"Striking out," Riveaux said on the way back to her truck. "Just about closing time for me too. You must be beat."

Sure, I was beat. Torn apart. And renewed by purpose. Fleur had been dead for about twelve hours, but the menace, the potential for more death, was a dark current forcing me ahead.

"I should check in with Moose," I said, "ask him for some medical insight."

"Brosmobile still up?" She rubbed her eyes with her knuckles.

"Shift's ending soon. Maybe he has fresh intel. He must see the fallout from these drugs."

"Medics see everything."

"Can you drop me at the firehouse?" I asked.

The firehouse was Riveaux's old HQ, before she was essentially pushed out, but she held her head high and said, "Yep. Just don't let my fan club spot me. I can't sign any more autographs."

11

MY BROTHER, MOOSE, TAPPED me into the city's erratic heart-beat. He was a good medic, too. A career as an EMT was his spin on ministering to people in crisis, the half-dead and the dead-dead. He had strong hands and wrecked nails that he couldn't stop chewing. I went on a ride-along with him one day last month and was amazed by his calm. A bedside manner so chill it bordered on confusing. He cared so much he couldn't show it. His emotions were so big he'd sealed an airtight lid on them.

Riveaux deposited me a block from the firehouse, intent on keeping her distance. When I finally arrived, I saw Moose in the ambulance bay doing two things at once, moving a gurney with his hip and bending down to restock a bandage supply. All six-foot-infinity of the guy straightened up when he spotted me coming. He was wrapped in his navy EMT garb with badges, patches, and pins. Moose liked wearing uniforms. Needed the creases, pleats, and rules. Structure. Guess we both needed that. Me in the convent, him, the army. Same as when we were kids, how he came out after I came out, enraging our parents but giving us another reason to bond. He couldn't find himself until I cut the path.

Or so I thought.

"Goose," he called, smiling like the edge of a smashed bottle.

Before I realized, I was smiling back. Moose was an A-plus person. A model human. A good guy. The most solid of the Walsh clan. He was a compulsive liar too. Had been since he was in second grade. Lied about what he had for breakfast. Lied about our cat's age. Stuff that made absolutely no sense. Once, when I was ten and he was a whisper short of nine, he faked a Russian accent and told all the kids in his class that he was a double agent living in Brooklyn under an assumed name.

In New Orleans, Moose just seemed to lie to himself. Or work himself into the ground with that crazy schedule. A tune I knew all too well. Loneliness also pinched at my own heart, when nighttime got too quiet and the past got loud. A war in the ear that you couldn't turn off, try as you might. Not that I'd trade it for complete serenity. What would I have to complain about if I did?

"You were right. It was fentanyl," I said.

He nodded solemnly.

"How fast does it hit?"

"Seconds," Moose said. "By the time we get the call, it's often too late. Sometimes Narcan can bring them back from the brink of death."

"The brink of death, yeah, but it can't undo—" I let the sentence collapse. Even my words had the vapors.

Every surface in the firehouse reflected red. Red from the exit signs. Red trucks. Too much red. "I was on a call last week," Moose said. "Teenager. Thought he was taking a Percocet at a party. His friends found him blue on the bathroom floor minutes later."

"Where's the epicenter?" I asked.

"There isn't one. It's all over the city. Every neighborhood." His cheek was clenched so tight it looked like he was going to shatter his jaw. "The knockoffs look exactly like prescription meds."

"Noticing any patterns?"

"Besides chaos? No. Fentanyl doesn't play by the rules," he said. "I'll keep my ears open, though. And take this." He pulled out a box from a nearby bag. "Narcan. Keep it on you at *all* times. It's only one dose, so don't test it." He mimicked the movements with his hands. "Spray it right inside the nose. Get up in there, in the nostril."

Narcan, the antidote the Diocese had banned.

"Thanks." It fit in the back pocket of my nun slacks. "Moose, how do you do this every day and stay sane?"

"One call at a time," he exhaled. "And a lot of coffee."

I blessed myself.

And then he blessed himself too.

"Why'd you do that?" I asked.

"You believe in it, and I believe in you."

Moose wasn't religious. He'd always loathed sitting through Mass and being forced to sing hymns. He'd wriggled through every minute of it. But sometimes praying together, even if you didn't have faith, offered a peculiar comfort.

"I know you've got a soft spot for the hard cases." He tugged his short beard. A few wisps of gray worked their way into his mostly chestnut hair. "This shit is very serious. I'd stay far away."

"Fleur died on my watch," I said.

Though, of course, it was about more than doing right by Fleur. Greater than vengeance or solving a crime. I needed to untangle the nest of pain and trauma, and suffocate the greed that fed it.

An alarm blared and three red lights flashed in manic unison. Moose said, "Hang on," and ran to the back to talk to firefighters who materialized out of nowhere. A group of men and women rushed to a fire truck and rolled out into the street. The siren screamed into the night. What hellscape awaited them at their destination? Would they get there in time?

My brother returned and looked at me for a long moment. "They're okay without me."

"You sure?"

"I'm off duty for the night. Going to head to Rouses. I could eat an actual moose." He smiled. "Join?"

"Only if you buy me coffee." I offered my most angelic smile.

"Wish granted."

Strong coffee would let me hack my own operating system, stay awake, and keep working through the night. But I knew we were fresh out of grounds at the convent. Moose and I slid into the market where shelves displayed multicolored boxes, jars, and cans of every size. So much choice. Too much.

As Moose waited for his muffaletta at the deli counter, I was going slightly insane, trying to locate the coffee Sister Laurel liked. The Community Coffee with the charcoal label.

But I couldn't find it. I was debating between two others—one in each hand—trying to imagine which one would taste less like a burnt tire in acid rain, when a familiar voice teased my ear.

"That one's the best."

I turned to see Rosemary Flynn holding a pack of sixty-watt bulbs in her left hand, her ruby red lips curved close to a smirk but far from what would qualify as a smile. As usual she smelled of rich soap. She reached across me and pointed to a bag of coffee on the shelf.

Staring at her finger, I said, "Thought you were a tea person."

"I'm full of surprises. And you need to use filtered water. Tap water is too hard."

"I'm less concerned with the mechanics at the moment. Just need a caffeine IV."

"Burning the midnight oil?" Her heat tore my skin off.

"Something like that," I replied, paying close attention to every word I said to betray none of the thrill at seeing this woman off campus, after work hours. I was glad Moose's sandwich order was ridiculously complex. Definitely didn't need him in that conversation.

"If you ever need an extra set of eyes," she said, "let me know."

That surprised me. "Didn't know you were into PI work."

"What do you really know about me?" Then she winked at me in a way that was somehow both innocent and X-rated. I had the sudden urge to grab her wrist hard, feel her pulse beating beneath my fingers.

Rosemary Flynn taught science at a Catholic school, not because she believed in God, but because she believed in proper lab procedure and getting a paycheck. Public and charter schools were "wastelands of expired chemicals," she'd said once as she poured her potpourri-smelling chai into her porcelain cup at the teacher's lounge table. Saint Sebastian's kids learned "titration and transubstantiation." The woman balanced equations the way Sister Rosetta Tharpe shredded the guitar. So what if it meant having to sit through a boring Friday Mass. She was either a good performer or enjoyed the challenge. There were other fun exercises I wanted to throw Rosemary Flynn's way. Including a blindfold. And other accoutrements.

"I didn't take you for the menial task type either." I nodded toward the bulbs she was holding.

"I'm pretty handy actually."

"I bet you are." My heart wouldn't slow down despite my deliberate efforts and internal threats. The ways the mind and heart double-cross each other.

The store's AC struggled to keep up and sent a rumble through the ceiling so heavy it swirled dust onto our heads. The tiniest dust devil in the world.

Rosemary looked up and shrugged. "Alex does things around the house too, when I remind him."

"Alex? Why would Alex Moore do things around your house?"

Still examining the ceiling, she said, "Alex moved in with me last month."

"Ah, living in sin," I said, seething.

Rosemary playing house with Alex? Well, fuck. The type of smug asshole who has a different bow tie for each day of the week but also knows every detail about vintage motorcycles. The kind of guy who helps an old lady cross the street, then takes to social media to proclaim about it to the world, chapter and verse. Alex was a tool and rarely a useful one. Though I had to admit, for all his annoying quirks, Alex might be an asset, if the Rebuild Fund tip didn't send us on a wild goose chase. Even a screwdriver could be used to smack a nail in a pinch.

Still didn't mean he was good enough for Rosemary Flynn. Basic men doing the absolute bare minimum and failing up, yet again. I wouldn't be surprised if it was written into the US Constitution, ordained and established for mediocre boys to rise to the top.

I walked to the checkout line so fast Moose had to jog to catch up. Tried to tamp down the urge to picture Alex's head getting crushed like a ripe cantaloupe.

Moose and I sat across from each other at a picnic bench outside the store. Though it was late, it was still sweltering. The moon was a high vowel sound.

"Here." Moose dropped half of the sandwich in front of me, then tucked into his half. He was eating so fast I was prepared to give him the Heimlich maneuver. I couldn't take one bite as sickness rose and I silently pouted about Rosemary and Alex.

I hated it. Hated feeling jealous of Alex.

"*Fugh.*" Moose gagged on his Big Gulp. "The 'ice' in the dispenser was melted."

"Another reason I stick to coffee. Just pour it out."

"But I'm thirsty."

"Yeah."

"I'm really sorry about your student," Moose said through voracious chewing.

I said "yeah" again, but I was still fixated on Rosemary Flynn's lips saying, *Alex moved in.*

"Fentanyl," Moose said, wiping his mouth, "is a dangerous drug sold by dangerous people. You need to be safe."

"Yeah."

"Are you listening to one word I'm saying?"

"I'll be safe," I said, but we both knew my definition of *safe* was a few ticks south of jumping out of an airplane without checking the parachute first.

"Eat," he said.

Food was the last thing on my mind, but I listened to Moose, for a change. After one bite I was so glad I did. It was rich, smokey and spicy, with juicy green olives that tasted like the sea. I said grace then inhaled the rest. Oil rolled down my wrists.

After we'd finished, Moose balled up the sandwich wrapper and lobbed it into the trash with precision. He stretched with his whole being. When he stretched like that, his hands were in different time zones than his feet. "Stay safe," he said one more time, and we parted ways with a hug that crushed the breath out of me.

Every time I said goodbye to Moose felt like it could be the last time.

I will be with you always, to the end of time. Matthew 28:20.

I had my Sisters, but Moose was the last of my nuclear family. Dad was still alive. Or he was in the category of the living. Not that living and being alive were the same. A choice was involved. Dad made it clear he wanted nothing to do with us, his gay son and lesbian daughter. He didn't have to pretend now that Mom was gone. Because of me, my mistake.

When I was twelve years old, before the wildness seized me, before the first taste of whiskey, the first ink, the first hit and first heartbreak, I came in second place in the Junior High Jazz Band Competition at the Brooklyn Music Teachers' Guild Hall. Why was second place so much worse than last place? I was crying my eyes out and Dad tried to comfort me in his typical fashion. "Sorry, kiddo," he said, "but every last Walsh is a loser. Better learn that now." He looked everywhere in the crowded auditorium except in my eyes and said, "We're a family of losers."

He thought he was doing the right thing, parenting with some kind of truth. And he was right—we were a loser family.

But a family of zeros was still a team. A unified front. Until we lost that too.

▪

I dropped the coffee grounds at the convent, placing the bag on the clean counter near the ficus. My mind was a five-alarm fire, my veins broiling. I needed to work and couldn't stay still. Staying safe, as Moose requested. Sorry. A clock was ticking. Waiting for reports, waiting for Riveaux, following proper clearance? Not with fentanyl selling for two bucks a pop. I had to throw rocks and break rules. Somewhere in the city, a dealer was snoring on a pile of money while Fleur's button nose was growing ice crystals in the morgue.

I crossed the street and walked to the back door of the rectory. The lock was child's play. A quick lift and a prayer, and I was in. Father Nathan must have been in deep sleep. I didn't hear any stirring on the second floor. If he did notice me, I'd spin a yarn about needing laundry detergent for Sister Honor's underwear. That'd end any discussion real quick.

His classic black-and-white shirt collars—starched so stiff they could peel potatoes—were hanging on hooks. A whole row of them. A priestly assembly line. I swiped one for the night and slipped out the door. I should have asked permission, but better to beg for forgiveness, given the circumstances.

I put Nathan's collar over my black blouse, a costume change to support a little fact-finding mission that Monday night. Clerical drag, why the fuck not. People talk to priests. They dish their dirt, confess their nasty sins. There's something about that little strip of white that screams "trust me." But a nun? We're invisible. Good for quick comfort, a sympathetic ear, ministering to the unhoused, holding a hand at hospice, carrying the donations of canned peaches up to the rectory. And we're there to absorb pain, to be a living landfill for your anger and sadness. Wing women for a homophobic pope.

If I couldn't beat them, I'd join them. Or at least look the part. I was a true believer anyway, apostolic AF. God knew I was all in, or would be soon. So that night I decided I'd do what it took. I'd be a mobile confessional booth, ready to absolve your sins, as long as you spilled the tea about the new drugs in town.

12

IN FATHER NATHAN'S PRIEST collar, I was me but not me. A different servant of God. Some animals live in disguise, surviving through deception. Camouflage of plain sight. The gnarly tree knot that's actually an owl staring into your soul.

Other creatures knew where to hide and when to run.

As I walked in the borrowed collar, I spotted a half-consumed cigarette some knucklehead had flicked into a hedge from a moving car. Still lit.

Yep, a burning bush. Miracles were real. You just had to know where to look.

I picked up the live treasure and took a drag. The smoke smelled like a new start, reminded me of morning sex. Smoking and sex. Dear God, I loved them both. Though now only smoking was an option. And a limited one. Dancing on the edge was fun, but it could also send you toppling into the sea below. Eating from the forbidden tree was Eve's "fall," our original sin. But wasn't that bite also bliss. A craving to see ourselves differently, free ourselves, fly close to the flame. Some of my benders opened new perspectives, breakthroughs on my first album, my best lyrics, religious epiphanies. Many others just ended in blackouts. And

Fleur's ended her. It wasn't a misfire—addiction—but a feature of us. The Bible says we're minted in God's own image. We're all micro-gods, wired for prayer, innate as instinct. We're preprogrammed to save, to need saving. Did that make our capacity for addiction divine? Did that mean God was addicted? To us? Was God just as fucked up as the rest of us? That comforted me more than I could ever say. Made me love God even more.

My legs moved on their own accord, down Decatur Street. The jasmine and eucalyptus in the hot wind gave way to the sour turn of sopping river air.

I trudged along until my soles blistered, until I hit a crummy dive in Saint Claude. *$3 special, whiskey and beer chaser* was handwritten on a ripped paper bag taped to the door. Perfect spot for lowlifes, the old Holiday, folks who need to disappear or slip under the radar.

Neon signs chewed the air with their dancing, warm light. My black gloves and priest collar drew curious stares and some head turns. Female reverends weren't uncommon outside the Catholic Church. But in that bar, I might as well have been carrying John the Baptist's head on a tray. Some moron in a jester hat straightened up real quick when he saw me, like I was his drill sergeant. Though I wouldn't have minded screaming in his face and demanding he drop and give me twenty while reciting the Beatitudes. *Blessed are the poor in spirit. Blessed are the meek. Blessed are they who mourn. Blessed are they who hunger and thirst for righteousness.* Thirst was right, fuckers. I ignored the chumps and snaked my way to the bar where the bartender had big eyes and bigger fists.

"Would ya look at that," the bartender said. "A lady priest in my bar."

"Reverend," I lied.

"What'll it be, Madame Reverend?"

"Water," I said, though I would have loved to murder a double whiskey. "And just Reverend will do. No Madame."

"Holy water coming right up, Just Reverend."

The woman on the next stool rubbed her eyes. Was she crying? Sweating? Both?

"Rough night?" I asked her.

"Rough life," she replied.

"Seems like the whole city's hurting."

"You're damn right about that," she said.

The bartender set down my glass of water a touch too hard and liquid splashed over the side. "On the house," he said.

Free water. What a gentleman. I raised my glass to the sad lady next to me. "A toast to healing."

"I need a whole bucket of healing," she said with a wince.

"Been hearing about a lot of pain lately."

"I can't get a break," she said, then sipped her drink. A Malibu and Coke, from what I could gather from the smell and color of the liquid and the patron's fashion choices. God help me but I was still a judgmental bitch on occasion. "My husband's such a jerk."

"Hurt people hurt people," I recited.

"Don't have to tell me," she said, and left greasy prints on her glass as she rotated it.

In a quiet voice, I said, "I'm here to listen." *And collect info,* I thought. "What's on your mind?"

"I'm all talked out." She grabbed her drink and left, barstool spinning in a lopsided rotation. She relocated to an empty back corner.

First fail of the night. I downed the water in two gulps and thanked the bartender.

At the other end of the bar, an older guy in a black and gold veteran cap kept rubbing the top of his shoulder like he was trying to start a fire. The way he scanned corners reminded me so much of Moose. Preparing for threats, expecting danger, alarms always incoming. Always real.

I moved toward him with my hands in prayer position. "Mind if I sit?"

He looked at the barstool then back into his glass. "Free country. That's what they keep telling me." If the priest collar bothered him, he didn't show it.

"Army? Navy? Marines?" I asked.

"Army, '69 to '70." He fidgeted with the useless straw in his drink. "Was a medic. Now I mostly medicate myself."

Another medic. That hit like a boot to the throat. Moose had said something like that once. How combat medics spent their army tours patching up people, only to come home broken themselves.

"My kid brother was a medic too. Afghanistan."

"Made it out?"

"Yes, thank God. And thank you for your service."

"Service. Sure." He scratched at his shoulder again.

I watched him drain his drink, feeling a sideways kinship. His drinking, my addictions to sex and substances. The temporary fixes of self-destruction. They were all medicines of a kind, in the moment. Attempts at a cure, rather. Every stranger's bed I'd ever crashed in. Every bar I'd closed down.

The vet ordered another Jim Beam and mumbled, "Helps me relax."

"A little self-care's good for the body and mind," I said. "What else helps?"

"What's it to you?"

"A lady of the cloth has to live vicariously." I pulled at the collar.

A barely there smile crossed his face. Not enthusiastic. Just slightly amused. "The VA can't get me a medical card. Said I should try meditation or church." The word *church* froze in the air. Like it was framed on a shelf. "Not against it or anything. Just not for me." He tilted his chin to indicate the collar around my neck.

"No medical card? You got a dealer?"

He shrugged as he took a sip. "Maybe." The brim of his hat drowned his face in shadow.

"Your contact sell anything harder than weed?"

"Maybe."

I leaned in. "Fentanyl?"

When his eyes went sharp, I knew I blew it. Absolutely tanked it. Sweat collected in the crooks of my elbows.

"Jesus fucking—" He set his glass down. "Why you asking about that?"

I blessed myself. "I'm trying to understand how good people end up in tough places."

"You got it backward," he said and downed the rest of his drink in one swig. "Tough places end up burying good people." After slapping a dollar tip on the bar, he stormed out.

The bartender gave me a consolation nod as he cleared the vet's glass and napkin. "Another water to wet your whistle, Just Reverend?"

"Bless you." I watched him fill my glass with his soda gun. How many bartenders had I sat in front of as they poured, uncapped, measured, muddled? How many noticed me unraveling? How many had pretended not to see as I followed strangers into bathroom stalls?

"You're a long way from church." As he set the water down, the scars on his hands and knuckles flexed. All the nights opening bottles, hauling cases, emptying trash.

"Can't be too different in here," I said. "Folks with a lot on their minds, stuff to get off their chests, prayers that need answering. I'm sure you've heard it all."

"At least your patrons come back every Sunday to see you." He sliced a lime into identical wedges.

"Well, I'm just the opening act for the ultimate headliner," I said, which got a laugh. *Good*, I thought, *building a rapport.* "Local bar like this? Lots of repeat customers, right?"

"Here?" He plopped two impossibly small straws into a glass and slid the drink to a patron three seats down from me. "A mix, but folks are mostly passing through. Ghost tour drop-off site's across the street."

"Even so, I bet you've got a front-row seat to real troubles."

"Amen to that, Just Reverend. Even their troubles have troubles."

"Hard to see people at the end of their rope."

"Hate it." He blinked quickly.

I leaned in, lifting off the barstool. "Any of your clientele getting mixed up with fentanyl?" Apparently the last exchange had taught me nothing.

He shook his head. "Don't know a thing about that shit," he said. For all the money in the world he wouldn't meet my eyes. "And if I were in your collar, I'd leave it in God's hands."

The momentary lull ended as a rowdy group stumbled in, demanding Jack and gingers. "Coming right up," he said.

Leave it in God's hands. Honestly, I'd love to. Except God gave me hands of my own, and I'd be cheating us both if I didn't use them to get some fucking answers.

I stood and walked in a slow circle. Then another arc in the opposite direction. Covering the entirety of that bar. That's how I caught the attention of a group of men near the dartboard.

"Get a load of this one," said a weaselly guy with wire-thin arms and cheap ink, the kind you get after too many Jell-O shots and not enough consciousness. "A High Priest*ess*. Forgive me, hot mama, for I have sinned!" He fell to his knees and raised his hands high. One of his whiskey-soaked buddies laughed so hard he sloshed his drink on the already sticky floor. Another doubled over whooping, slapping his thigh, trying to catch his breath.

At least someone wanted to talk to me. Not my ideal informant, but couldn't squander the chance.

"Well, aren't you entertaining, my child. But if you have something to confess," I said as I inched closer, taking in the evidence of his hard living. More track marks than Grand Central. "I'm all ears."

He slathered on a smile like I'd just flashed him my tits. "Got plenty, but what's in it for me?"

"Salvation." I blessed myself, my hands pruning under my gloves.

"Try again."

"Are you in trouble, my child?"

"You got that right." He laughed. "And I keep buying more." The guy exchanged a look with one of his buddies who was using his front teeth to tear open a bag of Fritos.

"Then maybe I've got something you need," I said.

"Oh yeah?" He perked up.

Another sloppy crew entered the bar, flooding the area, and the energy shifted. I was about to lose my already thin chance. Had to press on while I could.

"Let's go outside," I said.

He asked, "Whatcha got?" as he followed me out. A good shepherd, I knew what my sheep wanted.

Outside, the splendid smell of dumpster mixed with piss funk almost knocked me out. The music from the bar kicked back up, or maybe it never stopped. Memory is a bitch like that. Something to shape to our needs. What we perceive as the past becomes the content of the future.

"So whatcha got?" he asked again. I swore I could see his mouth watering.

"Absolution." I shoved him into the wall. The element of surprise, a major advantage. Then I whispered into his shut eye, as if it was a tape recorder, "Tell me everything you know about who's moving product in this town."

"What?" He thrashed.

"Drugs." I pushed him again.

"I don't fucking know." He fought back, swinging his arms. The alley cartwheeled as he flailed and hit my chin. I almost bit clean through my tongue.

But I grounded my feet, reset, and let the power seep up from the earth as I clamped down. The shock of it—of me—put him on defense, and I squeezed his throat until he groaned. He was so scrawny, it was almost unfair. Like choking a sunflower. But the feral part of me wanted to drain the life from him. Press my thumb into his windpipe until it popped like a balloon animal. Deep down, I wanted it raw, wanted to fight dirty, fingers in the eyes, hair pulled out in great chunks. I wanted to draw blood. And playing guitar all my life—shredding downstroke after downstroke—gave me unusually strong fingers. I gripped again.

"I don't know shit," he spat out.

"Your track marks say otherwise." I pressed harder.

"Fuck! All right."

Even in my gloves I felt his meaty arteries resisting my hand. "Start talking."

"Ease off."

Before I let him go I gave him one more good squeeze.

Rubbing his neck, the weasel yapped and yapped, reciting names that sounded made up and ordinary in the same turn. He listed locations. Parks, parties, and alleys where he'd scored meth, heroin, coke, and oxy in the past year. Intersections like Tchoupitoulas and Bienville. Abundance and Senate.

"What about fentanyl?"

"What about it?"

I grabbed his twitchy arm. "Who's your contact?" I paused between each word, enunciating each syllable like I was up on stage at a spelling bee in a fucking tiara.

"No contact. Just some guy who sold for the Royal Family."

"The what?"

"The Royal Family," he repeated. "Biggest game in town."

"What's the guy's name?"

"No idea. Met him on Bourbon and never saw him again."

Bourbon Street. Jesus H.

"Give me his number," I said.

"Don't got it. I couldn't even tell you what he looks like, I was so out of my mind."

"I need names."

"All I know is Ren's at the top," he said.

"Ren? What's the story there?"

"Nobody messes with Ren."

I let the weasel's arm go and he stepped back like he'd been nicked by a flamethrower. For a moment I leaned against the wall to collect my thoughts. The bricks looked different up close. Tiny air bubbles. Bits of sparkle in no particular pattern. Air pockets like miniature caves.

Ren. Ren, the alleged top dog. Not that you could trust a dive-bar nobody's word. I should know—I'd only started to trust myself. But the fear in his eyes. Like true love, true fear is hard to fake.

I watched the weasel rejoin the clamor of the bar, and I left the alley in a complete daze. Like the breeze had picked me up, floated me out to the street.

How could I track down Ren?

What—who—was the Royal Family?

Were they based on Royal Street? No, too easy.

Prince Dempsey was a royal pain in my ass, but part of a gang? Trish said he wasn't going to repeat Daddy's mistakes. And I'd baptized that kid months earlier in the Mississippi. A scrappy baptism in disgusting river water, but a genuine moment nonetheless. Unless I got played. Was I that naïve?

I was so lost in thought, I didn't notice two cops until they were almost walking through me. Seemed fitting. I did feel like a ghost.

"Hey, there," one of them—a runt with a boyish grin—said. "Out for a stroll in the wee hours of the morning?"

I turned to face him. We were nose to nose. "Officers," I said, wondering what wall they were going to drive me up. "Good morning. I trust you are having a blessed start to the day." I backed up two steps.

"Would be nice," said the other cop. He was a beefcake with a nose that looked like it had been broken annually since age ten. "More of a bullshit close to a lousy shift."

"Hard night?"

The smaller one nodded. "The usual drunks, a lost senior citizen, and a stolen Toyota Corolla."

"May God grant us a brighter dawn."

"You preach around these parts?" the little guy asked, scratching his temple.

"Uptown at a small Episcopal church. Saint Clare's—you probably haven't heard of it. But I bring the Word to the city. Street outreach."

"Uptown?" The bigger guy stepped forward like he wanted to tell me a big bad secret. "Do you know that bitch of a nun? The one who ratted out Reggie?"

"You're barking up the wrong denomination," I said, letting a deep breath in, centering myself. Though my vision swam and my head was about to roll off my shoulders. Fun. The police were after me now? The last thing I needed was a cop's foot on my neck in some off-script revenge.

For as scared as I was, though, my rage was bright. It flamed with a shade of red that had its own shadow. The men were stronger than me, but I was crazier.

The bigger guy opened his trout mouth. "I got a bone to pick with that holier than thou piece of shit. I'm gonna—"

"Simmer down, Jennings." The nice cop wiped sweat from his cheeks and behind his ears. "Grogan was dirty as hell. That nun did us a favor."

"Favor?" he spat. "She destroyed a good man's career."

"A 'good man' who was on the take," he said, then he turned to face me. "Look, sorry for any trouble. We're almost done with our rounds. Been a day."

I weighed my options, ran some scenarios in my head. It was obvious that I couldn't wait around for this good cop/bad cop duo to put two and two together. Had to get out of there fast, so I offered a tight, pious smile to keep my gold tooth concealed. "No worries, gentlemen." I made the sign of the cross and turned my torso in the direction of the street. "If you'll excuse me, I have a service in just a few hours, and I must prepare."

But the big guy was in my face again. He was faster than he looked, and his breath was rancid. I mean, the type of rot that cooks in the basement of hell for fifty millennia. "If you run into that nun, tell her payback's a bastard."

The runt pulled at his partner's massive arm. "Let's go."

"May the Lord be with you," I said, then walked away.

Clearly some of the New Orleans brass wasn't elated that I helped bust their detective, golden boy Detective Reggie Grogan. Guessing Jennings wasn't alone. But why blame me? Grogan was gambling away kickbacks from the Diocese to cover their decades of abuse, disappearing the evidence. Until one day, when Grogan's monthly payments stopped, he snapped and became a killer. Of course, his life had hit the skids. Up to his eyeballs in debt, marriage falling apart. Everybody felt pain. Cut anyone and they'd bleed. But white men navigated a small fraction of the troubles that women and people of color had to scale on the daily. Dudes still convinced they're the rightful owners of everything. Real estate, schools, the law, the country, faith itself.

Cosplaying in Father Nathan's collar, was I any better? Praying, pushing, manipulating, and lying to get what I needed. Then I remembered Fleur's lifeless eyes. Maybe to fight evil you had to become it. At least have a taste of it.

Honeysuckle licked the air as I walked home. Every keyhole blinked. Footfalls echoed. I couldn't see anyone trailing me, but I *felt* tension in the atmosphere. A spasm. Like a car full of goons could screech to a halt any second to wrestle me inside. And beneath my fear lived something else. Reverb. A hiss. A spark. I had a lead. The Royal Family. Ren.

My obsession—investigating—maybe it was misplaced righteousness. So what. The racing thing inside me refused to play it safe, to stop. Something that every martyr, every stubborn fuck, feels on her march to get burned alive or stoned to death.

In the shadow of an overpass sprawled a tiny town of tarps. A city within the city huddled beneath the expressway. There must have been twenty tents and sleeping bags with sleeping people tucked inside. A silent, strangely beautiful scene. Precious people who needed care taking care of one another. People who my church and our country kept failing.

There were countless reasons why folks ended up unhoused. Abuse, addiction, undiagnosed or untreated mental illness, cycles of poverty. Shelters were full. Safe houses had waiting lists longer than Sister Honor's grievance digest. The Archdiocese had dozens of empty churches. Empty schools too. Meanwhile people slept outside, in the heat, rain, and wind. My own convent bed felt selfish, like a sin. Every person at the encampment was someone's child. Each one a child of God. But try telling that to the bishop. Being poor wasn't a crime, but people sure loved acting like it was. The real criminals were the 1 percent. The grifters who made Faustian bargains, who Monopoly Man'd their way to power and refused to share. WWJD? Can't speak for the guy, but I'm pretty sure Jesus never said, *I got mine, now you get yours.*

Fucking asshats.

I took off the collar and looked up for a sign in the night sky. Must have been five in the morning then. The first hint of dawn let glimmers of light poke through navy. I finally reached the convent and slipped inside.

In the foyer I leaned against the heavy door and used every ounce of my strength and prayer to shut it quietly. The Lord worked in mysterious ways, that much I knew. But was complete chaos one of them?

Riveaux's words were heavy, dripping with sleep, when she picked up my call. "Better be good, Goldsmobile. It's not even six."

I kept my voice to a low whisper. "Got a lead. The Royal Family is moving fentanyl."

"The Royal Family?"

"Heard of them?"

"Yep. Local crew. Weed dealers, before medical cannabis was legal. Meth pushers before meth got supplanted by opioids."

"Guess they're branching out," I said.

"Who's the source?"

"Some junkie at a dive in Saint Claude. Said someone named *Ren*'s in charge."

"Ren? Okay. What were you doing at a dive in Saint Claude?"

"Stretching my legs. All the genuflecting's rough on the knees."

Silence on the other end. Then an agonizing exhale. "You're taking precautions, right, when you're 'stretching your legs'? Keeping your nose clean, following the PI method? Staying in your lane and whatnot?" Her tone was different. Deep worry coiling underneath the annoyance. The rare experience of vulnerability was a shiver in every cell. My mind melted into my body, like water seeping into cracks. Riveaux kept people miles away and wore her cynicism proudly. Maybe I was starting to break through. Maybe.

I said with closed eyes, "Obviously, but thanks for your concern."

"Thank me by staying on the right side of this."

"Always," I said. "Next rendezvous?"

"Let's check in after the Mass," she said. "Watch for any shifty behavior in your flock. I'll run down some leads on my end." She hung up before I could say bye.

For all my little tricks, games, routines, and prayer, sleep was torture. I couldn't relax enough to let sleep inside. Our flesh has to ask for rest, just like the mind. To invite it in.

I prayed for one hour of sleep, for one hour of dreamless dark, for anything to slow the motor. I'd have taken fentanyl myself if it were in reach. My skin felt radiator hot and frostbite cold at the same time. With my eyes open or eyes closed, all I saw was Fleur's face, forever leaving. Even trusting that God held her close, I'd still failed her.

Addiction was a hunger that could never be sated. The chance to be part of something good, to help—that's what brought me to the convent. To find meaning in the loss.

Before I'd quit Dr. Connie, the therapist Riveaux basically forced me to visit if I wanted to apprentice her at the agency, she kept asking, "And how did that make you feel?" and "What does it feel like?" She told me that letting go of trauma would feel warm, freeing. But I felt numb. No one tells you how jarring *nothing* can feel.

13

TUESDAY MORNING, THREE SLEEPLESS hours after my dive bar mission, I dragged my ass to Mass. It was a quiet reset and painful tribute to Fleur. Class was canceled for a day of mourning, as Sister Honor had proclaimed. But school would be back in action on Wednesday and Thursday. And by Friday, graduation would be a week away.

Fleur'd been gone only one day, but it'd felt like a thousand years. Serrated seconds that drew blood in new places every time I replayed the grisly discovery of her dead body. How I'd tried and failed to trick her heart back into beating. During her Mass, I made space in my prayers for my anger. I prayed for the strength and the focus to exact revenge. Against greedy dealers. Against the systems that fail people who need the most help.

"We remember Fleur's everyday kindness." Father Nathan's voice was so earnest. Each word a prayer of its own. "We remember her infectious smile. We remember the colorful earrings she always wore and the way she brought creativity and brightness to every room she entered."

Tears.

So many tears. There were wicked rushing rivulets and deep hiccupping wails. Mrs. Benoit cried stoically. Ryan Brown's body quaked as he open-mouthed sobbed. Shelly wept so hard, she'd passed out. Rosemary fanned her with the prayer missal until she blinked back to consciousness.

Some students cried silently, like leaky statues. A grief so deep it bordered on shameful. Some blew their noses with loud honks. I turned right and left, studied their expressions, tried to gauge who was feeling what, who knew what, who could have been a link in the fentanyl chain. And who was slinging those counterfeit motherfuckers?

But all I saw was pain. Fear. Illegible heavy-lidded eyes.

As I scanned the rows of fallen faces and bowed heads, I was desperately hoping I'd see Prince Dempsey. Anxious wasn't the word for how I felt. Competing worries buzzed through my body in combat. I looked through the pews twice, hoping I'd missed Prince on my first sweep. But there was no sign of him.

No Bernard either. Prince was flighty, sure, but Bernard was a creature of habit. So where the hell was he now? Finding Fleur's body probably turned him upside down. Might have been a crisis of faith.

Then came the singing. A gathering intensity of voices. Each person melding into the next then all as one. No individual, only collective sound. Except Sister Honor, who unleashed her pitchy notes with a scowl. She looked like she was getting electrocuted as she led us in Saint Sebastian's cover of "On Eagle's Wings."

Despite my appetite for thrashing in a mosh pit, I couldn't deny how much I loved singing that hymn. Sure, I changed *He* to *We* in the song. Refused to sing it any other way. My religion was real to me because I kept it real. Rediscovering it over and over. My faith was like a contact lens, invisible, but it changed the way I saw everything. Including myself.

When it came time for the Sign of Peace, Father Nathan paused and did a quick priestly review of the congregation. "The peace of the Lord be with Fleur, always. Peace be with you," he laid it on us, our cue, and waited for our staggered reply.

"And also with you." I started passing the hand-shaking peace around the pews. For a minute, I was okay. It was all okay. I was just another human animal looking for the feeling of hands clasping, for comfort in a pack. Something inside me realigned, snapped back toward surrender.

A horsefly buzzed lazily around the candles, high enough to avoid the flames.

"Peace be with you," I said to Sister Laurel and then to Sister Honor who jerked back like I'd just spit in her face.

She barked, "And with you," accidentally elbowing Sister Laurel in the gut. As Sister Honor straightened her spine with slow, deliberate effort, neck powder caked in the folds of her skin. Her breathing was labored, like she had to coach herself to get back up from the kneeler. Pain. Too much of it. Probably a sign she'd been pushing herself too far for too long. We all were. But I knew she wouldn't admit it if I asked or offered help.

Joey Delachaise shook my hand. Then Trevor O'Keefe, the budding artist who took my class last year. Then Ryan Brown. Ryan Brown, whose eyes were red goggles. "Peace be with you, Sister," he choked out. "And with Fleur." A flood of tears as he said her name. I held his hand, trying to feel for any wavering in him through my glove, like a hand-to-hand polygraph test. Was his distress the purest sign of innocence? Of true love? Was it an act? Or was it guilt? I pulled him in for a hug, whispering, "If you have any pills, dispose of them immediately." He pulled back alarmed, but I quickly moved on. Couldn't risk anything more with Sister Honor there.

I sent a silent prayer to Father Nathan. *Peace be with you.* He stood behind the slab of our altar with a marble certainty. His collar, a twin of the one I'd just borrowed. The crucifix hung above him with an elegant Christ casting shadows so heavy they could crush jasmine. Father Nathan was riding out a storm. Not just the congregation's grief that morning, but Saint Sebastian's stability itself. Churches across the country were shuttering their doors. Sold, demolished, and paved over to make way for high-end condos with indoor lap pools. Or empty, crumbling museums of ruin. Our convent was practically a historic landmark already, with just three of us nuns remaining. I hated the image of our school abandoned, grown over with weeds, so quiet, like time itself had been detoured around it. Father Nathan kept the ship steady. No *Mary Celeste* adrift with him at the helm.

Just as I sensed the last rounds of peace making their way through the crowded church, I spotted him—Prince Dempsey in the last row.

Shock and relief, raw currents, lifted me out of the pew, into the aisle, to the back of the church where he sat in shadows. He was loose-limbed, relaxed, like he'd been chilling there all week. Not bedridden. Like Prince on any other day, except his face was a mess. A black eye, smear of a bruised cheek, scars over his blond eyebrows.

"Peace be with you," I whispered and slid into the pew beside Prince, "and also with your face. What happened?"

Prince looked away and threw gum in his mouth. "Bad luck." His jaw was a hammer as he chewed. "Leave me alone."

"You know I can't do that, Prince."

BonTon sat between his feet. She could tear my ass to ribbons in one second if I made even one wrong move toward her person. I could relate. The dog and I were both rabidly defensive of the select few we claimed as our own. Her haunches held odd markings. Dark blobs. Like Father Nathan epically missed a forehead on Ash Wednesday.

The congregation recited: "O, God, we pray," and, row by row, people began to rise for the Eucharist.

"Where've you been?" I whispered. "You okay?"

He poked the rosary hanging from the wooden hymnal holder. "Busy. People to do. Things to see."

A child began to cry in the front but the sound quickly muffled.

"What about all those doctor's notes? Your mom also came by, said you've been sick."

"Mom was here? When?"

"Yesterday." With a quick glance at the altar, I saw Father Nathan performing the Fraction Rite, breaking the host. The sacred body, severed, torn into pieces, to be reborn in us. "She said your blood sugar has been out of whack, and you're safer at home."

Prince laughed.

"Why's that funny?" I asked, but Prince was a million miles away. All ten of his fingernails were dirty, but his knuckles were clean, smooth. "You and Fleur were close," I said, eliciting a *whatever* shrug from Prince. "Did you know she was using?"

Prince tilted his head. "What you on about?"

The organ swelled as the long Eucharist procession snaked around the sanctuary.

"Drugs. Fentanyl. Fleur got mixed up with some bad—"

"Spare me the scared straight speech," he interrupted. "Don't have time for that shit."

"Listen." The Communion line shuffled forward, so I spoke softly. "If you have orange pills, flush them. Promise."

Prince bent over to scratch BonTon's head. She was a crescent moon, all white, save for her dramatic black snout and those very weird marks on her fur. When I took a closer look, what I'd thought was dirt on her hips was singed hair and blackened skin. Marks with stories to tell.

"You think you know me so well," he said finally, "that you can save me?"

"Save you *again*, you mean?"

"You can't do shit. Go save yourself." He pointed at the altar, in front of which students were taking Communion.

"Some part of you still cares. That's why you showed up today."

Another shrug. The confessional booth's curtain spasmed but there was no breeze in there. No air moving at all.

"Stay here," I said.

Prince offered no reply as BonTon plopped her wet black nose into his sweaty hands. I dashed into the aisle, walking right up to the altar, cutting ten people in the Communion line. Father Nathan looked bemused as I girls-to-the-fronted myself ahead to receive the sanctified body of our Lord. He placed a holy wafer on the palm of my right glove, and I stared at it, then let it dissolve on my tongue. A two-cent disc purchased from the Guild that tasted like a sugary nothing, sweet paper, like the flying saucer penny candies Moose and I loved back in Bay Ridge. But the feeling was real. The shiver in my blood was real. The pain and sacrifice of an anointed person had transformed from fable into sacred metaphor, a symbol breathing itself alive.

Thanks to Jesus, life's greatest mystery felt less scary: When and how we die doesn't matter; it's when and how we *live* that makes our story happy or sad. Unutterable pain is unfair and cruel and illogical. But pain is also the price of new life, like a woman in labor, Jesus on the cross, the birth of a new idea or work of art. Divine needs awakened in me during Mass—to be, to see, to help. To fight.

Before I could make my way back to the pew, I saw Prince slip out the side door, BonTon padding silently beside him. After resting my face in my hands, letting Communion pour itself into me, absorbed by every artery, the congregation stood for the final blessing, and I watched through the stained glass as their shadows dissolved into the green beyond.

▪

As I left the church, holy water a wet promise on my forehead, Rosemary Flynn and Alex Moore walked toward me, arm in arm. Still couldn't believe she'd shacked up with that goober.

I couldn't avoid them, so as they approached, I put on my best smile, which surely looked like a hastily painted clown face. Here I thought my day couldn't get any better.

My two years in the convent had sharpened my ability to read people without them clocking it. I noted the tightness in Alex's expression, a telltale stress cue. He tried to flash his usual big smile, but it never unlocked, leaving crow's feet conspicuously absent.

"This just feels like a mistake," Rosemary said, her eyes thundering. "Fleur of all students. It's unjust, frightful. Almost perverse."

"It doesn't feel real, and I hope it never does."

You'd think they'd be old hat, the Remembrance Masses at Saint Sebastian's. Services and prayers for people we'd known and lost. We cried, we beat our heads, asked "why, why, why," then went back to business as usual. But there's no usual. I hated the sense that grief had a schedule and normalcy was some kind of mercy. Time should pause. The world should stop. Whenever someone precious is torn from the earthly plane, the ground should tremble. The sky should crack.

I stared at Alex, and his face went from pale to positively vampiric when he noticed me scoping him. "Let's get going, babe," he said to Rosemary, tapping the tip of her nose like she was his labradoodle, "breakfast at Brennan's waits for no one."

"Don't let the memory of Fleur stand between you and your waffles," I said in a voice hard enough to skateboard on. How satisfying to see Alex uncomfortable.

Rosemary stared at me with the most egregiously inscrutable look. Like she wanted to slap me or eat me or marry me. Honestly, I'd have taken any option.

"*Sorry*, not to be insensitive"—he placed his hand on his chest—"but a guy's gotta eat." Alex smirked, meaning he wasn't sorry. Couldn't be less sorry.

As I watched their retreating figures, I imagined hitting Alex so hard he choked on his own teeth. His bow tie was too bright. Smile too showy. Voice too punchable. What was he hiding behind his wraparound sunglasses and a cappella crimes? There was something I needed to rip out of him. Not just because of Fleur's death, not just because Rosemary was his "babe." Gag. It was something I couldn't yet grasp.

But, yeah, jealousy twisted the knife. Exquisite envy like the taste of blood after getting a tooth knocked out. The masochistic streak in me couldn't resist pushing further. I didn't want to know more about them, their life together, and yet I kept picturing them. Alex Moore and Rosemary Flynn. In their kitchen shaking up martinis. Them naked in their goddamn bedroom, him on top of her like a rock crab, all awkward claws thrusting—uh uh uh—while she stared up at the ceiling praying for it to be done, enduring all two minutes of his "lovemaking." Or she closed her eyes and thought of me on top of her, fucking her in a way she didn't think was possible, especially with two women.

My grinding teeth sounded like a truck rolling over a curb. I shook myself out of it. Way more important things to worry about than Rosemary Flynn and Alex wafflefucker Moore.

I needed to refocus, so I popped by the rectory to see if Father Nathan was back in his office yet. We had a bond few understood. Most thirtysomethings couldn't fathom an hour without their phone let alone opting into a life of duty and service. My old bandmates had called me insane; they'd had a field day with my faith. Father Nathan, from what he'd shared, had fended off similar naysayers. The Diocese didn't understand us either, our hot takes on Catholicism, liberation theology, and, oh how radical, general goodness. The bishop tried to cover up decades of suffering. Father Nathan and I wanted to pull back the curtain.

Despite it all, we were believers. Deluded, maybe. True believers all the same. And after my permanent vows, we'd be even closer.

As I knocked on his office door, it swung open. The phone was ringing, but he wasn't there. Probably still in the sacristy, changing out of his vestments. Safer bet to wait for him in his office, so I sat in the chair in front of his desk, where I spotted a jar of peanut butter with a fork sticking out. Dunking a tined utensil in Skippy was his trademark move. The guy owned a wholesome vibe that could power a small village. Not a punk like me. A polite badass. He wasn't a wilting lily to be screwed with, and he had a sad edge, a darkness all his own. He never cursed, never took the Lord's name in vain, but I'd seen him shoot a man without a second thought. In the name of justice, but it was still a wild card I'd never thought he'd play.

A few minutes later, Father Nathan walked in. "Tough morning," he said, ignoring the ringing phone and grabbing for the Skippy.

"When will this get easier?" I asked.

"Let me know when you find out." He smiled such a hurt smile I wished I could rewind it from his face.

On Monday he'd asked me to keep him apprised. So I did. I confessed about playing dress-up in his priestly garb, which tickled him. Told him about my tangle with the weasel and cops at the dive bar. How I couldn't sleep. How angry and scared I was. I talked until I ran out of words. Father Nathan listened in silence, like he had all the time in the world. One of the few men besides Moose and Bernard who listened like it was an active verb.

"Just spoke to Prince Dempsey at the funeral," I said.

"Glad he could make it," he said, his mouth still sticky with peanut butter.

"But he'd had his clock cleaned. Black eye and the whole nine." I grabbed a domestic violence pamphlet from a stack on his desk.

"Prince is a tough cookie. Don't put your energy into worrying, though." Father Nathan tapped his forehead. "He's got a mind of his own, which can be challenging in the present but a blessing in the long run."

"What do we do?" I slipped the pamphlet into my back pocket.

He laughed, but not in a mean way. "Focus on what we *can* do. Stay strong for the people who need us."

Tears blurred my vision like I'd just kicked back a fifth of whiskey. Finally. Tears, for the first time since losing Fleur. God, how I hated and loved crying, how it reduced me to my kid self, my essence, pure shapelessness, formlessness. A self that I'd carry with me always. Everybody was a nesting doll of everyone they'd been.

"What if I'm not enough, or too much?" I flexed my toes inside my shoes to feel more of me. Feel the ground under me too. "Too fucked up?"

"Our pasts, our scars, our demons, they don't get the last word. They're chapters in a story that's still being written." He placed a hand on the Bible like it was a confidant. "Let's focus on the future with a quick rehearsal. And do it like a real nun this time."

Twelve days until my final vows. But who's counting?

We went through the ceremonial motions twice. I recited the permanent vows of the Sisters of the Sublime Blood that would link my mortal self, my flesh and blood, in service to God and the Church for eternity. I touched the crucifix hanging on my necklace, imagining the surge of all the heartbeats and heartbreak that it had absorbed in my fevered life. Soon I'd make my new life official. A forever Sister. Infinite spirit inside a finitely celibate body. Every hour of every day of every week would officially belong to prayer, teaching, service. My time would be carved up nice and tidy, like lines of coke. But this bender wouldn't destroy me. No more lost hours. Never again to spend money from guitar lessons on whiskey and lap dances. The selfish child who stole makeup from Duane Reade and crowd-surfed at midnight would be forever riding the divine current.

▪

I left the rectory feeling like my heart was knifed down the middle. Not a clean break like those best friend necklaces. A messy, rough cut. I needed a minute to slap myself together. Or as together as I could possibly get myself after Fleur's Mass and the impromptu rehearsal. Crying was exhausting. Every inch of me was drained. Like I'd gone too deep and had to float back to the surface slowly. Or risk combustion in my veins.

Prytania Street stretched ahead lazily like it was still thinking about which direction to take. Deeply worn out, I walked toward the convent to call Riveaux, update her on Prince and the service. And make space for some emotional whipping. Self-flagellation was a cheap workout and damn, did it burn.

That's the moment I heard the scream. High and piercing as instant regret. My pulse triple hammered as I turned the corner into the parking lot.

There was a tangle of limbs on the asphalt—a body—surrounded by students and congregants.

It was Trevor O'Keefe, collapsed and drained. I'd just given him the Sign of Peace.

"Dear God," the words tore from my throat. "Trevor!" I raced over, fell to my knees, and tried to wake him. I slapped his face, thumped his sternum, and shook his shoulders, which was like trying to rouse a glacier. Pressed my ear to his chest. No heartbeat I could hear, but the faintest pulse twitched in his wrist.

"Wake up, Trevor."

No sound in return. Just disgusting stillness. His skin was as veiny and thin as watered-down paint.

"Wake the fuck up," I roared into his ear, into the next dimension.

I grabbed the Narcan that Moose had given me, thanked God I'd kept it in my pocket. It was easy to peel open. Easier than I'd expected. I tilted Trevor's head back like Moose said, shoved the nozzle up his nose, and plunged a spray into his nostril.

"Call 911!" I barked at the crowd without taking my eyes from Trevor, waiting for any blink, any tell, any spark.

"Already on with them." A voice behind me, one I couldn't recognize. I heard them pacing left and right, relaying our location to dispatch.

"Trevor," I called and called, sending my energy into his ears again and again, into any porous place, to pull him back.

Parishioners. Students. Neighbors. Spectators gathered, filling the lot like floodwater rushing a breach. Snippets of frenzy and panic sailed around me.

What happened?

Wait, who's that?

Oh, damn—Trev?

Is he breathing?

The silence stretched on and on. Nothingness as a presence, a solid thing, like a glass box. A pause you could feel. *Hail Mary, make this work. Mother of God, help me save this fucking kid.*

From nothing to something. A sound so quiet I thought I'd imagined it. Couldn't trust it. But it was real. A weak breath. Then another, and another. His spirit returned. Trevor was breathing. Trevor was back.

It worked. That God in liquid form. That miraculous Lazarus magic of Narcan. It fucking worked.

I rolled him to his side. Curled in the recovery position, he looked like he was napping. Just a tabby snoozing in a sunbeam.

But he still wasn't responding. Eyes closed. Soul trapped in a space between worlds. The kid who haunted the back row of study hall, bent over his sketchbook scribbling, pencil flying up and down like he was channeling seismographic drama on his pages.

A siren in the distance inched closer. From a whisper to a scream. Above us, the sun was a fireball, its heat crawling down in slow and violent streaks, as if the sky itself was being torn open. A raw wound between heaven and earth, bleeding light.

Then there was Moose cannoning over. He checked Trevor's vitals and strapped an oxygen mask on his slack face with machine-level focus.

As Moose worked, I scanned the crowd. Kids still in church clothes, their good shoes, ironed shirts, tied ties, clean hair. All looking so young. How many other students had ticking time bombs in their pockets?

Father Nathan appeared. "I heard the sirens," he said, panting. "Is he—"

"He's alive," I said.

"Have mercy, good Lord. 'This sickness is not unto death,'" Father Nathan recited, his hands extended toward Trevor's chest.

Yeah, I knew the Gospel of John. But it hit different after seeing it with my own eyes. After being part of it. The return.

Trevor came back. Back from the beyond. But Fleur was still gone. The approaching police lights striped the scene demonically.

Before Moose left, he placed another container of Narcan in my hand. For something so powerful, it was achingly small. Whimsical, even. "Some days we save them, some days we don't." Moose bit his thumbnail with vigor. "Today was a good day. Proud of you, Goose."

"Just trying to show you up." I stared at the Narcan. It fit in my palm like a Ring Pop.

"As if."

"Before you go," I said, "need to ask something."

Moose tugged his short beard. "Shoot."

"Just saw Prince Dempsey with a troubling black eye."

"Got into a fight?"

"Not sure. His knuckles don't show any signs." I stared at the church door, the stained glass, the spire. "Can I call social services if a student's in trouble?"

"We're both mandatory reporters for child abuse," he said, "but isn't Prince an adult?"

"Technically. But he's still a kid. The dog's hurt too, and his mom's arm's in a sling."

"I get why you're worried." Moose thought about it for a moment. "But if an eighteen-year-old is getting abused and not pressing charges—"

"We can take action for them."

"That's not how it works, Goose."

"That's how it *should* work," I said. "The system's a joke."

"Trust your instincts, but be careful." He gave me a goodbye hug.

As if my instincts had ever been trustworthy.

14

I HAD NO CLUE what to do with myself after Trevor returned from the brink, after he was driven off in the ambulance, after I'd filled out another witness statement with the police. Still no sight of Decker.

So, I waited. Trevor's parents called the convent from the hospital at lunchtime, saying it was "touch and go," promising to keep us updated. His mom's tight, high-pitched gratitude failed to mask whatever rawer emotion she was dealing with. His father's lawyerly control cracked every third sentence. With Sisters Honor and Laurel praying in the parking lot, a spontaneous novena to Saint Jude, begging for his divine guidance, I seized the opportunity to ask the parents candid questions. But they didn't reveal much. Over and over they'd said how thankful they were that their son was alive, avoiding using the word *overdose*. No mention of a tox screen. "We'll need discretion, of course," his father added. "For Trevor's future opportunities." It all had the sheen of a problem they didn't understand yet. But I could feel their rage, sharp and real, growing under the surface, waiting to be unloaded in the way only desperate parents could deliver. And I wasn't in the mood for any of it.

I talked with Riveaux next. As I told her about almost losing Trevor, she barely made a sound.

"Still there?" I asked.

"Yep," she said, "you all right?"

"Managing," I said. "You?"

"Running on coffee and carbs," Riveaux said. "Spent most of the morning getting familiar with the Royal Family's franchise. Found some relevant connections."

"Relevant *how*?" I asked.

"Kenneth Dempsey ran their meth enterprise and got snowed by an informant a decade ago. That's why he's in prison."

"Prince's dad was in the Family?" The snap of the info coursing through my brain was hard and quick, like pool balls colliding. "Holy hell. We have to pay him a visit."

"Already have those wheels in motion," she said. "Been chasing forensics too. Finally got a minute with Beth at the lab. Guess the quantity of the east wing batch?"

"Ten pills each?" I asked. "Dozens of baggies. So, two hundred pills?"

"I don't have to worry about you counting cards. Try 720."

The number was cataclysmic. 720 pills. That could have been 720 people dead. The number was inconceivable. 720 chances to OD. Each pill no bigger than a bird's eye, each one potentially holding enough fentanyl to lock the lungs. 720 funeral arrangements made by families too shocked to cry.

"Can't wrap my mind around it," I said.

"Each pill weighed around four hundred milligrams," Riveaux said. "Only two milligrams of that was fentanyl. The rest, some speed shit. But trafficking charges are based on over-all weight."

The figures were abstract, horrifying. "Translate that for me?"

"The contents of that locker could send somebody to the slammer for life."

Something so profoundly dangerous hiding in a locker, an ordinary, mandatory aspect of the school day, of teenage life. The violation of it made me sick. *Please don't let the dealer be Fleur or Prince.* "Street value?" I asked.

"Low end, fifteen hundred. High end, twenty grand. Could buy plenty of Honey Buns with that."

"Checked in with Mrs. Benoit?"

"Since she calls me every two and a half hours, yep. She cries or just breathes into the phone."

"So rough. I'm sorry."

"I hate hearing somebody fall apart." She sent a raspy sigh right into my ear. "Anything else to report?"

"Prince showed up at Fleur's Mass with a nasty shiner. The dog looked injured too." My reflection in the window shocked me. Not exactly runway-ready myself, with eyes like holes punched through paper.

"So Prince and the pupper had a beatdown, plus Trish's sling equals possible domestic abuse via her mystery man, question mark?"

"That's what I'm worried about," I said.

"Let me do some digging."

"And let's head over to the garage where Trish works, tomor-row after school," I said. "See what she knows about her hus-band's old gig. Maybe talk her into getting help while we're at it. A small diversion but it feels important."

"Sounds like a plan."

I wished I felt more confident as we hung up.

My hands wouldn't stop shaking. Sister Laurel came back inside and tried to hand me a glass of iced tea. But I couldn't grip it right, spilled some of it in my scarf and smelled like lemon for a while. Could have been worse.

Hoping to clear my head, I hid in my empty classroom around 2 p.m. The changing light coated everything in silver with that New Orleans afternoon glow that makes even grass look secretive. A hidden agenda, a trapdoor under every blade. My guitar felt like a stranger to me. I hugged it anyway. Staring out the window at the traffic calmed my heart a bit. Seeing people in motion made me feel less alone. It was stillness that scared me.

The classroom door creaked open and I didn't have to turn around to know who it was. Palo santo an olfactory hello.

"Yo," Bernard said.

I didn't answer at first.

"Heard about Trevor," he said. Bernard's body, his words, his energy were all deflated. "You're a superhero."

"Not feeling all that super."

"You losing it?" he asked. "I'm still losing it."

"Don't think I ever had 'it' to lose. What a mess."

Bernard took a step closer and stuffed his hands in his pockets. "But messes can be cleaned up." He tapped my elbow with his. "Without them, I'd be out of a job."

"Same here, I guess," I said, bringing my hands into prayer position. "Where were you during Fleur's service? Expected to see you there."

He hung his head and shook it. "Couldn't stomach it. The whole thing's fucking with me hardcore."

"Sorry," I said.

"Me too."

"It's like a slasher movie I keep rewinding and watching, hoping for a different ending," I said. "I'm glad I could help Trevor but I hate that Fleur's gone."

Some hearts could be forced back to beating. Others were already too far across the river.

Bernard nodded. "Last night I dreamt Fleur was standing in Jackson Square selling spooky dolls to tourists. Except the dolls all had *her face*, and the eyes opened and closed on their own, like this." Then he acted it out, blinking slowly, creepily. What the fuck was up with him? He was all kinds of addled and bizarre, like he was possessed by guilt or something. But guilty about what?

"Grim," I said.

"I'm afraid to sleep tonight."

"I can't sleep either, if it's any consolation."

"All aboard the insomnia train," he said.

I pictured it in my mind's eye. A train with me and Bernard and other exhausted passengers, all clammy, in the terrifically nauseous state of sleep deprivation. "Gotta go wait by the phone," I said. "Really hoping for another call from Trevor's parents."

Bernard walked me back to the convent with his arm around my shoulder, as if I'd float away. I looked at the silhouette of the church, how it punctured the sky. Lines, angles, and intersections perfect enough to solve some equations and keep others mysterious.

I gave Bernard's arm a hard press, willing him to be his usual self the next time I saw him. *Sort your shit out*, I wanted to say, but I just offered, "Take care of yourself."

Just a week and a half before graduation, before my permanent vows. Kids would be gone on summer break soon, at camp in the Ozarks and vacationing in Corpus Christi. A mixed blessing. No need for study buddies, but I wouldn't have eyes on them. Only a few would be back on campus for summer school in mid-June.

For the rest of the day and night I waited in the convent kitchen, by the phone, for a Trevor update. The light above the sink shivered, making shadows jump like hunted things. Besides a soft debate between Sisters Laurel and Honor about the Vatican, the only sounds of that night came from the fridge. That tired rondo of *click*, pause, *click*. I prayed the rosary, I lit candles, the hours passed, but Trevor's family never called back. The phone never rang. An infuriating, bullying silence.

15

ANOTHER MIRACLE. ON WEDNESDAY morning, I woke. Which meant I'd slept. For the first time since Fleur died, I'd managed to glue some hours of unconsciousness together. Maybe it was the accrued cost of running myself into the ground. My brain had no other choice but darkness. Dreamless, colorless, consuming. Amniotic quiet. I'd returned to my body.

Then I brushed my teeth, showered in cold water, dressed, and made a fresh pot of coffee. It was good and strong. The first sip was the punch I'd needed. It coated the back of my throat perfectly.

Outside, I heard streetcar wheels screaming against the tracks. A warning call. The sky was the color of antifreeze. The kind of blue that bends weather to its will.

After the twisted break of the past two days, class was back on. The whispers about Fleur and Trevor seemed to quell when I walked into school. In our shared classroom, Rosemary graded papers on her side, and my students were quiet. Ryan Brown dozed in the back row, using his khaki L.L.Bean backpack as a pillow, wearing a hobgoblin smile in his sleep.

Prince's guitar case and empty chair bothered me so much, I wanted to hurl them through the window and watch the shattered glass rain down. In my old life, I might have done exactly that. I thought of that particularly bloody show back in Brooklyn. Frozen February outside and Original Sin shredding the innards of a dilapidated venue. My amp cut out mid-song, dead mid-lyric, and I was so mad I yanked out the cables and threw it into the pit. Someone leapt on stage and punched me, busting my bottom lip open. Smiles, five-foot-nothing, never stopped singing. Later, in Nina's bed, I realized I had blood all down the front of my T-shirt.

In the too-bright, too-quiet present, I scrawled notes on the board. "Sister Holiday," Ryan Brown said, "can we get a curve on finals?" I hadn't realized he'd woken up.

Others joined in the tired protest.

"Finals?" I asked. "What is a final anyway?" The air was tight as a rip cord.

"Uhhh, what?" Ryan asked.

"No final exam," I said. "Everyone passes. Everyone gets an A. Thank Fleur for that."

Behind me, somber murmurs started up, and a quiet crackle of uncontainable excitement about a canceled exam. But just as quickly the voices dissolved into our classroom, into space, and how generous the air was to accept them.

■

One hour to fill until Riveaux was free. A visit to Crescent City Repair was our priority, but she was wrapping up a quick job—the low-hanging fruit of an infidelity case. The city's baked-in debauchery and paranoid spouses meant steady PI invoices.

I walked to the convent garden, where I knew I'd find Sister Laurel. Day after day, she tended to our plants and trees. And to me.

Being outside in the afternoon heat was like being slow-roasted on the devil's rotisserie. The air was heavy enough to choke on. Ninety in the shade. Even the breeze from the river was hot. Sweat collected in the small of my back as I knelt, tugging weeds with a vengeance. Weirdly it wasn't boring. I needed to tear, to rip.

The garden was a fury of color, scent, texture. Stone saint statues governed beds of basil and mint. Spiny tomato vines dripped fat red globes around wooden trellises. Executive-sized mosquitoes harassed the air. I thought about Fleur. Her soul was everywhere now, in each evergreen needle. In every cypress root. New life growing in the darkness.

"Careful, dear, make sure you're only pulling weeds." Sister Laurel's voice was warm but stern. And there was wisdom behind her eyes. The kind of understanding that comes from riding sidecar with loss.

"Got carried away." I sat back on my heels and wiped muddy sweat from my forehead.

A grackle bathed in a fresh puddle nearby, flinging droplets of water so joyfully I swear I could see a tiny smile on that beak. I watched the bird's simple existence. A marvel. Freedom in a world of no words. Or words I couldn't decode. With no feral cats around, the bird relaxed in a lake all her own.

"We all have our own relationship to pain and working through it," Sister Laurel said.

That lady knew. Fifty-some years she'd spent as a nun. And decades carrying the weight of abuse and all its consequences, its downstream churn. "What if I *can't* work through it?" I kicked the watering can.

"That's where God comes in, dear," Sister Laurel replied, but, from her faraway look, I could tell she was wrapped up in a thought. What was she tracking in the there-but-not-there? Spirits among the flowers? Sight is a funny thing. The mind's eye can deceive. When you get stuck in a memory, you can miss what's right in front of you.

Up in the palm tree at the edge of the garden was a web worm's lair. A hovel, woven thick. Hidden in the shell, a growing colony, an army ready to slowly kill the tree. So many ways to be a predator.

So many ways to fall prey.

Just then, Sister Honor stomped out of the convent's side door, her face the color of gangrene, her lips puckered with extreme disapproval. Would she hate me forever? She surveyed the garden, then leaned against the satsuma tree to catch her breath and yell at our hens, Frankie and Hennifer Peck, who were clucking in what I considered an endearing way. "Lord give me strength, but these creatures are a test of my Christian charity." She was noticeably more winded, the heat a worthy foe for even the strongest Sister. "If Saint Francis could hear your infernal racket, he'd exclude poultry from his mission." She lifted her chin and fanned herself with her hand.

"Birds will be birds," Sister Laurel said with a smile and the subtlest eye roll in history. "Perhaps our feathery little Sisters haven't mastered their hymns yet."

"Quite obviously and much to my chagrin," Sister Honor sneered. "Sister Holiday, I see you're up to your neck in filth, as usual."

"Staying busy, Sister Honor." I raised my palms, splaying my tattooed fingers. "Idle hands and all." Any hint of personality was unsavory to Mother Superior.

"The devil's workshop must sorely miss you." She sniffed. "If *he* does not pull you back in for another shift, the church woodwork needs polishing." She blessed herself and said something under her breath. Latin? French? A prayer? A curse?

I drove my tongue into my gold tooth until I felt blood about to break through. "Will do. And Sister Honor," I added, "is there any word from the Diocese about when the east wing rebuild will actually start?" It was a Hail Mary, but I had to try to get something useful from the vault of Sister Honor.

"We must let the Diocese handle the matter in due course."

"No timeline at all?" I asked. "No plan?"

"The only *plan* of your concern is God's plan. Remember your place, Sister Holiday." She turned to Sister Laurel. "A word please? In private."

Sister Laurel sailed an apologetic look my way and followed Sister Honor inside the convent. I caught snippets of their conversation through the open window.

"Can't keep covering for her irreverent attitude, especially not right before she takes her sacred vows, which frankly, I don't think she will ever be ready for," Sister Honor said in a whisper-scream that every skeleton in the mausoleum across town surely heard.

"She's doing her level best." Sister Laurel's tone was pleading.

I dug my hands into the earth, feeling the vibrations of death and renewal, pebbles and dirt, the damp cold against my ungloved skin. It smelled sweet, seductive, like black licorice and salt. Mud caked into my lifelines. The earth is alive with what burrows and hides inside it. We go on, not despite loss, but because of it. Rhythm of decay and rebirth, the tight cycle of dark and light.

"If Sister Honor spent more time talking out here, we wouldn't need to water a single plant," Sister Laurel whispered as she walked back outside. "She's like a sprinkler system." She cupped a hand to her mouth.

So much coiled tension melted from my shoulders as I laughed. Sister Laurel knew what to say to make me smile. Then and there I caught a flash of her as a child, my eighty-year-old Sister as a ten-year-old girl. Could practically see her skipping. We carry every age inside of us, for better or worse.

But a coughing fit seized her, so intensely, the bench wobbled. Her body shook with each inhale. Maybe Sister Laurel needed me as much as I needed her, and, with my permanent vows, I could care for her in her last chapter. She was frail, but her eyes were still incandescent. Wisdom lived in her thin frame, slight as a secret. Our elders offered a unique way of knowing, a special mode of freedom. If only people were smart enough to pay attention.

After she caught her breath again, she said, "God is with you, dear. And your Sisters are too, even the ones who'll never say they love you out loud." She meant Sister Honor, but she wouldn't explicitly out our Mother Superior for caring about me, the misfit. The oddball. The punk. The nun who was always one fuckup from getting tossed out.

16

RIVEAUX'S RED TRUCK APPEARED at the campus entrance around 4 p.m. for our field trip to check in on Trish Dempsey.

"Peep the iPad," Riveaux said, nodding toward her satchel sitting near my feet.

I woke up the tablet and a mug shot stared back at me. "Hello, Kenneth Dempsey."

"He's over at the Chêne Facility." Riveaux slid her hand down the steering wheel as she took a corner. "Got a little confabulation with him on the books tonight. At least two Dempseys on the schedule today. Three, if we're lucky."

"Nice work. Kenneth's been out of the loop for a long time, but maybe he knows some of the players from back in the day."

"He could still be connected, Goldsmobile. Chêne had an inmate OD last week."

This web was more complicated by the hour. Was Prince's dad involved? Still pulling strings? What the hell did that mean for Prince?

Kenneth looked annoyed in his mug shot, a fucking-get-this-over-with attitude. I could see Prince's angry eyes in his dad's. Fierce blue. I put the tablet to sleep.

We cruised through side streets to the Crescent City Repair & Autobody Shop, past markets and theaters and apartments. The balconies revealed personalities, individuality, neglect. Some dripped with tangles of Christmas lights that never came down. Some held thriving ferns and flowers in colorful pots.

With the windows rolled low, cicadas treated us to their screaming contest. Railroad tracks yawned into the distance under green canopies. New Orleans stretched itself out in rings and orbits, so different from New York's vertical fetish. The desperate climbing of skyscrapers.

"Spend any time with the Rebuild Fund files?" I asked, feeling my words melt into the air. That day, my skin, the motion, the cigarette smoke, it was all porous, connected, dissolving at the edges.

"Not yet," Riveaux said. "Even though I'm a freak in the *spread*sheets."

"The morgue called," I said. "Need you to stop by and ID your joke."

"Must be a case of mistaken identity," Riveaux shot back.

We ribbed each other until we arrived at the garage. There were three small steps up to the front customer door; along the north side was a wheelchair ramp leading to a side door. Inside, we found Trish Dempsey standing behind the front counter, flipping through a catalog, her eyes glittering like windows in a lightning storm. The kind of storm where trees explode. I noticed Riveaux studying Trish's pink sling.

"Well, I'll be," Trish said. "What can I do ya for, Sister? Didn't know you were in the market for a car repair."

"I'm not. Prince around?" I was trying to focus on her face and scan the shop interior at the same time. An impossible task that made my eyes burn. "My associate and I were in the neighborhood, and I wanted to touch base."

Riveaux gave me a sideways look then introduced herself with an outstretched hand. "PI Magnolia Riveaux."

"Trish Dempsey. And sorry, I can't shake with this contraption." She motioned to her sling. "And Prince isn't here. Like I told you before, he's home."

"Here's the thing"—Riveaux kept her vibe casual like she was ordering a café au lait—"another one of Prince's classmates got their mitts on bad drugs. Sister Gold—" She caught herself. "Sister *Holiday* here wants to make sure your son's not jumping on the bandwagon."

"My boy would never, I assure you." Trish's face was calm. Warm, even. But her tone, the energy under her words, was caustic. "I know what y'all think about me."

"I promise you don't," I said.

"Y'all think I'm some kind of trashy-ass bitch that doesn't know *come here* from *sic 'em*. Let me tell you what. I kept my boy safe during the storm. And after his good-for-nothing daddy went up the creek."

"No doubt. And I know you love Prince. We're just trying to help you both."

"*Help?*" She laughed. "One thing's for damn sure, I'm not used to help of any sort. Never expected it. On my wedding day, my mama—you'll never believe this—she took me aside and she said, 'Patricia, you're going to be alone all your life.' And she was right."

"You don't have to go it alone," I said.

"Look here, little miss church lady and PI whoever, we ain't perfect, but we're a family. I've got things under control. Prince is all good."

"How often does Prince visit your husband in prison?"

She pulled her left earlobe like it was a latch that could teleport her to a different hemisphere. "Oh, they don't get on well. Not at all. That ship sailed long ago. Hell, at this point, it's at the bottom of the Mississippi. Same goes for me."

"So, no contact whatsoever?"

"Not so much as a whisper."

"Any gentleman callers knocking at your door?"

"Not anymore," Trish said, impatiently, "and the second my boy's feeling better, he will be at school. Cross my heart."

From the corner of my eye, I saw Riveaux tense. Peripheral vision was the real vision. She was also searching the shop, scanning wall to wall looking for anything notable. I spotted only one security camera, above the cashier desk. A dusty dog bowl sat by the door.

"Hey, since we're here, wondering if we could run something by you." Riveaux's strategic nonchalance was an art form. "We know the Royal Family was Kenneth's dealio, but did you happen to overhear any watercooler talk about a Ren?" Riveaux asked.

"A *what* now?" Trish rested her hand on her hip.

"Somebody named Ren? Kenneth might have known him in the old days?"

"Sorry. Never met 'em." Her fingers splayed wide then curled in, like she was working out a hand cramp.

"No worries," I said. "But if you ever want to talk, call the convent. And here's Riveaux's number."

I gestured for Riveaux to give Trish a Redemption business card, but she'd already done it. Set it on the counter near the register like a poker chip. One step ahead.

"Call us," Riveaux said.

"Anytime," I added. With the image of Prince's black eye looping, I said, "And if someone's rough with you or Prince, call the police."

"Hey, now, I'm tougher than I look. Everyone forgets what I've been through." Trish tossed her hair. "Y'all need anything else?"

"Can we see the repair bay?" Riveaux asked. "I'm a bit of a gearhead," she lied.

"Sure thing. Want a job?" Trish asked. "Can't keep good help these days."

"If this PI situation doesn't pan out," Riveaux said, "I'll know where to go."

I quietly dropped the domestic violence pamphlet from my back pocket on Trish's desk as she led us through a side door. The repair bay held two cars on lifts. A PT Cruiser the color of a dill pickle and a spunky fuchsia Miata. Riveaux picked up a tire gauge lying on the concrete.

"Subtle choices," Riveaux said, then tossed the tire gauge Trish's way, which Trish caught with her good hand. "Nice catch."

"Our clients are a hoot and a half," Trish said. "I must say that Miata over there sure is a looker." She pointed with the gauge.

"A real prize," Riveaux added.

Just then, Trish's phone buzzed. "Shit. This is a VIP customer. Gotta take this," Trish said, cheeks red. "You'll see yourselves out?" She fluffed her atomic-blond hair and quickly headed back into the office.

After I shut the passenger door, Riveaux adjusted the smudged rearview mirror. "I threw Trish that gauge to see if she'd use her dominant hand." She turned the key in the ignition. "She didn't. That arm's really hurt."

"Smart thinking, Riveaux."

"Don't sound so surprised. We need to stay smart."

I nodded, though smart wasn't exactly my strong suit. Action was, leaps of faith.

"Time to pay Big Papa Dempsey a visit," she said.

As Riveaux drove us to the prison, I lit a cigarette from her pack. The cherry glowed with a mystical complexity. It wanted to tell me something. "Let's call Moose," I said. "See if he's got any news."

Without taking her eyes off the road, she handed me her ringing phone with the speaker activated and BROSMOBILE dialed.

"Hey, Moose," I said, when he picked up. "You're on speaker."

"Brosmobile," Riveaux shouted.

"Good news," he said, and I heard a smile behind his words. "No ODs today."

"We'll take it," Riveaux said. "Slow shift?"

"Hardly. Some frat boys who needed their stomachs pumped after mainlining Hurricanes, a lady who took too many edibles and almost drowned in Bayou Saint John, and a fistfight at a bachelorette party, but no ODs."

"Sounds fun," I said.

"I'm doing my mindful breathing." Moose's voice carved air. "Any updates?"

"Nada. Trying to hunt down Prince and maybe a lead or two. His old man's a former dealer."

"Hopefully former," Riveaux added.

"Don't bite my head off," Moose said, "but what if Prince is laying low because he's involved?"

Riveaux hummed.

"You both were there when I baptized him." I took a deep breath. No point in shouting. "I hear you, loud and clear. But you're wrong. If anything, he's at risk of ending up like Fleur."

"I'm just saying—the kid's not a saint." Moose's airy, chill reply pissed me off even more.

"Why can't you trust me on this one?"

"Easy, Goose. I'm looking out for you."

"Night, Moose." I smashed the red button, hanging up. Then I stared out the window. The stoplight changed, green to yellow, exactly when I knew it would. As if I'd done it. Maybe I did.

"Family," Riveaux said. "Can't live with them, can't bury them in the backyard without neighbors asking questions." She pinky-pushed her glasses up her nose with a flourish. "My mom's too much like me."

"Stubborn? Annoying? Mom jeans?"

"All of the above," she said.

The city looked dirty through the truck's windshield, everything washed in a silty bath. The peat of burning rubber and a nearby crawfish boil drifted through the open windows. A train sang its metal tune on the river side. There were sirens too, as always. One close, one far. I prayed it wasn't another of my students keeling over. Riveaux turned on her scanner but we couldn't capture anything of note.

"Mom's gifted, too," Riveaux added. "Spent half my childhood watching her mend strangers, and the other half as the audience to her soliloquies." She let out one dry laugh. "My mother can heal anything in this world but her own narcissism."

"Lucky for her she's family."

"Too bad that luck skipped a generation," Riveaux replied.

Luck was an illusion at best. A false promise. And I'd been like Prince once, and Moose had seen it firsthand. When I was young and broken, excited to break myself. To set the world on fire and cheer on the flames. Staring into the abyss. A deep deep vicious *yes* like getting swallowed whole.

17

THE AIR-CONDITIONING WAS CONDITIONING nothing at the Chêne Men's Correctional Facility. Seemed like even the most powerful HVAC system would buckle in this ridiculous heat.

"The clergy can come in too." The CO's badge read LANGLOIS, and he had the radiating red face of a guy who spent all weekend fishing with no sunscreen. Raring to go. He spoke only to Riveaux. His lack of attention was a blessing. Maybe he wasn't among the uniformed men in this town with a grudge against "that bitch of a nun."

"You're the best, J. J.," Riveaux said as she ushered me to the checkpoint. She had a shorthand with Langlois. Small nods of friendship or reciprocity. Both were necessary for private eyes.

Even with Riveaux's friends on the force—beat cops, detectives, lab techs, correctional officers—who expedited our clearance, we still had to wait. And show IDs, sign logbooks, empty our pockets, and consent to searches. The sunburned CO inspected my shoes like I might've smuggled a nail file in the rubber sole. By design or staffing shortages, it seemed like the prison wanted visitors to move through the space slowly.

I entered the visiting room the way Sister Augustine taught us to proceed into Mass. Step by step, one foot in front of the other, with intention. My crucifix chain pressed its cold comfort against my collarbone as I moved.

There was still no sign of Kenneth after one rosary—the Holy Wounds. The room reeked of old mop water and armpit musk. Decades of smoking hadn't dulled my olfactory senses too much. As I prayed and we waited, I thought back to eighth grade, when my Bay Ridge church youth group reenacted each Station of the Cross. The incense was so strong I hallucinated. During the crucifixion, a mulleted boy named Daniel something played the role of Jesus. I helped him affix the crown of thorns and apply the fake blood running from his eyes. I starred as Virgin Mother, with black eyeliner and black nail polish. After the Mass, Daniel's older sister let us crash her party behind the abandoned Red Hook grain warehouse where I learned how to shotgun a PBR.

Then the visiting room frequency changed, crackling like the moment before a gully washer ripped the sky open. Kenneth Dempsey filled the frame on the other side of the cloudy plexiglass. He walked to the partition, and his stormy-blue eyes found me first. Then he sized up Riveaux's unimpressed stance.

Prince's dad was lean, like Prince. No massive muscles. No tatts. But he had swagger. The confidence of a man convinced he'd win any fight. Even in prison. He wore a faded blue jumpsuit with a black inmate stamp. He snatched the phone and I picked up my receiver at the same time.

"Don't believe I've had the pleasure," he said.

"Sister Holiday." I met his gaze and tried to hold it. "I teach your son in my music class." The flimsy plastic phone in my gloved hand felt like a toy. Make-believe.

Kenneth perked up. "Music? Last I remember, he couldn't so much as hum a tune."

Riveaux lifted the third receiver to interrupt. "Hey, Kenneth." She leaned toward the plexiglass. "PI Riveaux. I'm going to cut right to it, then Sister Holiday can tell you anything you want to know about your son. You're probably dying for information, with his mother icing you out."

"How you know that?" He leaned forward in his chair.

"One look at the visitor logs. Need to ask you about the Royal Family. We know you were their top man way back when."

"Ladies, that's all in the past," he said. "Been inside three years and five days, paying my debts to society."

"So, no contact with the 'Family' since then?" Riveaux outlined an initial, or a code, *PS*, scratched into the counter.

"Not one lick. Check with anyone and everyone in this fine establishment."

"Any cousins of the Family in here?" Riveaux asked. "Heard someone OD'd last week."

"I'm too busy to keep tabs on any of that claptrap. Not that I'd ever rat, mind you."

"Why so busy?" I asked.

"My healing journey." He tapped his chest. "Not for the faint of heart."

Riveaux narrowed her left eye. "Look, we get you're on the straight and narrow now, and we're not here to cause trouble. We're not cops—just working our own investigation."

"PIs," I added. "Redemption Detective Agency."

"Yep, that's us." Riveaux forced a smile. "One last question and then we can talk about Prince. The name Ren mean anything to you?"

"No, ma'am," Kenneth repeated. "Like I told y'all, me and the Royal Family ain't kin no more. Not one person had my back. I've forgiven their sorry asses but never will forget."

"Wait." I leaned back in my chair. "How'd you know Ren was Family?"

"A hunch. I have a bit of that sixth sense, if y'all know what I mean. Always did serve me well. Until it didn't." His charm was like a smoke bomb. It filled space too quickly and made me sick. "Alls I know is I didn't have time to select my replacement. No ceremony or nothing. Whoever stepped into my role, maybe this Ren fucker, he'd have to have been at the right place at the right time. A power grab like that's gotta be quick."

Riveaux shifted gears. "What detail you working?"

"Maintenance. Seven to four every day. It's a daily grind, lemme tell y'all, but I'll be if I don't love working with my hands. Bible study on the weekends is the real jewel." He spoke loud and proud, like he was recording an audition tape for a reality show. Or practicing for the parole board. "I know y'all know what I'm talking about. Right, Sister?"

"What Scripture's lighting the fire in you these days?" I had to push, find the seam.

"Oh, all of 'em books. The good ones. Judges and what not."

Book of Judges. Nice choice. The concubine, the mob, some dismemberment, lots of warring. But for every bastard abuser using some verse as a shield, there was a Judith. A Lilith. An Esther. A Ruth. A Naomi. A whisper of female revenge, of dissent, scribbled in the margins.

"Now, about Prince, what's junior getting up to?" Kenneth asked. "Haven't seen my boy in an age."

"Looks like someone beat the hell out of him," I said.

"A fight?" He blew air slowly, like he was cooling a steaming bowl of soup. "Never was a chip off the old block. Gotta toughen him up. Defend himself proper, like. Boys need quick reflexes these days. Talk soft but carry a big stick. Y'all know that line?"

Kenneth kept talking, the charm flowing relentlessly, deflecting, redirecting, the *y'all this* and *y'all that* a smoke screen.

"Doesn't it concern you," I asked, "hearing your kid got roughed up?"

"Sure does concern me. Any daddy wants the best for their child. But Patricia has a tight leash on that boy. It could break your heart. He never visits. Never sent a single postcard. I was wild, yeah, but I'm walking the proper path now. I'm the example he *needs*." He pounded the partition with his tight fist, ensuring the swift arrival of two guards. "My apologies, gentlemen and ladies. My sincere regret to y'all." He spread his hands wide, palms up, like a dog rolling over and showing his belly. The regretful, wounded father. "Working on my grief. I miss my son is all. Miss him so much."

Kenneth was good. A smooth operator, but scary too. Expecting sympathy. Three years inside, claiming total detachment from the Royal Family, no knowledge of Ren, feigned concern for a son he'd just dismissed moments before. Could he be orchestrating a fentanyl ring from behind the heavy Chêne walls? Did he know the current players? Probable? Unlikely. Possible, of course.

"We done here?" he asked, but signaled toward the guard station before we could answer.

"For now," Riveaux said.

"Stay safe, Sister." Kenneth winked.

A hand on my shoulder made me jump. It was Langlois. "I'll show you out."

"Charming," I said as we collected ourselves outside.

"Alarmingly. Who knows if any of it was true," Riveaux said.

Overhead the moon refused to blink. A celestial staring contest.

The sick rumble of the truck's engine matched my jumbled thoughts. Knowledge, I'd realized that disturbing week, doesn't exist in a straight line. It's a web. Layers, each level, each turn, revealing new torments, new questions, new flashes of insight—and new clouds that obscure the breakthrough, the aha, the clue. You're grasping, fumbling, ready to give up, but then, a fit, a foothold, the luscious consumption of inner knowing. One moment lost in limbo, the next, lucidity. Epiphany burnt like hellfire.

"You heard what he said about the succession. What if Prince picked up where dear old dad left off?" Riveaux's eyebrows lifted ever higher, practically floating above her head. She checked her mirrors, about to reverse.

"Just don't think he would," I said. After that day's parent-teacher conferences, seeing the roots of that particular family tree, I felt like I had to believe in Prince. Who else would? The kid deserved someone in his corner.

"Maybe he'll be home this time. Back to the Dempsey digs?"

I nodded. But before we exited the parking lot, I saw the telltale red and blue of a police light scooch behind us.

"What the fuck." My throat closed.

"Chill," Riveaux said, then rolled down her window.

My heart jerked to a stop as I heard a familiar voice stalking up to the driver's-side window. "Well, what do we have here?" It was Sergeant Ruby Decker, one of my many uniformed haters in New Orleans. "Sister Holiday and her apostle." Her face contorted like she was passing a kidney stone.

"Doing the Lord's work," I said, projecting my voice over Riveaux. A wave of nausea rolled up my spine. "Wanna join us?"

Before Decker could answer, Riveaux said, "Ruby, lovely to see you. How can we help?" Her hands gripped the wheel at ten and two.

"Get out of the truck, Sister," Decker said, sailing her words past Riveaux. "You can stay put, Maggie."

"May I interest you in a high-protein snack?" Riveaux held up a Slim Jim.

"Head on back to your little agency," Decker said. "Sister Holiday, you're coming with me."

Riveaux looked terrified, angry, and confused. "But—"

"Head on back, Maggie. The Sister and I need to chat, and I know you're a busy woman."

"So sorry. It's not a good time for—"

Decker smiled. "Your choice. My car now, or a call to the bishop about your escapades."

Sometimes you have to take a punch to stay in the fight.

"Fine. Riveaux, I'm all good."

"Hey," Riveaux whispered, "call me if you need me."

"She will be just fine," Decker said.

Before she got into the truck, Riveaux recited, "'Always try to keep a patch of sky above your life.'"

"Pardon?"

"Proust!" Riveaux hollered as she rolled up the window.

Decker said, "Get in the back," and I did.

"Where are we going?" I asked, violently dizzy as we took the on-ramp to the interstate. My saliva was hot. Someone in the clink must have called her, tipped her off. Fuck.

"The station."

"Why?"

"Quiet," she replied. "I have a headache."

I said six Hail Marys and thought about Acts 2—tongues of fire, so comforting—as we drove through the lush night. Even in terror, the outrageous beauty of New Orleans was impossible to ignore. Dark and light, pleasure and pain. A peculiar energy woke up in me on that drive. I felt my guardian angels fume, flex their exquisite wings. Draw their swords.

18

I SLOUCHED IN A chair in front of Sergeant Decker's desk, waiting.

Waiting. Waiting. Always waiting. But inside the waiting, planning.

The door flew open. Decker's eyes were the unyielding brown of a pickax handle. She tossed a bottle of water at me like she was aiming for my head. "You still haven't learned to keep your nose out of places it doesn't belong."

"Thought you'd forgotten about me." I smiled and drank some water which tasted like plastic. "I'm touched."

"Forgotten? The 'nun' who got my wife killed? You're an ever-present stain on my psyche."

"I get that a lot," I said.

Ruby Decker had every right to hate me. Sadness was too hard. Anger was a more delectable blade. Sue should never have been caught in that whole godforsaken mess. I couldn't blame Decker for wanting me to rot in one of the city's soggy mausoleums.

Hell, I wanted to keep myself in a crypt most days. No judgment, free rent, peace from Sister Honor's pitchy singing.

"Grogan went down because of you," she said. "That's your only bit of good history."

"As much as I'd love to gallivant down memory lane with you, I'm betting you didn't bring me in for a girls' night." I looked down and tracked three distinct scratch patterns radiating from the chair legs.

She glared at me with disgust, like I was a clump of hair clogging her shower drain. "The thing is, I got the strangest call from Chêne. The team said some PI requested access to Kenneth Dempsey and showed up with a nun. Thought I'd see what Redemption was up to."

"Living the dream."

"More of a nightmare. Lucky for you, I can give you a much better pursuit." Decker thumbed through a box filled with binders and files. She flipped one open, sailed past a few pages, and pointed to a mug shot of a nasty white boy with a patchy beard. The guy's smirk declared "repeat offender" and he had canyons where eyeballs should be. "Meet Lenny Mastoni."

"Looks like a dumbass."

"He's a lieutenant with the Royal Family," she said.

"The Royal Family," I repeated, sure to sound intrigued, like I hadn't already heard the name at the dive bar, hadn't already rolled it around in my head.

"Sure, let's pretend that I didn't just pick you up from a fireside chat with their former meth mastermind. They're a small but savvy local gang," she explained. "And getting more ruthless as they grow. Locking up new territory fast." She pointed to the picture of the human dumpster fire.

"This is the guy behind the fentanyl?" The adrenaline. The rage. I wanted to reach into the picture and break his nose.

166 = MARGOT DOUAIHY

"That's what we need to confirm," she said. "NOPD's been after the crew for years. We grab one low-rung soldier but two more pop up. They're a step ahead. Can't get anything that will stick to the new boss."

I let out a low whistle as I flipped through four pages of Lenny's rap sheet. "Dude's been busy." Assault, weapons charges. In and out of prison. Maybe Lenny and Kenneth knew each other. Hell, maybe they were bunkmates. "Any known associates?" I asked. "Our friend Kenneth, perhaps?"

"Unlikely," she said. "The known associate of *interest* is someone named 'Ren.'" She scratched behind her right ear. "Word on the street, Ren's the top of the food chain. Lenny Mastoni's worked his way up to second-in-command."

Naturally, Decker already had some of the puzzle pieces that Riveaux and I'd been busting our asses to find. But at least it validated the intel we'd landed. And maybe this Lenny character would lead us to Ren.

"Climbing the corporate ladder," I said.

"We need details of how the Family works. Evidence. That's where you come in."

I leaned back with my hands behind my head like I was sunbathing. "What I'm hearing is, you need my help. I'm flattered, but—"

Decker slammed her right palm on the table. "I don't *need* anything from you."

"Then why am I in your office?"

"You're a mess. A disaster, actually, which could make you a convincing undercover option."

"A convincing *what*?"

She repeated "undercover option" loud enough to make my sternum vibrate. "You can make nice with the crusty punks and junkies in a way no badge could ever dream of. And you can help us understand exactly how they operate. They'll never take a second look at someone like you."

"Even if I could find an in—and I'm not saying I could—why would I help the cops? After everything that went down?"

Decker leaned back and brought her hands behind her head to mirror my own screw-you body language. "Come on. You're already working this, so I'm not putting you out. We have common goals—cutting the fentanyl supply off and keeping people out of the morgue. Plus, you owe me. Sue too."

She was right. A chance to punch up, out of purgatory. Right a few wrongs. God, I wanted it so bad I could taste it, salty and raw as a nosebleed.

"And if I say *no thanks* to this little deal?"

"You walk out of here, and I walk out of here," Decker said, "and we let the chips fall where they may. No hard feelings. No heat."

"Okay."

She rolled a pen. "And I'll just sit back and wait for more of your students to OD, for your congregants to get hooked and then die choking on their own sick. And for your own bloated corpse to float up the river in a few years' time. Because that's our reality now. People will die while you sit on your hands and say Our Fathers."

"You're stone cold, Decker," I said, impressed.

"Sue kept a RENEW flyer," Decker said, "up on our fridge with a magnet. I haven't been able to take it down."

I lowered my attention to my own gloved hands. Was this my penance? I wished I could chew through the leather to bite my thumbnail.

Decker's eyes drifted. "She said you were proof that 'faith was personal.' Not some one-size-fits-all commodity."

When I looked up, I caught it, the familiar loss in her eyes. But just as quickly as Decker let it surface, she slammed the shutters closed.

Leaning over the table, she said, "This is a limited time offer, Sister. You'd go undercover to get productive leads on the Royal Family. Check in and debrief with me daily. No exceptions. You in or out?"

In or out, she asked. But it's not in or out. It's in *and* out. A split screen of my selves. Holiday Walsh and Sister Holiday, side by side. Haven't I always been both? Wouldn't I be both forever?

"I need to use the restroom," I said. But really I needed time to think.

"Take a left and then another left," she said, staring at the picture of Lenny and his felony of a beard.

The station bathroom was empty. In the least horrific stall, I kept replaying the word: *undercover.* Like prayers hovering above doubt. Like ink stitched into skin with gloves pulled on top. Deception to dredge some truths. Sometimes a lie was the only way to grow and reach toward transformation. Like the violence of a seed splitting its shell. Grasping for God through darkness.

When I returned, five minutes later, as I pushed open the door, the sharp burst of citrus surprised me. Decker was peeling a clementine as carefully as an archivist handling fragile paper. "Well?" she asked, still staring at the picture of Lenny.

I closed my eyes and felt the texture of a hundred mistakes and regrets. Riveaux once told me we had sixty thousand thoughts a day. I wondered how many of my sixty thousand were self-hating, how many were self-destructive. "Fuck it." I opened my eyes. "I'm in."

"First good call you've made in a while." Decker snatched the folders and slid them into their box labeled, in all caps, the police siren of fonts, THE ROYAL FAMILY.

"I'm going to need to read all of that," I said.

"It would take you months. I'll get you up to speed."

"I'm a quick study."

"Sure. One more thing before we get started, and it's nonnegotiable."

"What?"

"I'm not telling the brass. You're not exactly popular around here, and my squad wouldn't be able to see the bigger picture. Definitely not looping in PI Magnolia Riveaux. She gets one whiff of an undercover job without a fully trained operative, and we're both done."

Riveaux was my partner, my friend. The Louise to my Thelma. The idea of going undercover was intoxicating, but the thought of deceiving Riveaux made me ill. If I didn't take this chance, though, if I didn't try, could I live with more dead kids on my conscience?

"Fine. We'll do it your way, but I have an ask too."

"Of course you do. What?"

"I need to see Grogan's file. *All* of it. That's my price."

"You can read it here, but you can't have it."

"Fine." I crossed my arms.

She reached into her desk drawer and plucked out a thin file folder and dropped it in front of me. *GROGAN* was handwritten on the front in large letters. "Not exactly *War and Peace*," Decker said.

"A page-turner nonetheless." Opening the file for one second and seeing Grogan in an orange jumpsuit was a prayer answered. If only the Diocese were behind bars too.

"Seriously," Decker said, "not one word of this op to anyone. This is deep cover. Say it with me." She stuck out her hand for a shake.

With my heart like a saw blade spinning inside me, I reached out, shook Decker's hand with my own. "Deep cover."

Decker checked a box on her form. She handed me a prepaid phone with a charger. Even had a camera. "In case you see something interesting," she said, "grab a pic."

It felt alien in my hand.

"My number's in there," she said, "under MOM."

That was a minefield I wasn't prepared to cross. Maybe never would be.

"We're starting tonight." She tossed me a pile of mildewed clothes. "Change. I'll be back in ten." Decker nodded with what could easily be mistaken for respect, then walked out.

■

The clothes were hilarious, Central Casting for Street Punk #3. I shimmied into the black tank top with fabric so thin it was almost see-through. The denim skirt was soft and faded, a size too small, molded to my ass. The leather jacket was buttery soft in places and hardened with scars in others. Pocked with nicks, cracks, and slashes. Wide pockets that cut deep. A pair of black boots that could probably kick through a brick wall. And to complete the look, makeup. Old eyeliner, mascara almost dried out, eye shadow, and lipstick that held someone else's touch.

Decker returned and made no comment about my getup. "Up in Smoke is Lenny's hangout. It's a hookah lounge that the Royal Family uses as an HQ."

"So you're asking me—a real nun—to go *undercover* in a lounge. Like a reverse *Sister Act*?"

"You better do right by Sister Mary Clarence. Ingratiate yourself with the crew, get to know them, pal around, listen in." She got clinical and laid out undercover protocol like a field manual. "First test, walk across the room."

She watched my posture as I strolled.

"Not bad, but you need a harder step. Put lead in every movement. Again."

One step, then another. I tried to remember how gravity felt on stage, how it felt before Sister Honor seemed to legislate the laws of physics themselves. It was thrilling, being confronted like that. Forced to loosen up and let my new life go for a minute. Let everything go.

"Strip it all back, really feel the grunge."

"Punk, you mean?"

"Whatever gutter you slithered out of. Now your voice. Say, 'Fuck you.'"

"With sincere pleasure." I locked a laser stare into her eyes. "Fuck you."

"Again."

"*Fuck you.*" I luxuriated in each word.

"The student has surpassed the teacher. What's your alias?" she asked. "What name you wanna use?"

"Name? Definitely not *Sister Holiday*."

"Has to be something you'll respond to instantly."

After a moment it was there, in my ear. Already inside of me, fully alive as a furnace fire. "Tammy."

Tammy. A name. A song. A riff on "For Tammy Rae" by Bikini Kill. And the story of Tamar in Genesis, a badass who disguised herself as a harlot to get what she needed.

"Hey, Tammy." Decker's voice was bright.

"What'ya want?" I responded exceptionally fast. Not one ounce of hesitation.

"Good. Now, Tammy, say you see Lenny or someone you maybe think is in the crew. What's the play?"

"Stay quiet, look bored, play hard to get, let their big egos do the heavy lifting."

She nodded, then said, "But don't be shy." As she circled me and pointed to my right hand which was playing with my rosary, and my jacket sleeves which, I didn't realize, I'd pulled down to conceal my tattoos. "Be loose and messy. Look ready to fight if somebody fucks with you."

"I *am* ready to fight."

She nodded. "Say some crumbum has a bad look."

"They all do."

"True." She slow nodded. "But say you see one and think, 'I just got made.' What's your move?"

"Keep an eye on the exits, back to the wall, never a door. Watch their hands. Let them talk."

"Good. Squad car drives by when you're talking to Lenny?"

"Don't look away but don't look too interested. Curse the cops under my breath, count to four, breathe."

"Right. Any chance you'll ditch the rosary?"

"You mean Tammy's grammy's?"

Decker chuckled. "All right, that'll work."

Another check on Decker's form. Another box filled. Another level unlocked.

Decker ran vice drills until I felt dizzy and my stomach growled. Brooklyn-era Holiday Walsh didn't need to resurrect through the crack in the cave of Sister Holiday—the old and new me were always together, always roaring and ready.

"Final test." Decker stood about an hour later. "Tell me about Sister Holiday."

"Who's she?" I said.

■

Ten blocks away from my target, my mark, Decker dropped me off. I heard toads purring and croaking but couldn't see them. They were working undercover too. The subtropics bred various kinds of sweaty divinity, hidden magic, and legends. Locals swore the rat king was real. A generation of rats tangled their tails into a knot. An underground Ren. Gris-gris pouches dropped on stoops with no footprints, like they were spirited there.

I made my way to Up in Smoke looking like '80s Madonna if Madonna'd done time, donated too much blood, and did harder drugs. Bleached blond over dark roots. Blue eyes ringed by supremely smudged eyeliner. Full lips that could recite the Letters to the Ephesians and Lunachicks lyrics in alternating breaths. Strong dark eyebrows. Leather jacket, and under it, a black tank and a body covered in ink, from my jawline to my toes. One me drowned inside the other me.

Inside, the lounge was exactly the kind of hellhole time capsule I'd expected after seeing Lenny's mug shot. "I Want to Sex You Up" pumped through a tinny sound system. Hallucinogenic colored lighting attempted to mask the menacing interior. The north wall had a neon sign—FOMO with a strike-through. Twentysomethings drank Red Bull and vodkas, and sucked on ornate glass hookahs. A woman slowly danced alone with her hands clasped tightly across her chest like she was practicing for her own funereal sojourn in a coffin. The air choked with the deathly sweet smoke of apricot tobacco. I scanned the room, taking in every annoying detail, every tormented person, every potential clue or suspect. Two men near the exit looked like cartoon extraterrestrials in the green light. Did anyone spot me spotting them? Shocking what people will allow, will overlook, when you're sporting a resting bitch face.

The bartender, a wall of a man with more ink than our Sunday hymnal, held my gaze. The nonverbal translation: time to order. I hadn't thought that far ahead. Hadn't rehearsed that step with Decker. My heart kicked against my ribs. Sobriety and staying honest were promises I'd made over and over.

My options were to drink water and look like a narc, or pick up the glass and be who I used to be. Who I still was. It was my best chance to nail a key player. Maybe the entire Royal Family. Would halting the fentanyl scourge cancel out the relapse?

With wrinkled bills, courtesy of Decker, I ordered bourbon. No brand name. Just bourbon. The first taste was painful. A shock. Too sharp and way too strong. But it was a job. I stayed in character.

The second sip went down easier.

Third swallow, well, that felt like coming home.

The bourbon was good. As I drank more, I felt my insides melt. Helped me feel more me. The right person for a fucking change. And Decker's money made it okay.

An hour ticked by. No sign of Lenny Mastoni. Plenty of garden-variety losers, but no one I'd pinged as a player. Only regular drunks doing regular damage.

The bartender looked like he bench-pressed Harleys for fun. A real demolition derby of a dude. Maybe he was muscle for the Royal Family, or maybe just a guy working to make rent and pay the bills. Difficult to tell in the foul smoke, under the attitude. And what did the bartender see when he glanced at me? Dye and roots. Biblical tatts. Dark circles under blood-shot eyes. Another hard woman at *rock bottom*, to quote dear Bernard.

The ventriloquist of my past self, in my same voice, ordered another drink for me. In the corner some guys were raising their voices. They weren't shedding blood, but they weren't playing rock-paper-scissors, either.

Then, drumroll, another drink. Still no Lenny.

I held it together, channeled Holiday Walsh channeling Tammy. But for a moment it was too much, too confusing. Even my internal monologue was starting to slur. I was too vain to be a messy lush. But too fucked up to be sober.

Finally, I drained my glass, dropped a five-dollar tip on the bar, and slunk out into the muggy night. First day undercover, first slip off the wagon since the Communion wine on Easter. And all for nothing.

I texted Decker from the burner. How cliché. Kept it brief. *No luck.*

She picked me up ten blocks away. I wasn't sure what was louder, her disappointment or the rusted muffler. I chewed the inside of my cheek as we drove.

"No mark?" she asked.

"Not yet," I said as I stretched out in the passenger seat. "Rome wasn't built in a couple of hours."

She laughed. Was Decker warming up to me? "We'll try again tomorrow," she said. "Regularity is key. You'll need new clothes to keep up your cover. I'll take care of that." Her wedding ring gleamed.

I leaned my head back. A steady pain beat my temples from the inside out. All that secondhand hookah smoke, the tutti-frutti vortex. If I could pull this off, maybe Fleur's mom would have a shred of closure. Maybe the ODs would stop, and I could balance the scales. *Maybe.* And maybe the pope would be the next grand marshal of the NOLA Pride Parade. Still, I had to try. For Fleur. For Decker's wife, Sue. For every person winking at obliteration.

19

THURSDAY MORNING, I SHUDDERED with the fallout from my boozy Tammy time. Only two hours of sleep. I could hardly hold my head up let alone run a class that morning. I'd hugged my guitar tight as if it could steady me. But the vibrations made me nauseous and the metal strings bit my skin. I'd spent a lifetime building calluses to protect against pain, but it kept showing up uninvited.

"G to D to E minor," I instructed in a rough voice, like I'd been swallowing sand. "And try to watch your fingers this time, Ryan. Keep your grip loose, let them float. What'd the D chord do to hurt you? Ease up."

Buzzy frets. Sloppy chord changes. Pathetic timing. My students seemed determined to tank it. I wasn't much help either in that sorry state. Wasting God's gift. The magic of creating a perfect thing—music—from nothing. From empty space. From the void between strings.

Prince Dempsey wasn't in the void, but he still wasn't in class. Since seeing him on Tuesday—alive enough to give me shit in the church—that particular worry had shifted from desperate to merely urgent. I told myself to believe what his mother had said, what Father Nathan'd said, that he was fine. I had to focus on one thing at a time, and right now, that was the Royal Family.

"Stop, everyone." I put my guitar down. "Graduation's next week, and this song is the centerpiece. Please don't give Sister Honor another reason to hate me." That got a laugh. "Let's remember which strings are which, all right?" I held up my hands. "Right hand, left hand. Yeah?"

Hail Mary, please grant me a handful of Advil and forty nights of sleep. And maybe a forty if you're feeling generous.

The hall echoed with the sounds of Father Nathan's graduation practice. First the valedictorian, then the salutatorian learning how to project. Swaths of their speeches, laughter, and clapping bled into our various mutilations of the Beatles' "In My Life." Weeks ago, he'd asked me to be the faculty speaker during the ceremony, and I'd agreed, as long as I could skip practice.

All of our seniors would be walking the stage soon, with the exception of Fleur. "Summer" meant different things now. For some twelfth graders, it meant graduation and maybe college. For others, summer school. I thought about the graduates heading toward that mysterious thing called "the future" while I nursed my homicidal headache from the hookah lounge. Kids were asking me questions about tablature and timing while I thought about hunting down Lenny Mastoni. And I couldn't tell anyone. The feeling was as ropy and tense as scar tissue.

I picked up my guitar again. The neck felt light and too honest. "From the bridge, count it in." But the bell ended my misery. Students packed their guitars in scuffed cases and left.

Rosemary Flynn wrapped her lecture about cosmic collapse and event horizons on her side of the classroom. In that hangover haze, I'd appreciated her presence more than usual. Just knowing she was there. Smelling her rose perfume with the chalk dust. A tiny spring-loaded coil of energy in my chest with Rosemary near. A gold, hopeful surge.

Twelve hours until Tammy strolled back on stage. Until Sergeant Decker expected a check-in text.

■

Riveaux barely looked up when I entered the office. "Nice to see that you're alive," she said. "Thanks ever so much for checking in last night."

"Sorry, I was busy."

"Nun on the run," Riveaux said. "What'd Decker want?"

"To throw me a ticker-tape parade. Needed to make sure I was available."

"Long overdue." She looked at me finally, and crossed her arms. "Hope they can loan you the popemobile."

"God willing." I made the sign of the cross.

"Really, though. You okay?" Riveaux asked.

"She had questions about the east wing. Nothing major."

"Mhmm." She tipped a cigarette out of her pack. She had my back, and I wanted to have hers too. But being a good undercover operative for Decker meant being a good liar to everyone. No exceptions. I loathed every second of lying to her. Hated myself for it. But I had to do it right.

I unrolled a tiny scroll Riveaux had meticulously crafted with a straw wrapper. "She really looks at details, you know. Careful. Thorough."

"Maybe you should take some notes." She stretched and rolled her shoulders.

"You're one to talk, Riveaux." I pointed to a tower of old coffee cups. Something fuzzy was growing in one. Looked like the cleaning company hadn't been by in weeks. Good move on their part.

"Mayhem and entropy keep us sharp," she said.

"Let's put that sharpness to the test." I grabbed the papers from my desk. The printout from international superspy Alex Moore and the folder of fiscal docs I'd lifted from Shelly's filing cabinet, near her framed tuxedo pope cat. "Finally time to slice into this hot tip."

"Ready for some *gross* profit?" Riveaux bit her bottom lip as she wheeled her chair over and spun it around.

We dove into the documents, and it was immediately clear that Alex "Deep Throat" Moore had just looked at the Diocese's annual grant budget. From the URL at the bottom of the page, it seemed that the info was all public. Available online. Riveaux confirmed it with a quick search on her phone.

If that shit was so easily accessible, why'd Alex make it seem like the Pentagon Papers?

We scoured the fiscal documents. Riveaux breathed with her mouth open. "Look at this one." She pressed her pen against form A-459, the payout disbursement record. "So, the insurance elves disbursed six hundred and fifty K for Saint Sebastian's, all itemized under the property damage claim."

I pulled out the invoices, estimates, and contractor's work orders. One was stamped with a cartoon hard hat logo. We cross-referenced each line item from the insurance stack with the bank statements for the disbursement account: $18K for industrial dumpsters and $127K for debris clearance and smoke mitigation that had already been completed. No discrepancies there. More than $500K sitting pretty in the bank.

"Check this out." Riveaux tapped an estimate for around $700K in major structural work. "Looks like the east wing needs specialized restoration. Historic buildings always cost more. The designer handbags of architecture." She circled a figure with her pen, and the black ink made a tiny halo. "Total costs: eight hundred and fifty K." She grabbed another form from the stack. Her inner nerd was rejoicing. She pushed her glasses back up her nose, her eyes dancing up at the corners.

My head felt exceptionally light. "Damn. The cost of rebuilding's a hell of a lot more than what the insurance policy paid."

"Not uncommon. Policy holders get left in the lurch all the time. But here's where it gets really interesting." Riveaux grabbed the Diocese report from Alex. "Your BFFs at the Diocese approved a grant for exactly that amount—two hundred K to bridge the shortfall."

"So, thanks to the generosity of our dear friends at the Diocese, there should be just enough money to cover all the costs, but *still* no rebuild? Did the bishop ever sign the check for the grant? Or did he just line his pockets?" I thought back to our rectory search over Easter. The freezer full of steaks for Father Reese. The bishop's Bentley in the parking lot. That slimeball probably chalked the leather seats up to God's will. The heated massage feature a divine right.

"Curious case of the missing money," Riveaux said as she flipped through the file.

"Oooh, what's this?" I asked, picking up a plain white envelope from the fiscal folder. It was relatively thin. Ordinary. I pulled out the pages and unfolded them. The first document I read was a bank statement from another account. The numbers spoke their inanimate language under my gloved fingers. "Here's the elusive grant. It was deposited three months ago. But only a hundred K remains from it." My eyes sizzled—I could feel red veins webbing—as I read.

Half of the grant money was gone. No wonder the rebuild hadn't started.

"So, a hundred grand unaccounted for?" Riveaux twirled her pen around her knuckles with exceptional skill. "Didn't y'all take a vow of poverty?"

Then the other contents of the envelope. An invoice for a bizarrely expensive hotel reservation at the Big Easy Inn. Its letterhead on paper so thin and cheap, it made the parish bulletin look like the queen's royal stationery. "Five rooms at the Big Easy Inn are booked. Every night of every week. For twelve months." My two hours of sleep gave my words a dramatic squeak, like I was talking through a kazoo that was run over by the Muses float. Father Nathan's signature on the hotel invoice changed the emerging picture with vulgar specificity.

"So, why are Father Nathan's sticky fingers all over the collection box?" Riveaux leaned back and spoke to the ceiling. "Five rooms at a shady motel. That's a lot of square footage for spiritual guidance."

"Who's checking in?"

"What if Father Nathan has a wife and some poppets tucked away?" Riveaux asked.

The idea of him with a secret family was ludicrous. Although it wouldn't be the first time a servant of God pulled the wool over our eyes at Saint Sebastian's. Men thinking their titles gave them get-out-of-hell-free cards.

"Riveaux"—I held her eyes—"there are five rooms. That'd be one forest of a family tree."

"Maybe he's got a crew. A sister wives kinda situation. And they're playing house on the Diocese's dime?" Riveaux twisted her face up. "Or maybe prostitution? Human trafficking?"

"Not a chance," I said.

The rules we expect humans to follow were sometimes binding and serious. Or, they were suggestions, temporary promises with contracts signed in invisible ink. And sometimes, for the really sick fucks, double-dog dares. But not Father Nathan.

"What about kickbacks? Some kind of embezzlement cover-up? Our Father who art misappropriating funds?" Riveaux's smile was wild, ready, and, well, delighted. She'd derived a strange sense of joy imagining all the ways Father Nathan, my friend, was transgressing. But it was also the tonic of the hunt. The undeniable thrill and rush. It had a clarifying effect, the way a good fever boils a virus out of the blood.

"These are legitimate rooms," I said, "blocked out night after night. Standing reservations, under his name."

"Wait a sec," Riveaux said. "Sounds like a sweet setup for moving product."

"Drugs?"

"Warrants are harder to pin down if someone's got multiple hotel rooms booked." She reached across her body to massage her back. She dug just below her shoulder blade, groaning with the pressure. "Besides, management's not asking questions if the bills are paid and tips are good. Then you factor in the east wing stash. Could Father Nathan be working for the Royal Family?"

"Doesn't make sense." I stared at the hotel letterhead. The fleur-de-lis springing ever upward. A spear. A weapon. "Why not use an alias? Why keep the invoice?" Drug ops needed deniability, not a paper trail so clear even Ryan Brown could follow it.

"What if someone's forcing his hand? Extorting him?" she asked. "And he's keeping a record in case it gets dicey."

The floor felt like it had tilted at a sick pitch, and my head filled with static. I rooted my heels down, watching the empty jalapeño Zapp's bag on Riveaux's desk blur and sharpen, blur and sharpen. No breath I took reached my lower lungs. I studied his signature, the same flourished *N* on every piece of paper.

Riveaux retracted her pen with a decisive click. "What do you think's going down?"

"Not sure." I grabbed my guitar case. "But I'm going to find out."

"Make *him* confess for a change, question mark?"

"Exactly." The Diocese grant had split like the Red Sea. I hated that Alex Moore was right.

"I'll give you a lift. Then I'm going to swing by the lab," Riveaux said. "Doubtful they have anything new for us, but can't win if you don't play."

We drove in strange silence down Carrollton, shadows dappling the dashboard. At Napoleon, we idled at a red light. I imagined telescoping my arm up, through the window, to touch a tangle of moss. Sweat rolled down my neck, but I didn't adjust my scarf. Some discomfort you earn. Some you choose. We passed Palmer Park with a yoga group huddled under a tent. I saw a woman walking fast with a go-cup in front of a pack of jogging teens.

As we turned onto Prytania, Riveaux broke the quiet. "Whatever hole you're getting yourself into with Decker—"

"Stop digging?"

"Not saying that. Just make sure you can climb out." She turned her head to look directly at me. "But if you hit bottom, holler, and I'll throw a rope."

I nodded and stepped outside. She drove off, leaving me with that familiar feeling I'd just failed a test.

The central wing hallway stretched endlessly with pictures of Saint Sebastian's graduating classes through the years. They eyed me with each step. Such young and hopeful faces frozen in time before the world showed them the price of love. Of caring. Of living.

I dashed past the main office—couldn't risk a therapy sesh with Shelly. Father Nathan's classroom was empty but alive with an invisible presence. Like the altar between morning and evening worship. His desk was tidy. I flipped through an essay collection about Corinthians marked with Post-its.

The walk across campus to the rectory took five minutes, but it felt longer, slower, like I was trudging through the sludge. A quick afternoon shower had left puddles that trembled when cars passed, each one a mirror. So many watching eyes. The dark sockets of water. Saints in their niches. Mary on her pedestal. I jumped into a puddle and savored the storm.

The rectory was for fathers, but my mind kept circling back to the mothers. Fleur's mom who'd never see her kid walk the graduation stage. Trish Dempsey on her roof after Katrina, holding baby Prince so tight, so close, he could have been her pacemaker. Women like my mom, with rosaries draped around wrists or car gear shifts, praying their kids have good days and make kind friends. Such simple asks. Mothers lighting candles and saying novenas and working overtime shifts at the hospital.

At the entrance to his office, Father Nathan's smile brightened, even as I blasted past him. "Hey, your vow ceremony is—"

"That's not why I'm here."

"Oh, okay." His eyebrows stitched. "What's up?"

"Five rooms at the Big Easy Inn." My hands shook as I talked. "Booked every night. For a year."

He took careful steps to his desk, like he was avoiding wet cement. "Who told you?"

"Does it matter? A hundred grand from the Diocese grant is gone."

He raised a hand. "Hold on. Do you need a drink of water?"

"I don't need a fucking drink of water. I need answers. Why is a hundred thousand dollars missing from the Rebuild Fund? Why are you booking hotel rooms?"

He inhaled. "Those rooms"—he leaned forward—"are lifelines."

"Who for? Your secret family? A drug ring? *Who?*"

His head shot back like a PEZ dispenser. "Drugs? Secret family?" He laughed. "You have lost the plot. The rooms are a *safe house.*"

"A what?"

"A Saint Sebastian's shelter for the vulnerable, but through a hotel. A motel, technically."

"Wait, what?" It was suddenly so clear. So astoundingly obvious, like a Communion chalice to the back of the head. The domestic violence brochures. His office phone ringing off the hook. Ringing like the Saint Roch church bell on Easter morning. I was gobsmacked. Impressed. But still alert to the fact it could all be a ruse. "Why pay for it with the Rebuild Fund?" I traced the outline of the scar on my chin. A crescent moon, forever waning or waxing.

"The Diocese wants to renovate space we don't need and will never need, while people sleep in their cars."

"Or in tents."

He nodded energetically. "Why not use the money to help our community *truly* rebuild?"

"Wouldn't the bishop go hog wild over that? Throw money at it so they can feel like they solved something?"

"If only. The Diocese rejected my shelter proposal three times. Said we needed to focus on 'property improvements' instead of 'social services.' Last month, a woman came to confession. Her husband had put her in the hospital twice. She had three kids and nowhere to go. So, I made a call."

Father Nathan was diverting Diocese money to shelter people fleeing abuse. Why was I surprised? Father Nathan, our avenging priest. No stranger to drawing outside of the lines. How could I not have seen this coming? How could I fault it? Can't call it fraud when you're stealing from corrupt fuckers to protect the vulnerable.

"Why didn't you tell me?"

"Sometimes we have to keep secrets to protect people," he said. I saw past the collar, past the title, to the human, a man who'd chosen the priesthood, the church, when others ran from it or delivered it as comic relief. "Don't we?"

The blow landed with magnificent precision. I was running yet another undercover operation, though he couldn't possibly know that. I sank into the chair across from him.

"How are you finding folks in need?" I asked. "Just in the confessional?"

He nodded. "People who need help know where to go. Like your very own truant, perhaps." He smoothed his right eyebrow with his thumb, only to muss it up again a moment later.

I thought back to Easter. The river. It clicked right there, right then, with Father Nathan's strong incense burning. "*Prince Dempsey.* Prince is in one of the motel rooms?"

He shut his eyes and nodded.

"You should have told me."

Father Nathan raised his hand like he was about to launch into the Gospel. "Not my secret to tell."

"He's *my* student." My voice broke. "I've been worried sick."

"He's an adult. And he didn't give me permission to disclose."

"Except you are disclosing," I said, "right now. So, who beat him up? Who hurt BonTon?"

"He didn't tell me, and I didn't ask. He clearly needed immediate help."

"You're Robin Hood in a starched collar."

"More like a desperate man with a creative accounting strategy." His smile had an edge. "And one that I could get excommunicated for. But every penny's tracked. These folks are running for their lives." The chair's frame shifted as he crossed his legs. "One woman had to move piecemeal, one bag at a time, because her ex-husband was stalking her. He'd know if she left with a suitcase. For weeks, she moved her clothes, pantry staples, and family heirlooms in a tote bag."

"You could have trusted me, brought me in on this." As I said it, I felt the tar of my deep cover slosh around inside me, pulling me down.

"Like you trust me? I told you not to worry about Prince. And you seem cagey yourself lately."

"Maybe we're both trying to right some wrongs," I said.

"You're not going to say more, are you?"

I shook my head.

"There are worse sins than bad choices for a good cause." He drummed his fingertips on his desk. "Just don't get caught."

"The Diocese will crucify you if they find out."

He laughed. A wild deep contagious real laugh that had me laughing too. "They definitely will find out. I've kept all of the records hiding in plain sight for a reason. I am not being forth-coming about it, but I'm not hiding anything either. Perhaps that will help my case. But I answer to a higher authority. I'd rather face their questions and judgment than explain to God why I had the means to help but *chose* not to."

"What now?" I asked.

"Help me help people," Father Nathan said, with his pulpit voice. Devoted. Knowing. A Sign of Peace with a spear secreted inside. "And soon you'll fill me in on what else you've been investigating? Before you take your final vows."

I headed for the door. "Soon."

"Grace isn't a given," he said. "We have to fight for it."

20

"FATHER NATHAN'S RUNNING A guerrilla domestic violence shelter out of the Big Easy Inn," I told Riveaux, my voice a severe hush on the convent kitchen phone.

"Didn't see that coming."

"Playing Robin Hood with the Rebuild Fund." The rotary dial had left a pink indentation on my finger. A kiss. A bite. "The Diocese will be pissed."

Riveaux exhaled. "Father Sticky Fingers is sticking it to the bishop. Good on him."

"I'm praying he doesn't get caught too soon. That's where Prince Dempsey's been staying."

"Well, well. The plot thickens."

"Can you pick me back up?"

"Gimme fifteen." She groaned, sounding like she was pulling on her boots. "Just wrapping up an invoice, putting the financial ducks in a row."

We chain-smoked as we drove to the Big Easy Inn, the motel-shelter off Tchoupitoulas. Father Nathan's vigilante ministry. Sure, he said to drop it. But he also knew I wouldn't. I prayed a quick penance with my rosary wrapped around my fingers. Impromptu brass knuckles.

Riveaux tapped ash out her window at a red light, and a green parrot swooped between trees. A tall man walked a dog so small it had to run on triple-A batteries. There was a person on stilts trying to catch up with a trio of ladies in sun hats. One woman had dollar bills safety-pinned to her vest by strangers—a beloved local birthday tradition.

"Here's a riddle," Riveaux said. "What gets longer as night falls but vanishes in complete darkness?"

"My eye rolls? Definitely not my patience."

"A shadow. Poetic, no?" She flicked her cigarette butt into a puddle, where it died with a hiss. An American Spirit drowning.

As we pulled up to the dimly lit motel parking lot, we saw Prince walking BonTon. "There's our man." Riveaux slid down in the driver's seat. "And his little dog too."

BonTon sniffed, then selected a patch of grass for her duty, number one, with the discernment of a Michelin reviewer. Prince looked away.

We exited the truck and approached calmly, slowly, quietly. But Prince turned in a panic at the sound of Riveaux's footfalls.

"Fancy meeting you here," I said, waving away mosquitoes and gnats trying to smother me.

"You've got to be kidding me." Prince gave BonTon a hand signal, and the dog sat. "How'd you know where I was?" he asked.

"Doesn't matter," I said. "We're not telling anyone."

"Fucking better not." Sweat beaded on his forehead.

"You okay?" Riveaux asked.

"I was, until you showed up."

"We need to talk." Riveaux cut right to it. "About Fleur. About your face. About your mom's sling."

"Can't help you."

"Why not?" I asked.

"I'm having a medical emergency," Prince said.

"Your blood sugar?" I asked.

"No," he said. "Just deathly allergic to your bullshit."

I couldn't let the moment pass. "Is your mom's boyfriend beating you?" I asked. "You can tell us."

"Did you not hear me?" Prince over-enunciated. "I can't help you."

I studied him. And then it hit me. "Prince, does your mom know you're here?"

He leaned in. "It's better for me here. That's all I'm saying."

This was more complicated than I could fathom.

"We want to help."

"Don't need your charity."

"How 'bout your buddy there? Canine cuisine's on me. A dog's gotta eat," Riveaux said.

Prince looked down at BonTon.

"Why not just accept a damn gift for God's sake?" I said, straining the frayed end of my unraveling rope.

"Jesus," he whined. "Fine." He was posturing, for sure, but the instant relief in Prince's eyes was unmistakable.

BonTon leapt into the truck bed like she'd been born to ride and swiftly settled in.

"We can all fit in the cab," I said to Prince.

"Naw," he said, then settled into the back with BonTon, her tongue out in a big pit bull smile as the wind whipped her ears.

At least one of us was having a good time.

Twenty minutes later, we stood in Harvey's Pet Heaven. Judging from the one guinea pig enclosure, the empty birdcages, sad amphibian tank, and post-rapture inventory levels, Harvey's lil slice of heaven had major cash-flow issues.

Prince was amped up the moment we entered the shop. He cursed at the guy behind the counter, maybe Harvey himself, and made him check the back for some kind of special organic, grain-free dog food. Once the coast was clear, Prince grabbed a bag of small mammal treats and, sneakily, emptied it into the guinea pig hut. Riveaux and I watched, impressed.

"You like animals better than people?" I said, more than asked, as I followed him and BonTon down a dusty aisle.

"Animals don't lie. Animals don't break promises." He studied the ingredients on the bag of kibble like he was proofreading a PhD dissertation. "People blow." He grabbed the bag and powered on, stopping abruptly in the back of the store. A single bullfrog sat in a cloudy tank no bigger than a shoebox.

"Fucking criminal," Prince said through his teeth. "No filtration." He pointed to the top of the tank. "No companions. No basking spot."

"No 'Rainbow Connection' here," Riveaux added. Her face was genuinely pained.

Prince pressed his palm against the sad glass, and I stared into the glossy wide eyes of the frog. That tiny creature of God looked horrifically aware of its prison.

"Fleur would've hated this." Prince's nostrils stretched wide with fury. "She loved animals."

"You and Fleur were close?" I asked.

"Sure," he said. "She didn't ask me a million questions."

"Did you know she was in trouble?" Riveaux asked.

"Who isn't?" he asked, still looking at the frog, his fingers leaving ghostly smudges.

Each fingerprint was a story. An echo. A confession of a sort. I stared at the tanks and cages, imagined all the footprints left by crawling creatures. The feathers dropped by winged things. I was about to lose it in Harvey's Hell. Clearly, the sleeplessness was eroding me. Or it was the release, the relief, knowing Prince wasn't sleeping on the street.

Prince headed to the counter with BonTon trotting behind him. Riveaux paid, and I noticed Prince's stomach looking oddly bulky. A bulge near his belly button.

Outside, after the door of that hellish heaven slammed shut, Prince set down the dog food, smiled wide, and held up the frog he'd just covertly liberated.

"Hello, my ragtime gal," Riveaux offered.

"We're taking her to Madame Chartres's courtyard," he said.

"In the Quarter?" Riveaux protested.

"Short detour," he argued.

"Then you'll tell us what's been going on?" I asked.

He scratched his jaw. "Only one way to find out." Prince nodded, but at me or the frog, I wasn't sure.

It was a quiet drive, with Prince and his menagerie in the back, and me and Riveaux in the front. Only the ambient sounds of the ever-present street jazz. Sadly no "Michigan Rag" from the emancipated frog.

Prince led us through an iron gate, into a dark, narrow pathway. I had to duck and collapse my shoulders to fit. The passageway opened up into a most unexpected garden. An enchanted microclimate, degrees cooler than the stifling streets, with scents sailing around in spirals.

"Here," Prince said. We stood around a moss-covered fountain with a large basin where a stone statue of a mermaid rose from the center. Water shot from her mouth.

BonTon whimpered as Prince carefully placed the frog at the fountain's edge. "Go on," he said to the frog sitting immobile. "Go be a frog. For Fleur."

"For Fleur," I repeated.

A moment passed. Prince stared at me, miffed. "*C'mon*," he said.

"What?"

"Fucking bless it." He pointed at me then the frog, gesturing angrily, slapping the air. "Bless the frog, to protect it and shit."

"Oh, sure." I made the sign of the cross over the green being. "May you live well, God's creature, free from the hands of anyone who'd seek to cage you. Free from hurt."

Free from hurt. I thought of Prince's bruises. BonTon's burns. Trish's sling. Moose's scars. Riveaux's broken and healed back. All of us desperate for ease, for feeling at home in our own skin.

I said, "Amen," and the frog kerplunked into the fountain basin.

"Happily ever after," Riveaux said into the water. Then she turned to Prince. "Now, you're up."

"For what?" Prince's smile faded. "An award?"

"You can tell us," I said.

"Tell you what?"

"Your eye. Your mom's arm. Who did it?" I asked. "Your mom's been seen around with some guy. Is it him?"

After an uncomfortable silence, Riveaux said, "You can talk to us."

"No," Prince said.

No. A brick wall.

I stood up straight and held his eyes. "I understand your—"

"You don't understand shit." Prince leaned down and wiped crud from BonTon's dewy eyes. "I got nothing to say to you."

"Careful," Riveaux warned, "or we might think you're involved."

"Listen, Prince," I interjected, "if you're mixed up with the wrong people, we can help make it right."

Prince didn't miss a beat. "Real interesting story you got going on there. But keep my name out of it." He grabbed the big bag of dog food, slung it over his shoulder, and turned toward the garden exit. "And don't talk to my mom either." He and BonTon walked in perfect sync as they left.

"Swing and a miss," I said.

Riveaux, ever pragmatic, responded, "Win some, lose some." But her eyes followed Prince and the dog. "We'll try him again soon. Persistence is key with a kid like him."

"Don't I know it." The Saint Louis Cathedral bells made the air shiver. Ten o'clock. I needed to get it together, prepare for the Tammy show. "Need my beauty sleep," I said.

As we walked to Riveaux's truck, a crow dive-bombed an alley cat near the dumpster. Two brutes fighting over scraps. Two animals unwilling to yield, doing what it took to survive.

"You all right?" Riveaux asked suddenly, throwing me a dubious look.

"Just tired," I said. "Long day." Not to mention the night that lay ahead.

21

WHILE MY ACTUAL GUITAR watched me from the corner of my room in the convent, I packed my case with Tammy's jacket, combat boots, and makeup. The burner tucked into the jacket pocket like a Cracker Jack prize. Sisters Honor and Laurel were asleep, but if they did startle, for any reason, and see me in the hall, they'd never question me carrying my instrument, my ever-present companion. Hopefully they wouldn't enter my room and see my caseless Fender in the corner.

I met Decker on Prytania Street. She listened to Sweet Honey in the Rock as I changed in the back of her cruiser. Then she dropped me off with a reminder to check in and avoid "candy from strangers." As if I didn't learn lessons of survival the hard way back in Brooklyn, where there were unfounded rumors of razor blades hidden in Almond Joys.

I crunched over a broken bottle as I neared Up in Smoke. A street band was playing a devastating number. Aching and sweet. "Killer tune," I said to one of the buskers. "What's it called?"

"'Gimme Toulouse,'" he said, smiling over his mandolin.

I kept walking and a roach the size of a jeep darted past like it was late for a very important date. As I shook out the sleeves of the leather jacket, the once-supple hide flaked fiercely. In the pockets I found a tube of blood red lipstick, a small comb with some missing teeth, and a travel-sized can of hairspray, no bigger than a roll of quarters. With maximum hold to boot.

A lifetime ago, the jacket could have been Nina's. I could practically catch a hint of my ex's clove cigarettes if I buried my nose in the collar, felt the phantom charge of her fingers laced with mine. Memories somersaulted back, each image punching me. Nina, my first love. The bass player in Original Sin, our band. All the benders we shared. The sleepless blur of days spilling into nights. All the weekends I wore the same black jeans and ripped T-shirt and washed my underwear and bra in her sink. We met as teenagers, riot grrrls who found each other. We dated on and off for more than a decade, until she married a pretentious fuckhead named Nicholas. Though that didn't stop us from fooling around. My provisional vows did.

Me and Nina. I remembered sitting with her, in her West Village loft, one of her many cult books open in my lap. She'd read it out loud like it was *Goodnight Moon*, saying, "The bodies of thirty-nine members of Heaven's Gate were found in matching purple shrouds, tracksuits, and black-and-white Nike Decades." She'd wax poetic about Ti and Do with gory details about "their last supper"—potpies from Marie Callender's. She was amazed by the lengths people traveled for their beliefs. I was amazed too. But not by cults. By her. The way her eyes burned. Feverish. Dizzy. I remembered how she looked when she'd said, "What if love is a cult. Total devotion and sacrifice." She'd drawn a heart on my thigh with her index finger.

"I'll *chug* that Kool-Aid for you." I'd smiled.

"Heaven's Gate used applesauce for their curtain call."

"I'd mainline applesauce, then."

"You're fucking warped"—she kissed my knuckles, one by one—"and I love it."

The memories made my teeth clack. Sparkling tension in every muscle before one of our shows. The beauty mark on her neck was shaped like a shooting star. A tiny Hale-Bopp.

But like the comet, Nina was gone, and I was in New Orleans, going undercover as a new version of my old self. As Tammy. To bust up a drug ring. And walking into Up in Smoke, the past still breathed inside me.

I shoved through the door of the lounge and coughed. Toxic fruit tobacco held any available oxygen hostage. In the corner, a sunburned man watched a silent TV. A miracle hair growth serum infomercial. The sound system was a midlife crisis in audio form. Ginuwine's "Pony," a timeless composition, played as clientele mummified at the bar. I surveyed the space, replaying Mark 13:33, *Be on your guard and stay alert*, and Decker's psalm, *Check for exits and potential threats*. The Eve tattoo on my throat itched.

Near the pool table, I set my eyes on a guy with his back to me. The pack of losers orbiting him had various degrees of greasy hair. Some with hilarious steroid arms. Some spoke only in grunts. Guys like that were why the nuns of Bishop Shannon High School gave the girls "rape whistles" to wear around our necks. Violence was the victim's fault—that was the message they sent us. Thanks for nothing.

The man holding court turned. A white guy. Slimy. Grimy. His eyes were chips of ice. Cold, hard, ready to cut down to nothing. It was Lenny Mastoni, a.k.a. my mark. Decker's POI with the Royal Family. This time we had gotten lucky.

I walked over while rehearsing my lines in my head like a set list before a show. You'd think I'd be as smooth as stucco when it came to cisgender men, but I could code-switch with the best of them. Weaponize high femininity? Sure. Femme fatale? With pleasure. Leading on a lowlife for the greater good? Count me in. It was like walking on air.

I was good at being bad.

"Buy a girl a drink?" I asked Lenny. So cold my tongue stuck to each word.

Lenny peered up from his game. Through the apricot smog, he raked his icepick eyes over me like I was a used car he was considering buying for parts. I wondered what my translucent tank top and smudged eyeliner looked like to him. I could smell the tired misogyny seeping off him as he consigned me to the slut column in his mental Rolodex.

He chalked up his cue and puzzled out his next move. "I look like an ATM to you?"

I leaned my hip against the table to crowd into his space. His cologne, with notes of a gas station burrito and wet dog, burned my eyes. "Forget the drink," I said. "How about a smoke? No vape or flavored shit."

A muscle ticked in his stubbled jaw. Finally, he grabbed his hard pack of Parliaments and tipped one out for me.

"You're a legend." I made sure to let my finger brush his hand as I took it. Had to suppress my reflex of revulsion. Never missed my gloves more than that moment.

Lenny flicked open a scuffed Zippo and rolled the wheel. The flame shivered as I leaned in and let the first taste of smoke bite my tongue. I once asked Nina to suck on my tongue, and figured she'd say, *You're a freak*, but she did it and she loved it. It led to an hour-long make out session in her shower. I quickly stuffed that memory down and planted my feet. No more Nina. Back on target. Back to Tammy.

I took a drag and sent a silent prayer of thanks that New Orleans was gorgeously lax on public smoking bans. "I needed that. Ever need something so bad you can't think about anything else?"

Lenny ignored me, focusing on his game. It was as if I never existed.

"I'm Tammy," I said. Couldn't let him slip away. I blew a stream of smoke from the lower corner of my mouth.

"Lenny," he said, watching a striped ball skip helplessly past his intended corner pocket. His opponent smiled into his flat beer.

Clearly that game needed all his focus. So I stepped aside and watched him bomb miserably. He wielded the pool cue so clumsily. A caveman discovering a tool for the first time. His shots ricocheted off the rails with extreme prejudice. It was painful to witness—the slow death of hand-eye coordination itself. Another slippery white guy came up to him and they chatted about the Saints' odds next season.

After the pool table slaughter, I went to the restroom to check the burner and freshen up my makeup. It was more fun than I remembered, the makeup. Drawing, shading, applying, reapplying, puckering, kissy face. Looking at myself straight on and then in profile, left and right. Wearing the drama. The mask. From a stall covered in passionate graffiti, I texted Decker: *Nothing yet but Lenny here.*

She texted *K*.

No *okay* or *OK*. Just *K*. No pep talk. Thanks, Decker.

A minute later, I slid onto a stool beside Lenny who had migrated to the bar, letting my knee graze his thigh. His jeans were the kind of overpriced designer denim that tried too hard to look distressed, like they'd been mauled by child laborers before being sold for a small fortune. "Come here often?"

Lenny tensed his forehead, pulling his bushy eyebrows low over his eyes. "You trying to pick me up, sweetheart?"

I laughed the way I used to laugh when I was trying to get out of a speeding ticket. "Lemme get back to you on that one."

"You're new around here," he said with his black eyes on my knuckle tatts. He seemed to be taking a good look at me, for the first time since his initial appraisal.

"Tried on Memphis for a minute, but New Orleans kept calling me back home," I said. Decker wanted me to let him do the talking, but it's hard to tango solo. "Ever been to Memphis?"

"Memphis." He inhaled, held his breath for a moment. "Once or twice."

"Well, it's boring as death," I said. "Now I'm back where the air feels right. I'm a musician. Work's better here."

"Whaddaya play?" he asked.

"Guitar."

"What kinda songs?"

"Whatever people want me to play," I said.

"What's the top request?"

"'House of the Rising Sun.' By far the most requested song here."

He nodded. "What was it in Memphis?"

I searched my brain. *Don't overthink*, I heard Decker's voice. "A cover of a tune you've probably never heard of." I was buying time.

"Try me."

Nothing came to me. Absolutely nothing. I was blank. Lungs in a muzzle. Then I remembered the buskers. "'Gimme Toulouse,'" I said.

"'Gimme Toulouse,' huh?"

Lenny's expression rippled. A brief lightning flash of knowing claimed his face. But it was there and gone far too quick to parse. Interest? Suspicion? The wiry understory of a hunter silently turning toward a scent, locking in. Hard to say. "Good tune," was all he offered in reply. His shoulders rolled back and he hooked one boot on the bar rail.

I lit a new cigarette from Lenny's pack, exhaled a smoke ring, and tried to shape it, like packing a snowball. As if I could hold smoke. As if wanting a thing badly enough could make the impossible possible.

Lenny asked what I was having and ordered us a round. An out-of-left-field white wine for him and a bourbon for me. He slid the tumbler of Bulleit my way like he was dealing cards, and I said, "Thank you kindly."

Soon I'd learn what hand Lenny was really dealing.

Game on, motherfucker.

22

FRIDAY WAS A NEW day. A fresh start. But still performing the magic trick of balancing my four roles: nun, teacher, PI apprentice, undercover agent. A kaleidoscope of fucked-up me's.

I was drinking coffee in the convent kitchen, eyes closed, when Moose called. The receiver felt heavy. A beautifully designed functional sculpture you could bludgeon someone with.

Moose exhaled. "Prince okay?"

"Not exactly sure about that," I said, "but he's out of harm's way."

"So, he wasn't willing to share?"

"No," I said, "but I'll keep trying."

"Of course you will," he said. "Let's grab breakfast before your Mass on Sunday."

"Sorry, I can't." Even my words were exhausted, collapsing. I felt guilty, pathetic, for drinking undercover. Couldn't face him. Not to mention he'd sniff me out in a second.

"Why?"

"Too much going on," I said.

"Too much of what?" He was annoyed. Had that queeny edge in his voice I usually loved, unless it was directed at me. "Don't get in too deep, Goose."

"Stop. I'm fine."

"Don't avoid the question."

"Me?"

"You know what? Forget it. You *always* do this. You shut down and I'm supposed to just sit here and watch you self-destruct?"

The line went dead.

I couldn't argue or lie. It was better if Moose thought I was the same shitty sister. If he knew what was actually going on and what I was trying to uncover, he'd really have something to worry about.

■

I was lobbing exercises at Ryan and showing Rebecca the chromatic run in the bridge of "Minor Swing," when Sister Honor's shadow darkened my classroom doorway, eclipsing the hallway light.

"A word?" Sister Honor shifted her weight off her right foot. Maybe her plantar fasciitis was acting up again. I held up a finger to tell her to give me a minute.

"Why can't I play something cool like Rebecca?" Ryan Brown wheedled, then butchered two notes in a row. I'd been so busy riding out the hurricane in my house of cards that I still hadn't flagged his wack thumb technique. Carpal tunnel was imminent.

"Intonation, Ryan. Can't have Django up there weeping on cloud nine." I touched my right temple to quiet my internal percussion section as I followed Mother Superior into the hallway. "You got this."

"Your beatnik cacophony is highly disruptive. Do put bet-ter choices on your curriculum." Sister Honor rested one hand against the wall, giving her foot a break, but her voice didn't soften and her uptight BS never loosened up.

"That's why you're here? To review my syllabus?"

"Not *only* that. Trevor O'Keefe."

"He's awake?"

"Yes, and he is recovering, thank the Lord. But he won't be returning to school. His parents feel he needs a more structured environment. Away from certain influences." Her eyes raked over my gloves.

I opened my mouth to ask more, but she steamrolled on. "Your permanent vows are approaching," she said. "The bishop and I are watching very closely to evaluate your dedication to the parish standards. Now more than ever, proper decorum and piety are required."

Like I could ever forget the constant scrutiny. I fought to keep my eyes focused while my brain slowly poured out of my ears.

Through the door, Ryan hit a perfect chord. For the first time maybe ever. *Praise the Lord.*

"Go with God." I shot Sister Honor a smile despite the stab-bing pain behind my eyeballs.

"Very closely," Sister Honor mouthed the warning again.

■

The school day was a high-wire walk between vice squad and catechism. One minute I was teaching three-chord progres-sions to juniors, the next imagining taking a pipe cutter to a drug dealer's fingers. I popped into the library to grill Alex Moore, but he wasn't there. Did he know anything concrete about Father Nathan's covert ops, or did he just wonder why the Rebuild Fund wasn't rebuilding jack shit. Or worse. What if Alex was the Diocese's bitch boy snitch boy, setting me up for a grand fall? Eve style. A tale as old as Genesis.

Between third and fourth period, I caught myself daydreaming of simpler times. Playing my guitar in pajamas at Nina's, not worrying about student ODs. Would full commitment, life after permanent vows, be easier, or harder? Every time I thought I'd figured it out, doubt crept back in.

I spotted Bernard as I walked through the courtyard. He was striding toward Prytania, leaving campus early. Very early. Maybe he was on an errand. Or just stepping out on the second half of the school day. I stood under the sycamore, in the shade of its lobed leaves, watching him step farther into the distance.

▪

I held the convent phone gingerly like a complex ecosystem hid inside it. "Tell me something good."

"Define 'good.'" Judging by Riveaux's voice she was on her fifth cigarette. "I'm meeting with Mrs. Benoit later. She's probably bringing in Fleur's baby footprints in plaster of paris to cry over. Crazy Friday plans here. Wanna join?"

"Have to rain check that one." I pressed my forehead against the stone wall. So cold. The temperature of holy water.

"You busy Little Johning it for Father Nathan? Can't see the Sherwood Forest for the trees?"

I could hear her *gotcha* smirk through the curlicue phone cord.

"You've had that in the back pocket of your mom jeans for a minute," I said.

"Nah. Improvisation is one of my many gifts. For real, what's the vibe there?"

"I'm one rosary away from a nervous breakdown. My vows are next week."

"Cold feet?"

"Freezing," I said.

"One minute outside will warm you right up. Snap out of it. Lots of work to do."

"Thanks for the encouragement."

"Now hang up before Sister Honor tries to exorcise me through the phone."

▪

That night at Up in Smoke, Lenny joined me for a cigarette outside. Sure, we could smoke inside. But I'd wondered if, on the street, away from the bartender or other patrons, he might talk more freely. We leaned against the brick and did the useless small talk thing between drags. Lenny needed to start dishing, but teeing him up would take time.

Time I didn't have.

I'd honed the art of the long game in the convent. Polishing the stained glass, pane by pane. Wiping down baseboards. Replacing novena candles. Dusting the Saint Lucy statue while her eyes stared at me from the plate. Losing myself in prayer. The rosary beads laced through my fingers, each day a different mystery. Joyful on Mondays, Sorrowful on Tuesdays, Glorious on Wednesdays. My life as a celibate queer.

Lenny's pager—cliché, ornament of hilarity, '90s tribute but not in a good way—chirped every two minutes. He'd silently check it then stuff it back down in his front pocket like the device was annoying him. That's when I clocked the gun tucked into his belt. Had to look away instantly.

"Mr. Popular, huh?" Light touch, couldn't possibly be more relaxed. Decker'd be proud.

He yawned. "Everybody wants a piece." He lit another cigarette and examined the flame too long.

"No surprise."

Playing it too eager would tip him off. Playing it gray rock would also clue him in. So I nudged him back inside for the theater of another pool game. He held the door open for me, a chivalrous move of which I took close note.

Inside the grubby hookah lounge, my dignity was violated when "She's Like the Wind" came on the shaky sound system. Patrick Swayze's lethal foray into song that I hadn't heard since the first and last time I was stuck in a Macy's elevator. Lenny mouthed every single lyric and hummed the segue. Forget the worry of a stray bullet or undercover screwup delivering my early death. That song was nailing my casket note by note.

When Lenny missed another easy bank shot, I couldn't help myself. "You're murdering that table."

His head shot up. "And you got game, Miss Gimme Toulouse?"

"*Gimme* the cue next." I delivered it bored. Unimpressed. "Though watching you lose is entertaining."

That got him. Nothing hooks a certain brand of dude, especially a self-styled romantic with a taste for white wine and melodramatic "music," like a slight. He said *hi* to some fool walking by with a woman twenty years younger. The gal gave me a wink.

Lenny gestured to the table with his cue. "Show me what you got, sweetheart."

I took my time chalking up, highlighted my tight ass as I leaned over the table. Thanks, convent chores. Then I ran three balls clean before deliberately scratching. "Ah, well. I'm a little rusty too." I stuck out my bottom lip and felt the lipstick I'd applied too heavily.

He grunted and his bushy eyebrows seemed to spawn baby eyebrows above them. Unibrow level. "Where'd you learn to shoot?"

"Around. Used to make quick cash hustling frat boys up Saint Charles." I lined up another shot and banked it.

He rewarded that story with a howl. "I'd pay to see that. Better than a movie."

I blew chalk off the tip of my cue. A perfect kiss of air. "I like movies with explosions."

"I like anything with a car chase." He flubbed again, blasting one of his stripes two inches too far. The ghost of my beloved childhood cat Marple would have rocked a tighter game than the Royal Family's lieutenant. I kept an eye on my guitar case, which I had to lug around everywhere. A vital accessory in my real life and undercover life. Lenny inhaled the bouquet of his wine before he drank some. I imagined a nose of Welch's white grape juice and envelope glue. "What's a nice girl like you hustling frat boys for, anyway?"

"Who says I'm nice?" I made sure my tank top rode up, exhaled a snake of smoke, and watched it disappear in the faux fruit carcinogenic air.

Lenny's laugh was a dying chain saw. He had a gold tooth too. Way duller than mine, but it still stole the light when he opened his nasty mouth.

Lenny sipped his Chablis and moved closer. I, in turn, put my own whiskey down to keep from knocking the whole tumbler back. I took off my leather jacket instead, and Lenny leered at my neck ink and full sleeves. He let his eyes stay on the tight fit of my threadbare shirt. Then the rosary around my left wrist. "Religious?"

"Ha." I forced laughter but me forcing laughter so badly made me laugh for real. "Tammy's grammy. I mean, it was my grandma's. Though I did go to Catholic school for a year."

Fuck. I'd slipped. But he didn't catch it. I saw it in his eyes. No change. Close call.

"Catholic school, huh?" He tugged at his earlobe and paused. But it was a different kind of shift. "Still have that uniform?"

"And the knee socks and the big cross necklace."

He drew his cheeks in severely. Another vast pause passed in which the earth turned at least ten thousand times. "Big cross, huh?"

"You know what they say." I batted my eyelashes as I pocketed his lighter from the high-top table. I swiped it to test to see what he'd notice. Not a thing, apparently. "The bigger the cross..."

Lenny's smile was a very slow, very infected thing.

"Be right back," I said. "Order us another round?"

In the restroom I sent my check-in text to Decker. She replied, as usual, *K.* I stared into the mirror, which showed how my darkness loved to push through. Black roots grown out, black eyeliner, black sea of pupils. My hands shook. From the rush. Seeing Lenny's gun. Drinking without eating a proper dinner.

I walked to the bar where Lenny stood, proud of the two drinks in front of him. "Chocolate martinis," he said, like he just cashed his Skee-Ball tickets for a stuffed dolphin.

The drinks congealed in front of me. A staggering concoction of fudgy swirls that tasted like burnt rubber. I choked it down with a silent Hail Mary.

"Good, right?"

"You got a sweet tooth," I said.

"Sure do."

I wasn't sure how much longer I could keep doing this, feeling the chocolate martini rotting my molars. It was time to be bold. "Happen to know where a nice girl could get some harder candy around here?"

Lenny went still. Dead still. Not even a breath. For a scorching moment, again I thought I'd overplayed my hand. Burned myself. Came on too strong. He'd made me for a narc and was about to rain hellfire down.

But then he pulled back, and I saw some strategy in his hooded eyes. "Might know some people," he said.

"Mr. Popular strikes again."

He licked the toxic chocolate rim of his glass. "I'll hook you up, if you can make it worth my while."

"Name your price."

Lenny stared at my lips, my chin, then lower. He leaned in. "I need my lighter back." He *had* noticed. "And a taste."

One horrific finger reached out and touched my jaw. My earlobe. I had an urgent need to snap his finger in half. It was a particular and detailed vision. But I held myself in check—another small miracle from God.

His fingers rested on my throat. My tattoo of Eve. "Bet that's one sweet apple," he said. "I need a little taste."

"What do you mean by—"

Before I finished my question, Lenny pressed his mouth against my throat and started licking, then sucking. His lips were wet and sticky. His beard, old Brillo. His breath. Lord, no. Like something had died in his mouth before the New Testament was inked. He started moaning slightly, really going at it, sucking my neck, probably leaving a mark. The scrape of his teeth made me think of a rat gnawing through insulation.

I shut my eyes so tight I surely burst a blood vessel. Tried to ease the nausea by imagining Nina. I clawed at any memory. Any shred. Any image of her I could reach. Her mouth on my neck instead of Lenny's.

But it didn't work, and I was shutting down. Tried to conjure Rosemary instead. Her smell, rose petals and satsuma peels, new lipstick, strong soap.

None of that thrill was on offer. Nothing sexy or fun. Only a man who really needed to floss.

After a minute, probably less, which lived in my cellular layer like sixteen consecutive eons looped in a Möbius strip, Lenny pulled away. His face, like the cat who caught the canary. "Guess the doctor's not coming for me today."

"Yeah?" I tried my most sincere attempt at a sultry smile as I tried to puzzle out whatever inane joke he was making now. Wished I could bathe in Clorox, do a shot of arsenic to destroy any trace of him. But the mission. The orange pills. Fleur's button nose, Trevor's metallic blue skin. "Why's that?"

"Apple a day keeps the doctor away," he beamed, happy with himself, his conquest.

"Well, Johnny Appleseed, now it's my turn for something sweet." I leaned in. "Got an angle on anything orange?"

"Easy there, Gimme Toulouse." The Royal Family lieutenant dragged two fingers inside his glass to grab the last smear of chocolate syrup. He sucked them clean.

"You said—"

"Everybody wants something." He laughed silently. "Have patience." He turned and walked back to the lounge.

I watched him go, imagining taking a machete, lopping off his bearded head, and placing it on a spike at the Ursuline Convent in the Quarter. I'd gotten closer, though. Closer to the Royal Family. Closer to the source. Lenny's saliva was still on my neck, steaming. If he kept his attention on me, it could be a bonus. A fast track to the inner sanctum.

But I'd just made a deal with a devil. And every devil collects.

23

WHATEVER THAT PERFORMANCE WAS—DIVINE deception, holy duty, low-key sex work—it left me spinning. Spun out. In the gross gas station bathroom on Elysian Fields, I traded Decker's boots and denim skirt for my nun garb. Gloves, pants, blouse, scarf.

My cringe elevated as my buzz faded. I decided to walk instead of summoning Decker for a ride back. Needed to get my head straight. Each step toward Engine 29 was heavier than the last. I hated that Moose was so upset with me earlier, on the phone. The perennial needle to thread, needing to see Moose, to be in the Walsh clan, while lying to his face. If he wasn't too pissed with me, maybe I could twist his arm into buying me dinner. My stomach rumbled. It was worth the risk of discovery. I needed creature comforts, and I needed them soon.

Cicadas echoed in the elaborate dark. I walked through the Bywater for fifteen minutes, past shotgun homes with tiny orchards in their front yards: quince trees, strawberry patches, rose hips, loquats, all distinct, even in the inky night. I noticed a tree with particularly ripe apricots dangling off. As I crossed the yard, I tripped over a root and tumbled face-first into a kiddie pool. Fully dunked. After I emerged, drenched, I still grabbed an apricot. I ate it quickly—better get the booze off my breath. Then I grabbed one more.

Post splashdown, with Decker's money in my pocket, I hailed a taxi. The driver's eyes in the rearview mirror widened at the sight of me, with my soaking scarf and wet hair and guitar case.

"Engine twenty-nine," I said, ending any possible conversation.

Moose was playing bourré when I found him. That rhythmic card game looked fast and competitive. Ideal combo for a Walsh. "Goose, what's wrong?" He slapped down a card. "You all right?"

I rubbed my eyes so hard I felt them slide back into my head. "Fine."

"Ya sure?"

"Just saying hi. Here's an apricot."

"Guys, this is the sister I complain about all the time. Goose, meet the guys."

The men kept their eyes and energies tied to their game, slapping more cards down and grunting a quiet smattering of heys without lifting their heads. Moose walked to the sink, washed the apricot, took a bite.

"I'm going on my break," Moose announced, then turned to me. "Let's get something more substantial to eat."

We walked down the block to the twenty-four-hour diner, Night Owl, with coffee that could make a corpse stand and testify. Moose and I had been there once before. The waitstaff should have been canonized for all the varieties of drunk revelers they'd served bottomless coffees.

"Hey, Gabe," said Miss Nora, a white woman in her late thirties with a crooked name tag and an excellent manicure. "Grab any table you like," she said. I was surprised she knew him by name and was glad—and a tinge jealous—he was regularly getting out, making friends, living life. He deserved it.

"Thanks." He nodded. "Any satsuma cake left or are we too late?"

"Right on time," she said.

"Two of those, please." He smiled at Miss Nora. "I'm paying, Goose. Order up."

"Sweet potato pancakes for me." I picked the first thing on the menu. "And a coffee, please." I needed the coffee to hit hard and hurt a little and make me want to punch back. "And a seltzer."

"Seltzer?" Moose smiled. "How refined. Though it's just anxious water."

I kicked him under the table and said "thank you" to Miss Nora, and, "God bless you."

"And bring my sister some last rites too, if you've any in the back," Moose added, which pulled a smirk from Miss Nora's mostly no-nonsense face.

"Fresh out of those, I'm afraid."

He leaned over the table and whispered. "Miss Nora's a gun-carrying mother of five who has a master's in anthropology and wears a different mix of power patterns and animal prints every time I'm here."

"Icon."

"If I wasn't as gay as a three-dollar bill, I might be in love with her."

"No way. I call dibs," I said.

"You got it. You need more fun, Goose. When's the last time you did anything for yourself? Something that didn't involve a fire or flood or some case?"

I opened my mouth to rib him in return, but he stopped me.

"Don't." He rotated the saltshaker. "You crack jokes instead of talking about real things. I never know how you're feeling, and it's tiring."

Such a serious man now. As a kid, Moose collected moonbeams in jars, convinced he could use them as night-lights. "Okay," I said. "Sorry. I'll try to be less hilarious." But I wasn't ready to tell him. I didn't want him to stop me, and it felt like if I could crack this before I took my permanent vows, it'd be okay. And I could have a fresh start. Moose sighed in response to my evasion.

"What's really going on?" he asked me. "Kinda late for a drop-in." Moose nodded at Miss Nora as she brought our coffee in thick mugs. Moose dumped two tablespoons of sugar in his and watched me, waiting. Miss Nora set down a gigantic seltzer. The cold bubbles scraped my throat as I drank.

"Any ODs today?" I asked, afraid of the answer.

"No, thankfully."

The ceiling fan loped in wobbly slow circles. Looked like it would spin to the floor at any moment. A transformer somewhere in New Orleans was on the edge of blowing. You could feel the staticky crackle in any old break. In any healing seam. A message sent from the future. Or the past.

"Now quit sidestepping," he said. "What's really up?"

"Besides seeing Prince, nothing new," I said. "But you know. All the things, all the time."

The chrome diner felt like being back in Brooklyn again, like being twenty and sharing drunk-serious rants at three in the morning, solving the world's problems over grilled cheese, fries, and hot coffee. Except now Moose and I weren't kids, and the problems were killing people.

"There's one thing that's been really nagging me," I added.

"What?" He twirled his arm hair in that absent-minded frenzy that drove me nuts.

"Bernard has been acting incredibly squirrely," I said. Not that I was anywhere close to rock solid. After my little tumble from the wagon, the undercover sideshow, I needed to make sense of just one thing.

Moose flicked me an unreadable look. "Yeah?"

"Yeah. And I found his lighter next to Fleur, that day in the gym. I'd never suspect Bernard of being involved in something so awful, but . . . he's acting off. So strange, just not *him*. Starting to think he—"

Moose waved his hands. "Hey. Hang on. You're a million percent wrong."

"How do you know?"

"I actually do know what's been up with him."

He was about to say more when the food arrived. I said a silent grace for the pancakes before drowning them in syrup. They were crisped on the edges but lazy and pillowy inside. I would've been happy to perish right there, on that plate. Moose's stack of pancakes was dusted with crushed pralines and topped with ladles of cream and butter, New Orleans–style. If you're going to sin, sin well. The satsuma cake rested between us like two shards of caramelized light. Sunbursts. I stuffed a forkful in my mouth and citrus bloomed in layers. The first taste was a little spicy, then it was a bright smack in the face, then, a warm hug.

"Wait," I said with my mouth full. "Spill it."

"We're dating," he said.

I stopped mid-chew. "You're *dating* Bernard? Bernard Pham? Our Bernard?" My voice reinvented his name each time I repeated it.

Moose blushed in a way I'd not seen in a while. Or ever. It made me want to laugh and fall apart and cry my throat bloody. It was real. Moose was really living. He'd stepped into his life. With someone amazing to boot. And there I was, lying to him and to everyone who mattered to me.

If pressed, Father Nathan and Riveaux'd say I was doing God's work, trying to stop drug dealers. But nobody knew I was getting blotto after midnight with a gang lieutenant lapping at my throat like an ungodly anteater.

"I'm really happy," I said, "for both of you. But why haven't you told me?" I took the last bite of the revelatory pancakes.

"We didn't want to tell you before we knew if it was serious. But it is, I think. You're not mad?" Moose asked, pouring more sugar into his coffee. The earnestness in his eyes startled me.

I shook my head. "Not mad. This explains why he's been so weird with me, aside from the Fleur of it all. And why you asked about Bernard on Monday."

"I knew it'd be tough on him," he said, "and I was right. He's been so upset. Just stares off into space. And then the lighter, which totally freaked him out. Like, what are the odds? But I know he lost that months ago. I even bought him a new one, because I'm sweet like that."

What an ace PI apprentice I was turning out to be. Training to track and investigate, but I'd completely missed love blooming right under my nose. Too wrapped up to notice subtle changes in my brother. An energized air about him. Easier smile. It was so clear, there, in the Night Owl. His joy was real. A comfort too. Compounded with the relief of knowing true-blue Bernard had only been hiding good news.

"See? I was right. There really *is* a God." I blessed myself. Since he and Dennis split, Moose's love life was as dry as the martinis Nina used to make. I preferred my martinis salty and dirty as tears.

"Guess you picked the right line of work."

"There's a major problem though," I said.

"Oh no." He set his mug down and gripped it hard. "What?"

"I'll have to get used to not being the center of your attention anymore."

Moose smiled. "You'll always be center stage."

"If Bernard can handle your weird pinky toe," I said, "he's a keeper."

"My feet are perfect, thank you. And you're so bad."

"I am." More than he knew. How dangerously alive I felt undercover. The beautiful and crazymaking high of lying, possibly breaking something. Sister Honor would classify this kind of thinking as Satan's honeypot; that curiosity was a fast track to hell. But wasn't the expectation to be good and obedient every minute of every day a failure of imagination?

Moose held his own face for a moment and scratched his fingers through his beard. "It's been hard, you know. Letting someone in."

Oh, I understood. Nina had obliterated my heart when she chose Nicholas. Not that it was ever that simple. Nothing was.

In a fit of fidgeting, Moose knocked over his coffee. The mug tumbled off the table but didn't break. "Sorry sorry sorry," he said as the coffee pooled.

"Let me." I grabbed napkins. As siblings we took turns being the fixer. We were both pros at mopping up messes.

I downed the rest of my coffee as Moose paid the bill, and we stepped out into the humid night. He stuffed cash into my gloved hand. "Taxi it back to the convent."

Before I could thank Moose for the miraculous food, cab fare, and the time with him, his phone buzzed. His entire magnetic field changed.

"An OD," he growled, "I'm on," and hurtled back into the firehouse.

Holy Mary, Mother of God. I get that you're out of miracles. But help a Sister out—don't let it be another student.

24

SATURDAY, 6 A.M. WAS there an almanac, a world record, for not sleeping? If I wasn't so wrecked, I'd have looked it up. I was gutted, bone tired, but the smell of Sister Laurel's chicory coffee helped me move. Her Saturday ritual started like always, by measuring grounds and saying the Angelus.

The sky awoke anxious, with bruised tones. I lay on my bed in my spartan convent room. My old digs in Brooklyn was a pit. Bras hanging on every doorknob. Fossilized tangerine peels. A cactus tall as the ceiling. A stolen traffic sign wearing my first leather jacket. Tampons and prayer cards and photos spilling from the same shoebox. Zines Scotch-taped to the wall. Patti Smith posters. Sticky bottles of black nail polish leaving lunar prints on the windowsill. A place to play guitar, sleep and not sleep. Random hookups. Countless nights in bed with Nina, with her intermittent handstands. Fueled by cheap coffee and cheaper whiskey.

The convent, in contrast, was a declaration of anti-pleasure. Or, rather, the luxury of freedom from superficial concerns. No mirrors. None of that savage union of fact and falsehood, reflection and distortion. Even before they were invented, mirrors stalked the human mind. Narcissus, undone by his own reflection. My bedroom wall was a shade of off-off-white that managed to be exceptionally blinding and bland at the same time. A single wooden cross praised itself above my narrow bed. My dresser leaned against one wall. Inside were my pajama set—the soothing color of a straitjacket—socks, underwear, bras, and the black scarves I used to cover my neck tattoos. My closet was mostly empty, apart from the rotation of five black blouses and five pairs of black trousers.

We mixed our weekend breakfasts with morning prayers. Sister Honor started her riff on Prime as I took my spot at the worn table. "*Gloria Patri, et Filio, et Spiritui Sancto.* Amen," Sister Honor said with her eyes closed. A bit of Latin kept it edgy. Looking at Sister Laurel's sweet face, I felt last night's whiskey bite back, the guilt burning my throat. I was disassembled. Nauseous. My body a runaway train. A tank engine that would never stop, never sleep.

Our little Lord Chucky, asleep on the hay.

The shower ran cold—always did. I brushed my teeth in the sink and then scrubbed my skin red in the numbing shower. After I wrapped up in a towel that hadn't quite dried on the clothesline, I dashed to my room and threw on my generic garb. The sun scored my sole window into a spotlight.

When the kitchen was free, I called Moose who had, thankfully, brought someone in the Ninth back from the brink with Narcan the night before. "No ties to Saint Sebastian's," he said, exhausted. A prayer answered.

Desperate to give Bernard a hug after Moose's reveal—and throttle him for not telling me himself—I walked to school. He usually mowed the grass on Saturdays, and I figured we could talk in privacy.

Even at 8 a.m., the heat was juicy. Sweat stippled my hairline. Catalpa trees rained neon blooms in the convent garden. I stepped over white and blue flowers as big as fists on the broken sidewalk. Sprays of sweet jasmine climbed the iron gates mischievously. A Bunny Bread delivery truck rolled by, lacing the air with butter.

Almost with indifference, like it had no choice, the wind poured through the fountain of the weeping willow. To my mind the most beautiful trees were the emotional ones. I touched the willow's bark as I had done so many times. I swore a small indentation had formed, a worn spot where my index finger rested, trying to feel the voice that connected it to the invisible pathway. The gardenias were so gentle they were loud. I knelt to inhale the black-pepper breath of nasturtiums, to make sure it was all real. That early summer heat. That TKO of a hangover. That ripe city.

The sky was striped with flat, thin clouds, and I followed the path into the school's central wing, surprised to see a light on in the weekend emptiness. As I reached my classroom—my shared classroom—I found Rosemary Flynn sorting through a stack of photographs, her back to me.

I moved closer to her, and in a quiet voice said, "Hello."

"Oh." Rosemary popped backward and her face flushed.

"Didn't mean to startle you," I said. "Didn't expect you here on a Saturday."

She gently rested the backs of her fingers to her cheeks, like she was checking for a fever. "I could say the same. What're you doing here?"

"Looking for Bernard," I said. "You?"

"Catching up with grading. After losing Fleur, almost losing Trevor, and some familial issues of my own, I can't seem to cross anything off my list." When she shook her head, her bangs didn't move. Not a strand out of place. Such quiet control.

"I know what you mean." A heavy breath left me before I realized it. I stared at the floor, following scuffs and shadows. Sure as hell didn't want to hear about any domestic drama with her Secret Agent Man, Alex. But Rosemary seemed low. Pulled down. The usual spark in her gunmetal gray eyes dimmed. "Hard to focus with everything going on," I said.

"Found these photos of my father the other day. He attended Saint Sebastian's in the late sixties."

"Hope he didn't have Sister Honor for religion." I imagined Mother Superior back in the day, buoyed by youth, spine straight as her ruler, in a crowded convent of more than twenty nuns.

"Look at how *young* he was." Rosemary held up an image. "He was just admitted to a memory care facility last week. Alzheimer's."

"I'm so, so sorry," I said, blessing myself, then glanced at the photo of her teenage dad outside the east wing. Time traveled with that face from the past. A piece of history, but the same glowing ferocity of teens like Fleur and Prince. He was forever sealed in that moment, grinning, proud. Personality clawing through the photo's paper and sheen. I remember that feeling. As a girl, I was a bottle rocket screaming into the sky. Unfair we can't get back to that age, before life dropped its anvils of truth on us. Before we learned how many ways a heart could break, how sharp the splinters could be. "He looks like the life of the party," I said.

"He could talk the stripes off a tiger."

Even in the black-and-white image, I could see where Rosemary got those dreamboat eyes. "Must run in the family."

Rosemary didn't smile at that, just released a deep sigh that seemed to relax her. She reached into a paper bag on her desk and pulled out a shiny cherry with a dark green stem. The cherry was perfect, so real it looked fake, the color of a drugstore valentine, lipstick kiss on a collar. She placed it in her mouth, then carefully deposited the pit in a petri dish. "Science says it's just neurons misfiring, tangled proteins. But then there's this—" She pointed to the crucifix on the wall. "The soul. Where does the soul go when brain functions stop, when the body fails?"

I was close enough to Rosemary to count her nose freckles. Close enough to react to the hitch in her breath. "The soul can't be measured by any equipment you have in the lab," I said. "It's a feeling, a mystery. Energy can neither be created nor destroyed."

"Can't argue with that."

"*You* can argue with anything."

"I draw the line at scientific law." Rosemary tilted her head, and the pale curve of her neck was unbearable.

"Science isn't my bag," I said, and took a seat on the piano bench. "Music is."

"Don't I know it," she said. "My dad loved music."

"What kind?"

"Jazz. Every type. Old, new—didn't matter really."

The ache in Rosemary's voice. I knew that pang. An absence that never stopped expanding. On impulse, before I could think it through, as instinctually as eyelashes closing in a blink, I reached out and caught Rosemary's hand in my gloved hand. Her fingers were long and slender, not like my hands, with my busted knuckles, tatts, and mutilated fingernails I had to hide. She didn't move her hand away.

"What was he like when you were a kid?"

She sat beside me on the keyboard bench, so close I could smell her rose perfume. So light and bracing. I let her hand go. "He worked double shifts cleaning at the airport." She bit her lower lip. "He'd spend half his paycheck at Louisiana Music Factory, then we'd eat red beans and rice for a week."

"Priorities." I pressed middle C, but the synthesizer wasn't on, so the key sank silently beneath my finger.

"And Sunday afternoons"—she smiled that sad smile again—"while the rest of the neighborhood was getting 'saved'"—she raised her hands—"we stayed home, on the porch, listening to his latest treasures. Jazz on Sundays. Scandalous."

"Heathens."

"Preacher walked by with his hellfire and damnation, and my dad just turned the music up louder." She laughed. "Every last neighbor was on our steps by sunset."

"Sounds fun."

"It was. Until Katrina came to town. I was fifteen at the time. Felt like everything got washed away."

"Except you."

"Except me," she said. "My dad rebuilt the house. He was good for a long time, until a few years ago. His mind's gone now."

"I'll pray for him, Rosemary," I said, and I meant it.

"Please do," she said, and I was slightly surprised. Her fingers hovered over the keys, cherry stains on her fingertips like red ghosts. I wanted to rip my heart out of my chest and present it to her still beating. Rosemary was the only woman in my new life who came close to making me feel how Nina did. Rosemary, who played aloof but dissected me with her eyes. Rosemary with her scientific formulas, her hypotheses, her precision.

Her voice slipped into my eardrums. But I wanted to feel all of her, not just her voice. Her body. The body is God's gift for us to enter the world, to feel ecstasy and bewilderment and pain. To feel life itself. Some saints told us our bodies were stained, weak, and flawed. That we could liberate the soul by denying the flesh what it wanted, subjugating physical cravings, whipping ourselves into salvation. But we met Christ in *human* form, as a helpless baby. An all-powerful God could have sent Christ in any shell, any packaging, as a twenty-foot colossus, as a volcano, but he didn't. Jesus was sent to us not just as spirit or ether or a beam of light, but as a tangle of muscle and joints. A body that was tortured for us. Jesus broke bread and he ate it. He drank wine and he slept and he dreamt. He wept real tears in Gethsemane. He felt the nails driven through his lifelines.

On that bench, with Rosemary's thigh against mine as she placed cherries on her tongue, my desire felt sacred. One soul reaching toward another soul through flesh.

For years I'd had to be like Mary, like Saint Lucy, women you can see or hear but never touch. Because it's scary to want something. It's terrifying to dream and dream and dream, just to wake up in the dark, reaching for what you can't grab hold of. Rosemary was too good for that snitch Alex, but was I any better? She was too smart to get buried under my avalanche. No matter how she tempted me. Or I tempted her.

But could one bite be so bad?

I blinked back to the present moment. "I have to go," I said.

"I should be grading." She stood and smoothed imaginary wrinkles from her pencil skirt. Ever the picture of poise and confidence. Not the whore or the Madonna, but both. We all were. The scripts written for us girls, gals, dames, nasty women, sluts, angels, goddess-mothers—the tropes that predated us and would outlive us, if men in power stayed in power. Spoiler alert, they're locked in until the end.

"Thank you for asking about my dad," she said, and sent a look from beneath her tidy bangs. The light turned her eyes to quicksilver. "Most people don't know what to say, so they say nothing. But it was nice to talk." Then and there, Rosemary Flynn had never been more real to me. Too real. And, like so many heaven-sent things, I left her behind.

Hail Mary, full of grace. Keeper of lost causes. The you who knew a celestial announcement meant earthly pain. I need you.

No more wallowing in what-ifs and could-have-beens. I had work to do.

■

I left Riveaux a quick voicemail telling her I'd be busy that night. "Father Robin Hood needs me," I lied. "You do your internet sleuthing, and I'll pray we don't end up on an FBI watch list."

I did chores for the rest of the day. Polished the wood into gleaming mirrors, high on lemon Pledge. Dusted picture frames and statues. I swept, mopped, and washed sheets. Cleaned the church stained glass, pane by pane. My eye to Mary's eye. The worship of breaking my body. Until it was Tammy time.

25

IN MY NUN UNIFORM, I slipped out the kitchen's side door. I held my guitar case tight as I crossed the shadowy seam of the courtyard. In the low light each brick looked demonic.

I let Decker know my plan for the night as I changed in a gas station bathroom. She sent a generous *OK* in reply. Twice as long as her usual *K*.

"There's the apple of my eye," Lenny said as I walked into Up in Smoke. I was barely through the door when he turned me around and led me outside. "Got a surprise."

"A pony? You shouldn't have."

"This is better."

"Sweet ride," I said, as we approached a cobalt abomination of a sports car. A piranha on wheels. Louisiana license plate 2ND2NO1. *Second to no one?* Wow. Subtle. What would Decker advise here? Getting into the car of the Royal Family's arrogant lieutenant, the same dude who went to town on my neck like a billy goat at a salt lick, was dubious at best. But I was on a mission, and increased access was worth the risk. The suede seat was so soft it was dry. I imagined it shedding all over the ass of Tammy's black jeans.

"Corvette," Lenny said, chin high. "Stingray."

"Sick."

With no back seat in that clown car, my guitar case rode in the trunk, my Guild uniform still warm inside. The presence of a newspaper in the car, *The Times-Pic*, surprised me. Didn't take Lenny for a reader. But I had a minor seizure when "She's Like the Wind" came on and Lenny started singing. Were both the car and bar loaded with his personal, punishing playlists? Or was God screwing with me? In a voice like a cement burn, Lenny belted out, "She's out of my league."

League? Like I played by any rules. *League.* He didn't know the half of it.

"Smooth suspension right here." He patted the dashboard with his big hands. Mitts that could crush and crack and choke things. "I love driving." He gripped the wheel. "You?"

"If I had a ride like this. Or any ride at all."

"I know people who can hook you up." Cars and drugs. Lenny sure was a jack-of-all-trades. He was looking straight ahead, but I could still feel Lenny observing me, analyzing, taking note. "You in the market?"

"Not for a Stingray, but sure."

At the red light, Lenny grabbed a lounge matchbook from the glove box, his elbow grazing my thigh. He scribbled something on the inside of the flap and handed it to me. At first it looked like a child's squiggles. Then I saw the 504. Local area code. His phone number? Or a friend of the Family?

"Like I said, I know people," he said, gunning it when the light turned green, "who can set you up with something good."

"Mr. Popular," I said, my new nickname for him. I'd be texting those digits to Decker soon. "Thanks."

"Don't lose it. Good deals don't last."

Through the windshield, New Orleans performed its nightly surrender to darkness. We drove down streets tourists never saw. Past sad oceans of concrete and dogwood petals so pink they cast polka-dot echoes. At the edges and in the center of it all was black. The black night. Black was a blessing—a smudged cross on the forehead during Lent. Only darkness births stars. Black is God showing us that nature holds secrets. Nina's black lipstick. My black boots, black jacket, blue-black ink sewn into my skin. Father Nathan's black-and-white collar. If I survived the mystery tour with Lenny, a black habit would soon tell the world I was a bride of Christ. Black wasn't absence—it was power distilled. In a country bleached of meaning—Botoxed and over-filtered into a facade—darkness was honest. Every shadow was a shelter. A way home.

We pulled up to a club in Saint Roch. At first glance it looked abandoned. Second-floor windows boarded up. But inside was a teeming mass. Unwashed bodies and big moods. The tile as slick as a slaughterhouse floor. Even the peeling concert flyers were crying. Toner running in streaks of coal tears.

I shouldered my way through the crowd, and everywhere I looked, the past and present barreled into each other. Drunks, lanky mall punks, real cut-up hard kids, and trust-fund-suckling nepo babies. Like any given night in the East Village.

Lenny left to grab drinks but it was also a business trip. I watched him work the room. A quick nod to the bouncer. A passing whisper with a pompadoured dirtbag near the DJ booth. He was Ren's second-in-command, which meant he let others down the food chain work the mean streets as he sipped his Chablis. Including whoever it was who'd served the kids at Saint Sebastian's. Did Lenny care how old the buyers were? Did he care who died next? What did he care about other than his Stingray, white wine, and music from the deepest circle of hell?

As Lenny liaised with potential clientele, a mohawked girl in Docs crashed into me.

"Shit, sorry." She grabbed my arm. "Everything's upside down."

"Easy does it," I said, trying to keep her upright. "You okay?"

"Just have the spins."

For a second, I saw myself in her, and I prayed quietly. A silent Hail Mary.

"What'd you take?" I asked.

"What didn't I take?" She started swaying, eyes fluttering, a woozy jumble of a person. I prayed harder. Then I said *fuck it*. "Let's get you some fresh air." I hobbled with her to an exit, looked around for Lenny, hoping he hadn't seen us. Not that he'd lose his shit over Tammy helping someone. But I didn't want to draw attention to myself. This girl was loaded though, and really needed support.

Once we were outside, I propped her against the tagged brick wall. "Throw it all up, kid." I held her hair back as she retched. "Drive it from your body," I said, like we were exorcising Beelzebub. She hurled and shook, tears soaking her face.

After two vile and exceptionally fragrant minutes, she stood up straight and wiped her mouth with the back of her hand. "Jesus, that was rancid."

"Been there plenty myself," I said. I wanted to grill her. Have her detail exactly what she took and where she got it, but she needed care, not an interrogation. Plus, asking too many questions could blow my cover.

"Sorry for ruining your night."

"Takes a lot more than that," I said.

"Thanks for the help. You're a godsend."

A godsend. A nun. Tammy. Who was the real me or the fake me?

I walked the girl back inside. "Thanks again," she said as she disappeared into the fray.

A minute later, Lenny popped up with two drinks, his white wine and a whiskey for me. Neat as a pin. "Been looking for you," he said. "Thought you bailed."

"And miss all the glitz and glamor?" I gestured to the squalor of the club. The moldy bar rag air and weeping walls. The floor had to be sentient, based on the sheer amount of bodily fluids feeding it.

He laughed hard, like he was trying to dislodge a chicken bone, like it was life or death. Lenny was an asshole who facilitated the sale of lethal pills to kids, but at least he laughed at my bad jokes. He sipped his white wine and said, "Good thing I didn't bring you here for the ambiance."

"We're here for what, then?"

A stunning woman in a dress made entirely of duct tape danced into someone banging their head, sending a beer bottle crashing onto the syrupy floor.

"Damn, Tammy's all business tonight," he said. Lenny talking about me—the fake me—in the third person made me want to drop-kick him. Restraint. Breath. Decker's training. One, two, three, four. "How 'bout I sweeten the deal? Ran into the candy-man earlier."

"Candy sounds dandy." I held out my hand, palm up.

He carefully set down a white pill and his ogre fingernails scraped my gloveless skin. "This is the good shit."

"What is it?" I stared at it. A miniature full moon. A tiny big bang, ready to detonate.

"Don't want to ruin the surprise." He checked his pager.

"Where's this Willy Wonka anyway? Think he might have something in a nice shade of orange?"

"Orange?" He shook his head. "This right here is the money shot."

"You gonna partake?" I looked at the tablet—the dot of the *i* in pain. "Can't let the lady dance alone."

He smiled with too many teeth. "Not tonight. You'll have plenty of fun for both of us."

My dread and excitement swirled with Decker's cautionary words. Our training. My vows. I kept staring at the pill. How could something so small stop a heart?

The section of my brain dedicated to rational thinking screamed at me to stop, drop, and roll, to crush that mother-fucker of a pill under my heel, to walk—*run*—away. I hadn't touched drugs for so long. I'd made promises. I'd be making more promises next Sunday.

But the other part, the animal part, said *yes*. The elemental me that chased oblivion. I'd asked Lenny for drugs, and he delivered. Mission possible. Plus, I doubted it'd be lethal if it had made its way up the Family tree.

A bitter squeal scratched my tongue as I dry-swallowed the mystery pill.

I felt it sink into my insides. And then, about twenty minutes later, the length of Team Dresch's *Personal Best*, like falling backward into a pool, the real world disappeared, and I started rolling. Silent thunder hummed behind my eyelids.

My hands dripped disco balls as I moved them, mesmerizing trails of sparkler light. My brain blinked like it'd been maced. Each thought was a glow-in-the-dark star from my childhood bedroom ceiling. Music pinched the air, then dyed my veins the silver-gold of a sun-shower.

Lenny said, "Seeing double yet?" His face stretched, auto-tuned.

"I'm seeing everything twice except for what matters."

"What you looking for, exactly? Thought you were here to have fun?"

I tried to say something coherent, something Decker would rubber-stamp, that Father Nathan would approve of, but my tongue was wrapped in cellophane. My ribs throbbed with each heartbeat, but I was alive, so free, living the mission twice, as me and as Tammy.

I tried to clock Lenny, watch him. But I was also watching the door. Watching every door. Each foot tapping. Eyes too wired to blink. I was the deer unable to dislodge itself from the silent roar of the headlight.

My first high since Brooklyn, and I was the same old tangle of limbs. I wanted to grab the duct-tape woman next to me, wrap one arm around her waist, grab a fistful of her hair and kiss her. I wanted her to hold me like an infant and sing to me, to tell me it was going to be okay. I wanted to climb onto the stage and dive into the crowd, feeling a hundred strangers lifting me.

The future, present, and past were all there as I rolled in that grimy club. Time lost its spine and its forward thrust. It spiraled into a crown of thorns, then a lava lamp from Spencer's, and then it became pure sound. And every color.

As the room carouseled, the duct-tape woman turned to me and said, "Your pupils are eating your face, sweetie." Her mouth was a heart-shaped perfume bottle, and her breath smelled expensive. Very expensive. "You okay?" Her hands were surprisingly strong on my shoulders.

"Honestly, never better," I replied, and truly meant it.

"Dance with me." She pulled me into the swarm of bodies, and every motion left contrails in the air. Her hands found my hips, steadying me when the floor tilted. I was winged and weightless. The woman was perfect. A perfect riddle. Her laughter, a chain around my neck.

Up and down I swung on a swing of rapture. I was Eve and I was Lilith. Every cedar miracle in Psalms. I was every sin in Leviticus. I was a bonfire and holy water and a Communion wafer melting on my tongue. A rosary bead tickling my stomach.

Until the ride of the high bucked me straight to the ground. And reality came crashing back.

A man in a navy suit stood out from the swarm and walked toward the exit. Was it the candyman? The owner of the club? Ren? Was he even really there? Was I really there? The ground rippled under me like someone had tossed a stone in still water. I shoulder-checked my way through the crowd to follow the suit, bodies both solid and liquid, trying to keep navy in view. Until someone grabbed my wrist—Lenny.

"Little girls' room's the other way," he said.

I yanked my arm free and shifted course, bumping into a speaker, stumbling toward the club's criminal tribunal of a bathroom. My stomach flipped as I crashed through the door and fell onto the piss-wet tiles. Felt like I was about to heave my guts up, into the apocalyptically stained toilet bowl. But I didn't. By some miracle my stomach settled, and my insides stayed inside. I sat, breathing slowly, the back of my head pressed against the sticker-covered wall, trying to anchor myself inside the spin. I had to look up, not down. Definitely not left or right.

I studied the underside of the empty paper towel dispenser until I managed to stand.

At the sink, cold water on my face felt miraculous. I dried my hands on Tammy's jeans, a human towel. Tammy wasn't in the mirror. It was me, but a me pulled from an archive.

Back near the bar, Lenny said, "Didn't take you for a lightweight."

"I'm good," I lied, "just had some sketchy leftovers earlier."

Each blink produced a new frame of the story. The club. Me. Lenny.

Whatever Lenny had put in my palm, the Royal Family menu item, was a fueled-up jet with no landing gear. A spectacular high with the comedown of a cheap shrapnel bomb. Nails, screws, and ball bearings packed into a pressure cooker, designed to shred. Raw and merciless.

I looked for my duct-tape dance partner again, but she was gone. Her touch had felt more real than anything in my life.

Was there any truth left in me? Or was I just a walking lie? Only the void at my core knew for sure.

26

OUTSIDE, MY SHADOW STRETCHED out before me, then behind me, then split in two. After a Solo cup of water, I had pulled myself together, back from the astral plane. Lenny and I now huddled in the shadow of Saint Roch's bell tower and passed a joint back and forth.

I'd lost track of the cumulative sum of my relapses, which added up to bad math. Not your typical devotional practice one week before taking forever vows. Going undercover was my Rumspringa.

"You really know how to work it on the dance floor." Lenny grinned like he'd just found extra fries at the bottom of the bag. "Tammy the twerker."

"All of those moves were the candy's, not mine. This weed's more my speed," I said.

"I know how to show a lady a good time." A big stretch made him shiver, and I saw the gun in its usual spot, tucked into the small of his back behind his belt.

Night deepened. The streetlight melted a gloss over every haunted corner, every chained-up bike wheel. Every delectable petal. I ran my fingers along the bricks and peeled moss away.

Lenny's eyes were the color of bleeding gums. "Ever wonder"—he passed the joint—"why we're here?"

"In New Orleans?"

He smiled and swatted a mosquito. "No, *here*. Alive."

"Yeah. All the time," I said, "but it sure beats not being here." In my mind's eye I saw my mom. Fleur.

The new, chiller high crept through the web of my veins. The weed was strong but soft. It padded the comedown and blurred all the razor-sharp edges. Drugs and prayer served similar functions sometimes. They both let me hover in a corridor below or above awareness, where all realities were possible. Part of me fought to stay alert, to fake inhaling from that joint, but I needed Lenny to buy Tammy. To trust her—*me*. To cozy up to the Royal Family so I could take them down, one by one. Top to bottom. From Lenny and Ren to the jackasses peddling counterfeits to kids.

The drugs had made everything at once surreal and too real. Couldn't help but laugh hysterically at the absurdity of the moment. A lesbian nun getting high with a light-rock-loving thug who, as deranged as it was, as crazed as it was, had started to feel like one of the Gowanus Boys back home who'd let me bum cigarettes. We'd talk about music waiting for a bus or huddled under an awning waiting for the rain to clear. Funny how just waiting for the next moment to arrive creates some of the most indelible memories.

Lenny seemed amused by my unhinged laughter. "I gotta say, you're not like everybody else."

"Yeah?"

He took another hit. "We're a lot alike."

"Pool sharks, great at smoking." I took a deep drag.

He smiled. "That's why I'm gonna let you in on a secret"—he looked over his shoulder—"but if you breathe a word of this to anyone, I know lots of ways to slice up a Red Delicious." He exhaled through his nose. "Clear?"

My skin prickled with fear—the whiplash of jumping to the worst-case scenario. My default setting. I envisioned ants crawling over my future grave, worms oozing through the eyeholes of my skeleton.

"Clear as crystal," I said.

"So, here's the deal. If everything goes to plan," he said, "I'm moving up in the world real soon."

"What world?"

Again Lenny glanced right then left as if the roaches might snitch. "Ever hear of the Royal Family?"

"Like Prince William and Kate Middleton? You in line for the *crown*?"

He shrugged. "In a manner of speaking. But not those royals." He leaned in close. "The Royal Family runs a lot of operations in this city."

Taking it all in with a relaxed face, I said, "Guessing from the Stingray, the Royal Family's not a nonprofit."

"Far from it." He put on that dumbass smile, like he was getting a blow job.

"What kind of operations?" I exhaled a smoke ring. "Girl Scout cookies? Tupperware parties?"

"Don't be cute." He ran his tongue over his teeth.

"Can't help it." I bumped his shoulder with mine. "Look at me." He blushed five shades of red.

"So, the thing is, I'm getting a promotion." He laughed. "Nuh-uh. I'm *taking* a promotion. They have no idea what's coming."

If the second-in-command had plans for upward mobility, things weren't looking too sunny for Ren. Maybe the Royal Family needed some family counseling.

I had to update Decker immediately. And I had to tell Riveaux as much as I could, without revealing my source. The Royal Family's lieutenant was about to launch a coup.

Decker's caution be damned, my theory was bearing out: Cultivating intimacy with Lenny, a romantic gangster whose club played Toni Braxton and Color Me Badd, was getting us somewhere.

"When're you moving on up?" I asked.

"Real soon." He cracked his knuckles against his chin.

"Sounds serious."

"Taking no prisoners. Hold tight." He looked at his phone. "I'm getting a call."

The high made everything too sharp, too real, too slow. After Lenny strolled to the corner, his phone to his ear, those words remained, *no prisoners*. I drifted to images of Fleur. The birthdays she would miss, tilting her head and smiling for photos—good side forward—as the crowd sang that awkward-ass happy birthday song. Pretending to not make wishes but making them anyway. The festivals and parades, dehydrated from day-drinking, the miracle of feeling the sun on your face. The pizza parties and road trip sing-alongs and bleary-eyed check-ins at gross hotels. The anniversary dinners at the Italian restaurant with the nice tablecloths. Taco Tuesdays, new sneakers, *A Christmas Carol* on Christmas Eve. I played the imaginary tape forward. All the major joys and gutting sorrows, all the mundane and forgettable moments, growing up and getting old around the dining room table. All the large and small things that give our lives shape, chapter headings, and reasons to say *wow*.

Lenny returned from his call but didn't sit back down. The vibe shift was immediate, hard, an instant freeze, not just on his face but his entire aura. Maybe Ren'd put him in his place, gave a verbal swat on the nose. "Let's get back to the lounge. Wanna show you something."

"You've shown me a lot already," I said, in character, patting the spot next to me. "Much rather hear about those moves you're making."

"Let's go."

His flat tone let me know it wasn't up for debate. Fine. I'd play along and pry him for info on his home turf. I walked ahead of him, hand on my burner, letting my body soften. I knew Lenny was watching me, closer than ever before. Could he feel the lies rumbling around inside? But I didn't look back. Looking back turned you to salt.

Lenny drove crazily from the club, then insisted on carrying my guitar case for me as we reentered Up in Smoke. I'd never been there this late, 3 a.m. the Bud Light clock on the wall told me, and the hookah lounge was empty save for the bartender, me, and Lenny who sat on a stool that screeched every time he so much as breathed. My elbows stuck to the scarred wood of the bar top.

He raised an intimidating glass of white wine to his mouth and pounded it back. Surely an entire box of Franzia in one vessel. His eyes caught mine in the cracked mirror behind the bar. "Been thinking about your 'Gimme Toulouse' cover. Said you played it in Memphis?"

"Huh? Yeah. They loved that tune." I was blinking one eye slightly more than the other but I couldn't stop it.

"When you first mentioned it, I got a kick out of it. You know why? My cousin Spider—he wrote that song." The bar light hit Lenny's wine with a blaze, a soul had just slipped inside it. He traced the tip of his finger carefully around the rim of his glass.

"Small world." I felt like I'd just been dropped through an elevator shaft. The savage quickness of the change in temperature and pressure. The gun in his belt ready and waiting.

"Thing is. Spider plays it in the lounge on occasion, but mostly on Frenchman. Plays on the corner too. Maybe you've seen him? The guy with the mandolin."

"Lots of guys with mandolins around."

"But there's a problem. So, Spider's never *left* Louisiana. He's got that condition where you don't like new places and you can't travel far. What's it called?"

"Being American?"

He let out one sharp inhale or a laugh, couldn't tell. "Spider just gave me a call back at the club. I mentioned you—my new little friend who loves 'Gimme Toulouse.'"

"First cousin or, like, twice removed?" I asked, trying and failing to derail Lenny. Didn't like the look in his eye.

Ignoring my question, he said, "You know what he told me? Turns out that song, it's a local legend. But no one else even knows it, just Spider."

"Music travels wherever it pleases. Music is *free*." I refrained from drinking more whiskey to preserve any quick thinking I had left. "I have absolutely played that song. Fan favorite."

"How'd you even learn it?"

"I'm a quick study. Got one of those ears where I hear a song once and pick it right up." I scratched my throat which was suddenly unbearably itchy. Eve screaming. The apple pulsing a warning.

"Then let's hear it. Let's hear 'Gimme Toulouse.'" His *s* had a distinct slur. He was piss drunk. "Play it right now. You got your guitar."

"All right, showtime. Won't even make you pay a cover." I got on the ground with the case, full well knowing it held my nun uniform and no guitar. I had to milk it, drag it out, click open the latches one by one. Let Lenny think my fingers were clumsy with whiskey. His fishbowl of Chablis perched on the edge of the bar like an invitation. Like blood becoming sacred. Transubstantiation in the Bywater. And then I opened the case, making sure the lid blocked his view of its contents. "Ah, damn," I said, like a foul-mouthed kitten who lost their mitten, as I pulled out one of my spare strings I had blessedly left in the case. "Looks like my G string wasn't too happy in your trunk. It broke."

"Huh?" Lenny asked as I handed him the string. I settled back in on my stool, the guitar case still unlatched but closed, letting my knee bump the bar, sending the wine glass into a wobble. Almost there. I reached to grab the string back, making sure my elbow caught his glass. "Oh shi—"

The Chablis tsunami hit him and he jumped up.

"Jesus! Sorry." I reached for napkins and yelled to the bartender who was off in the back. "Some help over here."

"These pants are dry-clean only."

"Quick, to the bathroom. Cold water before it sets." I cashed in my gambit by latching up the case and moving it out of eyeshot.

He looked utterly helpless with wine dripping from his crotch. "Song first."

"With a broken string? No can do. Spider'd never forgive me." I shook my head and followed it up with an *oh well* shrug.

"You're full of shit."

"Relax." I couldn't dial my voice down lower if I tried. "You're full of wine." Lenny looked back at me, helpless. He was an afterthought of a guy with delusions of grandeur. A middle man. He was a sad loser, but he also once was a scared little boy, with a pair of worn-out lucky socks or a pet rock or whatever.

Pride finally won him over. As he staggered off to the restroom to unstain his crotch, I grabbed my case and sprinted out of the godforsaken hookah hole. I called Decker from the street as I hauled ass. My lungs were on fire. Had to make it fast.

"What?" Decker's voice punched me through the phone.

"Royal Family drama. Lenny's making a move"—I took a breath—"says he wants to take over the whole op."

"Put Ren out to pasture?" she asked.

"Seems like it."

"The loyal lieutenant pulling the rug out."

"He tested me tonight, hard." I scanned the street behind me, saw only an orange cat crab-crawling under a car.

"You pass?"

"Pretty sure I'm burned."

"Great." Decker's voice was barbed wire through the phone. I could feel her knuckles around her cell phone. "Just fucking great."

"And he kinda made me do a hit. Just one pill but it was—"

"A hit?" The explosion of her voice. "You ingested drugs from a mark?"

I rubbed my eyes so hard I worried I pulled out an eyelash. "What was I supposed to do?"

She exhaled. "Think before you act."

"I wasn't going to tank the case when we're just getting started," I said.

"Won't matter if you're dead in the gutter. Go to the Circle K on Kentucky." I felt her growl. "I'll be there soon."

Outside the gas station, my body shook as I sat against the wall and wretched on the sidewalk. Sweat burned my eyes. My duet with Tammy was done, but I'd scored. Decker might not think it was enough, but I had intel. A coup in the works. And, for the first time since meeting Tammy, Lenny'd lost his cool. What would he remember in the morning?

Before any clarity, there was a hand, and skinny white legs. Some guy in grubby jean shorts and an Insane Clown Posse T-shirt grabbed at my guitar case, but I wouldn't let go. "There's nothing of value here," I said, but the Juggalo moved at me again, shoved my case against the brick wall, hard. Each letter inked on my left knuckles sang with pain. I finally posted up and hit the clown with the case—one smooth, holy swing, socking him squarely in the sacraments. The Juggalo fuck bellowed and galloped off as I crumpled on the ground. I must have looked ridiculous, monstrous. S-O-U-L bled into the night. Even my shadow tried to run away.

27

A FEW HAIL MARYS later, Decker rolled up to the gas station, an annoying angel in a practical car. "You look like shit."

"Bad comedown and worse luck," I said, leaning through the passenger window to talk to her. The world spun and my legs gave out. I was so light and unsteady, I felt like a hallucination of a human. Had to hold onto the car to stay upright.

"I'm taking you to the hospital to get a once-over. God only knows what was in that pill you took." Decker's face set hard. "You could die from that shit. You *know* that."

"But I feel fine now."

"You don't look fine."

"My brother's an EMT; he'll fix me up."

"So, you're not fine then?" Decker's eyes flashed, and I could see two or three rants forming in that head of hers, but she didn't push any further. I tossed my guitar case in the beige back seat.

We drove through the city, dodging frat boys and conference tourists in lanyards and bachelorette parties that dappled the streets. I prayed Moose would be home and I kept replaying, *Vengeance is mine; I will repay, saith the Lord.* Romans 12:19.

That was the problem with the New Testament. Too much forgiveness—not enough fire and brimstone. The God of floods and locusts spoke to me that day. The God of salt pillars and smited firstborns.

In front of Moose's house in the Marigny, Decker and I hobbled to the door slowly, dejected, empty, like gamblers who just tanked it and lost their rainy day money at roulette. Pink house numbers gleamed under the porch light. I knocked and knocked. For a moment I panicked, thinking I'd have to make a trip to Urgent Care. But the door gently opened.

"Jesus Christ, Goose." Moose shuffled in his slippers. Fancy. I'd never seen him in slippers before. Just like Dad's. "What's going on?"

"She's all yours," Decker said, then walked away shaking her head.

"Bernard here?"

"No. What are you wearing?" He made way for me to enter, and I headed straight into his foyer. "What's happening?"

"So, don't worry, but I've been undercover, and I took some kind of pill."

"*Drugs?*"

"And I fucked up my hand." I presented my bloody knuckles.

For somewhere between four and six minutes, Moose refrained from lectures and commentary. In the spotless kitchen, he worked on my wound quickly, efficiently, and quietly, like I imagined he did in the army. I cursed when he poured peroxide on my knuckles. Not the unholy grind of nerve or bone pain. But antiseptics kissing an open wound was no fun.

When he finished cleaning and bandaging my hand, he presented me with a bottle of Smartwater and two pills. "Take these." Over the counter to combat under the counter.

We walked into his living room. Track lights clicked on in sequence as we moved through the space. So spare. Not like my convent, though, more like a mod furniture showroom in DUMBO.

I sat on the leather sofa. "Thanks."

"You're not getting off that easy. Drugs? *Undercover?*" He sat next to me and slouched. "That's why you've been so weird?"

"I have to stop the supply."

"You took *fentanyl*?"

"No. Just Molly. At least, I'm pretty sure it was Molly." I sounded so far away, even from myself. "My students are over-dosing, and I have to stop it."

"Getting yourself killed helps them how?" The anger-as-love show was grade-A Walsh sibling repertoire.

"Not exactly part of the plan."

"You could've told me about this before," he said.

"So you'd tell me to stop?" I asked.

He grunted. "I would've had your back. Like Easter. Like now."

"Sorry," I said, but I didn't have the energy for another dressing down. "Take me home?"

"You should change first," he said, frustrated.

"Let's just go now."

On our ride from Moose's to the convent, I was captive to his meandering monologue about wound care and honesty. I said "I'm sorry" and "I know" sixteen hundred times. It reminded me of all the apologizing I'd done. How many times I convinced my brother I'd meant it. Convinced myself.

Once, I shared a hospital room with an addict so gone, with a stampeding need so raw, the only place they could give him an

IV was the bottom of his foot. That was my path until I changed course. And then the course changed on me.

Every drop of whiskey at Up in Smoke had fucked more than my sobriety. Every sip a gigantic cannon of self-sabotage, a middle finger to Father Nathan, my Sisters, and the permanently binding vows I was supposed to swear next week.

Jesus said, *Take me in, I'm yours. I need you as much as you need me.* At least that's what I felt in my soul in the hard pew with my face in my hands every Sunday, electrified after eating the son of God, after drinking his blood. Everyone who received Holy Communion became another Mary with another sacred being inside. Transubstantiation was as desperate and real and true for me as the living ember of the sun. That's what my bandmates back in New York and the scumbag Opus Dei fucks always missed. Religion was personal. Private. No one had the right to tell anyone what they should think or feel. No one, not the bishop, not the pope, not the president, could dictate what I believed.

At the red light, my vision drifted to a live oak. Its gnarled branches and roots dripping color. Prayer cloths, Mardi Gras beads, memorial ribbons tied to places where a loved one shed their mortal coil. The color story of a thousand different people, a thousand different wishes. Each bead, every shred a monument. If those scraps could weather the storm, so could I.

Finally, the campus was visible through the windshield. Then the convent. The home of the Sisters of the Sublime Blood. My home.

"Promise me," Moose said as we parked.

I sighed. "No more undercovering."

"That's right. If you are even tempted to do this again, call me first. I'd rather know even if I can't stop you. And don't fucking lie to me. I'm too worried. You'll make me go bald like Dad."

"Much easier to maintain," I said. "But I promise."

Sister Laurel appeared as Moose helped me inside. Her insomnia worked in my favor that night. She looked so tired, as if she'd been waiting at the window like some lovelorn sailor's wife. She shook her head at the sight of me. "Lord have mercy. Get in quick before Sister Honor sees you. You look like you've gone ten rounds with the devil." She blessed herself.

"I stopped counting after the eleventh."

"I'm not even going to ask." Her buzzed eyes danced slightly up at the corners.

"Good idea," Moose said, and gave Sister Laurel some knuckle care instructions. Seeing Moose interact with one of my Sisters was a small comfort. Family.

I noticed Sister Laurel's brightly colored socks, the pair she wore at least once a week, claiming they kept her toes smiling. "You've got more guts than sense, my dear," she said, "and a heart too big for this world. Don't forget that you aren't as alone as you think. Go and rest now." Sister Laurel made the sign of the cross—up, down, left, right—over my bent head.

The quiet moment was capsized when Sister Honor whirlpooled into the foyer. Moose blocked me strategically so my Mother Superior wouldn't see the bandage on my gloveless hand.

"Where on earth have you been?" Her voice could have made a hurricane apologize and turn back. "And why in God's good and perfect name do you look as if you have just ridden on the back of a cloven beast in a rodeo?" Her rageful eyes lasered all over me and the Tammy jacket. She could not have possibly blinked harder.

I forced a smile so fake it pinched a nerve in my jaw. "I was offering spiritual support at the encampment. One of the folks has a job interview tomorrow, asked if we could exchange outfits."

"The Christian choice," Sister Laurel said, covering for me. She then led Sister Honor into the kitchen so I could walk upstairs. "God's presence was particularly *vital* tonight," I heard her saying.

Moose and I looked at each other and laughed. Finally, the tension between us had broken. He squeezed my shoulder and I play-punched him. A pretend hit with genuine affection.

"Get some rest, Goose. I'll swing by tomorrow," he said, then left.

Sister Honor's sourpuss announced that she was clearly unsatisfied, but, thankfully, she seemed unwilling to pursue my lie. Perhaps she could tell I'd taken enough licks for one night. For a lifetime.

28

SUNDAY CREPT IN LIKE a slow-boiling fever. It was a clear day, except for one quick-moving summer storm. Rain came and went fast, pounding the stained glass so hard the saints appeared to duck, lightning stabbing sideways behind Mary's translucent eye.

The drug-addled club, the spat with Decker, the heart-to-heart with Moose, the close calls with Lenny and Sister Honor, and wiry sleeplessness compromised the usual peace of morning Mass. My double life was crushing me. Graduation in five days. Vows in a week. The world spun faster than prayer could keep up.

"From the Gloria," I said to our small church choir, eyes fixated on the pew where Prince and BonTon slept during the Easter lock-in. We'd track him down again soon enough. At least I knew Father Nathan had his eye on him.

Our holy water fonts seemed to levitate. Prayer lives in that space too, between knowing and terror, between the pause and restart of breath.

After Mass, after the congregants and my Sisters and Father Nathan left, I stayed behind.

My bones ached, knuckles still raw, but I had to keep busy. I kept my left glove on, scrubbed the marble floors, and washed the baseboards until my kneecaps burned almost as much as my hand. I polished the pews to a sleek shine, until a haggard ghoul with hair like burnt straw stared back at me. My reflection. Just a few days late on the ask from Sister Honor, but after last night's close call, it was time to suck up a bit.

Then, a voice tumbled and echoed from the main door to the altar. "Hello! Anybody home in this house of the Lord?"

I looked up to find Trish Dempsey in the vestibule, blond hair sprayed to Jesus, mascara already running at eleven in the morning, bubblegum-pink earrings to match her sling. My white cloth fell to the floor.

"Oh, well, *there* you are, Sister Holiday. Just who I wanted to see."

"I rarely hear that." I gripped the pew's edge. Couldn't let on. Not one centimeter of knowing. Last time I saw Trish, she'd lied to my face. Why? Did she know her son was in a domestic abuse shelter? Was she protecting him? "What's up?"

"Haven't seen hide nor hair of my boy this weekend."

"You mean he's not at home?" I knew he wasn't, but I needed her to do the talking.

"In fact, he's not, and I'm worried sick. I called that private-eye-whoever lady, from the card. She said to talk to you. Said y'all saw him Friday night. But she wouldn't tell me where, like I don't have the right to know the location of my own child, my literal flesh and blood. Like I don't deserve to know." I said a silent prayer of thanks for Riveaux's stonewalling. If Trish couldn't keep Prince out of harm's way, then he needed to stay hidden. For now.

"I don't know where he is right now," I answered, honestly. "Trish, I—"

"No." She pointed at me. "You need to tell me everything."

"I'm trying—"

"Now. Before *God*. You waltzed into my place of employment, not four days ago, asking all kinds of questions of me. So now here I am, in yours." Her arm sling was pumping like a bellow.

I picked up the rag and started wiping circles on the wood, needed to give my hands something to do. "I'm worried too. But for now, he's safe. The Lord has—"

"Don't give me that horseshit. And you should be worried. This fancy-pantsy school's turning out to be a drug den. I heard what happened to that O'Keefe boy. And it makes me wonder— *really* wonder—who's pulling the strings?"

"What are you saying?"

"All's I'm saying is that *you* need to get your house in order before you start coming for mine."

Trish strode away, then I attacked the floors until my wounds opened. My LOST SOUL wanted to bleed out.

■

A mourning dove sang its dirge as I walked across the street to the convent. That elegant sadness. Nearly a week without decent sleep was dragging me down, wrapping me in a weighted blanket. Could hardly keep both eyelids open at the same time.

Back in the kitchen, I dialed Riveaux.

After two rings she picked up. "No ODs on the blotter." Riveaux was a pro at skipping pleasantries. "Just a van lifted in the Ninth."

"Wonderful to hear your voice too. Sure beats getting bawled out by Trish Dempsey." I brushed my eyebrows against the grain, which felt stranger than I thought it would. "She laid into me after Mass."

"Shit," she said. Then I heard a quiet *click*. Was she systematically snapping a chopstick? "Probably my fault."

"Definitely your fault." I pantomimed an E chord with my injured hand to make sure it still worked.

"She called in a tizzy, asking about Prince. Told her we saw him Friday. Avoided details. She was seriously pissed."

"This is serious."

"We don't have to share Prince's location. He's an adult." Riveaux sipped something. Could've been old coffee, could've been fresh. Didn't matter either way.

"Yeah, but I feel bad for the woman—she seems genuinely worried," I said, thinking of her frantic expression. "But we're not saying shit until we know what's going on."

I stretched the phone cord, desperately wishing I could tell Riveaux everything, hear the thrill of good intel coursing through her, my mentor, my friend. Wanted a verbal high five, wanted to celebrate actually chasing a lead instead of my tail for a change. "But if Trish comes around, again—"

Another call bleeped in.

"Gotta take this." Riveaux sighed. "Mrs. Benoit again."

■

They arrived at the church for the final dress rehearsal of my permanent vows. My Sisters, Father Nathan, Moose, Rosemary, and Bernard. Sister Honor had insisted on one last run-through before next week's vow ceremony because she didn't want me to "bring embarrassment on the Order." No Sister of the Sublime Blood would be ill-prepared on her watch. I'd recited the sacred words with Father Nathan until my tongue went numb. Moose kept clearing his throat during my responses. I didn't wear the white tunic Sister Honor had picked up for me from the Guild. No more costume changes. Even if the costume reflected the role I believed in. The role I was terrified to accept. That's why I needed moral support from friendly faces, though I couldn't bear having Riveaux in the mix. One less plate to spin. Inviting Rosemary was equal parts nonsense and nerve. Maybe I asked her to attend to make it really real. No more delays or flaking. Time to put up or shut up.

After the rehearsal, Father Nathan and Sisters Honor and Laurel stayed behind for vespers. Back in the convent kitchen, Moose and Bernard cooked collard greens, beans, and rice, an explosion of sumptuous smells. Oil, garlic, and onions. Simmering greens. As Rosemary started making a pot of chamomile tea, I ran up to my room to check the burner phone.

One message from Decker: *Hang tight*

When I got back, Bernard was stirring and chopping, seemingly at the same time. "Pass the cay—?" But Moose was already handing him the jar of cayenne.

I stole a forkful of beans, and they fell apart in my mouth. Garlicky and rich. Kept my gloves on, my knuckles chewed up like roadkill.

Then Moose presented a plate of Hubig's Pies he'd brought. "Made sure to stock up on lemon. I know it's your fave flav, Goose."

I tapped Bernard on the arm and pulled him into the laundry room, where I gave him a big hug. His tense demeanor evaporated in my arms. He smelled like Moose's beard oil and palo santo. "I'm so happy you're dating my brother," I whispered, "but I swear to God, if you don't keep me in the know on stuff that matters, I'll go full Judith on your ass." I mimed slitting a throat, and Bernard let out a fierce squeal.

"Pinky promise," he said, looping his little finger around my gloved one. His pinky was twice the size of mine.

Something unwound in me during that meal. Maybe it was Bernard's hypnotic chopping. Maybe the delectable smells. Or seeing the relaxed way my brother and Bernard moved around each other. Dinner conversation was easy too.

"I have some news." Rosemary rested her fork on the edge of her plate.

With my eyes closed, I said, "Please tell us it's good news."

"Very. I landed the science grant," she said with a shy smile. "The only one citywide. And the Diocese doubled my request."

"Take a bow," I said. "Not that I'm surprised." A win for Rosemary felt like poetic justice.

"We should be the ones bowing," Bernard said. "Queen coming through!"

Moose swallowed, patted his mouth with his napkin, and raised his glass of water. "Cheers to things working out." And we all clinked our cups. I would have loved to slam back a Wild Turkey in one slug, but iced tea was a decent substitute.

Bernard offered some bad nun jokes. "What's a nun's favorite car?"

Definitely not a Stingray, I thought.

"A Christ-ler," Bernard said, supremely satisfied.

Moose groaned then caught my eye across the table. He mouthed, "You good?"

I nodded.

Then with the suddenness of a punctured tire, the electricity went out.

One blink, light. The next, complete darkness.

A blackout. It was bound to happen eventually, with such vicious heat.

"Whoa," Moose exhaled.

"Moon's full tonight," Rosemary said. "Let's go outside."

In a single-file line we felt our way through the dark, our hands gliding over doorframes, the convent's skin, the cracks in the walls. Pain made permanent.

The rising moon scored the darkness of the convent garden. There are few places you go in the world, close your eyes and know exactly where you are. New Orleans was one of them. Ripe blueberries, blackberries, raspberries, and cherries hung heavy on gnarled shrubs and branches. Honeysuckle and magnolias sweetened the air. Lavender. Shadowy petals like velvet.

Bernard winked at Moose, a small moment, a casual intimacy that told a bigger story. The guys made it look easy. Flirtation. Spontaneity. Like it was the most natural thing in the world. Envy kicked me in the teeth, even though I was happy for them. I looked away so fast I got dizzy.

Moose laughed straight from his heart as Bernard started to vogue to the sounds of the night. I always took Bernard for more of a snobby sound guy. His last industrial noise album was eleven hours long. But he was ballroom ready.

Moose joined in. Moose, who carried stretchers, whom I'd seen lifting Trevor's fragile body, was popping and locking as he danced through the musicless garden. Couldn't remember the last time I'd seen my brother dance like that.

In that instant of that natural high, of movement, the worship of Being, I knew Tammy was toast no matter how hard Decker wanted to try to resurrect her. No more drinking. No mystery pills. Sobriety was a sucker punch of reality. Big girl molars pushing through gums. But it was an honest pain. Time to turn the page. The ends didn't always justify the means.

It was harder to turn the page on Rosemary. Her skirt rode up and I fought the urge to sink my gold tooth into her thigh. To claim her as mine. Commit her body to memory. I imagined the life we could never have. Farmers markets for strawberries. Subtitled movies at the art cinema, though she'd surely complain until the credits. Walks through the spidery drapes of Lafitte Park.

"Penny for your thoughts," she said. Her bedroom eyes looked more excruciating in the dark light. Her radiant red hair.

I couldn't fess up about any craziness of the past week, so I swallowed hard and said, "Just thinking about Fleur."

Rosemary moved closer to me, and the air itself tasted bewitched, infused with some dark and dazzling enchantment. I wrapped a vine around my fingers and studied the fuzzed anatomy of the tree above.

"Better not to think sometimes," Rosemary said.

"Isn't that all you do? Scientific method?"

"I can do so much more." Her words held a shifting, breathing urgency, like leaves trapped in a gale. "Let me show you." In the darkness Rosemary's eyes were on fire.

A twig snapped in the bushes and I went stiff. But it was just the stormy heart of the garden. Fruit aching to be eaten. I shot to my feet. "I should go. Prayers."

"Pray later," Rosemary said. "Stay with me."

But I'd chosen to seal my fate. With a vow. Rosemary was a temptation I couldn't fall for. The apple I couldn't bite. A reminder of the person I couldn't be.

"I have to go." Before I left, I picked a plum from a low branch. It fit like a tiny abyss in my palm. Of course Eve reached for forbidden fruit. She was hungry to know, to feel. To be more than a rib-born second fiddle. More than an add-on. Eve wasn't a sinner. She was a seeker. A boss-ass bitch who dared to take a bite. If only I had that courage.

29

WHEN THE SUN BROKE through the horizon, an ever-moving blade, the sweat in my narrow convent bed could fill a baptismal font. The power was back on. So was the chorus of Monday morning worries. Was Prince in trouble? Was Tammy in trouble? Was Lenny looking for my alter ego? I stared at my burner, which didn't chirp or chime. Decker hadn't written anything besides "hang tight." Not knowing where things stood, I had to lie low. Not my forte.

After I took a quick shower and changed, I sipped coffee in the garden before school. Felt like I was knee-deep in hot water, scaldingly rough, shooting up my nose. Time was running out. But time was also nothing. An invisible force. We can't see it, can't touch it. Only the clues of its effects. Representations. Clock hands. Sundial shadows. Crow's feet. Tree rings. Kids getting taller. Or dying too soon.

Between fevery daydreams, class continued. Graduation at the end of the week, thank Christ. I caught Rosemary's gray eyes across the classroom. When I sent her a hello wave, she nodded and went back to organizing papers and index cards on her desk. We'd have to recalibrate, find a new way forward. I listened to my students butchering "In My Life." Ryan Brown's timing was particularly egregious and throwing everybody off. "It's okay, try again," I heard myself say, though my voice seemed to come from somewhere else entirely. I was phoning it in, and so were the students.

Before I left school for the day, I made sure to corner Alex Moore. A library come-to-Jesus moment. "The Rebuild Fund," I said. "Why so insistent I look into it?"

"Find something interesting?" He sounded almost surprised. "Verdict?"

"Forget it," I said. "It doesn't concern you."

"This school's future is of *great* concern for me," he said. "That's why I brought it up."

"That's why?"

"That's why."

Yet another man asking a woman to do his heavy lifting. Shocker. I left Alex in the reading nook with his malevolent bow tie, another riddle I didn't have time or mind to solve.

■

The rest of the week continued uneventfully. Riveaux was busy with requests from Fleur's mom, agency paperwork, and other Redemption duties. She kept me posted on anything relevant, but our investigation stalled. And that was fine. Hated to admit it, but I'd needed a break, a beat, a chance to reset, figure out what the next move was. Being on campus, keeping a vigilant eye on the students—the living, breathing students—felt like the most important thing I could do. Sister Honor might have even been proud. As for Prince, I didn't dare approach him without Riveaux. He had crucial info to spill, but it had to be on his terms. At least he was relatively safe at the motel.

The hours had melted that week, dripping in catatonic school days, waxen daydreams, night terrors. I kept seeing Lenny's wine tsunami morphing into the frog freed by Prince transforming into Fleur at the water fountain.

I'd surface long enough to notice changes in the light, sometimes clear, and sometimes thick as cake batter.

On Thursday morning, one day before graduation, Bernard popped by the convent with Vietnamese iced coffees, his favorite. Condensation cried down the sides of the plastic cups. How perfectly sweet and strong. We sat in silence in the garden, drinking our coffees, not talking. And everywhere I looked, into the earth, into the branches, up into the breath between the trees, it was like staring into deep time. Every bit of matter, a clock.

Last class, I let the seniors play charades. Kids being kids. Silly, ridiculous, sad, mad, wonderful kids. Prince'd missed his last chance to graduate. Rebecca surprised me with a present, a card and a box of marzipan wrapped in silver paper. "Oh." I was too shocked to say more as I opened the box. Each morsel, a masterpiece. Tiny pears with blush-pink cheeks, roses so lifelike their thorns could draw blood, and an absurdly detailed marzipan lamb. The kind you'd expect to see in a fine shop window on Magazine Street. I left the edible rose for Rosemary, on her desk, near her prized Erlenmeyer flask.

▪

At 9 p.m. that night, the kitchen phone rang just once, then I heard Sister Laurel calling out to me to come quickly. She was up late again as usual, a blessing. The last thing I needed was a ringing phone waking up Sister Honor, who'd surely emerge irate from her sepulchral sleeping quarters. I ran down the steps in my white pajamas.

"Hey," I said, expecting Riveaux.

"Stay there." It was Moose. "Don't go anywhere," he ordered.

"What's going on?"

"I have something for you."

Moose showed up two and a half rosaries later, his uniform dark with sweat patches. "You're going to want to sit down," he said.

"Why?" I asked as I slid out a kitchen chair.

He stared at me, his voice fell into a serious-whisper. "Do you know a Joseph Delachaise?"

"Joey, sure. Saw him at Fleur's Mass and at school last week. Why?"

"Sorry, Goose." He put his hand on my shoulder.

"What?"

"It's bad.

"*What?*"

"He OD'd tonight. I was on the call, and I swear to you, I tried everything."

"Joey? No fucking way. Not Joey. I warned him!"

Joey knew the pill might kill him and took it anyway. And that's what made addiction so devious. So impenetrable.

A cockroach crawled up the wall of my skull. That's what it felt like. Every hangover I'd ever survived had all resurrected and cut through me, slicing every vein at once.

"I'm sorry." Moose wiped his forehead with his forearm. "I saw a Saint Sebastian's uniform in his bedroom, figured he was one of yours."

"How much more fucked can this get?" I was too angry to cry.

Hail Mary, fix this right now. Please make it untrue.

"Remember how I said I've got your back?" he asked.

"Of course." I was terrified of what he was going to say next.

"Here." Moose pulled something from his pocket. A plastic bag, with a phone inside. "It's Joey's. I took it from his desk."

He handed me the iPhone. No passcode, 9 percent charge. The screen's sick blue light glowed in my face.

"You miraculous motherfucker," I said.

He couldn't resist smiling. My brother had stolen evidence for me, put his job on the line. Moose, Gabriel, my guardian archangel.

"I have to get back to work," he said, rubbing his face. "Call Riveaux, tell her. Everything."

"But—"

"Tell her everything," he said. "All of it."

"I can't."

"You can," he said. "You investigate this *with* her, or I'll take the phone back."

"Fine."

He nodded, not quite convinced. "Don't tell anyone else about the phone. I could lose my paramedic's license. Maybe a whole lot worse."

"I promise."

"Go get 'em, Goose."

A quick prayer for Joey, another kid gone way too fucking soon. Who died for no reason. Another family torn apart. But there was no room, no time for grief. We had to move.

Cascades of messages lived inside Joey's phone, but one thread screamed loudest. A group text titled *Brain PWR*. Power?

Brain power. The blue bubbles burned my retinas as I scrolled up, stopping as soon as I saw one name.

FLEUR: Hi! Anyone have study buddies left?

RYAN: yo big sleazy is done! says we r on r own!

JOEY: WTF

TREVOR: Shit. I'm out. Finals in like a fucking week.

RYAN: yo need study buddies! imma beg da sleaze!

FLEUR: I found some!

So many explosions inside me, I couldn't keep track. I became each detonation then a meadow of them, a field of sunflowers on fire.

Study buddies. Like Sarah'd said. Who or what was Big Sleazy? The dealer of the east wing stash?

I found some.

I looked through Joey's camera roll. Concert pictures and selfies in his bedroom. I saw his trumpet case in the background, as he crouched to show off his white sneakers. Still pristine because he cleaned them obsessively, like every teen trying to control their little corner of the universe. When everything's possible and impossible. We can't stop making movies about that time, that age, writing books about it. We're all chasing that lightning. The fury and madness and beauty of feeling alive. The big, bold verb of being.

And while we're romanticizing teenage lives and pain, we're
failing teenage bodies. Failing their minds. Colonizing their
attention. The men in power—cannibals with long résumés—
see kids as demographics, users, followers in the Pied Piper's
death march, new consumers to bring online, future workers
to exploit. Unsullied lands to strip-mine. They didn't see Joey's
polished Pumas. His trumpet case, covered in stickers from
every NOLA jazz club that let him sneak in. They didn't see
the perfection of children who enter this earthly realm pure,
dimpled baby hands reaching for warmth and care. They don't
see the suffering. Or maybe they do and they feed on it. Because
in a system that rewards groupthink and carnage, kids with
empathy, curiosity, and free spirits are the biggest threats of all.

Hail Mary, please. Burn it all down.

Next, I called Riveaux on the kitchen phone. "We lost another
one. Joey Delachaise," I said into the receiver.

"Goldsmobile, I can't—I'm so sorry."

"Me too," I said. "Nice kid."

"Even if he wasn't," she said in a bright, clear voice, "it still
wouldn't be right."

"I have his phone."

"How?"

"Moose grabbed it," I said. "He was on call."

She let out a long whistle. "Brosmobile with the assist."

"The phone's got texts about 'study buddies' and somebody
the kids called Big Sleazy."

"Easy Sleazy beautiful," Riveaux said, making absolutely no
sense and all the sense in the world. "How do we run with this
scuttlebutt?"

"Graduation tomorrow. There's one kid on this text thread
who we can corner. Let's dish out some Redemption."

"Pomp and circumstance it is," she said.

"One more thing."

"Lay it on me."

"I've been working undercover with Decker."

"What in the? Wait, pause, rewind. *What?*"

"I've been working undercover with Decker," I repeated, hoping for calmer acceptance. Confession without the bite of surprise. How wrong I was.

"So, you've been lying to my face and sleuthing behind my back?"

"Decker made me promise to tell no one. To keep it totally on the down-low. But you get it, right? I had to do it. I had no other choice."

"We all have choices. For instance, you could've broken that 'promise' sooner." Riveaux cursed.

"At least I'm telling you now," I said. "Right?"

As I updated Riveaux on Decker's training, Tammy, Up in Smoke, Lenny, the Royal Family, I dodged her F-bombs, her spears through the heavy receiver. Joey's phone's battery indicator blinked urgently. Two percent. Another end in sight.

30

BY 9 A.M. ON Friday, there were fifty twelfth graders fidgeting in their graduation seats. I tried to look at each face as I stood on the rickety auditorium stage. The polyester sin of my academic regalia stuck to my arms, my back, my legs. Our paper programs warped dramatically in the humidity. The kids sweat through their rented gowns. I imagined how pissed the Guild clerks would be when their sopping capes were returned.

When Father Nathan had asked me to deliver the talk, I'd resisted. "Speak from the heart," he urged. "Just be real."

Sister Honor's cavernous face had acted out all five stages of grief during that meeting. She'd pushed for Sister Laurel as speaker, of course. But Father Nathan knew me, and he'd observed enough of my music classes to see what happens when you talk to teenagers like human beings, not toddlers at the day-care in a "Wheels on the Bus" sing-along. Not that my Sister was condescending, but the students needed real talk.

I leaned into the mic. No *one two one two*. Just jumped in with, "Here we are." Feedback turned "are" into an orchestra. *Are are are.*

A few scattered *mmhmm*s, a ripple of unease. The members of that audience knew the deal. A scary year. A dying planet and billionaires rocketing to space (good riddance). They were inheriting a wounded city and stepping into uncertain futures. The barbaric news of Joey's OD hadn't wound its way through the community yet. A stony resolve to keep up the business-as-usual front until the last mortarboard was tossed.

"Been a biblical year, hasn't it?" I asked. "Fire. Flood. Hard goodbyes."

A sniffle from the audience then a choked sob.

"We still have a choice," I said. "We can let this world raze us to dust or we can fight back. We can fight for hope."

Bernard sat in the third row with his hands clasped in his lap. I could practically hear him telling himself not to cry. My chosen brother, now my actual brother's boyfriend. Bernard wore his good suit, the charcoal gray one that made him look like one of the TCM noir detectives I'd loved watching as a kid. Every few seconds his eyes would dart around, then back to me. I smiled at him, sending him an energetic hug through the ether.

The microphone felt hot, holding all the ghost voices of everyone who had ever breathed into it. "When Father Nathan asked me to speak today, I almost said no." In the front row, I saw Ryan Brown and stared the sharpest daggers his way. As soon as this was over, I was going to grill him for specifics. Finally, I caught him in a verifiable lie, with a direct connection to Fleur, Trevor, Joey, and "study buddies." Ryan was the last man standing of the Brain PWR group. The nanosecond I left the stage would be a holy war.

I cleared my throat. "Because, really, what should I say today? That everything happens for a reason? We all know that's bull—" I stopped there, averting my imminent damnation by Sister Honor. "Our faith isn't a bulletproof vest, but it can be a life raft. And here's what I do know. You've all survived. And I don't just mean passing Ms. Flynn's final exams." One laugh for that one. Bernard, of course. Bless him. "You've survived loss. Navigated grief. We have to hold one another now. Always."

Sister Honor shifted in her seat like she was sitting on a pincushion.

Despite Riveaux's presence, the gaps in the crowd stung. Wounded Prince Dempsey, whose absence was a hiss. A live wire that would happily electrocute anyone who looked at it let alone touched it. He'd refused to talk.

The kids needed truth, not pathetic fiction. But my words—any words, really—were cold comfort. "You are capable of more than this world will ever give you credit for," I said. "Don't give in. Don't give up, or I will never forgive you."

After I wrapped, there were quiet rumblings of assent. Coughs. A lone "amen" rang out in the back. Sisters Laurel and Honor, and Father Nathan, sat for a moment in quiet prayer.

As the graduates shuffled across the stage to grab their diplomas, their eyes were still haunted but alive. It was a fragile and resilient thing—life. Beauty you could crush if you held it too tight. Every breath was a miracle and a punishing reminder of the thin line between here and gone.

"In My Life" came together in the end. The caps flew. Ritual complete.

Parents rushed forward with sagging carnations, hugs, and demands for pictures. The scene was surreal and sweet and awful. Sister Honor shook hands with graduates and family members, seeming incapable of lifting the corners of her mouth as she posed. The comfort and warmth of the road trip with Sister Honor to Ascension Parish on Good Friday felt obscenely far away. Rebecca's grandmother kept touching her face—her eyebrows, high cheekbones—and crying like she couldn't believe her grandkid had grown up so lovely, so accomplished.

Near a D.A.R.E. poster, Ryan Brown had no idea what was coming. I moved toward him like a jungle cat. "Got a minute?"

He backed up sloppily, dropping his program. "Mom's waiting over there."

"It's okay, Ryan. Just want to talk for a sec."

His face relaxed and he stopped his reverse retreat, his backward salsa.

"I'm so proud of you," I said, and hooked my arm over Ryan's shoulder, walked us a step toward the exit. The deafening rush of blood in my head, hard enough to crack bone. "You lying little bitch."

He tried to wriggle away. "I have to—"

"What you have to do is tell me everything. Right now."

"About what?"

"Don't." As I led him up, into the stage wings, out of sight, my shoulder embrace became a full-blown headlock. "I saw your group text. You've been lying to me."

"Here." Ryan produced a pack of cigarettes from his back pocket. A bribe. "I'm sorry."

"Joey and Fleur are *dead*, Ryan. Trevor barely made it." I took the cigarettes. "Talk."

"Wait—Joey?" Ryan's body dropped instantly, with shock, with fast pain, like he'd just had his Achilles tendons sliced.

"He OD'd last night. He's gone." The pain moved stealthily inside of me, one nanometer at a time. A consumption so quick, I didn't feel my own heart breaking. It had broken a million times since Mom died. Then a million more times since Shelly said my name over that damn PA.

Ryan clutched the back of his neck. "Fuck. *No*. Really?"

"I wish to God I was lying. Tell me now, who was your supplier?"

"I don't know what you mean," he said.

"Bullshit." I tightened my grip. "Talk."

"It's graduation day and my grandparents drove from Shreveport, and—"

I stepped closer. "Who's Big Sleazy?"

Ryan jolted at the nickname. His face went through several emotions, surprise, panic, and then finally resignation. He shut his eyes and said, "Alex."

"Alex Moore?"

Ryan nodded. "He's Big Sleazy. Fleur nicknamed him. But don't tell him!"

Alex Moore. The name pounded my chest all at once and in staggered hits, like buckshot blooming out, out, out in excruciating, infinitesimal fragments.

The Big Sleazy, our very own librarian. Our steward. Our Dartmouth grad. Our resident know-it-all, Alex Moore. Not some menacing outsider from a seedy crime family. Just a cappella crime.

"How'd it start?"

"Alex was just helping us get through midterms and finish college applications. When we had a test, he'd give us two or three pills, to focus."

"What a champion. Then what?"

"A couple weeks ago, he stopped. Said we had to talk to a doctor and get real meds on our own." Ryan tried to turn away but I wrenched him closer.

"On the text thread, when Fleur said she 'found some,' where'd she get the pills?"

Ryan was scuffing his right loafer with purpose, with intention, like his life hinged on each scuff. "I don't know—she didn't say. She gave me one the day she died, but I flushed it like you told me."

I led us down from the stage, flagging Riveaux and Bernard over. "Mr. Brown has valuable information for the NOPD, isn't that right?" I quickly filled them in.

"But Mom's right there." Ryan pouted. "And my grandparents."

"Bernard, can you please alert Mr. Brown's family and escort them to the station? And give the police this?" I handed Bernard Joey's phone in a plastic bag. "Guard it with your life."

"Downtown Ryan Brown," Bernard said, "how about it?" He ushered Ryan toward his family with a jaunty smile like they'd just won Jazz Fest tickets in a raffle.

"Riveaux, want to visit the library?" I asked.

"Let's book it."

31

EVERY MUSCLE AND LIGAMENT screamed as I sprinted to the library, Riveaux a few paces behind. The predatory bird that lived in my rib cage pinched the air with her talons. God was present, after an out-of-office stretch. God was alive inside me, the velocity hurtling me forward. I took the stairs two steps at a time.

As I was about to torpedo my body into the library, Riveaux said, "Hold up. If you go in too hot, you might put him on the back foot."

"That's right where we want him," I said.

"Let's think about how we—"

Before Riveaux finished her warning, I dashed in. Alex Moore was exactly where I saw him on Monday, sitting in the one comfy reading chair in the corner. The chair—a green leather wingback with classy bronze tacks along the seams. His computer-screen tan was alarming. Dude needed some sun on that skin. But he was a man at ease. His knees were spread so wide they could've spanned the Esplanade. He'd wasted no time to skip back here from graduation. Surely hoping to offer guided tours of the library—*his* library—to any graduates who stopped by with their parents. Thankfully, none were in sight.

"Bringing me my teacher of the year trophy?" His voice was a human pan flute. I wanted to rip his tongue out of his head and bury it in the convent garden.

"We need to talk about Fleur." I posted myself directly in front of him to drench his books in my shadow.

"What about her?" Alex closed his journal with baroque slowness.

"And Ryan and Trevor and Joey," Riveaux said.

"Anyone else?" Alex blinked and exhaled through his nose. "The bishop? Sister Honor? Jesus himself?"

"Tell us about the pills," I said.

"Pills?" Alex tilted his head and adjusted his bow tie.

"The ones you've been pushing," I said, spelling it out.

"Are you accusing me of dealing *fentanyl*?" Alex played incensed but his pulsing left eye sent strobes. Riveaux and I had his stupid back against the gorgeous ropes.

"Worse," I said.

"What's worse than that?" He sniffed.

"Playing pharmacist to the study group," I said. "You supplied them with pills—study buddies—then cut them off after they got hooked. Ryan Brown's outed you."

"Wait a minute." He stood. "It wasn't like I *sold* them anything," Alex said, in a sensationally condescending tone. Alex touched his bow tie again and straightened his glasses, like he could buy himself time with lots of teeny tiny useless movements.

Riveaux interrupted his strategic fidgeting. "How'd it start?"

"Start? I just gave them a few Adderall from my *prescription*. Totally legitimate—not street drugs."

I balled my gloved hands into symmetrical fists. It felt dangerous to stand close to him when I wanted to wrestle him to the ground. But somewhere in my mind was an internal voice that sounded a lot like Riveaux cataloging the assault charges that the fucker would levy. Couldn't risk it. My fist met the desk instead, and it felt good. A sad stand-in for Alex's nose, which, from that angle, looked like a bony butt.

"I was helping them." Alex's shoulders collapsed. "Giving them a little boost. Just a few pills for each of them. It was honestly nothing!"

"Whoa there, drugstore cowboy," Riveaux said. "That's not nothing. Unless jail time is no biggie to you."

He turned even paler. "It was a baby dose! Those kids were so scared of failing."

"So you turned to drugs?" Riveaux huffed. "Ever hear of studying? Like, flash cards?"

"You make it sound easy. But I wouldn't have gotten into Dartmouth without medication."

The bitter twist. Riveaux had been hooked on meds herself, after her ladder fall. And me, with my laundry list of addictions. We all needed something to handle the pain. Too bad the fixes could lead to new problems.

"My brother takes Ambien," I said. "He'd be screwed without it. But you can't just set out prescription meds like a bowl of M&M's. What happened next?"

"Then, they were acing exams. It was clear they needed this medication. So I said it was time for them all to get an official diagnosis and prescription."

"Which can take months," I said.

"Yes but—"

"You cut them off cold turkey?" Riveaux cracked a knuckle and rolled her neck once, like she was limbering up for a fight she didn't want to have.

"I never meant to—" Alex's breath was so rotten and scum-thick that it made me wish I was dead. "There weren't nefarious intentions here. I swear to God."

"Keep God's name out of your mouth." The room held every visual echo, every memory of kids from all the years, the decades. All the backpacks and hats, headphones and water bottles. "Maybe they spun out on their own, but you put it in motion."

"And then cut the brakes," Riveaux said, sliding her hands into her mom-jeans pockets.

Meds were modern-day miracles for so many. But Alex fucked it. His performative despair wasn't even a perfor-mance. It was a stroppy and sad little tantrum. How pathetic. A middle-aged man trying to be relevant, trying to matter to teenagers who'd never remember his name after graduating. A boring-ass manchild playing Dead Poets Society, desperate to be anything other than basic. The kind of guy who loved Rosemary Flynn because she was so pretty and he thought he deserved pretty things. A man who'd jeopardize everything for what, high school cred?

Riveaux added, "Since you forgot to mention any of this in your statement to the cops, they'll be here shortly to help you make edits." She had her phone out. A quick nod from her, another from me. It was a win for us, backing Alex against the wall like that. We had a good rhythm, me and Riveaux.

Alex lurched forward and snatched up a pair of scissors from the reference desk. He made a fine show of splaying the scissors open and holding the blade to his neck. "I cannot go to jail," he said. "My father's a *judge*."

A thin red line appeared beneath the metal. Not blood, just the red promise of a cut. He'd never do it, though his melodrama was slightly entertaining, I had to admit. Nothing like real pain. Nothing like the damage I left in my wake. Nothing like the desperation of the new mothers in prison, after their babies were ripped away. Nothing like Mrs. Benoit crying herself to sleep every night on the rug of Fleur's bedroom, breathing into the phone with Riveaux.

"Put it down, Alex," I said. "You're not going to kill yourself with scissors."

Riveaux didn't even look up from her phone. "Though you might need a tetanus shot." She yawned and snatched the scissors with ease.

Alex wanted to matter so badly. Maybe God would have some mercy left for him, but I was fresh out.

■

An hour later, the bittersweet joy of graduation depleted, and Ryan Brown and Alex Moore coming clean to the cops, Rosemary and I sat at the convent kitchen table. I laid it out for her. "Your boyfriend supplied Adderall to students. The study group got hooked."

"What?" Rosemary seemed to speak without moving her lips. "Alex did *what*?"

"But he stopped giving them pills, told them to figure it out for themselves," I said. "You know the rest."

"He lied to me." Rosemary's words held no charge. No rage. No surprise. Nothing. She looked empty. Her tea cup trembled against the saucer—Sister Honor's favorite set. "I asked Alex what he knew," Rosemary said, "and he lied."

"He'll likely be facing charges," I said.

Rosemary evened out her already too-even red bangs. "*Alex*." I swore I heard a transformer blow three blocks over as her face fell. "I knew he took meds. Everyone takes something. But he should have never *given* his medication to students."

"It's not your fault. It's his," I said, trying desperately not to gloat.

"I need some air," she said as she walked outside. She opened her mouth but couldn't say any more.

In the garden we sat side by side on the bench. I lifted my head and took in her rose perfume, her stoic profile. "You okay?"

"No. Not even close." She stared ahead. "I'm obviously going to end it with him. He has to move out today. I don't even want to look at his stuff."

I thought of the Big Sleazy nickname but held my tongue.

Sitting next to her, I felt her heat, which sent shock waves through me. "Sorry," I lied.

"Don't be sorry. He was just"—she looked down—"a place-holder. Like everything else here. Temporary."

"Except permanent vows."

"True." Rosemary exhaled slowly, then flicked a mote of gold pollen that had landed on her skirt. "Frankly, this almost makes me want to be a nun. Just feel so lost right now. I hate being lied to."

"Sometimes people lie for good reasons," I said, trying to convince myself. "But this isn't one of those times."

"I feel so guilty." Rosemary's voice wavered. "I should have seen through him. If I had, Fleur and Joey would still be alive."

"We do the best we can every day. That's all we can do." I pulled off my gloves and took her hand, laced our fingers together so tight it cut off the blood flow.

"I'm not sure I'll be a good guest at your ceremony. Two days from now, right?"

"Don't worry about it."

"Are you worried about it?" She let go of my hand.

"Nope. Of all the forms of human sacrifice, this one's the least messy."

The world sparkled around us, cicadas found the dial on their ancient lifting song.

"Gallows humor," she said.

"Without the humor, it'd just be the gallows."

We sat like that for a moment, saying nothing, breathing together. I felt her warmth through my uniform. A skinny garden snake slithered past. It knew me. It *knew*. We were all helpless creatures crawling through our miraculous, scary planet. Our lives just blips in God's never-ending timeline.

32

ONE DAY UNTIL PERMANENT vows. After I showered, I stood naked in my bedroom and conjured Nina for what might be, should probably be, the last time. Her hands on my body, the body she all but owned. Nina who tasted like Camel Reds and Big Red cinnamon gum. Nina, who made music with me at seventeen, who'd bite my neck and slip on handcuffs and fuck me until I saw God. The same God I was about to marry. The same God that politicians like Governor Baptise and pathetic priests said would condemn me to hell for loving her.

I remembered her voice. "I can't do this anymore," she'd said, our last winter night together, the air frozen, brutal. "I can't live two lives."

"Then don't."

"I'm not like you, Holiday. I can't walk away from everything I know. And *you always leave.*"

Nina was right. That was the truth. I had started it all. I'd set the terms of our love when we were seventeen, when I sat her down and said with outrageous clarity: "I will hurt you and leave you. No strings, ever." I never gave myself to Nina fully or asked for the same in return. Because I was afraid. I was afraid of love. "No strings," I repeated.

"Okay, no strings," she'd said all those years ago. "No strings, but what about cuffs?"

Faith and danger. Putting yourself in someone else's hands. Wasn't that what I was doing now, with God? But the memories of Nina. So gentle and real despite the uncrossable bridge between past and present.

You always leave.

Yeah, last I'd heard, Nina was getting divorced from Nicholas. But I'd ended us before we had a real chance to begin. I'd written the end before the start. Locked myself in my own purgatory with her, and I had to own it.

▪

Father Nathan's office door was open when I arrived.

"Tomorrow's the big day." He stood at his bookcase. "Still time to back out."

"Does the eternal ring have a return policy?"

Father Nathan laughed as he shut the door and glided to his desk. In his black cassock and clerical collar, maybe the same one I'd worn at the dive bar, he cut a severe figure. Young, tall, not your average priest. Neither of us fit the mold of average. Thank God for that.

I held his eyes. "Need to ask you something, off the holy record."

"When have we ever been on the record?"

"May I smoke? I'll make sure no blowback reaches Sister Honor's nose."

He winked, shut off his sad AC, and opened his window. "Only if I can have a sip."

"You smoke?" I was glad I brought the pack I'd confiscated from Ryan at graduation.

"Once upon a time," he said. "When I worked as a line cook for a summer in Toledo. And yes, let's keep Sister Honor's bloodhounds off the scent."

I lit the cigarette, took a hit, then handed it over. "Forever starts tomorrow, but I can't find any peace, and I don't want to. I can't stop thinking about Fleur and Joey, why I couldn't save them. Why tragedies like this terrorize us. Why any tragedies happen at all. Why suffering exists."

"What I'm hearing aren't really questions," he said, and took a pull of the impounded Dunhill.

"Right."

"I struggle with the same non-questions, if that helps." He tapped ash into the lid of his peanut butter jar.

"It doesn't." I took a fast drag and it hit wrong. My cough was boiling and sooty, and in a second, I was wheezing. Father Nathan slapped me on the back.

"Breathe," he said.

"I can't."

"You can and you will. With you fully committed here, we'll make Saint Sebastian's mean something."

"The church needs to evolve or die." I stared at the crucifix. "We both know which of those the bishop prefers."

"So let's keep our focus on change," Father Nathan said. Heat leaned on the windowpane hard enough to crack it. "And keep fighting."

"Keep fighting." After I repeated the words, I realized I wanted to be part of something living. The church's next chapter. For more than two thousand years, people held on to a promise, a story, trying to do good in a hard world, reaching for a better way. I tapped more ash into the lid. "Two underdogs reforming the entire Catholic Church."

"Look at Jesus's disciples. Fishermen, outcasts, rabble-rousers. We fit right in."

I mashed out my cig and stood, stretching with a different set of exhausted muscles.

"You ready?" he asked.

"Ready."

I needed to retrieve my printed copy of the vows from my class-room before the next day's ceremony. Sister Honor'd crucify me if I fucked up one word of it. But really, I needed time to think. Time alone. The empty school was like a carnival after closing. All the rides quiet and still. Graduation was done, summer term weeks away. I left the spooky emptiness as quickly as I'd entered.

In the courtyard, hibiscus and crape myrtle dripped their obscene beauty. A boot print in cement was filled with fallen petals. Spanish moss swayed and leaves rustled under branches. Then a most unexpected sight.

Rosemary Flynn.

On our campus on a Saturday night. She was quite literally reading a book—Carl Sagan's *Contact*—and walking at the same time, and she bumped right into me as I was lighting up the last of Ryan Brown's cigarettes.

"Careful," I said. "You might stumble into salvation next." I pointed to the church's stained glass windows, which, even at night, gleamed.

"Smoking before your permanent vows?"

"My bachelorette party." I exhaled a curl of smoke.

"Let me buy you a drink then," she said. "I'm killing time so Alex can move his stuff out. Glass of milk?"

"I quit years ago," I said, my heartbeat throbbing exquisitely in my wrists. "But we can have iced tea in the convent."

"Let's party," she said.

As we walked from the alley, across the courtyard, Rosemary looked so composed, so put together in her smart outfit. Nothing out of place. Not even a bra strap. Rosemary never let a bra strap show. Crisp sleeveless top, pencil skirt. I bet she carried a lint roller and tiny iron in that bag of hers.

"Last fling before the ring," she said, as we reached the street.

"Last fling."

Then a bolt of sound. One bang. Quick and hard as a pipe against steel.

Was it before *fling*, or after? During? That echo marked the instant when a bullet tore through Rosemary's throat, her perfect porcelain throat, and exploded out the back in a fountain of blood.

She crumpled to the ground and her book hit the pavement. Rosemary was down. Too fast for me to catch her or stop it.

Then, another hard crack, like a thunderclap.

My head whipped toward the sound, toward the street, where I saw it. The Stingray speeding away. That cobalt abomination, shark massacre on wheels.

Shock at first. My two lives had collided. And then, the terrible realization. Lenny had put it together. He'd made me. After the club and spilled wine. And he'd come for me, but the fucker hit her.

Rosemary's feet had landed at different angles. I got on the ground with her, pulled my gloves off and cradled her as she sputtered blood. From her mouth and throat, the blood poured. I rocked her, prayed for her. The brutal wrongness of her inner world pushing out.

"I'm with you," I said, then screamed for help, my voice sawing the night air.

Sister Laurel materialized, flushed, terrified, but still a steady vision in the panic.

"Call 911," I said, "and stay inside."

Lenny had sped off but he could come back.

Rosemary was bleeding out as I talked to her, held her, squeezed her hand. Every minute, an eon. I kept repeating, "I'm with you," I kept talking, though she couldn't reply. Her lips moved but she couldn't form words. Her throat a gaping wound. Her circuits cut.

"I love you," I said, and brushed grit from her forehead and face. Her impossible cheekbones.

She couldn't speak, but her eyes fluttered. Slow, heavy blinks. Rosemary's right hand still twitched in mine.

"Wish we met before." I kissed her right temple. The fragile skin and faint pulse beneath.

A sound left her throat. She didn't *make* the sound, it escaped from her. It wasn't a pretty whisper or a sigh, but a rip. Not human or animal. Beauty itself was dying. Pain finding a voice in that pit of night.

Infinite spirits inside finite bodies.

"It's okay," I told her. And she felt heavier, sinking back, letting the current take her. Matter speaking through her, reclaiming. "I've got you."

May the Lord bless you and keep you.

Her hand went slack. Thick stillness settled.

"You're okay," I said. "You're going home."

I'd seen death before, but nothing like that. A sick, slow quickness.

She was gone. All gone. No do-over. Every word she ever said to me hammered my ear. Her tea snobbery. The story about her dad. Our classroom spars. Our almost-kiss in the church. The hot-as-hell woman with vintage pearls and too-even bangs was the same woman choking on her own blood. How, how, *how* could this happen?

Minutes later—ten? thirty? five hundred?—sirens announced their presence as cops descended on us, their walkie-talkies leaking phrases and instructions that made no sense, sounded like a different language, a different reality.

A cop with a shiny face appeared. Couldn't have been much older than Prince. "Are you hurt?"

"She's dead."

"Miss," he said, "I need you to step away from the body."

"The body? That's Rosemary Flynn."

"Please step back from the body, ma'am," the officer continued, and if he said one more thing to me about *the body*, I was going to break his. "We will need you to—"

"You want a statement? Lenny Mastoni did this, and he works for the Royal Family. *Lenny Mastoni.* Go to Up in Smoke in the Bywater and arrest him."

"Your name?"

"Tell Sergeant Decker this was Lenny Mastoni."

"What's your name?" he asked again.

"Sister Holiday."

"*Sister?*"

I zombie-walked to the convent shrouded in Rosemary's blood. Not just balancing on the knife's edge, I was the blade, ready to kill Lenny. I didn't even remember the police taking my official statement. Nothing felt grounded or real.

How could I take my permanent vows now?

How could I not?

33

I PACED MY CRAMPED bedroom, punching the wall, reopening my knuckles, crying myself into exhaustion. Felt like a wood chipper was eating each nerve. I kept seeing visions of Rosemary, the blood gushing from her throat. Blood unlike any liquid I'd ever seen. With a will like it had its own mission. Like it wanted to devour her, devour us. I rehashed it all, over and over again, how I held her hand, cradled her, cleaned her face, kissed her, tasted her blood. I'd never been closer to her than in that moment. Her presence was as strong as a slap across the face.

It was so unreal and sickening I couldn't even call Moose. Had no idea how to tell him. I laid on my bed and closed my eyes. When I brought both hands up in the air, I could still feel her ragged breath through my fingers.

Rosemary was gone, but I refused to accept it.

I refused the *idea* of it.

No more indecipherable looks from her in the teacher's lounge. No more vexing flirtation. I'd never get a chance to talk to her again, argue with her, count her freckles. My body refused that reality, rejected it violently. I wanted to set myself on fire. I wanted to stand at the top of the Superdome with a key around my neck, a human kite to taunt lightning or whatever plague I could summon. I wanted to put the past in a meat grinder and crank it, break it all down. The pointlessness of it all. The sheer outrage of finals and vows and worrying about decorum or anything really. About warranties and bank accounts. We'd all be dead someday. Sure. But Rosemary was dead because of me. I couldn't forgive myself for letting it happen, letting her die. Her rose perfume was still in my nose, though, so a part of me was convinced she was alive.

All that to say, I was losing my mind.

But God taught us that grief is a test, access to the life force of empathy. Without grief, we'd be psychos. Robots with no remorse. AI. Grief was an invisible heart, a secret mirror. Like the Ghost of Christmas Future, grief showed us the depth of our character, who we could be.

Or grief just woke us up screaming.

And if the dead never truly left the world—just our instantly perceptible realm—would I be able to communicate with Rosemary, to talk to her, the same way I spoke to Jesus and Mary and Mom? I'd have to learn. In my new-new life, in my veil, I had a lifetime ahead to attune, break the code.

But I didn't want peace then. Or prayer. I wanted revenge. Lenny was dumb but not dumb enough to return to a campus swarming with cops. He wouldn't be at the lounge. But I had to find him, draw him out. There was only one way.

I shot upright, dizzy from the glow of it. Grabbed Decker's burner then dug through my guitar case until I felt the matchbook, the one from Up in Smoke with Lenny's scribbled number.

It was the only lead I had. No backup plan. Just rage and a phone number.

My fingers shook as I dialed.

It rang twice.

Then: "This number's outta business," came a sarcastic voice on the other end.

Click.

The line went dead.

And my legs gave out. I had to hold the doorframe to stay upright, because I knew the voice.

Prince.

My brain erupted in my skull. Maybe Moose was right all along. In any case, Prince was closer to it all than I'd thought. Closer to the Royal Family. Closer to the drugs, to the bullet through Rosemary's throat.

I called Riveaux from the burner.

"Redemption Detective Agency, Magnolia Riveaux speaking, who the fuck is this?"

"We have to find Prince." My voice was shaky, but alert in a blazing new way. "The motel. Now."

"Be there in ten, unknown caller."

I would have vowed obedience for three lifetimes if it meant Riveaux got there faster. Four lifetimes if she brought me a carton of cigarettes.

Certain that Sisters Laurel and Honor were in a deep sleep—shattered by their own grief—I waited in the foyer. I kept seeing flashes of Rosemary. Her blood on my skin even though I'd washed it off. She'd soaked into me on a molecular level.

Riveaux looked like hell when I slipped into the truck. Her usually tidy ponytail lopsided. Almost a side pony.

"Goldsmobile, I'm sorry. Your girl—"

"Not my girl." I stared at the dashboard, meters, needles, ways to measure distance and speed and time. "Not anyone's." The clock blinked 11:11, and I wished for Rosemary to breathe again, to annoy me again, to not be dead.

"The best lights burn too bright to last."

"Please," I begged, "don't talk about her. Don't say her name. Don't say anything."

"Noted."

The world outside had no shape. No patterns.

"I'm going to kill Lenny," I said. And I meant it. *God forgive me.*

"Your mark did this?" Riveaux asked. At the red light she took her hands off the wheel and cradled her elbow in her opposite hand.

I was glad she knew. Glad Moose made me fess up.

"Yeah. It was so stupid to think he'd let Tammy go. But when he's dead, it won't matter."

"The night before your vows?"

The light changed, and she was trying so hard to comfort me, and it hurt to feel it—her care. The truck swerved whenever Riveaux'd look at me. But at that moment, I couldn't have cared less if she sailed us off a bridge, into the heart of Lake Pontchartrain.

Was Lenny still hunting me? I'd hoped so—would be easier than finding him. Every car looked like a Stingray. Every band on the corner seemed to feature a mandolin. Riveaux kept asking if I was all right, if I needed anything. I couldn't even answer. Couldn't even smoke.

Finally, the hotel. "Stay in the truck," I said, "please. I have to talk to Prince alone." I was so out of my mind, I was weightless.

"No way in hell, Goldsmobile. Not in your state."

"I have to talk to him, one-on-one."

"Going rogue's not the way."

"He's involved somehow."

"Good thing I'll be with you then. C'mon." She led me up the steps, practically carrying me, and I banged on the first door of the five listed on Father Nathan's receipt. Nothing. I tried the next. Still nothing.

At the next door, a bark before we knocked. BonTon must have smelled us. I heard a shuffle and muffled cursing. The hotel room door cracked open, and there was Prince looking even more frail. His white skin practically see-through, healing black eye, and sunken face. He kept one hand on the top of BonTon's gigantic head.

"What?"

I pushed past him into the roasting gloom. The drapes were the elegant color of gristle. BonTon tucked her tail between her legs. Riveaux said, in a low voice, "It's okay, pupper."

"Recognize this number?" I lobbed the matchbook from Lenny at Prince's head.

He dodged and missed it. "Should I?" he asked as he picked it up.

I jabbed my knuckle too hard into his frail chest. "Why do you have Lenny Mastoni's phone?" I breathed in and forgot to exhale.

"You know *Lenny*?" Prince mussed up his greasy hair and collapsed onto the sad loveseat.

"She went *nun*dercover." Riveaux whistled, and I gave her an eye roll. Put my whole broken body into it.

"Lenny's bad news." He wiped his nose, sending his weary arm jutting into a triangle.

298 ■ MARGOT DOUAIHY

"Why do you have his phone? I called the number—*you* answered."

Without looking up, Prince said, "Stop asking."

My strength was an uncaged thing. I grabbed Prince by the front of his sweat-stained T-shirt and hauled him up from the sofa to meet my eyes. "Don't lie to me." I felt his collarbone as I twisted my fist in his shirt. I could have broken his neck right there. So hideously easy. One little snap. The ultimate sin. One snap and he'd be dead. I grabbed his wrist instead.

"Hey," Riveaux said, staring at me with growing concern.

BonTon barked urgently and danced up on the very tips of her feet. So high she leapt off the ground. "It's okay, Bonnie," Prince said.

But the devouring need inside me wouldn't stop. It crawled out of me and before I knew it, I was bending his wrist. Prince was squealing, "Ow!"

Riveaux put her hand on my back. "Stop, right now."

I let Prince go and he tumbled. I didn't want to break his arm. I wanted to break the world. I wanted Rosemary back.

As he caught his breath, the intense effort of Prince's lungs startled me. He was so weak it was actually pathetic.

"Lenny killed Rosemary," I said. "Tonight. A drive-by."

Prince looked at me with horrid clarity. "Jesus fuck." He shifted on the loveseat, the springs creaking. He paused for a moment as if running an equation, or searching for a way to start the story. I felt it hum in my bones, saw the battle moving across his face. He was about to tell us everything. "It's not Lenny's phone."

"If it's not Lenny's number," I said, "whose is it?"

Then it hit me. Lenny had given me the number for a car hookup. *I know people*, Lenny had said. *Who can set you up with something good.*

"It's Trish's," I said. Every cell was a lit M-80. "Right?" Prince looked away as he reluctantly nodded.

"Trish's phone?" Riveaux was vexed.

Prince knitted his eyebrows together, and I could see a vein throbbing in his temple. "I broke into Crescent City last Sunday and stole it. Told her contacts to get fucked. I've been trying to stop her."

"That's why she's been looking for you," I said, and replayed the scene in my mind. My white rag. Trish's bubblegum-pink earrings to match her sling.

Trish Dempsey.

The Trish I'd thought to be a down-on-her-luck but invested mother.

"That chop shop's her pride and joy."

"Chop shop?" A sharp inhale. "But we checked the place," Riveaux said. "We were in the bays. Didn't see anything unseemly."

Prince shook his head. "It was under your feet. Mom had them build a hydraulic lift, looks like a service bay."

I've got things under control, Trish had said.

Riveaux was awed. "The concrete pad drops down?"

Prince nodded. "Like an elevator. Ten feet or so."

"But this town doesn't do basements." Riveaux looked at me. "It'd hit the water table."

"Naw, it ain't a basement. The street level was changed a long-ass time ago," Prince explained. "They brought it up, beams and shit. But the old ground floor is still there."

I recalled the ramp on the side of the garage.

The car thefts Riveaux'd heard on the blotter. The cops near the dive bar chasing an MIA Corolla. Amber's dad's car stolen by "some asshole." It was all connected.

"Your mom's been running a chop shop for the Royal Family? Since when?" asked Riveaux.

"Years—not long after Daddy went in. We were broke." He scratched his head, and I could smell his greasy hair from there. "But it's more than that. Mom climbed up. All the way up. Like, the Queen."

"What're you saying?"

"I need to spell it out for you, sis? R-E-I-N-E."

"What?" The shape of the headache forming behind my eyes was troubling.

"*Reine*," Riveaux said with confidence. Such expertise in her voice. "*Queen* in French. Of course."

"Trish is *running* the Royal Family?" I asked.

"Obviously," Prince said.

Trish, Ren, Reine. The Queen. Again, New Orleans high jinks never failed to impress. Words as code, names with double meanings. Each phrase, a portal, a riddle, a dare, like *fais do-do*.

Riveaux cleaned her glasses with her blouse. I could tell she was as stunned as I was. "What about Big Papa Dempsey?" she continued, trying to keep the interrogation on some course. "Does he know? He involved?"

"Naw. The only good thing he's ever done—stay away. He doesn't know shit."

That smooth operator had been telling the truth. And he had said whoever took over for him would've needed to get in fast. Who better to do so than the missus? I leaned against

DIVINE RUIN　■ 301

the dilapidated wall. The Royal Family stole nondescript cars, chopped them up and reassembled them at Crescent City, gave them a garish paint job, then the crew could transport drugs and ride with no identifying marks. And Trish was behind it all.

"If your mom's the queen bee of a criminal empire, why's she living in such modesty?" I thought of Lenny's Stingray and Italian threads.

"Like I said, the shop's her baby. Hydraulics ain't cheap. And she's building a compound in Baton Rouge."

Trish. Not some operatic villain but a worried mom. A canned peach angel. Beaten like a storm window by a slick, abusive husband, Trish found security, agency in the Royal Family. With Kenneth in the pen, she'd been put in a hard spot. But the ends sure as hell didn't justify the means.

"Three weeks ago, Mom said I had to start earning my keep in the Family business." Prince rested his elbows on his knees and stuffed his face in his hands. The motel room Bible was out on the bedside table. BonTon an expectant alarm on the cheap carpet. "Said she'd recruited Fleur after, uh . . . after—"

"After what?"

"Fleur was freaking out. Worried she wasn't going to graduate. Kept going on and on about the fucking 'study buddies.' So I asked Mom to help her out."

"Because you knew she had a supplier."

"Never supposed to be like this. I was trying to help Fleur. But Mom saw dollar signs and a big new market. Roped Fleur in, made her count pills and bag 'em. And told me to 'manage' her at Saint Sebastian's."

I thought back to the *B* lighter near her body. The baggies with one edge crimped, melted closed. Fleur must have used Bernard's lighter. That stash in the locker—her starter kit.

"But I said fuck that." Prince touched his bruised cheek. "Mom sure didn't like me telling her no. She beat the shit out of me with her fucking hairbrush. I just took it. But BonTon, she wasn't having it, not at all, and she went straight for Mom's arm. Didn't you, baby?" He lowered his face so he was nose to nose with his dog. "You protected Daddy."

BonTon's tail thumped once against the carpet.

"And that's why Trish's arm is in a sling?" I asked. "BonTon, not some bad-news boyfriend?"

Prince smiled like a proud pop, but the light didn't last. "Right after Bonnie jumped mom, she . . . she—" Half of his face hung lower.

"She what?"

"Took a drag of her cigarette and butted it out all over my girl."

The dog buried her head in Prince's armpit.

"Jesus Christ." I made the sign of the cross.

"Who hurts a dog? Psycho shit right there." Riveaux exhaled and shifted her weight, pressed her hands to her lower back. She was exhausted or in pain, or both. We all were. The shitty room had grown smaller, hotter.

"So I was done. Bounced outta there real fast. The next day I begged Fleur to stay the fuck away, even showed her the marks on Bonnie."

"What'd Fleur do?" Riveaux asked.

"What could she do?" Prince wiped his eyes aggressively. "She was on the hook. And wanted the drugs. Said she'd just do it till the end of the school year, and then it'd be over. We fought about it so bad."

That's what Amber told us last Monday. She saw that "sus guy" and Fleur arguing.

"Fleur said, 'They're just *study buddies*,'" Prince continued. "She thought they were legit meds, not like actually bad. Was gonna get a real script soon from her doctor, she promised." He started to sob, and it looked like he was biting the inside of his cheek. Hurting himself to stop the tears. "I couldn't believe how my mom had fucked up her head." He took a breath. "That's when I went to Father Nathan. He saw my face, knew it was bad. I've been here since so I can figure things out. Figure out how the fuck to stop her."

"Wheelin' and dealin'." Riveaux's dry laugh could refinish furniture. Sometimes I wondered what her wisecracks protected her from. I saw the way she recoiled when she heard about BonTon's burns. The deep well behind her eyes.

Prince's phone was sweaty in his hands. "But I have photos from the garage and can tell you all the ins and outs, everywhere you need to look. And I've been trying to figure out what to do with this? He pressed a button and Trish's voice invaded the hotel room. BonTon's ears pricked up. *Where's the fucking duffel, Prince? I'm sick of this shit. I'm not going to keep cleaning up your messes.* Trish was frantic, her manic need scratched through the voicemail. *You looked me square in the eye, and you swore. Run that smooth-talking mouth of yours all you want, but I'm done listening, and I'm done with you, you no good son of a bitch.*

Prince played it again. *You no good son of a bitch.*

Good Lord. That was the angry call we heard on Monday night, parked in front of the trailer. A message left for her son.

"What duffel's she talking about?" I asked.

"Her go bag," he said, "with a few pounds of product and two hundred and fifty K in cash. Just in case things went sideways."

"Your mom thinks you stole it," I said. "Did you?"

"Hell no. Think I got a death wish?"

"If you didn't swipe the go bag, who did?" Riveaux asked.

"No fucking clue," Prince said.

"Lenny," I said. "It was fucking Lenny. He's been planning a coup, making his move."

The scale and scope. It landed with the thrash of trees torn up by the roots. There was no "mystery man." Miss Mardi Mart had seen Lenny at Trish's side, the lieutenant. She'd said he was blond, though she forgot to mention the sports car. With the east wing stash in evidence, she owed her supplier some big bucks. She'd have to pay up or shut up. Eternally. By stealing Trish's go bag, Lenny was screwing *her*, royally.

"We could have helped you," I said.

Prince scoffed. "Not with this."

"But why cover for her for so long?" I asked.

"She's a bitch, but she's all I have. *Had.* Besides Bonnie. I've tried and tried to get her to stop." He kicked a chair leg. He kicked it again. He'd have kicked until he broke his toes. "But, I'm tired. I can't do it anymore."

I turned to Prince. "Grab both phones. We'll need everything you've got."

34

SOPHIA KHAN, LEGAL EAGLE in Chanel, the attorney who'd kept Prince out of jail last year and loved impossible cases, tapped her impeccable nails on her desk. A miracle she actually answered her phone at midnight. Another that she agreed to help. "Once more," Khan said. "Play it again."

Trish's voicemail squealed through Prince's tinny phone speaker again. Prince, Riveaux, Khan, and I stayed perfectly still as we listened to the recordings for the third and fourth time.

Attorney Khan glanced at Prince. "A quarter million in cash and fentanyl?" she asked, dry and wooden, as if she had a splinter in her tongue. "Your mom's quite the entrepreneur."

"Living the American dream," Prince replied.

I could see how hard it was for him to shake his loyalty to Trish. Even while he was trying to take her down.

Khan cracked her neck with shocking efficiency. Was she also a chiropractor? "So, there's a problem," she said. "We have photos and videos of the chop shop under the garage, VIN numbers. Slam dunk. But there's no evidence connecting Trish to the drugs. Or to Lenny."

"But she's running the whole show." Prince shook his hands in wild frustration.

"What about Trish's voicemail meltdown about the go bag?" I asked. "It's her *voice*. That's evidence, right?"

Khan shook her head. "She never mentions drugs, though. She never says what's in that bag. Hearsay won't cut it. We need hard *evidence* that will stand up in court."

Prince punched the air. "Then I'll fucking get it."

"Absolutely not," I said.

Khan looked at me solemnly. "The police will want to set up a sting, have Prince wear a wire. He's the only one who can convince both Trish and Lenny to meet."

I shook my head. "Dangle him like chum? No way."

Khan breathed hard. "He has the best chance at drawing them both out."

"I'm doing this," Prince confirmed. No hesitation or doubt. Like he'd already done it a thousand times in his head.

"Check the hero over there." Riveaux pointed at Prince. "Who's playing you in the biopic?"

His eyes bounced around, but I could see a distinct smile.

"These people are dangerous," I said. "They won't go down easy."

"Don't have to tell me," Prince said. "But I can't die with regrets."

"Better to not die at all," I said with a sign of the cross.

"If we do this, we have to do it smart," Riveaux said. "Coordinate with Decker and Narcotics."

"Make sure they don't hang the kid out to dry," I said to Khan. "Prince's safety is the priority."

"Always." Attorney Khan was confident and cool. "First things first, I'll secure immunity for Prince before he says a word."

Prince sat forward. "Still got Lenny's actual number. From when my mom was trying to get me to move product."

"Good," I said, though I still wanted to eviscerate Lenny myself.

"What's next?" Prince asked.

Khan jumped in. "The police will give you a script and mic you for the sting. They'll have you call your mom and Lenny individually and set up a meeting."

"And say what? I don't know Lenny that well."

"Tell him you'll help him take down Trish," I said. "Tell your mom you've got her bag."

Prince sniffed. "What if one of them thinks it's a setup?"

"They both think they can get away with anything," I said. I thought of Rosemary's perfect mouth sputtering blood. "Don't let them."

As we left Khan's office, Prince grabbed my arm. His eyes bulged, pupils inky, the size of binocular lenses. His beat-up face was still healing. "What if this doesn't work?" he asked. "What if it does?"

"It's going to be okay," I said, and squeezed his hand.

"Don't make promises you can't keep," he said.

It was 2 a.m. when we walked outside, toward Riveaux's truck. Sunday. My vow ceremony kicked off after 9 a.m. Mass. My world was falling apart, but I had to trust in God, in my friends, in perfect strangers. Trust. Such a small word for a dizzying leap. Prince had lied to me. I'd lied to Riveaux. Father Nathan and I'd lied to each other. But we were starting anew. Everything out in the open. We couldn't stop then. No second thoughts, no backward glances. The salt in our wounds was already enough.

35

THE DAY I MARRIED religion was clear. The light painfully bright. Sister Honor had bounced us from the convent early because an electrician was coming. Something got fried during the blackout. If only hearts could be fixed like fuses.

Prince'd cut a deal and was learning the steps of the sting from the cops, but there was no delaying my ceremony. Not with Sister Honor looking for *any* reason to bawl me out. Even Rosemary's murder couldn't derail it.

"We need you now more than ever," Father Nathan had urged that morning, grief dragging each word down. It was time. Time to pledge my life to the Sisters of the Sublime Blood forever, amen.

After Mass, before the ceremony kicked off, I flipped through a Bible. Proverbs 23:29–35: *Who has woe? Who has sorrow? Who has strife? . . . Do not look at wine when it is red, when it sparkles in the cup and goes down smoothly. In the end it bites like a serpent and stings like an adder. Your eyes will see strange things, and your heart utter perverse things.*

The sweat and haze spun me back to Original Sin's final show in wherever the hell Bushwick. The bar itself was a jumble of rotted wood with exposed nails. And the smell. My God. Warm beer, smoke, sweat. We skewered every chord. Hannah pounded the drums like she was running from the cops. Smiles clutched her own sweaty neck as she sang, closed her eyes like she was getting fucked. And I guess we were fucked. All of us. That's how it felt. Pure, unhinged, uncut. We didn't know it would be our last show. That pit before us was holy, Communion, strangers slamming their bodies into each other. One girl danced so hard she punched a guy in the teeth. He was just standing there. It was perfect.

That old me was still me now. Thirty-four years old and about to promise poverty, chastity, and obedience for life. The same me who used to think commitment meant a second date. Who only wanted to marry Nina when she was an already-married woman. Who kept Rosemary at arm's length until it was too late.

Showtime. I stood at the back of Saint Sebastian's, ready to roll.

The sanctuary was hardly a quarter full. Riveaux and Mrs. Benoit sat in the back. Moose and Bernard sat in the front row, beaming and looking sharp. The program Father Nathan had printed shook in my brother's hands. I knew my brother would rather have watched me walk down a different aisle, standing up front as my Moose of Honor, then making a teary toast, getting overserved at the open bar, and dancing like a ridiculous teenager.

And, Mom. If only she could have seen me then. Walking the same but different path. I told myself she was there. Believed it too.

Sister Laurel sat next to Sister Honor, while the bishop waited at the altar already drenched, either from pissing himself or sweating through his robe.

When the Litany of Saints started, I pressed myself flat on the floor. The certainty of marble against my cheek. My Sisters chanted, "Saint Francis, pray for us. Saint Clare, pray for us."

The words came easier than I thought. "I, Holiday Walsh, vow to Almighty God."

Father Nathan placed the black veil on my head. I'd have to get used to it, but it fit. It fit the me I needed to be. A better version. A switch from rookie Sister to lifer. Union of past, present, future. The fabric tickled my cheeks—it breathed when I breathed. In the veil, I was a superhero, a myth made real. A weapon disguised as submission. The veil itself quivered, and I felt my being change as it settled. It dimmed everything and focused me. Turned the world dark at the edges. Couldn't see left or right. Just a view forward. Only forward.

Sister Honor adjusted my veil and whispered, "Don't embarrass us."

"No promises," I whispered back.

The bishop slid the ring onto my finger. It was gold, simple, and much heavier than it looked. Was that pride in his face? Humility? Humanity? His eyes were bright as struck matches.

I nearly asked him, "Is this real?"

Almost said, "Hold on," but resisted.

You always leave. Nina's voice echoed. *Stay with me,* Rosemary had said.

"Amen," I said. "Amen."

The bishop replied, "You are now a bride of Christ."

No more escapes, no more borrowed wives, no more borrowed time, no more fake living, no more lies. I walked down an aisle without keeping an eye on the exit. No need for a way out. Not anymore.

■

After the ceremony, the scent of incense lingered like the fuzzy middle of a daydream. Maybe I was sleepwalking? Moose gave me a quick, wordless, teary hug. Bernard took in the veil, said, "Bitchin'," and they drifted off, down the steps. I looked for Riveaux and Mrs. Benoit but they must have already split.

My Sisters glided toward the convent in a state of calm delight. Before he left, Father Nathan'd said I'd "aced it."

I stood alone outside, on the steps of Saint Sebastian's, my new veil pinned, my habit crisp, sweat raining down my back. The backs of my knees were soaked. Then Riveaux appeared, rounding the corner. She hadn't left after all, probably just helped Mrs. Benoit to her car. She bent to inspect something on the ground. "Losing your marbles?" I asked, slightly worried about her reaction to the veil. To me.

"Not yet," she said as she flipped a penny from one side to the other. Tails to heads. "Leaving good luck for someone who needs it." Then she lit two cigarettes and handed me one without asking.

The breeze swirled and my veil fluttered slightly. Felt like I'd left the world only to resurface in a black-and-white cinema still, where nothing mattered and nothing made sense except the moment, the balance of light and dark. All that is seen and unseen, the Nicene Creed. We sat and smoked for a while on the puckered church steps in that creamy air. Riveaux glanced at me sideways, took in my new veil, and said, "Suits you."

36

THE INCENSE HOVERED AROUND my veil, right up until the midnight sting. Prince had called Lenny and Trish, feeding them different scripts, luring them into the same trap. It was all in motion. No turning back.

Midnight at the Crescent City Repair Shop. Sounded like the title of a 1950s tune, not a covert op. A sting on the same day I became a forever nun.

NOPD's Narcotics lead, Detective Mills, ran quite a team. There was a surveillance van, disguised as Bundle O' Joy, a cloth diaper laundry service. Decker and Mills hunkered down in the Bundle. Two plainclothes officers were stationed outside.

Riveaux and I weren't supposed to be there. But Decker convinced Mills, a young guy with an underbite like a bulldog, that Prince "needed" friendly faces nearby. Solid plan. So why did I feel like it was all about to go south? If Prince got hurt, I would never recover. But that stubborn kid had his mind made up. And I would have done the exact same thing.

Prince had been twitchy in the prelude to the sting, back at the police station. He was rocking BonTon like a baby, and I could see the veins in his neck, raised and pulsing. Mills had tested his audio and briefed him on the dos and don'ts of the operation. "Keep it vague and casual," Mills'd said. "Easy does it."

"This is gonna be fun," Prince'd said, trying to amp himself up.

I couldn't stop him from walking into danger, but I sure as hell wasn't going to let him go alone. "We'll be right outside."

"That's supposed to make me feel better?" He scratched the back of his neck.

"As soon as Lenny and Trish talk shop on tape, the police will swoop in and grab them."

"They fucking better."

Hail Mary, full of grace, bless this sting and the kid at the center of it.

At 11:42, Riveaux and I took position in her truck, way down the block. Tension tight as shrink wrap. The moon pinned itself low in the sky, eavesdropping. I felt different, sitting there in my veil, stronger. Older. More real. Sweatier too.

I was a living paradox no matter what side of the vow I was on. And everyone except Riveaux looked shocked when they saw me in the habit. Eyes shifted quickly, skittering away like water bugs on the skin of Audubon pond. I didn't watch them watching me, but I felt it. Their confusion. In the core of me, the punk core, I welcomed the horrified stares of "normal" society. Of regular people. What did normal ever mean? What power did it have?

Riveaux broke the silence.

"When I started the agency, I thought I'd be catching cheating spouses, not staking out a narcotics sting."

"You love the action."

"Maybe a little." She pinched her fingers.

"If this tanks, I—" Stopping mid-thought was the most honest reply I could give. None of us could pretend this mission felt anything other than batshit crazy.

The autobody shop was hardly distinguishable from the darkness itself. It melted and shifted with the night sky. The clouds were dark and heavy with rain.

Prince showed up right on time with a gait that hardly masked his terror underneath, but BonTon was a different story. She bounced beside him, tongue hanging out like they were strolling to a picnic. It had been easy for Prince to get Trish to meet. She'd been searching for him all week. Getting Lenny out of hiding, however, required a bit more fancy footwork. But Prince fed his ambition, said he could help bring the Queen down. For good. The fallout from the missing go bag would take time to catch up with Trish. Prince could guarantee a faster transfer of power. Of course that prick took the bait.

Mills's voice crackled in our earpieces. *"Subject approaching loading zone. All units maintain position."*

"Look at him," I said. "We can't just sit here."

"You thinking what I'm thinking?" Riveaux asked.

I nodded.

Against direct orders and our better judgment, we left the truck and slinked into the garage.

Mills was incensed. *"PIs, stand down immediately. I repeat—"* He'd have our heads. I could sense Riveaux was already regretting it.

"You hear anything?" I asked Riveaux, tapping my earpiece.

"Nope."

Lord, guide our steps, protect us, and forgive us our trespasses. Especially the ones we're committing right now.

We crept into the ramp side entrance. I imagined the chop shop below our feet, the tools and parts. The instruments and ingredients needed to retrofit, hollow out, and build secret compartments. The terrible artistry of it all.

The minutes ticked by with agonizing slowness as we crouched behind the PT Cruiser and waited. Trish Dempsey would be here soon. Queenpin, mother, survivor. And Lenny, that monstrous fuck, always the second string.

Prince, the bait, stood near the front register. BonTon by his side. No bag. Nothing to hand over.

Then, showtime.

A figure slid between shadows across the wide-open garage— Lenny. Walking easy with bravado, ready.

Then Trish—through the main entrance. I saw her pink sling in a whole new light.

Hard to fully take in Prince's expression from where we were hiding. Not hatred or heartache, but both. And even from our tucked-away spot, I could tell that Trish and Lenny were sizing each other up. Confused.

"Well, look what the cat dragged in," Trish said to Lenny. "My wayward boys together."

Lenny looked at Prince, confused. "What the fuck's she doing here?"

"Wayward, my ass." Prince ignored Lenny and went off script immediately. "Fleur's dead because of all y'all's bullshit."

"*Wrong opening*," Mills grumbled through our earpieces.

"Now, honey," Trish said, moving closer to him, "I'm real sorry—I know how friendly you two were."

"You don't know *shit*."

"But I need that duffel, sweet pea, so where is it?"

"That's a question for Lenny," Prince said.

"*Me?*" that fuckface Lenny asked with a fucked-up laugh.

Trish cleared her throat. "Prince, darlin', you said you had my bag. That's a quarter of a mill, shug."

"Naw. I said let's meet up so I can *get* you your duffel." Prince scratched his chest and I was desperately worried about the mic. "That's why I got Lenny here. He took it. He's been trying to drag you down."

"The kid has no clue what the hell he's talking about." Lenny talked to Trish like Prince wasn't in the room. "Telling stories to sound like a big man!"

BonTon let out a low growl which Prince shushed with a signal, a quick flick of his wrist.

"Thank you for telling me, darlin'." Trish tilted her head at Prince. "Honestly, that makes a whole lot of sense. Lenny, you've been getting sloppy lately. Heard you got jilted by some hot little number down at the lounge. Left high and dry."

Lenny's laugh sounded like choking. "Just some whore. Don't get it twisted, Reine. Like you know a thing about my end of business. The real work. I'm out there taking all the risks while you sit pretty. I'm sick of it."

"Says the man who *stole* from me? And how about that bad batch you got me?" Trish said, and lifted her chin. "You think you could run this business, *my* business, when you're getting product like that?" She turned to Prince. "Look, baby, your little friend Fleur didn't deserve to die, but Lenny here's the one to blame."

"What if that asshole got fucked-up pills on *purpose*?" Prince pointed at Lenny. "He knew you'd be on the hook, so he took the go bag."

"Well now, honey, that's a twist," Trish said. "Either way, I'd say it's about time I clean house."

They both drew their guns in an instant, Lenny aiming at Trish, Trish aiming at Lenny. The metal show.

"*Units hold,*" Mills barked in our earpieces. "*Hold position. Wait for them to spell it out.*"

But I wasn't going to let Prince stand in the cross fire alone.

We had precious minutes, seconds, maybe, before it all fell apart. I felt it as clear and real as the Eucharist. We had to get one of them on record saying the fucking word, *fentanyl*.

"Sorry to butt in," I said, stepping out of the darkness. Riveaux tried to stop me with a fierce grip on my elbow. Not tight enough. "But *this* isn't Lenny's coup."

"Sister Holiday?" Trish bucked back in shock, and Lenny did a such a hard double take he'd surely need a neck brace.

"Lenny's way too dumb for a smart move like that," I said.

"Huh? The Royal Family owes it *all* to me," he said. "If I'm so dumb, how'd I lock down the entire fentanyl game in the city?"

The magic words.

Two officers powered through the front door, one after the other. "Drop your weapons! Both of you on the ground!"

Decker followed in with her own piece raised. Mills and his underbite pulling up the rear.

"Calm down, everybody," Lenny said, and slowly brought his gun down, Trish following suit. He let it rest at his side for a moment, a long breath. Then pointed it at me, my third eye, so seamlessly and intimately it was graceful. "One last order of business," he said.

Lenny pulled the trigger the same instant BonTon launched. From nowhere. From heaven. That miraculous dog hurled her body into Lenny like a pit bull missile.

He fell hard under the weight of the dog, his shot going haywire, and the bullet bouncing manically off the ceiling. His gun clattered across the Crescent City concrete as the tide of police rushed into him. Riveaux sprang from the shadows and grabbed the weapon.

The fucking dog saved me.

"Lenny Mastoni," Decker said, "you're under arrest for the murder of Rosemary Flynn and trafficking of Schedule II narcotics."

In the melee, the chaos and screaming, Mills and the cops subduing Lenny, Trish took off with immortal speed. An awakened deity in a pink sling. Past the tool racks and lifts where she was building an empire. Away from the son she'd birthed and taught to ride a bike and throw pennies into lucky fountains. Through an empty service bay. Gone.

"Target on the move." Mills grabbed the officers, leaving Decker with Lenny, and the trio ran off after Trish.

Lenny was on his knees, his hands cuffed behind his back. He hissed at me, shouting all the nasty things he'd do to me if he could, spitting as he ranted. Curse after curse, threat after threat, and not even creative ones, until Decker'd dug her knee between his shoulder blades, shutting him up, forcing his cheek to the ground. *Hail Mary Mother of God, bless Decker and her sharp knees.*

BonTon headbutted my thigh. "Good girl," I said, giving her a tight hug.

"What a shitshow," said Riveaux, "but the pupper's got perfect timing."

"You'd be surprised at how many hand signals she knows," Prince said. We exchanged a look that said more than that kid had ever said and probably would ever say to me in his lifetime. He looked younger and decades older all at once. He'd done the right thing, but I was sure he'd carry some scraping guilt for snitching on his own mother. I worried for him that it would never fade. But I had watched his face, his wild eyes, as Trish'd escaped. Even after all the pain she'd wrought, BonTon's charred fur, Fleur's demolished heart, there had to be a small part of him that was hopeful.

Whether or not Prince was right about Lenny and the bad batch—if it was intentional sabotage, a lethal step in his plan, or just a royal fuckup—didn't matter. Trish was still complicit. In all of it. All the Family business. She had blood on her hands and death at her feet. Lost souls trailing her.

Trish was on the run. Good luck catching a woman like that.

37

IN THE BACK OF Decker's sedan, Lenny Mastoni sat like a chump. I saw it so clearly, even with him inside the car. That expanding black hole, the hungry poison at his core, growing ever outward. Like the corroded people who hurt others to pretend they're strong. I followed his stare to his Stingray, his hideous love, parked across the lot. He wouldn't be getting behind the wheel anytime soon.

"Can I have a minute alone with him?" I said to Decker and Riveaux. They looked at each other, then nodded in unison. No need to discuss it.

Riveaux handed me a cigarette and said, "You earned it." Then the women walked a few feet away, their own bond reforming in the win of the takedown. Partial win, at least.

"Hey, Tammy." Lenny smiled. "Can I still call you that? Too bad about your little girlfriend."

"Too bad about your little coup." I reveled in a split-second daydream. The astounding high-definition clarity of grabbing Decker's gun, pistol-whipping Lenny, and then emptying the entire clip into his head. Such a rich fantasy. I'd linger and take my time, pulling the trigger until the clip was empty.

But I couldn't. I couldn't kill him.

Dear Lord in heaven, I wanted to. But my vows. The ring on my finger, a steady pulse, an external heartbeat holding me back.

"You thought you were hiding behind a habit." When he scratched his eyebrow, the handcuffs caught the light. "But it was easy to find you. Saw your Church announcement in the newspaper."

Fuck. *The Times-Pic* in the Stingray. That's how the bastard tracked me down.

"What a surprise to see your picture," he said.

"No surprise you were so easy to play."

"Just sorry I missed."

"Says the soft-boy gangbanger with his sad-sack songs, expensive jeans, and offensive wine. You're not even a good villain. You're nothing. Fucking nothing. A pathetic middleman. A footnote that was never meant to be read. And you fucked with the wrong nun."

"Thought nuns couldn't fuck." The bozo winked.

Again, that temptation, the dazzling daydream of ending him in front of Crescent City Repair. I scanned the area. The parking lot, the street. Desperate to find one stick, one piece of glass, anything I could use as a shiv.

I moved across the lot and picked up a red gas can. And with fuel inside—perks of being at a car shop. I unscrewed the cap and walked over to the Stingray. That sleek, idiotic, odious fuckery. Lenny might've been crushing on Tammy, poor thing, but that Stingray was his one and only true love.

"For Rosemary." I held up the can.

Then I turned and doused the Stingray's windshield. A baptismal splash of gasoline. The rest followed in slow, wide arcs, so elegant, until the can was empty and the air glitched from the sharp fumes. I caught a glimpse of my reflection in the fuel-drenched window. A stranger in the veil, yet somehow more me.

That Up in Smoke matchbook was the gift in my pocket that kept on giving. I ripped off a match, lit it, and dropped the tiny flame into the puddle by the front wheel. Flames bloomed instantly. So greedy and beautiful. Dark and light—delicious annihilation. The Stingray lit up like it'd been waiting for that ending.

That new beginning.

Lenny watched the inferno from the back seat of Decker's sedan, wide-eyed, as the flames devoured his precious ride. "You fucking bitch!"

"Go with God."

The fire roared, hot and ravenous. So different from the incineration back in Brooklyn, losing Mom. That was all taking. Theft. This time it was a rebirth. A fever to burn out the poison.

I turned away from the blaze with a cigarette in my mouth and walked a slow stroll toward Riveaux and Decker. Feeling every pop and ember, carrying it with me forever. My veil trapped the heat.

They were all with me—Mom, Fleur, Joey, Rosemary. In the smoke and in the darkness. Shadows I could count on.

An eye for an eye.

Abyss for abyss.

Somehow, this felt more holy than anything else.

A purer path.

No, I didn't look back.

ACKNOWLEDGMENTS

Thank you to my agent, Laura Macdougall, and to my editor, Lexy Cassola, for your sharp wisdom, brilliance, magnificent humanity, humor, and general excellence. Thanks to the entire Zando/GFB editorial team, and to my hero and inspiration, Gillian Flynn, as well as the extreme delight of Kendall Sullivan. Mara Wilson, you are a noir blessing.

Thank you to my beautiful wife, Bri Hermanson.

My dear hearts, Todd Wonders and Marc Bardon, and my Scranton girlies: Pearl Bell, Rebecca Ferris, and Margo Fotta. Gratitude for Puya Abolfathi (who inspired Sister Holiday's musing during Communion), Brent Korson, Chris Fotta, Miriam Belblidia, Stacy Giovannucci, Jennifer Huxta, Lenore Mills, and Kelly Moore.

Thanks to Katie Williams, Mary Kovaleski Byrnes, Kirsten Imani Kasai, Lisa Dierks, Roy Kamada, Porsha Olayiwola, Raquel Pidal, Mako Yoshikawa, Julia Glass, and my students at Emerson College. Sincere thanks to Dylan Hearn for being a kind and hilarious soul, and to Karyn Hearn for your library stewardship.

Big love to Ana Reyes, Constance Adler, the Hermanson family, and Ben Pryor. Big thanks to Rob Byrnes, John Copenhaver, Lev A. C. Rosen, Robyn Gigl, J. M. Redmann, Greg Herren, Michael Nava, Rob Osler, Kelly J. Ford, and all the Queer Crime Writers for the love, courage, and inspiration. Tremendous heart-joy for Susan Larson, Summer, and Kit. Victoria Horn, thanks for the poetry. Maureen Corrigan, NPR, and PBS—thank you.

Thanks to Chalice Santorelli, Sarah Whalen, Jessie Dorne, Dr. Dardano, Dr. Weston, and all the nurses and technicians at Baystate Hospital who took care of me during my emergency-ish surgery.

Thank you to friends in the indie bookstore world: Andrea Talarico, Barbara Peters, Emily, Elisabeth, Robin, Roz, and the NEIBA. Major appreciation for Exile in Bookville, All She Wrote, and Ruby.

Eternal thanks to Mom and Dad, Christa, Lina, Sienna, and Barb Sabo. Thanks to the Publishing Triangle, and Lucinda, Stan, Grace, and the Left Coast Crime community. Thanks to Rosy Faver Dunn of the Norton Island Residency, the Waverly Comm and F. Lammot Belin Arts Foundations, Monson Arts, the Centre for Writing (UK) and Dragon Hall, John Pope and the Pinckley Prize team, and the Studios at MASS MoCA Residency for supporting the arts.

It's a gift to exist with you, dear reader.

AVAILABLE AND COMING SOON
FROM PUSHKIN VERTIGO

Jonathan Ames

You Were Never Really Here
A Man Named Doll
The Wheel of Doll

Simone Campos

Nothing Can Hurt You Now

Zijin Chen

Bad Kids

Maxine Mei-Fung Chung

The Eighth Girl

Candas Jane Dorsey

The Adventures of Isabel
What's the Matter with Mary Jane?

Margot Douaihy

Scorched Grace

Joey Hartstone

The Local

Seraina Kobler

Deep Dark Blue

Elizabeth Little

Pretty as a Picture

Jack Lutz

London in Black

Steven Maxwell

All Was Lost

Callum McSorley

Squeaky Clean

Louise Mey

The Second Woman

John Kåre Raake

The Ice

RV Raman

A Will to Kill
Grave Intentions
Praying Mantis

Paula Rodríguez

Urgent Matters

Nilanjana Roy

Black River

John Vercher

Three-Fifths
After the Lights Go Out

Emma Viskic

Resurrection Bay
And Fire Came Down
Darkness for Light
Those Who Perish

Yulia Yakovleva

Punishment of a Hunter
Death of the Red Rider